CAMERON DOUGAN

BECAUSE SHE IS BEAUTIFUL

A Novel

ATRANDOM.COM

NEW YORK

Copyright © 2001 by Cameron Dougan

Library of Congress Cataloging-in-Publication Data

Dougan, Cameron.
Because she is beautiful: a novel / Cameron Dougan.
p.   cm.
ISBN 0-8129-9168-0
1. Women—New York (State)—New York—Fiction.   2. Upper East Side
(New York, N.Y.)—Fiction.   3. Americans—France—Fiction.
4. Beauty, personal—Fiction.   5. Paris (France)—Fiction.   I. Title.

PS3554.O816 B44 2001   813'.6—dc21   00-052587

Random House website: www.atrandom.com

Manufactured in the United States of America on acid-free paper

2 4 6 8 9 7 5 3

First Edition

FOR HELENA

perhaps it is to feel strike
the silver fish of her nakedness
with fins sharply pleasant,my

youth has travelled toward her these years

or to snare the timid like
of her mind to my mind that i

am come by little countries to the yes

of her youth.
                                And if somebody hears
what i say—let him be pitiful:
because i've travelled all alone
through the forest of wonderful,
and that my feet have surely known
the furious ways and the peaceful,

and because she is beautiful

                                                e. e. cummings

PART I

A GIRL

That Sunday Kim lit a candle for her mother and prayed that her father would die. There was no war now for him to go to, where he might get shot, where his patriotism would mean something and he'd be a hero.

"To be brave like him," her mother said.

Kim watched her unwrap the blood-flecked paper bundle that her father had brought home. They ate filet mignon once a week whether they could afford it or not. Her father insisted on proving his expensive taste.

Kim sat on the floor while her mother cooked. She'd move and still be underfoot. They'd spent the previous afternoon at Woolworth's going through the racks. Her mother had bought a pretty new coral blouse specially for Sunday dinner. Her father drank scotch in the other room with the television blaring, an announcer's voice like a siren rising and falling to the pounding of horses' hooves. Her father shouted and her mother stopped and called out but he didn't answer. He'd been talking to the television.

At dinner he barked out grace and cut into his steak. He took a bite and chewed. He cupped a napkin to his mouth, then folded the napkin and set it down.

"Rare means rare," he said.

He threw the slab of meat off his plate. It hit the wall, leaving a mark, a trail of black flecks like running mascara. He grabbed her mother's arm and squeezed, knuckles white, tendons rising on the back of his hand.

"Three good pieces ruined," he said, staring at Kim.

She was only seven.

"You see what she does? You see?"

The front door slammed behind him. The sleeve of her mother's new blouse was grease-stained. She dropped the steaks in the garbage and stood at the sink with soap on her hands, the tap running, staring out the window for a while. Then she came over and rested her hands on Kim's shoulders. Her fingers smelled like lemons.

"I cooked the meat too long," she said, and left the room to put on a clean blouse.

—

Long after sunset, he sat with Kim on the stoop, staring hawk-eyed at nothing. Kim couldn't move until he gave permission.

"Did you see that?" he said, pointing across the street to some bushes that shot up at the back of an unused property. A full moon lit the ground.

"Did you see it move?" he said.

She focused all her energy, and finally she thought she did but wasn't sure.

"I hate the moon," he said.

She gazed at the flat white circle and the haze that spread across the sky. It made the crabgrass, the broken bits of wood and debris that littered the lot, silver between shadows.

"We all hated it," he said. "You could never tell in that light if something moved. You'd lie in a foxhole with your ears ringing, clawing at your eyes. When a tank was coming the bushes would start to shake."

Kim could see the Big Dipper. She traced it to the North Star. She stared again at the bush. She sat very still and waited. The bush never moved.

"There!" he said. "Did you see it?"

"Yes, Daddy."

"Are you sure?"

"Yes, Daddy."

—

He cursed fields of lush windswept grass, deceitful rolling fog, and God's bitter stars dangling in a smiling heaven. He told gruesome stories that her mom said she was too young to hear.

"She has to," he would insist. "To understand."

He'd tell how his best friend, John Consella, got his stomach shot out while playing cards. The sniper's gunfire ripped his side open. There was nothing there to bandage. He could have reached in and held the man's heart. Consella's cards were still fanned in his limp hand—three eights. He coughed and tried to speak. Blood splattered her father's cheek as he knelt. "I had you," Consella said. Her father had thought he'd been bluffing. For two months he didn't wash his face.

"Now do you see?" he said to Kim. "You really understand?"

"Charlie," said her mom.

He shot up a finger. "Why am I telling you these things?"

Kim looked from her mother back to her father.

"You don't understand?" he said. "You haven't heard a single goddamn thing."

"Charlie, I baked an apple pie this afternoon."

Again the finger, training on her. Kim watched her mother take a cardboard container of ice cream from the freezer and set it on the counter. She took down bowls from the cupboard and peeled the foil off the pie and licked her finger.

"I'll cut you an extra big piece," she said. "Is this big enough?"

She held up a slice. Her father's stare did not relent.

"What was Consella's hand?" he said.

"Eights," said Kim.

"How many?"

She couldn't remember.

"Go to your room," he said.

"But—"

"No dessert."

His hand tightened around his drink, the fleshy bulge at the base of his thumb wet where it choked the glass.

"I want you to think about what you've done here."

Her mother put one of the bowls back in the cupboard.

"You heard your father."

Kim ran to her room, swinging the door shut behind her. She flopped on the bed and pulled her hair into her face to cover her eyes. In seconds the door flew open.

"Don't ever do that again," he said, flashing the back of a hand. "No slamming doors. Do you hear me? Clear? Now, no dessert for a week."

He closed the door so hard the dresser shook.

—

If only she knew what bluffing meant.

It sounded soft, like stuffing, clouds or downy pillows, a drift of snow nestling against the side of a house. Somehow it had to do with her father's friend getting shot. She ought to know.

She fell asleep in her clothes and woke to her mother's coaxing voice. She sat up sleepily and straightened her arms so that her mother could pull the dress over her head. Then she lay back. Her mother tucked the blanket around her chin and kissed her forehead.

She woke again to a hand on her shoulder, the steely fingers of her father. "Shhhhh," he said, and motioned for her to follow. "Hup-two, get out of bed."

All the lights were out. She wobbled down the hall, rubbing her eyes.

"What is it, Daddy?"

Moonlight spilled across the kitchen counter, the dark shape of a bowl with a spoon sticking out. "Sit," he said. He carried the bowl to the table—two scoops of ice cream. He sat across from her and nodded for her to eat.

"Be very quiet," he said. "If your mother catches us, we won't be able to have ice cream for a month."

Her lips closed on the end of the spoon and she pulled it out slowly, shaping the ice cream to a fine point.

"Good, huh?" His smile was so broad she could see the fillings in the back of his mouth.

"Ummmm," she said.

"Our secret."

He went to the sink and looked out the window. He pulled his pajama sleeves up to his elbows and leaned against the metal edge of the counter. The muscles in his forearms shifted as he rocked forward on his feet. He looked tired.

"Dad, what's bluffing?"

"It's when you pretend, Princess. When you make someone believe something that's not true."

John Consella hadn't been bluffing. He hadn't been pretending and then he got shot. Was that the point—that he should have been? It didn't make sense.

"Do you see tanks, Dad?"

"What?"

"The moon."

"Oh. . . . No tanks, Precious. Hey, did I ever tell you the one about ol' Bert the cowboy dog? One day he comes into the saloon, his big ol' ears a-floppin' "—he put his hands at either side of his head—"ambles up to that ol' bar, tail a-waggin' "—he took a bow-legged step toward Kim, making his voice twang—"and orders himself a cold sarsaparilla."

"What's that?"

"What ol' cowboy dogs drink. Kinda like root beer. Now, turns out he can't hardly hold the mug, and that's when the bartender notices and says, 'Bert, what happened?' Ol' Bert looks down at his leg like so and says, 'Someone shot my paw!' Get it? Pa! You finished? We better get back to bed. Give me the bowl."

She got up.

"What are you forgetting?" he said.

He knelt and she threw her arms around his neck and squeezed. His chin was scratchy and she didn't want to let go. He hugged her back and she wanted to curl up in his arms, to sleep right there in the kitchen with the moon shining in and everything still about her.

"Okay, okay," he said.

She squeezed even harder.

"Okay," he said. "Enough. Time for bed. Shhhhh."

He had a smile that could stop time.

Her father trained men. Their family moved often, but things stayed the same: uniform houses with square, neatly mowed lawns. Wire fences kept the world out.

"Top secret," her mother would whisper.

Airplanes streaked the sky. They'd fly in tight formation, like praying hands.

One time her father planted a birch tree in the front yard. It took him a whole afternoon.

"Just like a foxhole," he said, shoveling the dirt, his undershirt dark at the chest from sweat.

She watched from the shade and kept his beer cold and brought him one when he called for it. When he was through, he took his undershirt off and wiped his forehead with it. He came over to where Kim was sitting and put an arm about her and admired the work. The dirt was patted down around the tree's slender base. The black and white stripes on the trunk were clearly delineated. He had always wanted a house with a birch tree, he told her, and now they had one. It would grow and sway in the breeze.

And then they moved again.

Those weeks after a move were the hardest—her mother unpacking, cleaning the new house. One time she caught Kim on the floor, surrounded by picture books, her Bible opened to an illustration of Noah's Ark, clouds billowing as though all the world were ablaze, water rushing in to swallow the earth, people hanging from treetops, a man on the highest branch pulling his hair, his open mouth a black hole, the darkest spot in the painting. Two of every animal were supposed to fit on the boat, but it didn't look big enough. Why two and not one?

"Looking at scary pictures?" her mom said, kneeling. "You should be outside making friends."

She closed the Bible and led Kim to the front door, prodding her out. Up the block, three girls jumped rope, two swinging the long cord in wide loops, the other, a flutter of white dress and hair ribbon, hopping from one foot to the other.

"See? Now go introduce yourself."

She gave Kim another push.

Kim walked slowly, knowing that her mom was watching, not looking back. She sat on the curb. The girls seemed to take no notice. She listened to the rope swiping the pavement, the girls' counting, singing. "Peach pie, berry pie, custard, and apple."

The girl in the middle looked over at Kim.

"Get-two-three, your-two-three, own," she huffed.

Kim didn't move. After a while the girls dropped the rope and came over to stare at her. One had a yellow dress with an orange daffodil stitched on the front. Her hair was drawn back in a long tight braid, which she pulled around and hooked under her nose like a mustache. She squatted and stared at Kim's shoes.

"They're like strawberries," she said, her voice nasal from the mustache trick. The other two girls got down beside her, careful not to let their clean, unwrinkled dresses touch the dirty street, and peered at Kim's shoes, their flushed faces twisted.

"Strawberries are sweet."

"Sugary."

The girls smelled of soap, rosy shampoo like the kind Kim's mom used.

The girl with the braid whispered, "She has strawberry shoes because she likes to lick her shoes."

She stared down her pointy nose and beamed at her friends. Their smiles were triumphant.

Kim clapped her hands. She'd seen an old woman on a park bench once shoo pigeons this way: confusion. Kim jumped up and clapped her hands forcefully.

The girls scrambled to their feet in a rush and charged to the door of the nearest house, bumping into one another, a tangle of bows and braid, fighting for the knob, stumbling through into the dark. The door slammed.

Kim waited. Out of the corner of her eye, she thought she saw a curtain move. They'd left the jump rope lying in the street and were probably worried, watching to see what she'd do. Several minutes passed. Finally the door opened: one inch, then wider. The girl with the braid came creeping out. As she got closer, Kim stomped and clapped her hands again. The girl grabbed one end of the rope and dashed back to the house, bounding up the step. The door banged shut behind her, catching the rope. It went limp across the stoop. All was quiet. Then the door clicked open, and the rope slithered in. Now the girls were watching Kim from the window.

The front door opened again, but this time it was a woman. She had on an apron and baking gloves and she glared at Kim through thick dark-rimmed glasses.

"Stay off our lawn," the woman said.

Kim got up and walked across the street and sat on the opposite curb, waiting for the sun to sink so she could go home.

When her mom let her into the house, all the books were put away and the floor had been vacuumed. "Did we play well?"

It was her mother's idea to make lists of reasons why their new homes were better than the ones before. They would remind Kim of the good things when it seemed like there weren't any.

"We'll stick this list to the refrigerator for when your dad gets home," she said, tearing a piece of paper from a note pad and handing Kim a pen.

They sat at the kitchen table and her mother stared at her, waiting for her to write.

"Only good things," said her mom.

Kim wrote:

> A bit of tar with a shoe print.
> Squirrels don't get dizzy. They like candy.
> Two white cars and then a red car.
> Flat stones are good fairy tables.

Sometimes a road has no line on it.
Cleveland Avenue has two.
I don't touch the lines.

She gave the paper to her mom, who read it and crossed her arms
and looked away.

"What about your new friends?" she said.

Kim said nothing.

"I don't like you playing near Cleveland Avenue. It's dangerous."

"I wasn't near there."

Her mother looked away again, then handed back the paper.

"We'll do it another time," she said.

"May I go to my room?"

"Yes, you may."

Kim went to her room and shut the door. She took a book from
her nightstand and climbed into bed and opened it. There was a picture of a fairy, kneeling on a lily pad. She had dragonfly wings and
long brown hair, bunched and braided and loose all together, falling
to touch the water. She was leaning over the edge of the lily pad to
stare at her reflection.

Kim folded the piece of paper and stuck it in the book to mark her
place. She went to her window and opened it a crack. While sitting
on the curb, she'd found an acorn, and she took it from her pocket
and placed it on the outside edge of the sill.

"In case you get hungry," she whispered, and shut the window.

She watched until she got tired. She'd read that fairies liked
acorns.

Kim's bedrooms would always have just enough space for a bed, dresser, and nightstand. Her father would inspect her clothes to make sure they were stored in orderly fashion.

One night the ceiling light startled her awake. For a moment she couldn't see. She could hear someone rattling hangers in the closet. Her father emerged and went to the dresser and started pulling out drawers, throwing clothes to the floor.

"What's wrong?" she said.

He rushed to the bed, the bulb of the ceiling light eclipsed by the dark of his looming frame. She pulled the blanket to her eyes. He smacked the side of her head.

"Look at me. Look at me."

He wrenched the blanket free and stuck his finger in her face.

"How many times?" He pinned her hands and slapped her cheek. "How many—"

Her mother was suddenly between them, a windmill of arms.

"Charlie, stop!" She got a hold of him. She fastened to him. "What did she do?"

His face twitched, shoulders heaving. His breathing slowed and he stared dumbly, bubbles of saliva at the corners of his mouth. His chin was wet.

After they left, Kim sat with her back to the cold wall, the thin blanket pulled over her legs. Pink shirts, ruffled socks, and flower-print dresses littered the room. She hated her clothes.

In the other room, her father was vomiting.

Kim's door opened a crack and her mother looked in, as if she'd expected Kim to be asleep. She came in and began picking up the clothes.

"Go to sleep, love," she said.

She tried to get the drawer back into the dresser. Her robe fell open. The light glared off her sagging white breasts.

—

If she wanted to, Kim could go days without talking.

Her mother promised that he was sorry, pleaded for her to forgive him. Kim clamped her mouth shut and stuck out her chin.

"He hasn't done that in quite a while," her mother said, smoothing her dress and straightening the buckle of a pink leather belt. "He's been so good."

Her slip was crooked and showed on one side, creamy silk that made her legs look pale.

Kim covered her ears and looked out the window at the fluttering leaves—alive, then perfectly still. Her mother glared and moved to block her view. But the glare lacked menace, and Kim could face her and not be afraid.

Her mother bustled about the kitchen. Pipes thumped. Water slapped the sink. A few minutes later, she came back and stood by the window, staring out over the patch of lawn and the street. A car drove past.

"It's supposed to rain tomorrow," she said.

She brushed Kim's hair from her eyes.

"Your hair's getting darker. Pretty soon you'll be my color. You have your grandmother's eyes, you know. Raw almonds, she always said. Do you remember seeing her? You were too young. That was . . . We'll visit her sometime, soon as your grandpa's feeling better. Would you like that? When we do, say raw almonds. She'll be proud. Yours are more pine-colored, though."

She stroked Kim's forehead.

"Don't take it out on me," she said, but Kim refused to speak.

Grandpa was always too sick to visit.

—

That night the table was set with plastic cups. Her father took her mother by the hair and dragged her from the kitchen. She struggled to keep up with his hand.

"We don't drink from plastic!" he said.

Kim remained at the table. She heard a crash and a slap but didn't move, because she'd learned that lesson. If he came for her, she didn't want him to have to search. She waited until her father left, then wandered to her parents' bedroom and pushed the door open. Knotted strands of hair fell into her mother's eyes. Her hand seemed frozen to her cheek, as though she'd forgotten it was there, and a thin line of blood ran from her nose to the crest of her upper lip. There were jagged cracks in the wall, radiating out from a grapefruit-sized hole. Powdered plaster coated her father's neatly made bed and the Bible that lay on the nightstand. Kim went to the bathroom for a washcloth and came back.

"He breaks all the glasses," her mother said.

—

In the morning Kim left for school but never got on the bus. As soon as she was out of sight of the house, she headed for the woods at the edge of the base. The road ended and turned to dirt. She followed bulldozer tracks past vacant lots, squares of poured concrete that would become houses like hers. Would there be a fence on the other side of the trees? Would she not be able to get out? She picked her way through gray thorny bushes, thick dead vines like cobwebs waiting to catch her. She stopped to listen, then started to run. Her coat sleeve snagged, and she wrenched her arm free. There was a tiny tear in the elbow where the stuffing showed through. Still she ran. The contents of her lunch box rattled. She saw light ahead. Maple saplings snapped at her knees and waist. She reached the open and found herself staring out over an airfield, only there were no planes.

She walked along the forgotten runway, grass sprouting between pancakes of cement. Some cracks had been repaired over the years, tarred many times, and finally left. She couldn't see an end, the runway was so long, and she walked and walked. Then she heard a motor, faint at first. She saw a jeep approaching. There was nowhere to hide. She walked quickly and didn't look back. Soon the jeep was beside her, moving at the same speed. From the corner of her eye she could see that the man driving was watching her, steering with his forearms leaned against the wheel. She stopped. He stopped. She started again and he touched the gas. When she stopped again, he shut off the engine. He had sergeant's stripes.

"Goin' for a walk?" he said, smiling. "You're out a long ways. I reckon you've come pretty far. You must be tired."

She shook her head.

"No?"

He took a cigarette pack from his chest pocket and patted it with his palm. He bent a wide face to the pack and plucked one out with a set of teeth that were big like a beaver's. He looked at her as he flicked on his lighter, got the cigarette burning, and blew smoke and waved it.

"Hey, aren't you supposed to be in school?"

She nodded.

"But you don't like school, do you?"

She didn't move. He smiled again.

"I guess your mom doesn't know you're skipping school." He dragged on his cigarette and tapped ash and looked out across the airfield.

"I'm not skipping," she said.

"It's okay. Hell, I used to hate school. I used to cut out any chance I could."

"I'm not skipping."

"No?"

He eyed her.

"I'm running away," she said.

"Oh."

His cigarette glowed red. The smoke disappeared into the clouded sky.

"From what?" he said.

"Everything."

"Everything? Are you running away from me?"

"No."

"Then you're not running away from everything. Who are you running away from, your parents?"

She stared at the trees on the outskirts of the airfield.

"Not much out there," he said. "Just more woods. Runway looks funny with no planes, don't it? They built a whole new airfield about seven miles from here. You should see it sometime." He patted the seat next to him. "Why don't you come up and sit a bit?"

She walked around the jeep, and he put out a hand to help her climb in. He hoisted her up and laid a hand on her shoulder. She sat very still. The hand was like her father's, fingers on the verge of tense, as though ready to direct her, ready to prevent her from moving. She was afraid that if she tried to leave he would chase after her.

"So what's a pretty girl like you running away from your parents for?"

His breath smelled of ash.

"What's your name?" he said.

"Kim."

"I bet your mom's gonna be awful sad when she finds out."

"I don't care."

"Not a little bit?"

She shook her head.

He blew smoke and flicked the butt to the pavement. He put his hands behind his head and leaned back, stretching. His helmet tipped back enough to show that he had no hair. He straightened the helmet, then put his hand back on her shoulder.

"You're a tough kid. How old are you?"

"Ten."

"Whew, ten? I bet you're strong, too. I bet you get that from your dad. Hey, let's see how strong you are."

He shifted and bent so that his elbow was resting on the seat. He nodded for her to grab his hand.

"I'll let you use both. Bet you can't beat me."

She looked at him.

"C'mon," he said. "What, are you afraid?"

She dropped her lunch box and clutched his hand in both of hers and began to pull. His arm hardly budged so she tried to use her body for leverage. She could see the surprise in his face when his arm started to move. She was puffing air through gritted teeth. His eyes grew wider. His knuckles were almost touching the seat. She held her breath and heaved. His arm suddenly gave.

"I'll be damned," he said, rubbing his hand as though she'd bruised it. "You're stronger than I expected."

She grinned.

"I'll bet your dad's a marine," he said. "Ten, huh? I know grown-ups who ain't half as strong as you."

He looked at his watch.

"Aw, hell. I better be getting back. I guess you'd better be on your way too. Kim, it was a pleasure wrestling with you. Maybe if we ever meet again, you'll allow me a rematch."

She wasn't sure if he was telling her she should get out of the jeep. She picked her lunch box off the floor and held it in her lap.

"I'd stay out here all day," he said, "but you know there're people expecting me."

She didn't move.

"Listen, if you're heading back to the base, I'll give you a lift, but . . . That's the direction I'm going. Otherwise I'd be happy to drop you somewhere else."

He turned the key. The motor sputtered on.

"You wanna lift back to your house?"

She nodded.

"You have to tell me how to get there. What street do you live on?"

"Lincoln."

"He was a great president. Must be nice living on a president's street."

He turned the jeep around and started back. A dirt road led through the woods. They passed open lots, houses that were just framed, and nearly finished houses, aluminum siding stacked at the curb, waiting to be hung. He didn't say a word until he'd turned onto Lincoln, and then he told her to tell him which house.

"There," she said.

He pulled into the driveway. The front door opened. Her mom hurried out, waving a tissue. The bruise on the side of her nose had spread onto her cheek like the beginning cracks in a mirror.

"Oh, God, oh, God!" she was saying. Her eyes were red. She clasped Kim's face in both hands and shook it side to side. "What were you thinking? I've been so worried, so worried. I thought something terrible—don't ever do that again!"

She held Kim's head to her bosom. The man got out of the jeep.

"Bill, thank you so much," her mom said, turning to face him, her hands on Kim's shoulders.

"Not at all, Mrs. Reilly. I found her out by the airfield."

"I'm sorry to have bothered you."

He tipped his helmet. He was staring at her bruise.

"Hey, Kim," he said, "no hard feelings. Remember about that second chance. I'll be gunning for you."

Kim looked down. He'd been bluffing.

"Where are your manners?" her mother said, letting go of Kim. "Thank Sergeant Jones for bringing you back."

"No need," she heard him say.

She sensed then that her mother was no longer at her side. She'd slipped away to stand by Sergeant Jones.

"Bill, you won't tell anybody, will you?"

He mock-zippered his mouth. Her mother seemed small next to him, delicate in a way that was unusual, and then Kim realized it was because of Bill, who was much taller than her father. A full head taller—he could drape a protective arm over her mother's shoulders and tuck her close to his side. The curve of her chin seemed to mirror the gentle bend of her eyebrows. Her eyes glistened, giving back light, but didn't they always? Trembling lashes, lips perfectly painted and fresh; even with the bruise, she looked as though she'd stepped out of a movie.

Bill started back toward the jeep. Her mom led Kim up the walk and pulled her into the house.

"When the school called, I nearly had a heart attack. Promise you

won't ever try that again. Mary, Jesus, I thought some—what if your
father had found out? How could you do that to me?"

She hugged Kim again and kissed her forehead and pinched her
cheeks.

"He won't know," she said. "Darling, I promise. What did you do
to your coat?" She examined the hole. "We have to mend that."

Secrets, Kim thought.

—

The next day an envelope lay on Kim's dresser. In it she found a
note, a hundred-dollar bill, and a medal. He'd won it for bravery.

For my most beautiful one, the note read.

She stashed the medal in her sock drawer but kept the money in
her hand. Either he'd had a good night at the track or his football
team had won. Once he'd given her two hundred dollars.

He brought home flowers that night, lamb chops from the
butcher, and a bottle of wine.

"Ummm, French!" her mother exclaimed, looking at the label.

She put on a yellow cotton dress and new stockings, makeup to
cover the bruise. He spoke contritely over dinner. He brought up
John Consella, pondering the details of his death once again.

After dinner he danced with her mom.

> Each kiss was divine, and with each glass of wine,
> I thought I could win you most any old time.

They were the same height, and she could lean her forehead
against his and gaze into his eyes. He dipped her slowly, his supporting arm showing no sign of exertion. Her hair brushed the floor.
He was lifting her on his fingertips.

Kim snuck off to her room and grabbed the medal her father had
given her. She crept back past the kitchen and went to her parents'
bedroom and crawled into the closet. She could smell her dad's shoe
polish. The greasy tin was wrapped in a plastic bag with an old

blackened rag, ridged and wrinkled, crusted like elephants' skin. She stood and pressed her face to his hanging uniform, breathing in the vanilla scent of his aftershave. She looked down at the medal in her hand, ran a finger across its dark ridged face. The back of her throat began to ache. She stuffed the medal in her dad's uniform pocket. She didn't want it.

She swore that when she was older she would live in a house with doubly thick walls that kept out the sounds of babies crying and glass breaking and the neighbor's dog barking. There would be no fences, only sprawling land, and horses maybe, and a grand stone house with great big odd-shaped rooms and winding endless halls. Her husband would be rich. He would build fires in a giant fireplace and wrap her in blankets and read her stories. He would take orders from no one, and his gifts wouldn't make her feel bad.

She heard approaching footsteps and froze. In a rush, she dug through the uniform pocket, jangling the jacket on its hanger, found the medal, and sprang from the closet just as her mother and father entered the room. Her father's brow twisted.

"What are you doing in here? You're not supposed—"

She dashed to his side and hugged his leg, pressing her cheek to the firm muscle of his thigh. She clutched the medal in her tight fist.

"I love you, Daddy."

"I—" He faltered.

Her mom stood back and smiled.

"We're so lucky," she said.

Her father got down on one knee and mussed Kim's hair. "Did you get my gift?"

"What gift?" chirped her mom.

"Yes, Dad. Thank you."

"Good. Off to bed, then. Your mom will tuck you in."

She left the room, her mother's voice trailing. "What did you give her?"

"Nothing," her father said.

"You're so spoiling."

Good moods lit up the night like lightning. Occasionally, they might last days, even weeks, and she could do no wrong. She would wake to the sound of whistling long before dawn. She could follow the chirpy notes to the kitchen, Mom cracking eggs into a pan, Dad shining a belt buckle at the table. Sometimes he'd be in the bathroom shaving, a towel wrapped about his sweaty skin.

"Morning, Sunshine," he said, when she walked in. "Don't let the steam out."

She'd close the toilet seat and sit and he'd tell her about famous battles, scraping foam from the sharp edges of his jaw and rinsing the razor under the tap. He told her about the Greeks and Romans, quizzing her.

"Thermopylae," he said.

"Monopoly."

He laughed. "Once more."

"The Battle of Monopoly," she said.

His shoulders jumped when he laughed. He wiped his face on a washcloth and took a green bottle from the medicine cabinet. He tipped the bottle to a cupped palm and slapped his cheek.

"Stings," he said, slapping his other cheek and leaning close to the mirror to examine himself. " 'Let me have war, say I, it exceeds peace.' " He was proud that he could quote Shakespeare. "You'll study him when you're older. You know why I'm teaching you these things? Because you're going to be the first Reilly to go to college. Your mom says there ain't a day that goes by that she isn't putting books back in the bookcase. That's my girl. Keep reading. And not just any college. I'm gonna send you to the best—Harvard or Yale."

He turned and looked at her.

"What happened to your hair?"

Her mother had given her a haircut.

"It dries faster now," she said.

Her father lifted her from the toilet seat and set her down.
"Now why'd you go and do that?" he said. "Girls' hair should be
long, like your mother's. Don't ever make yourself look less pretty."

—

That night, long after she'd been tucked in, there was something she
wanted to ask her mother. She went to her parents' bedroom and
pushed the door open slowly, expecting them to be in bed, but the
beds were empty, the covers pulled back and messed. The house was
dark. Was she alone? She thought she smelled roses, the strong
sweet scent of her mother's perfume. Then she noticed light from
the bathroom and heard the medicine cabinet clank shut. The door
was half open and she peered in, the rose scent powerful now like a
cluster of blooms. Her mother stood at the sink in a nightgown,
white with light, dark where it touched her skin, blurring the softness of her. She was putting on lipstick, first outlining the edges
with a pencil, hand steady, eyes fixed as though the world had disappeared, then the filling in, deep dark red, such a sharp contrast to
the sleepy haze. Kim rubbed her eyes and watched. How careful she
was, such purpose. Suddenly her father came into view. He'd been
behind her mother the whole time. He was wearing his blue pajama
bottoms with no top. The skin on his arms was tight. He put his
hands on her mother's shoulders and slid them down her arms. He
shut his eyes and pressed his mouth to the slope of her neck. Her
mother rolled her lips together and kissed the air. Her lips were perfect. Kim found herself dashing back to her room. She scampered
under the covers and pulled them up. She heard the light in the bathroom click off. She'd forgotten what she'd wanted to ask her mom.

—

Butch Sullivan was bigger than the other boys in class, thicker in the
head and chest. He liked to pull the wings off butterflies and shoot
BBs at dogs. He'd shot a bird once with a friend. Kim had found the
two boys laughing, the bird flopping at their feet, broken and bleeding. There was nothing she could do, and burying it only felt worse.

She tried to forget. A few months later, after school, she saw him take Jason Cooney's bicycle. Butch started riding it in circles, laughing as Jason screamed for him to give it back. Jason was something of a bully himself, with freckles and a gap in his front teeth. Every time he got close, Butch would accelerate, keeping a foot ahead of Jason's outstretched hand. A crowd of children was gathering, kids from her class and some older kids. They laughed at Jason, his clumsy attempts, his wet cheeks.

"Jay-Jay wants his bike back," Butch called.

Kim found a stone no bigger than a walnut. She waited until Butch circled around and stopped; then she threw it. It hit him on the side of the head and he went over like a carnival duck. The jeering stopped. Jason grabbed his bike off the ground. He swung his leg over the bar and pedaled off, hiding his face.

Butch lay on the ground. Everyone could hear that he was crying. The older kids began to laugh. Then Butch jumped up and ran away. It all happened so quickly. No one seemed to notice that it was Kim who'd thrown the rock.

But someone had. That evening Kim heard a knock at the door from her bedroom. Her mom called to her dad to see who it was. Footsteps moved through the house. The front door rattled. Kim stepped from her room to hear muffled voices on the stoop. Then: "Kim, get out here. Kim!"

She could see his dark form through the screen, standing on the step. The aluminum door squeaked when she pushed it open and stepped out. Her father waited with his arms crossed tightly as though holding himself back, struggling to swallow his rage. Mr. Sullivan was taller than her father, but not as well proportioned, a wide trunk of a torso sitting atop two toothpicks. He was a larger version of his son, with a round veiny nose and shiny cheeks, and he put a hand on Butch's shoulder. Butch had a bag of ice strapped to his head.

Her father's glare bored into him.

"You got nerve coming here to accuse a girl," he said.

Mr. Sullivan leaned forward, his shoulders rising and falling, deep barrel-chested breaths.

"Some girl," he huffed.

Her father's hand smacked Mr. Sullivan's cheek. Butch jumped.

"Don't ever talk like that about my daughter again," her father said.

"Dad," Butch whined. Dazed, Mr. Sullivan turned slowly and headed down the walk, Butch in tow.

Her father watched them go.

"Rotten apples grow on rotten trees," he said. "Dick Sullivan's a little man."

He looked at Kim.

"Did you throw that stone?"

"Yes."

"That was a hell of a bump."

———

He poured himself a drink, then another, never fully emptying the glass, each refill more generous. The neck of the scotch bottle knocked the glass rim as he poured, wobbled, then dinged it again. He touched Kim's nose. His finger was sticky. He settled into the leather armchair in the living room, and she crouched at his feet, leaning her chin on his knee as she spoke. He laughed, and the more he laughed, the more animated she became in her telling, jumping up, holding her hands out as though gripping handlebars. Her father called her mom out to listen and made Kim repeat the story. She tried to get Butch's look of surprise right—that moment the rock hit him.

"And he was moving," her dad said, gulping his scotch.

Kim didn't correct him.

"Not an easy shot."

"You shouldn't throw stones," her mother said.

"That boy had it coming." He got up to fill his glass. "The father too," he said, coming back, dropping into the chair. "You should have seen Sullivan's face. You saw it, Kim. Was that the face Butch made?"

Kim nodded. Her father laughed. Her mother didn't smile.

"Imagine, a girl standing up to that bully."

"Charlie—"

He pulled Kim to his knee and ran a hand through her hair.

"Your mother's right. We don't throw stones. Understand?"

Kim looked at her mom, who was frowning.

He put a finger under Kim's chin, coaxing her to turn back. He was all smiles and glassy eyes.

"This other boy, Jason," he said. "Was he worth it?"

He grabbed her mother's hand and pulled her onto his lap, nuzzling her hair.

"You're worth it, Charlie," she said.

Kim looked at her. "We're talking about Jason Cooney, Mom."

Her dad laughed.

Kim wished his good moods could go on forever. He walked her to her room and set his drink down on the dresser. He tossed her, giggling, onto the bed. She crawled back to the edge where he stood and jumped up, throwing her arms about his neck, dangling like a monkey. He backed away from the bed, turning so that her feet swung out and the room whirled.

"You're getting heavy," he said. "Okay, okay."

He kissed her on the forehead.

"Sleep tight, Princess," he said, his finger grazing the tip of her nose, and left.

She sat staring at nothing. What she'd done had made her father so happy, and she pictured his eyes when he raised his voice to her, acting like she was in trouble. She lifted her shirt over her head. She wrapped it around her fist and stared down at her white stomach, ran a hand over her ribs, counting them, two, three on one side, three on the other, more. She touched her nipples, the skin around them all twisty. She wrapped her shirt around her fist again, tight like a thick plaster cast, and thought how she'd never seen her father hit anyone else besides her mom. How strange it looked—the shock on the man's face, the sudden turn of expression. Was he scared? She hugged herself and glanced over her shoulder. Her father was standing in the doorway, leaning against the jamb. He straightened quickly.

"Forgot my drink," he mumbled, then stepped over to the dresser.

"Look, Dad." She held up her tightly bound hand. "Someone shot my paw."

He smiled and left.

She lay awake, the covers pulled up to her chin. She could hear her parents talking, her father's voice a warm hum. And she thought she heard her mother laugh. She listened, fighting to keep her eyes open, not wanting the night to end.

Bobby Streeber was older. He lived in the house across the street. Her father didn't like him. He had a motorcycle, and she'd sit and watch him working on it in the driveway. His hair was black and cut so short she could see his tanned scalp. He always had grease under his fingernails and a cigarette pack rolled into the sleeve of his T-shirt. "Just like the old son-of-a-bitch," he'd say. That was what he called Bobby's father.

Sometimes Bobby would give her a stick of gum. Sometimes he'd let her fetch him a tool from his tray. He'd ask her questions about her parents, and if she answered him honestly he'd get mad. When he saw bruises on her arm, he would kick the curb or throw a stone or spit. "Next time he does that, give me a holler," he said. "I'll nail the son-of-a-bitch." One time he was so mad he wheeled around and shattered his soda bottle off the side of a passing jeep. It screeched to a halt and the men who jumped out hauled him like a prisoner up his walk and rang the bell. He turned to see her before the door swung open. The mother stepped aside for the men to drag him in. Another time he put his hand on her back and took her hand and spun her. He winked as he backed away, cocking his thumb and firing his pointer finger.

The boys her age made fun of her bony legs and pudgy cheeks. Bobby never did. "Hey, Big Eyes," he'd call her, because big eyes were rare and big eyes were beautiful, and big eyes had brought down countries, he said.

—

"Mommy, how come I don't have a brother?" Kim said.

"You want a brother?"

Kim watched her mother at the sink. She finished the dishes and dried her hands on a rag and folded it over the handle of the stove.

"Maybe because you're everything we ever wanted," she said, coming over.

"If I had a brother, he'd stick up for me."

"You never need anyone to do that. Don't ever think you do."

"But he would. A brother would."

Bobby Streeber's mother was not his real mother, and his little brother was not his real brother. Their yard was always littered with toys. Kim heard Bobby's father yelling at him one time, screaming at him to clean up the lawn. It wasn't his mess, she thought. The mother never seemed to do anything. Supposedly she was pregnant. Kim wondered if Bobby ever hit his father back.

—

One afternoon he pulled his wallet from his back pocket and took out a narrow strip of paper. He flipped it over to reveal three tiny photographs of him in a row.

"I thought you might like one," he said. "Which one do you want? You want all three?"

She nodded, and he gave her the strip. It smelled like vinegar.

"If anyone ever bothers you, tell 'em to quit or else. Then show 'em the pictures."

He stared at her, then slipped a pale blue card from an inside pocket of his wallet. He held it a moment.

"I want you to have this too. It'll help," he said, and handed it to her. "It's okay. I got a new one."

The card had his name and address on it, and a long number with letters mixed in that didn't spell anything. There were smaller numbers and scattered letters typed in a series of boxes.

"Someone bothers you, show 'em this. Say I'll track 'em down. Okay? 'Cause you know me. The number's the same. That's proof."

When she went in for dinner, she hid the pictures and the card under her pillow.

—

The night Bobby Streeber's motorcycle went off a bridge, police cars and military jeeps lined up in front of the house. Kim watched from her living room. The red lights of the sirens went round and round. A small plastic wheelbarrow sat on the lawn in the flashing light. A woman began to wail.

"I knew something was wrong with that boy," Kim's father said. Her mother put a hand on her shoulder.

"When the soul goes out of the body," she said, "it leaves behind a shell."

"The temple," said Kim.

"Sometimes a temple is just stone."

Kim went to the bridge the next day and stared at the dent in the rail. There was no skid mark. A leftover piece of police tape fluttered in the breeze. She tried to imagine the impact—those few seconds that he must have been in the air and what he was thinking. The authorities hadn't taken the motorcycle away. She could see it sticking out of the water. It had landed so far from the bridge.

The older boys started gathering, standing in circles, smoking and drinking, staring at the bike as if it were a monument. Beer cans began piling on the sandy bank. One boy called up to her and pointed to his beer. She turned and ran until she couldn't hear their laughter. She dropped to the curb and hugged her bony knees to her face, to her eye sockets, squeezing until she saw color, not letting go.

A week later the motorcycle disappeared and the boys stopped coming. She kept Bobby's pictures and the card taped to the bottom of her dresser so her father wouldn't find them. When he wasn't home, she'd take them out and stare at the card, trying to memorize the long number, saying it over and over in her head because she knew it stood for something.

Midway through her high school, Kim's family was moved to West Germany. Kim and a handful of other Americans attended a tiny school on the base. The town was named Wildflecken. Wild fuckin', the students called it. Everyone smoked. She was skinnier than most of the girls, bony where they were not and smaller in the chest—cursed, she thought. She knew it was a gradual process, the growing there, but she'd never witnessed it in anyone but herself. She'd never known anyone long enough. Here everyone seemed finished. One girl had gigantic breasts. They were all the boys talked about. Another had no breasts at all. They were all the boys talked about. No one paid attention to Kim's.

Classes were harder, the teachers more strict. Their English teacher was a Frenchman who rolled his sweater sleeves up around his biceps like doughnuts. He made everyone write their essays on graph paper and criticized Kim if her handwriting got sloppy. They read *Othello,* and the teacher constantly referred to "green-eyed" this and "green-eyed" that, only it sounded like he was saying "grenade," and one of the boys, Vincent, would imitate him after class, saying, "Othello got blinded by a grenade."

They spent a whole class discussing the character Iago, breaking down his speeches, trying to identify his motives: hate, jealousy, evil. "Who is this man?" the teacher kept asking. Several of the students seemed to agree that he was the devil, manipulating everything to a destructive end. "Heaven is the judge," the play read. "I am not what I am." What was he then? An illusion? Nothing?

It was one of the only times Kim ever spoke out in class. "What if he's trying to say he feels like nothing?" she said.

The teacher turned to her.

When she spoke, her voice cracked. "Maybe he's trying to tell us that he's full of hate and jealousy because he feels like nothing."

A girl coughed. A boy in the back row laughed. The teacher moved on with the discussion.

After class, Kim heard a girl making fun of her comment. Vincent told the girl to go sit on a grenade. It didn't make Kim feel any better.

—

Those days her mother was always tired. Kim did most of the cleaning and cooking. Her mother would fuss with the pots and Kim would take them from her.

It was Kim who found her on the bathroom floor one night, the shower curtain pulled down around her. She had a cut above one eye. Blood had dried on her cheek, dripped from her chin, sluicing through folds of the plastic curtain to the white tile.

"Mother," she said, squeezing her until her eyes opened. Kim helped her into the bedroom and folded a wet washcloth over her forehead.

"My bicycle—" her mother said.

Kim went to the kitchen for ice and knotted the cubes into plastic bags and came back with towels and packed the bags around her mother's head and body.

"You're burning up, Mom."

"I fell and cut myself." Her eyes widened suddenly. "I thought you were my mother," she said.

—

Instead of calling an ambulance, Kim waited for her father. Long after midnight, headlights veered across the living room ceiling and a motor cut off. She opened the door for two men who shouldered her father into the living room and laid him on the sofa. His uniform was soaked. Theirs were unbuttoned at the necks and stained. One of them kept smiling at Kim. He wanted to say something, but his friend grabbed him by the arm and dragged him to the door. She could hear them snorting and laughing out on the street.

"You get a load of the daughter? What a knockout."

"Don't even think about it."

Kim dialed the operator and asked in English for the emergency number and waited to be connected. She told her mother that help was on the way and changed her washcloth and sat by the bed. When the EMTs arrived, she let them in and started for the bedroom. She got to the door and looked back. One of them had put his kit down and was leaning over her father.

"No, in here," she said.

The men glanced at each other and followed.

—

No one could say how long her mother had endured pain without telling anyone. Cancer had spread from her breast through her body.

Every day Kim rode a bus to the hospital. The buildings she passed had none of the quaint sloping roofs and crisscrossing beams she used to associate with that part of the world. They were factories, mostly, hulking brick structures with small dark windows, some of them broken, and inactive smokestacks. The hospital looked the same.

She would do her homework in a wooden chair by the bed. Chemotherapy pumped into her mother's arms, swelling her face to twice its size. If she rolled onto one side, she could not see the clumps of hair that remained on the pillow. Kim would brush the locks to the floor.

Each afternoon a nurse untied her mother's gown and sponged her flaking skin. She handled her mother too forcefully, Kim thought at first. But the nurse's hands moved with such confidence. There was a gentleness to her strength. Thin bits of rolled-up skin gathered on the sponge, and the nurse brushed them away, humming as she worked. This was her job, tending to the afflicted. How strange to see anyone taking care of her mother.

The nurse helped with the bedpan too, if needed, easing it beneath the dead weight of her mother's legs, then waiting, lifting the covers to check. After, she would empty the pan and replace it with a new one, setting it on the nightstand by the bed. Kim's mother stared into the metal basin long after the nurse had left. There were no mirrors in the room.

How different this person in the bed looked. Could her mother even recognize herself in the warped metal reflection of the pan? How beautiful she used to be, standing at the sink with a tube of lipstick, hair falling to her shoulders, skin so soft in the white light: the unspoken ideal of softness. Kim wondered about the time her father had been watching too. Why had she run back to bed? Perhaps his sudden intrusion had made her forget something important, like the answer to an exam that she knew but couldn't remember. That was a long time ago.

"Has he come once this week?" Kim asked.

"Yesterday," her mother said.

How could she forgive him?

Kim pored over the book in her lap. She enjoyed history. She imagined distant times and places. She remembered feelings. The pages transported her. She was studying the French Revolution, the passionate words of Thomas Paine, who supported the revolt, and the staying view of Edmund Burke, who felt the French had prostituted their past. He sounded stuffy, afraid. She was sad, though, that so many lives had been taken, even in the name of freedom. Somewhere she'd read that Marie Antoinette and Louis really loved each other and that, unlike many royals, they'd always been faithful. She wished they'd been spared.

"Kim," her mother said, "do you remember how you used to sit on the kneeler next to me when I'd pray?"

There would be droughts of silence, then questions, stories cascading like rain.

"Why don't you pray anymore?"

"I do, Mother."

"You're always so angry."

Kim closed the book and picked up a magazine that she'd bought at a kiosk outside the hospital. The ones she chose were usually Italian or French, filled with fairy-tale pictures, women wearing clothes that didn't seem to exist in real life. Her father called the magazines trash. She would leave them on the bus.

"What a marvelous dancer," her mother said. "He was so . . . I'd wait at the landing, listening to him answer all your grandfather's questions. Then I'd come down the stairs and Charlie would be holding his hat, like he was pushing a shopping cart."

"When's he coming next, Mother?"

"There were things he held sacred," she said, closing her eyes.

"What about Grandma and Grandpa? Have they even called once?"

Kim left the room and wandered down the long tiled hall, past the nurses' station, past vacant wheelchairs and open doors and the hard sounds of German. She took the elevator to the first floor and found the chapel, empty and quiet. A metal-lipped dais projected from the wall. On it stood a silver cross. Its facade was scratched, as though polished with a rough cloth, and she imagined the arm movements of the cleaning person that made them. A bucket and mop sat in the corner. Even here in this room removed she could smell antiseptic. Kim stretched her sweater neck up over her nose and covered her ears and tried to think of songs her mother used to sing as they walked home from Mass: "And little lambs eat ivy, a diddledy divey do, wouldn't you?"

Sometimes her mother would stop outside the church to talk. Kim would tug at her dress.

"Be patient," her mom would say.

Kim would balance along the curb, watching the women squeeze each other's gloved hands, their faces hidden beneath hat brims.

Her mother talked to these women on the phone, stretching the cord across the kitchen while she cooked. Kim would duck under.

"Pay with a kiss," her mom would say.

Kim would kneel on warm linoleum peeking through the dark window of the stove; three potatoes wrapped in foil, a meat loaf heating. "He said what?" her mother said, or "That's not what I would do, Love," or "I'll tell you later."

"It's ready," Kim would say. Her mother would give her a cookie and shoo her from the kitchen.

"Don't let your father see."

—

When Kim returned from the chapel, her mother's face was tipped away from the door.

"You're a good girl," she mumbled.

Kim opened her book and pretended to pick up reading where she'd left off. A round-faced nurse pointed to the clock. Her mother strained to turn.

"One minute more?" she said.

The nurse walked away.

Kim saved her place with a folded piece of paper and gathered the other books. She thought of all the lists her mother had forced her to write. She had read once that sacrifice was just a lighter shade of fear.

Her mother's hand crept out, exposing a bracelet of tape and gauze, tubes trailing away. She touched Kim's shoulder.

"Now go home and cook your father a nice dinner."

—

Kim baked a meat loaf. At seven o'clock he still wasn't home. At seven-thirty he walked in with a mustard stain on his uniform, his breath smelling of scotch. He went to the cabinet and took down his bottle and poured three fingers in a glass.

"What?" he said. "I saw her this morning."

"Bullshit."

"Where'd you get such a stinking mouth?"

"You've eaten already."

"Yes."

She put on a hot glove and opened the oven. She held out the meat loaf to show him.

"Mom wanted me to cook you dinner. This is from her."

"Put it in the fridge. I'll have it tomorrow."

He tipped back his glass. His cheeks bulged alternately as he swirled the whisky in his mouth. She went to the garbage pail and stepped on the metal pedal. The lid popped open. She flipped the pan, and the meat loaf dropped in. The lid banged shut.

"Do what you want," he said, and stomped from the kitchen.

She ran water in the pan and left it to soak. She put away the hot glove and cleared the table and went to her room to change into a sweater and pants. At nine the doorbell rang.

"Who's that?" her father called.

"Vincent," she said, coming out of her room. "He's helping me study for a test."

Her father stood in the entrance to the living room. The doorbell rang again.

"You've got a wop helping you study for a test?"

She opened the door.

"Hey, Kim—"

Vincent leaned toward her, then saw her father. Kim pulled him in.

"Dad, this is Vincent Lorenzo. His father's an engineer on the base. He's helping me with trigonometry."

"Hello, Mr. Reilly."

He put out a hand. Her father took it and squeezed.

"Are you a decent man, Vincent?"

"Sir?"

"I said, are you a decent man?"

"C'mon," said Kim.

She pried Vincent free and pushed him out the door.

"No dating on a week night," said her father. "That's the rule."

"This isn't a date."

"I want to see you studying, then."

"I'm going over to Vincent's."

"Like hell you are."

"Vincent, get the car started."

He turned, and she scooped her books up off the stand by the door.

"I'm warning you," said her father.

—

She got in the car and they drove to a place called the Point: a small clearing in the woods where the kids in her class would have bonfires on weekends and drink. A fallen tree concealed the dirt road that led to the clearing. Vincent jumped from the car and ran ahead and lifted the trunk out of the way. He stood in the headlights waving and she waved back.

"So strong," she said, sliding across the bench seat to feel his arm when he got back in.

They parked and he took a six-pack from under the seat and opened a bottle of beer with his teeth and chugged it. He offered her one, which she sipped. She was too busy talking. She told him about her mother, how she seemed to fade in and out now, and how her father lied about going to the hospital, at least she thought he did. She almost cried between sips of beer, apologizing for the way her father had acted back at the house and for being emotional.

"I swear he didn't mean it," she said.

Theirs was the only car in the clearing. Vincent chucked the empty bottles out the window and started to kiss her, his mouth opening and closing, sucking on her lip. His hand snuck under her sweater.

"He gets that way," she said.

"It's okay." He pushed on her breast. "You shouldn't worry. You're so hot."

"You're lying."

"You're the foxiest girl on the base."

He was unbuttoning her pants.

"Here," she said.

She slapped his hand away and did it herself. He unzipped his fly. He pulled her toward him, twisting her so that her back was to the door. At first they were only kissing. Then he slipped his finger under the elastic of her cotton panties. He pushed against her, rubbing back and forth. Her head bumped the armrest. Her knee scraped the dash.

There were tears in her eyes. Suddenly his finger was inside her, wriggling. There came a smacking noise, like a wet kiss.

"Sorry," she gulped. "I—"

"*Che bella.*"

He seemed not to have heard the sound, or he didn't care.

"Are you?" he said.

She could feel him, a pulse beating against her thigh.

"You want this?" he said.

She wanted him to hold her tighter and tighter and not let go. His breathing came in bursts.

He saw her nod and then he was inside her, ripping her with sudden shocking thrusts that burned and soothed. His face vanished. There was hair in her mouth and eyes. She didn't see his face again until the moment he jerked himself free, the moment he rolled his head back and howled and wet her thighs.

"So fucking beautiful," he said.

He reached back to open the door and scrambled out. He stood in the headlights with his back to the car, peeing. She looked down at her stretched underwear, the hot wet running down the inside of her thigh.

When he got back in the car she'd pulled her pants up. He drove her home.

"You'll pass trigonometry," he said.

She didn't say good-bye.

The lights in the house were off. She opened the front door and closed it quietly. Her father stood in the hall. His hand shot out and caught her on the cheek, snapping her head around. She staggered back against the door and clutched her face.

"Don't ever embarrass me in front of your friends."

She ran to the bathroom and locked the door. In the mirror, her one cheek glowed. She undid her pants and sat on the toilet. It stung and she didn't know how to stop it. There was no fleeting cool, only the burn, and a rust-colored stain like a splinter in her white underwear.

She heard cupboard doors opening and closing in the kitchen. A kettle began to whistle. There was a clank and scrape, the sound of one of the stove grills coming out of its notch and being put back. She pulled up her pants and left the bathroom. She went to the kitchen and saw that he'd filled two cups with steaming water. He was dipping in tea bags.

She watched with her arms crossed. He opened and closed a drawer, opened another, and took out spoons and set them on the table. He had a brown bathrobe on over his old faded blue pajamas, and he untied the belt and retied it, tightening the knot. He pushed up the sleeves and pulled back a chair.

"I talked to your mother," he said.

Kim turned and started back down the dim hall.

He called after her, his voice rising to a shout. "I told her what a fine meat loaf you made. Not as good as hers, of course, but right up there. Figured a little competition might give her some incentive to get better. I didn't mention your throwing it out."

She went to her room and took a pocket mirror from her handbag. Her cheek was darkening. She stared at the bruise, willing it to fade, thinking that it wasn't even there, how when she turned from the mirror she would no longer see it, and it would be gone. Then she pressed it to see if it hurt—to remind herself of the feeling.

Kim saw her mother folded in a coffin. Her father had picked out the wig, shaking off the saleswoman until finally he saw something in one of them. He provided a photograph so it could be styled correctly. They did a good job, except that the wig looked new and her mother was dead.

Kim's father sat in the front pew of the small empty church. A pockmark-faced sergeant she'd never seen before sat next to him. Two officers were in the pew behind.

Her father's parents had died long ago. He was the end of the line. Her mother's parents were living, although her grandfather was ill, supposedly too sick to make the trip. And there was the issue of expense. Certainly the military would have paid to fly the body back. Her grandparents couldn't understand why her father wouldn't want her mother buried in the United States. Now they called all the time.

"Is that you, Kimberly?"

Her grandmother sounded young on the phone.

"Kim?" Then, after a long silence, "Is your father there?"

"Raw almonds."

"What?"

"A long time ago, Mom wanted me to tell you my eyes—they're like raw almonds."

There was a thump as though the receiver had been dropped. Kim heard the muffled sound of sobs and a male voice growing louder, suddenly at the phone.

"What did you say to my wife?"

"Nothing."

"Kim?" Her father walked into the room. "Who is it?"

"Young lady," said her grandpa, "you listen to me—"

"I'll get Dad."

"Wait! Are you listening?"

Her dad put out a hand. "What's he saying?"

"That bastard stole your mother from us. You remember that, Kim."

"Feel better soon, Grandpa," said Kim, and handed the phone over.

She listened to her father becoming more steely as she imagined them pleading. His position in Germany was temporary, and it was only a matter of time before he was transferred back to the States. No matter, he wanted her buried there, near him. Period.

—

Now her father sat as if at attention, chest out, back as straight as the dark plank behind him. The priest rose. She took one last look at her mother, the frills around the wrists, gray fingers, now in death, unswollen. One hand was laid over the other, clutching a plain metal rosary Kim had never seen before. She looked appealingly at her father. He was staring at some point on the wall. She turned her back to the priest and reached into the coffin, trying not to touch her mother's flesh, clasping the small crucifix. She jiggled it once, then tugged. Her mother's hands broke apart. The loop snapped free, beads clicking. Kim stuffed the rosary in her pocket like a used tissue and tried to lodge her own in the gap between her mother's unjoined hands, racing because she could feel the priest approaching. The beads caught around a finger, and Kim let go.

"Come now," said the priest, peering over her shoulder.

She sat beside her father. He did not move through the entire service, did not breathe, it seemed. His face was taut, skin stretched thin over sharp-edged bones.

Afterward, her father talked to the priest. The men stood outside the church smoking, the butts glowing red in the gloaming. The two officers were younger than her father. One was ruddy-cheeked and impatient. His lip kept twitching. The other had curly sideburns and began to cough.

"I was supposed to pick her up ten minutes ago."

The other wiped his lips and drew on the cigarette.

"Charlene."

The sergeant blew smoke, a gray petal that curled into his nose and vanished.

"Want one?" he said, holding out the pack to Kim. "What are you, sixteen?"

"Seventeen."

Her father appeared at the door. The men flicked their cigarettes to the ground, and they all shook hands. Her father thanked them.

—

That night he wanted a drink. She watched him open all the cabinets, his movements becoming desperate until he looked at her, and she threw the bottle at him. He jerked his hands up. The bottle missed his head and shattered against the wall. Instead of lunging at her, he dropped to his knees and began to sob.

"*You* should be dead," she said.

He cried with his balled-up fists covering his eyes. Scotch dripped down the wall, thin tendrils of liquor seeping from one broad smear. A dog began to bark outside. She went to the sink for a rag and watched her father groaning on the floor, his Sunday suit rumpled and loose. She could feel her mother's presence then. She could sense her in the absence, the empty space at the sink, and she tried to see some sacrifice in her father's spasms of grief.

Her mother was buried a foreigner.

PART II

WORK

After high school, Kim became a stewardess. She rented an apartment in New York City but couldn't stay in one place. The earth was spinning. Some people hugged the ground; she wanted to fly. She would touch down in cities for the shortest pause and then take off again—no fences, no ties, always new faces. On one trip she sent a note to her father on a piece of hotel stationery. It gave her address but no phone number. Her number was unlisted. She dyed her hair blond.

—

Two months passed, two rent checks, but her belongings were still in boxes. On her first full weekend off, she put on a T-shirt and jeans and opened the windows wide. Air crept through the narrow living room and hall and escaped through the bathroom window, which looked out on an air shaft. She filled a bucket with soapy water and scrubbed the walls and the floor and threw the sponge away when it was black on both sides. No amount of cleaning could take the age out of the walls. She'd bought paint for the kitchen and set to mixing it, wiping her forehead with the back of her hand. She'd picked yellow, not lemon or sunflower or daisy-heart, or the famous brick road that moved the story along, ending at the beginning, or whichever way one looked at it. It was the shade of a mango, sticky-finger sunshine that made her feel tall, made her want to stretch even at four in the morning when all the city still lay in its own shadow.

She ate pizza from a flat carton on the living room floor and boiled water for tea. The four boxes contained everything she owned. She took out bundled stacks of fashion magazines and piled them against the wall. She took the remains of her clothes—the pants and shirts she had no use for now because all she ever wore was her uniform for work—and hung them in the tiny closet in the bedroom. The other two boxes held books, the scattered volumes her mother had left her: *Little House in the Big Woods, The Magical*

Land of Noom. She'd pored over the pictures so many times as a child that the plates were loose: the wooden box with wings that could fly all the way to the back side of the moon; and her favorite, the swarm of boxing gloves like a thousand bees and the man valiantly beating them off with his cane. She could shut her eyes and hear the smack of the stick warding off blows, knocking phantom gloves to the ground. Children's stories, she thought, all had their heroes. There were history textbooks from school that her father had forced her to save. She put them on the bottom and stacked the others on top, leaning towers that climbed the walls. Sticking out of the books were scraps of yellowing paper, some neatly folded, some torn. They were the lists her mother had forced her to make, lists that grew shorter as she grew older until they were just scattered ideas, memories, the closest she ever came to keeping a journal. She took one from a copy of *Charlotte's Web* and read:

Spiders can make webs when they are upside down.

Another read:

The bathroom sink smells like shaving cream.

She grabbed another, not paying attention to which book it came from:

Beth Steuben won't accept that we're all concealing something. Insisted three times that she believes in people. After class Jim Doherty asked if he could borrow her notes 'cause he'd been sick a lot. She told him to leech off someone else.

Not one of the lists was dated. Kim plucked them out rapidly one by one, not looking at them, piling them on the floor. She found a shoe box and gathered the bits of paper into it, trying not to care that she had just erased whatever connection there'd been between the lists and the books that had been their homes, telling herself it was best to forget, she would be happy if she could rid herself of the past. She stuck the box on the floor in the back of her closet and shut the door. Her thoughts were not meant for the light.

—

On short flights she was always too busy, racing against the clock to complete a regimen of tasks. But sometimes on longer flights she would meet men.

It was funny how they caught her eye: the businessman with his folded suit jacket in his lap, looking up from a paper as though to ask a question and then just smiling; the vacationer in Bermuda shorts and sneakers, looking to the aft of the plane to check the lavatories, then turning back, stretching, smiling, his wife asleep next to him—a whole production, to what end? Just to stare at her? There were no false smiles, though. She could see honesty in each of them.

—

Chaz had sideburns and listened to Chet Baker. He'd grown up on the California beaches and smoked and surfed and stared at the sun. He drove a pickup truck and wore sandals, even at night, with jeans and a sweater. She would look down and see his bare feet.

"Just breathing," he would say, wiggling his toes.

They'd walk on the beach and he'd teach her about waves, the ones to look for and the ones to let pass.

"The tides come and go," he said. "The waves keep coming."

He stored a sleeping bag in the back of his truck. Sometimes he would drive up to Big Sur. She knew where the spare key to his apartment was in case he was away. He'd come back with stubble on his face and a bag of dirty laundry.

One day she found an eviction notice on his door. She tried phoning. He never called.

—

Stanley was a doctor from Chicago. She'd met him on a flight to New York, where he was lecturing on breakthroughs in cardiology.

He knew so much. His beeper would sound in the early hours of the morning, and she would hear his grave professional voice on the phone, the one he used with administrators, and the more sensitive tone he used with patients. He used that tone with her sometimes. "There can be no emotions in an operating room," he said.

———

Jack sold insurance. At least he said he did. He had green eyes and talked about the future. Not family, but industry, society, the way things were going to be twenty years down the road. He'd spend an entire dinner discussing fuel prices and OPEC, then change the subject to electric cars and a guy he knew.

"I sell fear," he said once. "I know that's a harsh way of putting it."

"You trick people."

"No, they get what they pay for."

He was a true salesman. Everywhere they went, he always paid cash. She couldn't get over the fact. He'd pat the hood of his Cadillac and wink. "Cash!" If a dress was two hundred dollars, he'd ask, "How much if I give you cash?" The price never changed. "Never hurts to try." But she could see that it did in the way the salespeople regarded her after. She couldn't understand Jack's need to pay less than everyone, why he felt he deserved a discount. He called it "plain smarts." Then he would argue. "What do you mean it's unattractive?"

She kept seeing him, though. Perhaps because of his eyes. He had soft lips.

He left her, too.

———

Then she met Kurt. He had red hair and a chestnut beard that twitched when he smiled. He played professional baseball—a pitcher who had worked his way up through the farm system. The Yankees gave him his big break, then traded him to California. It was in all the papers, he said. He took her to pubs where the bartenders knew him and would give him free beers. He'd tip his cap and pretend to be throwing a ball, only he'd wind up pointing a finger at the man, mouthing exaggerated thank-yous. He'd slap the bar with relief, as though he'd come right from the plane—landed and stopped off to see his old buddies. He confided to Kim that he always forgot the bartenders' names. "Christ," he said. "I probably know one in every state—every time we travel."

"I bet you've got a girl in every state," she said.

He grinned and didn't deny it. He'd shake hands with the men at the bar, strangers. He loved the camaraderie as much as the game, the endless stories and discussions of numbers that meant nothing to Kim.

"How those kids of yours?" she'd hear him say to the bartender, or "You still getting out to the park?"

"Yanks coulda used you this year, Kurt. Any chance ya coming back?"

He'd return to the table with two sweating bottles and roll his eyes as though to apologize for the delay, the responsibilities of fame. She figured he had money. He just didn't know what to do with it. He wore jeans and drank for free.

She asked what it was like growing up on a farm, and he told her about early morning frosts and homemade sausage, work-filled days that made dinner taste like heaven. She asked if he was religious.

"Fuck no," he said. "The closest I get to religion is pitching a no-hitter. How 'bout you?"

She couldn't understand how he went from working on a farm to playing professional ball.

"Did you have to audition? They didn't just send someone out to the farm and offer you a job, did they?"

He tipped his bottle back and wiped his beard. His eyes widened suddenly and he rolled his head back with laughter.

"I was wondering how you knew I grew up on a farm," he said. "I'm thinking, Wow, does it show that bad? I guess you don't know about the minors, do ya? We call it the farm system. Christ, you're cute."

She started to read the sports pages, to see if his name was ever mentioned. Sometimes it was. It would show up in little print. A month later she read he'd been cut. It didn't say why, only that he'd been sent back to the minors. Back to the farm, she thought.

He wouldn't call. They never did. What was there to discuss anyway? If they no longer wanted to see her, did she really need to hear their reasons? She could think of a million, but they only needed one, and that one was always the same.

She remembered as a girl finding pennies on the ground. "Heads up," her father would say. "A keeper." She'd put it in her pocket. Now she couldn't remember the last time she'd seen someone stop for a penny.

After four years, she was promoted and moved to first class. The shifts were no better, but she traveled to exotic places. She sent a postcard to her father of a giant stone Buddha with ivy growing up its belly. "Still doing push-ups?" she wrote. She sent another of Big Ben, its spire silhouetted against the moon, and wrote, "I looked for Peter Pan. Couldn't find him."

Twice she tried calling her father, maybe more, not to talk but to hear his voice. The years made her reasons for not calling him seem less real, and then, possibly, there was the chance that they might talk, that she'd find herself in conversation without having to plan it. But the times he answered, she'd freeze. "Who's this? Hello? Hello?" he'd bark, then a click, as she stood there with a shaking hand covering the receiver.

—

One time on a flight, she wasn't paying attention and dropped a hot towel in a woman's lap. The woman swiped at the towel as if it were a live snake.

"Hot, hot!"

"It got away," said Kim, retrieving it from the floor. "I'm so sorry."

The woman adjusted her glasses and straightened the rings on her fingers.

The senior stewardess on board waited for Kim behind the curtain. "Those towels can be tricky," she said, clucking her tongue. "You'll get the hang of it, though."

The older stewardesses stuck together. She'd see them in the airport coffee shops—tight uninviting circles. One said to Kim, "They're talking about a revised mandatory hair length. If I had your hair, I'd just hate to have to cut it."

Her hair only came down to her shoulders. If need be she could pin it up under a hat. There was nothing she could do or say that would warm them to her, and she hardly wanted to make herself look less desirable.

—

She'd flown an extra shift. The terminal was deserted by the time she got off, and her feet throbbed. She couldn't wait to sit on the bus. She passed the bar, which was still open, and saw the stewardess who'd made the comment about her hair sitting over a drink. The woman spotted Kim and waved her over before she could look away. They were alone, save for the bartender and a janitor, who was cleaning the tiled entrance to the rest rooms with a bucket of water and a mop. The bartender was drying glasses, stacking them on a shelf behind the register. The woman's face powder had dried and caked around the eyes, and she looked as though she hadn't slept in days. She gestured to a chair, but Kim remained standing. She pointed at Kim with a half-smoked cigarette and blew smoke and tapped ash in an amber-colored glass ashtray.

"I've been watching you," she said, as though she'd been waiting for a reason to report Kim. "You don't want to sit?"

Kim knew to be careful. "It's late, ma'am."

"Ma'am?" The woman's lips curled. They were faded. Her lipstick had rubbed off on the glass before her. "You're like the rest of them," she said, slurring slightly. "What is it you want?"

"I don't—"

"What are your plans, goals?"

Kim shook her head. The woman smiled again, only the smile quickly disappeared. She ground out her cigarette.

"I've been in this business twenty years."

She signaled the bartender for another drink and took out a cigarette. She lit it and shook the match out and leaned across the table.

"You don't mind that you're a blank slate for men to write on?" She stared at Kim. "You want to be like the rest of them?"

"No, ma'am," said Kim.

"I'm sure you have your excuses."

The bartender came around with her glass and took the empty one. "Fifteen minutes, Pat."

She thanked him.

"Bit of advice," she said, turning back to Kim. "I've never relied on anyone but myself."

"Yes, ma'am."

"Why do you keep calling me *ma'am?* I'm not some dowdy schoolteacher. Let me guess: Don't speak unless spoken to, right?"

Kim didn't say anything.

"This is your first job, isn't it? Did you go to college?"

"No."

"All the excuses." She sipped her drink. "You do have a plan, though. Yes, you do."

"It's late."

"How do you live with yourself?"

Kim shook her head. What had she done for this woman to single her out? Who was Pat to tell her how to live or to presume that something was lacking from her life? Did she really believe that anything she could say might lessen a void or fill some sense of another woman's emptiness? No, it was pure spite, she told herself. She never wanted to see the woman again. She tried to stare as blankly as possible.

"You make me so angry," said the woman. "Hell, it's your life."

Kim nodded.

———

She took off her shoes on the bus and leaned her head against the window. When she got home, she hung up her uniform and put on a nightshirt and sat in bed. There was a note pad by the phone, and a pen, and she tore off a sheet and wrote:

Father once said, Women have caused wars, but none have stopped them.

She tried to think of one. She looked at the words on the page, then wrote:

Lemon rinds and pumpkin seeds.

She thought some more and added:

The second greatest commandment wasn't even a commandment.

She folded the piece of paper twice, got out of bed, and went to the closet. She dug through layers of shoes to get to the shoe box in the back, lifted the lid, and stuck the piece of paper inside. She went back to bed, set the alarm on her clock, and turned off the light. She had to get up in four hours.

It was summer, 1976. On the news one night she watched footage of square-rigged sailing ships in New York Harbor. They were honoring the country's bicentennial. She sat on her bed and ate salad from a bowl, the dressing sweet, puddled deep in the bottom, and thought how beautiful the tall ships were, their masts like stacked crosses rising to the sky, sails fat with wind, straining against their ties. "All the way from Norway," said the announcer about one. "That's a long trip home." The ships seemed displaced as they slipped silently past navy destroyers, tugboats, and modern fireboats vigorously spuming water hundreds of feet, soaring arches that wowed the commentators. The camera helicoptered up for a closing shot. It was far above the harbor, looking down, and all the boats seemed the same except for the sailing ships, which were still discernible because of their masts—quiet, prickly islands drifting. For one day they had their time in the light. Afterward they'd be put away like magnificent obsolete toys.

For weeks she thought about those ships, their melancholy stillness amid so much commotion. Nothing could touch them. Was it perhaps all they could do to stay afloat, to get through the day?

—

She turned twenty-three and then twenty-four. The senior stewardesses still considered her young. Her father sent birthday cards. Twenty-four came attached to a slim package. She opened the card first: a glossy photo of a cake that read *For my little girl.* There were five hundred-dollar bills taped to the inside, and she peeled the tape off carefully and put the money in her purse. Then she tore the wrapping paper off the package. It was her mom's leather photo album. She flipped it open to a sepia picture of a group of men and her father, shirtless, pants rolled, piling sandbags around a bunker. He was smiling, as though he were really enjoying himself, a cigarette tucked behind his ear. She stuck the card in the album and closed it. Then she took it back out. She went to the phone and dialed her father and stared at the shiny card as the line rang.

"Daddy," she said, "it's me."

There was surprise in the silence.

"I got the money."

"Oh, the money," he said.

"I miss you."

"That's for savings, now."

"I'm holding the card in my hand. Dad, do you have something to write with?"

"Are you listening to me?" he said.

"Dad, I want you to have my phone number."

She could hear grumbling, a drawer opening.

"Do you have a pen?" she said.

"Yes. Go, go, go."

She said the number and repeated it.

"What about the album?" he said.

"Yes, Dad. I love you."

She hung up and went to the refrigerator for ice cream. She sat on her bed with a spoon and a paper towel. She didn't need the approval of the older stewardesses. Or, if she had at one point, she knew she didn't need it now. At the end of the day, if a new stewardess approached her in the airport bar, starched from college, an unwrinkled smile, she would invite her to sit. The older stewardesses—they were bitter because they'd been at their jobs too long. She couldn't become like them.

An hour later her father called.

"Six years," he said. "Six years without a goddamn phone call. If your mother were alive—"

Kim didn't say a word. She just listened.

She met Sam in '79 on a flight to Paris.

"I'm from Paris," he said with a heavy drawl. "Paris, Texas."

At first she didn't like his laugh. It drew attention. He had a way of working his fingers when he talked, as though he were playing the piano. It wouldn't have been so noticeable if his hands weren't so large.

"He flies this route regularly," said one of the other stewardesses.

"I don't feel like talking to him," Kim said.

"He's one of the richest men in Dallas."

Kim peered back through the curtain. He'd stuffed his napkin into his shirt collar and was eating. His chin was soft, undefined.

"Suit yourself," said the stewardess. She was putting on fresh lipstick, staring at her reflection in the door of a stainless steel cabinet. "But if I were you . . ." She blotted her lips on a napkin and took one last look. "Remember, we're the next best thing to movie stars."

—

After lunch, Kim went to remove the Texan's tray. He reached out slowly and touched her hand. "They're nice," he said, taking her other hand.

For some reason she didn't pull away.

"I always thought you could tell a person by their hands," he said.

She found herself listening to the rhythm of his accent and his deep, soothing voice. He turned her palms up.

"Sad, though. Darling, I can tell. They're fragile and need looking after. Are these sad hands?"

She found her eyes filling with tears.

"This picture's all twisted around here. You should be sitting and it's I who should be serving you."

He smiled.

—

Their first date was in New York. He took her to a restaurant on the Upper West Side. She told him she liked lobster, and he ordered a seven-pounder to share. They drank salty dogs and split four desserts. Sam did all the ordering. They kissed in the back of his limousine.

He liked to say he'd made his money "drilling in all the right places." A little luck never hurt. He regaled her with stories using terms he'd grown up with, odd phrases involving cats in tall grass, and porches, and piss and rain, and hot kitchens, that she couldn't keep straight—a hundred Texas ways of saying "bullshit."

"You've never heard that one before?" he'd say. "Missy, I thought you lived in Texas?"

"Only for a short time," she said. "And no one ever talked like you."

He would call a few days ahead of his arrival to make sure she'd be in town. She would wait for him in the lobby of his hotel, and he would take her shopping at Macy's and Bloomingdale's. She would fill a dressing room with clothes and try them on and he would point at the ones he liked with his half-smoked cigar. He'd grin as he paid, and she'd hang off his arm and rub his stomach. As soon as they got outside he would relight his cigar and wave for the limo. He would drop her off with a tip of the hat and an hour or two to get ready for dinner. She'd lay the garment bags out and try on everything again, posing before the mirror on tiptoes, calves tensed, her image approaching, receding, looking back over the shoulder—the allure of the clothes and the curious reflection of herself in them.

—

The first time they slept together was in the Waldorf-Astoria. He was always smiling, but on top of her, with his hands moving down her sides, his face was all business. His eyes and lips clenched shut. He had hair on his shoulder blades and the back of his neck. His movements were jerky, disconnected. Yet there was something soothing about him, forgivable.

"Anything you ever need, darling, just call ol' Sam."

Months passed. The relationship was easy, until the first time she couldn't meet him. Then he was angry.

He shouted at her over the phone. "I make myself available to you when I come. You think you could do the same? Should I just not bother calling?"

They talked again later.

"I didn't mean those things," he said. "I was disappointed, that's all."

The next time she saw him he lavished her with gifts. "Give ol' Blue Skies a hug," he said, and she wrapped herself in his thick arms.

A month later, he stunned her by paying her rent. He never said anything. The landlord returned her check and she called to find out the problem.

"Your rent's been paid for the year," he said.

She called Sam and demanded he stop. He became obstinate.

"I told you. Trust ol' Sam."

"No one's ever been so kind to me."

It was only a matter of time before her schedule conflicted again with his visit. She waited until the last minute and called in sick. That night they made love on his hotel balcony. They were so high up, she was unashamed. She stood naked by the rail looking down on the city.

"Sweet child," he said, coming up behind her, "I could almost marry you."

What if he actually proposed? What if he asked her to move to Texas? She imagined his ranch: fields with grazing cattle, horses, a barn with a silo, wide-open land in every direction. She'd look out the window in the late afternoon and see the rising dust trail of a pickup approaching—Sam, back from a business trip, returning home to her. The scattered week nights and hasty hotel stays, the time they shared now would be time apart. She would no longer have to alter her schedule for their lives to overlap.

"You wouldn't like it," he said.

She thought she would.

"You'd get cow shit on them fancy heels. When I picture you, it's not with a pig, darling. It's with pearls."

A miss was as good as a mile. "Almost" meant never. Did he really believe she wouldn't be happy living with him, or was he content seeing her in New York only, keeping her caged to take out when he pleased?

—

Two years passed. She would study his face, the imperfections, and gradually his chin; the red of his cheeks began to remind her of the demands he made on her time.

Once, at a charity dinner, she noticed a man at a corner table, staring. At first she thought it rude. His hair was white with the faintest touch of blond. He was smoking a long cigarette and looked simply curious, as if he were trying to map out her story. A woman sat next to him, her hair pulled into a perfect French twist. Kim found herself looking more at the woman than the man, her black off-the-shoulder dress and diamond earrings. She had a way of tilting her head back when she laughed, as if on a hinge. Her shoulders came forward, exaggerating her cleavage. Her eyes were too close-set for the breadth of her lips and made her face seem bottom heavy. Yet Kim could see men staring at her. All around the room she could see them, glasses tipped to their lips, eyes cast sideways, laughing with the rest of their tables. Only the white-haired man she was with seemed uninterested—attentive but preoccupied. He was looking at Kim.

The band began to play. Sam asked Kim to dance. Everyone at the table smiled. He led her to the floor and fanned a hand across her bare back. He gripped her wrist and jerked her to the side, his thick interlocking fingers spreading hers wide. He looked down at his feet.

"You just follow ol' Sam."

He turned her, and for a moment she forgot about the white-haired man. She saw faces, ties, rings like flashes, a spark—then gone. She strained to see things longer. She'd snap her head the other way, hoping to recapture an image. Only Sam's face, red and shiny, remained constant. He hadn't been looking at other women. She was the sole source of his attention, and this suddenly repulsed her—this man with the gray bow tie and horseshoe studs. His hands were like paws. He never smiled. He leered.

Throughout dinner there were whispered asides of how good they looked together, assurances from the man sitting next to her that Sam's feelings were genuine, that she was the best thing to happen to him. As they went to leave, Sam had to use the "little boys' " room. She waited by the coat check, trying not to look at anyone. A hand touched her shoulder.

"I was afraid I wouldn't have an opportunity to meet you," said the white-haired man. His eyes were very blue. "Although if I were in his shoes, I wouldn't leave you alone much either."

"I'm glad you're not in his shoes," she said.

His brow raised. "They are boots, aren't they? Leave your purse behind."

He turned and she realized Sam was behind her. She set her purse down, her heart racing as Sam helped with her coat. He lifted her hair out from under the collar and draped an arm over her shoulder, pulling her toward the stairs.

"I can't wait to get out of here," he said.

"Miss," came a voice, "you forgot this."

The white-haired man was holding out her purse. The woman in the black dress was at his side, arm locked in his.

"Thank you," said Sam. He nodded to the man and tipped his hat to the woman and steered Kim away without further words.

"Child," he said in the car, "sometimes I don't know what you're thinking. Give ol' Sam a kiss."

She pecked him on the cheek. He leaned over and put his mouth over hers. The car reeked of cigars. She dug her nails into the seat.

Later, when Sam was asleep, she took her purse to the bathroom. She'd been afraid to open it sooner. She sat on the edge of the bathtub. Inside, she found a cream-colored business card. ROBERT SANDERS, it read, with a black fountain-pen stroke through the last name. She stared at it, then looked at her reflection in the mirror: her cheeks narrower than they used to be, but still round like a teacup, curved, flat at the chin, her mother's resigned lips and nothing nose, small but too wide at the bridge—she'd always admired a thin nose—and her almond eyes, big, unlike her father's, whose slits had recorded so much but shared little. What was it Robert saw? She took her hair in both hands and twisted it up and stared at herself, holding it there.

The following afternoon she called Robert. At eight, the buzzer rang, and she descended to the street to find a car waiting. She didn't know where she was going but didn't ask questions. She wanted to preserve the surprise.

It was a restaurant she'd never been to before, set in from the street with a low hedgerow in front that formed a boxed landing. Brass lanterns lit a heavy oak door. There was no sign that Kim could see to indicate the name. A set of roman numerals marked the address. The driver opened her door and extended his hand for support.

"Enjoy your dinner," he said.

She hesitated and started to unsnap her evening bag, then changed her mind and smiled.

Inside, the walls were painted olive with dark chest-high wooden wainscoting. Candles flickered in inverted bell-shaped sconces on either side of the coat-check door. A woman rose from a stool. She was already holding a numbered card in her palm. Kim started to take off her coat. A man hurried to assist.

"You are dining with Mr. Sanders," he said, passing the coat to the woman in return for the card. "He described you well."

"He did?"

"Only you are more beautiful."

He stepped back, half bowing, to usher her through a narrow archway. He followed her into the main room and stepped around her as she paused. A massive urn stood against the far wall, blue and green hydrangeas spilling over its rim in waves. Banquettes lined the walls—faces turned inward, the backs of heads reflected in a procession of tipped mirrors. Robert was seated at the first of four round tables in the center, reading from a leather-bound wine list. He noticed her and his face came to life. He folded his napkin and stood, eyes bright and inviting.

"Forgive me if I am excited," he said, stepping forward.

His hand found the back of her arm just above the elbow—a soft touch. His lips came delicately close to her cheek, and as he sought to kiss her other cheek, his hand slipped down to her wrist and then to her fingertips. The maître d' was waiting behind her chair.

"Mr. Sanders, enjoy," he said.

"Thank you."

Robert sat when she did. He stared. He wouldn't look away, and she tried not to smile. The waiter brought menus. Robert glanced at his, then retrieved the wine list.

"What looks good to you?" he said.

"The lobster."

"It is very good here."

"Should I have something else?"

"Only if you want to."

Robert's watch was thin, refined compared to Sam's. His shirt was striped, with stiff starched cuffs, held by enamel links and the tiniest of chains. She found herself staring at the buttons of his jacket, the crest on each, and then at his face as he concentrated on the list. His hair was the softest white, ageless, as though it had been that color from birth, parted just above the left eye, with square razor-cut sideburns. He could have been a pilot, or possibly a professor. He had that penetrating look, a patient look, as though he saw things far ahead but felt no rush to show what in time would reveal itself. The skin above his lips was smooth and unworried.

When she excused herself to go to the powder room, he got up. He stood again when she returned.

"You don't have to do that," she said.

"I do."

She watched him cut into his appetizer, one arm angled as if holding a dancer's hand.

"I'm happy," she said.

Robert raised his glass. "In unguarded eyes we remember how to love."

She offered her hand across the table. When he took it, she could feel the cool of a ring against her skin. She imagined living at the periphery of someone's life.

"You are very beautiful," he said.

"So is your wife."

For a moment he looked bewildered.

"That was not my wife," he said.

He sipped his wine thoughtfully, then added that she was simply the person he'd invited to that dinner. "She had a distinctive laugh," he said. He didn't mention Sam.

If Kim spoke, his eyes never strayed. When a busboy interrupted, Robert raised a hand and begged her to continue, refusing to acknowledge the man's presence until she finished her sentence. Then he thanked the man for waiting and nodded for more water.

Shortly after the main course arrived, the chef appeared. He put his hand on Robert's shoulder, and Robert stood to greet him. He introduced Kim. The chef kissed the back of her hand. She watched him return to the kitchen, not stopping at any of the other tables.

From where they sat, they could observe everyone entering the restaurant. More than once, couples came over to say hello: women with feathered necklines and freshly coiffed hair, men with striped ties and broad Windsor knots. Robert signaled a waiter. "A bottle of Cristal for the ambassador," he said. Minutes later, he lifted his wineglass. Across the room, a gray-haired man in a heavy gray suit nodded and raised his flute in return. He nodded to Kim as well.

When she turned back, Robert was staring again, smiling. There were more secluded tables that they could have sat at, tables that initially she might have thought were more romantic. Here they were the center of attention. Robert gazed at her as though they were alone.

———

After dinner he dropped her off. He walked her to her doorstep and kissed her. He waited until she found her keys.

Before bed, she boiled a pot of water. She put on a robe and sat at the kitchen counter, waiting for the pot to whistle. At last, she poured the steaming water. She wrapped the tea bag around a spoon, squeezing it against the side of the mug, strangling it with its own thread until the color swirled. The water darkened. Then she called Sam. She told him it was over, that she'd met someone.

"Sunshine, I know we're far apart."

"The distance—"

"Is controllable. You're right, right to be sore."

"No, my schedule—"

"The time apart."

"Forget time."

"You're not making sense."

"I told you!" she said. "I met someone."

"What do you mean, someone? Darling, *I'm* someone! Aren't I?"

She hung up. He kept calling and she hung up repeatedly.

"Stop!" she finally shouted. "I'm serious."

"Whatever I did," he said, "I'll fix it!"

"You can't fix not being right for me."

"After all—" His voice trailed away, then came back amplified, and she could picture the phone jammed against his reddening jowl. "Do I know him?" he said. "I probably introduced you."

"Don't shout."

"What's his name?"

"Stop being angry."

"We're not right?"

"No, Sam."

"You mean *I'm* not right. Tell ol' Sam why you're hanging him out to dry. I know I'm no prize. You got an itch I can't scratch?"

"Sam, you just . . . I won't get into this."

"Goddammit, girl. Tell me about him, then."

"I'm not—"

"Do I deserve this? Do I?" Then, after a long silence: "You're a cold one, girl. I'll see you in the sky."

He hung up. Her tea was still warm.

She'd never broken with a man before. Her impulse was to call back and say she'd think it over. She imagined Sam throwing back a drink from a glass that looked miniature in his grasp, pounding his fist, raising it to strike her. "That's what *you* deserve," he'd say, biting down on his cigar. She deserved to hurt, but she didn't. She dug her fingernails into her arm, looked at the marks, rubbed them, watched them fade. Nothing. She thought of Robert and his quiet confidence, and as the minutes passed she felt a sense of confidence too: enough to believe that no matter how angry Sam was, no matter how tempting or flattering his seeming desire was, she was right to have left him. He needed her, and she knew enough not to confuse need with love. She would not be like her mother.

There was a movie-ticket stub on the counter, and she took a pencil, tapped her lips, and scribbled:

Sam's inconvenienced. Tomorrow he'll realize I'm nothing, just the woman who came with the room.

That's all she'd ever been to him. She thought again of Robert, of his hand touching her arm. He didn't need her, so there couldn't be the same confusion. And she didn't need him either—was beyond wanting to be married, she told herself. She'd taken a risk. She'd stepped out on thin ice and it hadn't cracked yet. She was excited. Was this what it felt like to start loving someone?

She took the ticket stub and tore it, throwing away the bigger piece. She stuck what was left to the refrigerator with a magnet: *woman who came with the room,* it read.

Robert always sent his car. Joseph, the driver, was on call around the clock. He'd massage his brow with the heels of his hands at stoplights, crack his knuckles and stretch his fingers, and wrap them back around the wheel. Eventually he would ask how she was, how work was going. She wondered what Robert had told him, if Joseph knew she was a stewardess or if he was just being polite. She told him herself finally. He didn't seem surprised.

His father had driven a bus in New York for forty years. He could rattle off all the different lines his father had worked, a series of letters and numbers, like a secret code. He said some were crosstown and some ran the avenues. Joseph grew up in Gravesend, Brooklyn, went to Sheepshead Bay High School. He got his girlfriend pregnant at Jones Beach and married her. He started out driving taxis. He met Robert driving limos. "At LaGuardia," he said, "I got to talking. Told him how it was my twelfth wedding anniversary. He called the next day and offered me a job." It gave him the security to have a second daughter.

"Once my wife was sick and had to go to the hospital," he told her one afternoon as he drove her home. "Mr. Sanders paid for the whole thing. Didn't take nothing out of my salary. You're very lucky, ma'am."

She watched his face in the rearview mirror and wondered if he meant it.

"Do you like ice cream, Joseph? Pull over."

She hopped out of the car before he could come around for the door.

"What flavor?" she called. He was shaking his head.

She disappeared into the store and returned a moment later with two cones, already dripping. She licked her finger and handed him napkins.

"So the steering wheel doesn't get sticky," she said.

She sat on the bumper. Joseph leaned against the door. He gripped the cone tentatively, as though he were holding it for someone, and stared off. Ice cream ran across his fingers. A drop fell to the cement. He made no effort to wipe himself.

"You don't like coffee?" she said.

He looked at her and then at the cone.

"I don't know anyone that doesn't like coffee ice cream," she said.

He seemed to be sizing up the mess. At last he brought the cone to his mouth and bit with his lips. A dab got on his chin and she laughed.

"Don't tell Robert," she said. "He can't know my vices."

—

The sun was out, and she decided to walk the rest of the way home. She stopped at a deli for a newspaper and some fruit. The man behind the register was watching her in a convex mirror. It reflected the aisles and made her look fat.

A woman rapped the counter with her knuckles, startling the clerk.

"Am I standing here for nothing?" she said.

"Okay, okay, what you want?"

Kim picked out peaches and took them to the register. The woman ahead of her was buying a lottery ticket. She was going over the tiny numbers with a pen, picking randomly—or perhaps plugging in digits from somewhere in her life that had taken on significance—praying that this was the dollar that multiplied a million times, that would deliver her a new life.

The man gathered Kim's peaches into a bag and rang her up. His lips twitched into a broad smile.

"I think I have change," Kim said, digging in her pockets. "How much again?"

"No biggy."

She could only find a nickel.

"Here's another dollar," she said.

The man shook his head and closed the register. "For pretty lady, forget it," he said.

She thanked him and turned. There were three people waiting in line behind her.

Robert wasn't controlling the way Sam was. He planned around *her* schedule. He gave the impression that she truly added value to his life, that the hardness of her past provided meaning. He asked about her former lovers as though he were inviting her to confide some grave heartbreak.

"I was careless with my virginity," she said.

"Perhaps it's the one thing we feel pure ownership of at that age."

"It was meaningless," she said.

His smile suggested it was mild jealousy that made him curious, perhaps vanity.

"What we lose," he said, "and what we give up are two separate things. Looking back, the sex was only sex. Why we ever choose to equate it with loss of youth . . . I wonder what you were like. I wish I could have known you growing up."

He took her shopping at Bergdorf's. She mentioned Bloomingdale's.

"I'm going to arrange an account for you," he said. "Promise me you will shop here."

Within a week, a charge card arrived in the mail. She never received a bill.

At first, he accompanied her. He would call ahead. A woman would meet them coming off the elevator. They would sit and drink coffee as models glided through the room wearing suits the woman had preselected for Kim.

Robert withheld his comments until after she'd expressed hers. He didn't wish to taint her judgment. Yet he was not afraid to contradict her choices. He seemed aware of the fact that she wanted to dress for him, but he also wanted her to choose for herself and have fun.

"Perhaps you might show us four or five evening suits now," he said to the woman.

Kim began to see that statements like these were directed as much to her as to the salesperson. They were part of a subtle education, and if she said something to reflect her study—"Those buttons are too decorative for daytime," or "It's a gorgeous linen, but not for dinner"—his eyes would sparkle. He seemed to take the greatest pleasure in teaching her.

"Your perfume should be softer," he said. "I know a man. He will choose your fragrance."

She wanted to share Robert's taste. She would receive compliments from strangers—women behind makeup counters, in dressing rooms—even her tailor noticed the changes in her clothes. They were people who didn't have to say anything, but they did. It seemed that Robert was always correct.

—

The first time he visited her apartment was the first time they made love. He brought four bottles of wine.

"Are we going to drink all that?" she said.

"I want you to taste," he explained.

She went to the kitchen and smoothed her skirt. She looked through the drawers for a corkscrew, digging through handfuls of unmatching silverware. Finally, she found one. She bent to check her hair in a metal tray by the sink and returned to the living room and sat down next to him.

"What should we start with?" she said.

"I thought the La Tour. It needs to be decanted."

She hesitated.

"Shall I help?" He kissed her. "Come, now."

He led her back to the cramped kitchen and started to go through the cupboards. The paint on the doors was chipping, and a fingernail-sized fleck fluttered to the floor like a leaf. He seemed not to notice.

"Let's see what we can do," he said. He moved some glasses and took down a vase. "Perfect, right? You're blushing."

He touched her chin lightly, coaxing her face toward his. It was the purest gesture of tenderness, she thought.

"You look lovely," he said. "Now, glasses. Do you not have red?"

"Sorry?"

"That's fine."

He ushered her back to the living room and removed the foil from the neck of the first bottle. "After this, you will be spoiled. We'll finish the one you like best."

He got the cork off and poured the wine into the vase.

"That's splendid. We'll let it sit. I want to see the rest of your apartment. Do you have snaps?"

She showed him the back of her dress. "They're buttons," she said, and he laughed.

"Darling, I mean pictures."

She took out the photo album her father had sent and began to flip through it.

"Slower," he said, putting his hand over hers. "I want to savor them." He pointed to one. "Your mother and father?"

"Just after they married."

Her parents were holding hands. Her mother always looked great in photographs. It was a look she could sustain for the blink of an eye, without lines of worry—a dimpled smile that never appeared in life, only in pictures. It was how she wanted to be remembered. The smiles would endure. They would tell a different story. Her father was in uniform, dark jacket, white gloves, his head shaved to a bristle, a dusty shadow that would never again change length.

"He fought at Okinawa," she said.

Robert nodded gravely.

"I don't know why I feel I always have to say that," she said.

"You should be proud."

"I guess I am."

He looked at the photo some more.

"You say he fought in the Korean War, too?"

"Inchon."

Robert shook his head. "I have to confess, I don't know where that is. Was that a specific fight?"

"It's where the marines first landed, before we took back Seoul. Anytime there was an invasion, they'd send in my dad."

"I'm sure he's an honorable man."

"He says the military has changed."

Robert nodded as if he agreed. His eyes were unjudging. She wondered what he was thinking.

He turned the page to a picture of a young girl in a white dress, squatting in a sandbox with a shovel. A bow captured her bangs.

"Now who's that?" He grinned.

She liked the way he gestured, the way he held his wineglass, fingers split around the stem. The glass would tip, not out of carelessness, she thought, but playfully, as if he were teasing the wine to the rim. His movements were never sudden or distracting. She let his fingers trace the soft lines in her forehead.

"You're too young to have these," he said.

He stared and then turned back to the photo album.

"So thin—look here, like a little match girl. Those knees: I bet the boys teased you. If they could see you now. I try to tell my son—but he won't listen—'If they look like a pinup at twelve, they won't later on.' It's the ones like you. Time is an artist. You will become more and more beautiful." He paused and touched her forehead playfully. "Unless you worry too much."

She kicked off her shoes and folded her feet beneath her. Bit by bit, she began to lean against his shoulder. When she kissed him, she kissed softly, then forcefully. He allowed her to lead. He explained about the wines, their châteaus and the types of grapes used, what she should be tasting. Whispers tickled her ear. She began to undo his tie. His jacket slipped off. She unbuttoned his shirt and kissed the gray hairs on his chest and grasped his zipper. The photo album fell to the floor. She swung her feet out from under her and reared back, elbows digging into the buckling cushion for support. She began to pull up her skirt—the lace of her stockings, then white cool-bumped skin, revealed one walking finger at a time. His hands eased over the tops of her thighs. His jaw tensed. She could see the patience in his lips ebbing, the sudden pull-back nods of his head as he caught himself like a sleeper fighting for consciousness; only his face was alert, prickling with desire. His eyes were probing, she thought, even as his muscles grew taut, as he put himself inside her and pushed. It was over quickly. A rush of air escaped his lips. A strand of white hair fell into his eyes.

"I was too excited," he said.

—

She had on his shirt. They lay with their heads at opposite ends of the sofa, and he massaged her foot and sipped wine and looked about the apartment. A poster of Greta Garbo was pinned to the wall as carelessly as a note on a refrigerator: a shop girl turned beauty queen turned movie star, so full of sadness, so rich with knowledge, eyes gazing up as if the camera hung above her. A spider plant sat in a yellow bowl on the windowsill, one long dangling offshoot wavering in the draft. The heating pipes knocked, filling with steam. The creaks of the neighbor's footsteps, the wind rattling the window—all seemed amplified. Robert's eyes roamed. Stacks of magazines rose from the floor, old dog-eared *Vogue*s with torn-out pages protruding: pictures of Dietrich and Hayworth, studies in glamour; ads that she saved because of a specific haircut or pair of shoes. They leaned against the wall like the used collections of a street vendor. Then there were the towers of books. She still didn't have shelves or cabinets. The books climbed the walls, precariously balanced as though the removal of even one might send them all crashing down. Robert was used to so much better, she knew.

"Have you read all of these?" he said.

"I want to."

"*Treasure Island?*" He pointed.

"Yes."

"You read it?"

"Is that odd?"

He pointed again. "*Madame Bovary?*"

"Someday."

"You have many children's books. Is there something I should know? Someone hiding in an apple barrel?"

She shook her head and remained still.

"They surprise me," she said.

"Happy endings?"

"I know how *Madame Bovary* ends."

His forehead wrinkled slightly as he considered this, then relaxed.

"Our vase worked well, didn't it?" he said.

She swung her legs around and lay with her head on his shoulder. She curled his chest hairs between her fingers. His sweat had no scent.

"I'm not used to having company," she said.

"Are you happy here?"

"I feel safe."

"Back when I was in my twenties, before you were even born—"

"Oh, please."

"I was in Geneva."

He looked about suddenly and she sat up. "What's wrong?"

"Nothing, nothing." He smiled and kissed her forehead.

He got down off the sofa and pressed his cheek to the floor. His buttocks were pale and folded slightly where they joined the back of his thighs—two crescent shadows that twisted as he crawled. His hipbones protruded.

"What are you doing?"

"One of my links is missing. It must have fallen out—earlier."

She twisted the shirt cuff around and checked the empty eyelet.

"Don't you see it?" she said.

"Not yet."

"I think you just wanted to show off your bottom."

He looked back over his shoulder, and she laughed.

"A-ha!" He held the gold knot up to the light. He turned back and leaned against the sofa, resting his chin on her thigh. She held her wrist out and he worked to refasten the cuff.

"So where was I?" he said.

"In Geneva."

"That's right, at a dinner. There was a young woman sitting alone in a long hall, draped across a chair, wearing a white gown and gloves. I walked past her. I remember the way her elbow rested on the arm of the chair. Her one hand pointed up to heaven as if she were holding a cigarette, but she wasn't. Her dress pooled on the floor in front of her and I couldn't see her feet. Something about the angle, maybe the expression, her eyebrows—I had to walk by again, and then a third time. She finally noticed me and smiled, and it was one of those racking smiles, heartbreakingly spontaneous—"

"Do I ever smile like that?"

"Not that I've seen, but—"

She stood up sharply and went to the bedroom. She sat on her hands on the edge of the bed in the dark. She heard footsteps, a drawer in the kitchen, and then more footsteps—sounds that were strange because she was not making them, because in stillness she was accustomed to a mirroring stillness, not to movement and bumps and clicks that she could not control. She heard him sifting through plastic cassette cases; then music started and he appeared in the doorway, holding another bottle of wine.

"Let me finish," he said. He sat with the bottle between his thighs, working at the cork. "All I meant is that there's nothing more beautiful, more devastating, than a girl in a white dress, alone in a hallway in Geneva . . . and that I imagine you there . . . and how helpless you make me."

He kissed her.

"Are you going to decant that?" she said.

"You make me helpless, darling."

Kim would lay over a night in London, a weekend in Paris. She never stayed anywhere more than two days. She spent half her time in cookie-cutter hotels with a babbling television for company. She'd wake to language she couldn't understand, sometimes not knowing where she was. She'd open the curtains to still-dark skies and shuffle bleary-eyed into fluorescent-lit bathrooms in plastic travel slippers. Wrappers from used wafer-thin soaps stuck to the wet countertops like stamps. She'd run water and peel them off and throw them in the trash along with the scattered Q-tips and strands of floss, the mascara-stained swabs from the previous night's undressing. She'd go through the courtesy bags to see if there were shampoos worth saving or compact sewing kits. She'd remove the black and white threads and discard the rest. Always there was the disposable shower cap folded into a tiny square envelope like a condom. These were the souvenirs of her travels.

She remembered glimpses of cities like dreams: flower beds shaped like states, an iron statue of a horse running through a fountain of water, postcards of fairy-tale castles with pointed turrets, palm-tree sunsets, and Mickey Mouse greetings. She knew cities the way she knew people, always departing.

—

Jennifer was another stewardess. She'd grown up in a small town called Perdue, South Carolina. Her father had been in the Air Force, a decorated fighter pilot in Korea. He was shot down, his body never recovered. All her life, planes fascinated her, partly because they sent her mom over the edge.

"When she heard I'd taken this job," Jennifer said, "she wouldn't talk to me. Finally she broke down crying. She told me she'd been cheating on my father, right up to the day of his death. That's why she can't even look at a plane, she told me. I couldn't believe it, but I was proud of her for admitting it."

Jennifer knew about Robert. Sometimes when they worked the same flight they would share a hotel room.

"Robert finds the best of everything," Kim said. "He even suggested a hairdresser for me here in Paris."

Jennifer was painting her toenails, feet arched over the edge of the bed.

"Who cuts his wife's hair?" she said.

"He hates his wife's hair."

"He should make *her* change."

Jennifer flexed her toes and examined her work.

"He can't tell her things," Kim said.

On television, an actor was being interviewed. The dialogue cut to a clip of his new film—him running along a track in a tunnel, the light of a train behind him, and the grating squeal of metal wheels— then back to the studio, a microphone held close to the actor's smiling face, the interviewer mock-biting his nails.

"Do you think he'll leave her?" Jennifer wiggled her toes and put the cap back on the polish. "Do you?"

"I love the sound of French," said Kim. "Sometimes I make up what they're saying."

She stared at the television set, the actor's clean-cut features and the way he spoke. She knew he was promoting the film. Even if she couldn't understand the language, his words sounded confident, lighthearted. She shut her eyes and listened and felt she understood the man. Sometimes language didn't matter at all. Words only confused. There were other things to hear.

Jennifer turned to look at the screen. "Now, why can't I meet someone like that?" she said.

The words floated from the tiny TV speaker like a lullaby, but the audience was laughing.

For as long as Kim could remember, her grandfather had been dying. At least that's what she'd heard. She could still see her mother's stricken face as she clutched the letter telling of his first stroke. Somehow he kept going, outliving his daughter by twelve years.

Kim's father telephoned with the news of the death.

"Call your grandmother," he said. "Don't even think about not coming to the funeral."

She sat in the living room, stretched her feet to the floor, and pushed herself into the sofa cushions. Disdain for her father, not illness, had kept the man from his daughter's deathbed. Or was it pride, a grotesque stubbornness that had always kept him distant while his daughter suffered? Was it punishment? Should Kim now dignify his passing and comfort a woman who at the very least had remained in tow all those years, had done nothing? The rug bunched around Kim's treading feet.

"Don't start with that silent bullshit," her father said.

"Why would she even call you?"

"She has no one."

"He didn't go to Mom's funeral."

"He was sick."

"Oh, Daddy."

"She's your grandmother."

"I can't get off work."

She could hear him struggling to control his feelings. Work was the inarguable excuse. He would never force her to do anything that might jeopardize her career. All his talk of responsibility and duty; he'd preached himself into a corner, and he would die before he contradicted himself.

"I've been busy, Dad. Last week I had to fly two double shifts. I saw Hong Kong. It was just as you described it."

"Are you putting money in the bank?" he said.

"Of course."

"I don't believe you. When are you getting married?"

She imagined herself far away, farther than the miles that separated her from her father, because they were not enough. She projected sounds between them, noises to dampen his verbal grating—the rasping rush of a jet turbine spinning to life, sucking his words into a vacuous roar. With the sounds came smells, fuel, tarmac heat snaking to the sky, vibrating the horizon. She could feel the first bump of touchdown, the nose of the plane settling, the pop of her ears as she pulled the lever to release the door, fresh air stealing over her face, permeating her clothes in a heartbeat, and the glare of the sun.

"You could try calling more," he said. "Who else treats their family like you?"

"Okay, Dad. Did you see they sent a woman into space? The first American woman. It was in all the papers."

"Maybe if you'd gone to college, that would have been you."

"Maybe."

"I'll pass your condolences on to your grandmother. Is there anything I can help with? Are you still my Princess?"

"Yes, Daddy."

She left the receiver off the hook. There was wine in the refrigerator, an open bottle from the night before. She took the bottle and a glass out onto the fire escape and drank and listened to the birds and the rising and falling hum of traffic. Across the courtyard, on the fire escape of the opposite apartment building, stood a ceramic statue of a cat, one paw lifted to a window as if to enter. She'd thought it was alive at first. She couldn't imagine anyone wanting to live with that fake thing peering in.

Above and beyond the chipping brick row of rooftops, a skyrise cut into the sun, and then for a moment the sun was whole again and round. It bled into the uneven skyline slowly and disappeared, leaving the courtyard in shadow. Out there in space was a woman—Sally Ride was her name—and she was looking down on the world.

She was looking down on millions of people, families stacked upon families with all of their struggles and hates, their tiny lives in cities, in countries that from where she floated were nothing but vast swirls of blue and gray, a ball of color against a sea of black.

Kim gathered the bottle and glass and climbed back through the window into her apartment. She brushed soot from her dress and hung up the phone. It was teasing her, daring her to smash it, and she pictured it in pieces, bits of shattered plastic scattered across the floor like a thousand glittering stars.

A bottle of Sauternes chilled in a bucket of ice on the floor. A bowl of strawberries rested on the bed. In the glass against the sheets, the wine was like gold, honey to the lips. Robert and Kim were naked.

Robert had been married nineteen years. He had two children, a boy named Davis and a girl named Christine. Davis was a freshman at Deerfield Academy. Christine was three years behind him at Chapin. He never talked about them. His wife, Nicole, was an alcoholic.

"That doesn't give me an excuse," he'd said.

Do you love her? Kim wanted to ask. She knew it was best not to. He avoided such declarations. Kim respected him for this. It made the feelings he shared with her that much more meaningful.

Sorrow was safe ground, though. Occasionally, he allowed himself to discuss the pain Nicole provoked. That was not a betrayal to his wife. As months yawned and passed, she began to feel that it was not sex he sought in her arms but redemption.

He embraced her in foreign hotel rooms and in the backs of cars. He touched her under the table, kissed her by coat checks with the world behind them. He could neither shun the burden of his marriage nor draw security from it, and she saw his vows as his cross and conscience. In grief, he cared for his wife. It was Kim's role to show him his goodness in other ways. She could absolve him from guilt. She could love him; even the partial self that he offered was enough, was safe.

"Two nights ago," he said, "in front of everyone, she threw a drink in my face, then calmly gave the glass to a waiter."

Kim stroked his forehead. "I'm sorry."

He sifted through the bowl and held a strawberry out to Kim, who opened and closed her lips around it, kissing his fingers.

"I want to see more of you," he said.

She trailed a hand through his white hair.

"I want to see you more too," she said.

"These parties are a slow death without you. Even if we can't talk, if I could see you there, just to know you're near."

"Then invite me. I want you to be happy."

He took her hand and she sat up. The sheet slipped from her breasts.

"I hate that you're away so much," he said. "Sometimes I have no one to talk to."

"I want you to have someone to talk to."

He kissed her.

"You shouldn't have to work anymore. You need to be taken care of."

"Robert, darling, I have to work."

"You don't."

"I have to think of myself."

"Exactly."

"So many things could happen. What if you grow tired of me?"

"I won't."

"You can't say that. You may."

"No."

"Yes, Robert, and then what will I do? Get my old job back?"

He pressed her hand. "I swear to you, I will not let that happen. I'll take care of you."

She looked away.

His insecurity was comforting: to know that he wanted her that strongly, to see the tinge of desperation in his eyes. This had bothered her with Sam. Why not with Robert? She did not care about her job. Any hesitation was only to prolong the moment, to draw him out further, to hear him say things that now seemed freeing.

"Why?" she said. "What do I do for you?"

"It's not anything you do."

"What then?"

"Your eyes."

"That's no reason."

"The things you can laugh at. You laugh at me."

"That's easy."

"You accept who I am. You never ask for anything."

He reached under the pillow and took out a case. He held it open. It contained an emerald ring.

"I promise," he said. "Forever."

He took the ring from its case and slipped it on her finger. She could feel him growing hard under the sheets.

"I want you," he said.

He stared intently at her breasts as she straddled his stomach, lifted herself over him, and was still. He concentrated, held himself, and searched. She moved slightly to try to accommodate the misses. Then she took him in her hand. His brow relaxed. She settled onto him, sliding her legs out so that the lengths of their bodies touched. He pinched her breasts between the insides of his arms, hooked his feet around her, rocked to one side, and then rolled her over, hands now beneath her, working downward as he pushed. She held him as he shuddered. She was crying. She was happy. He kissed her fingers. He kissed the ring. She clasped him tightly and kissed his ear. She rubbed his back and pressed his face to her neck and whispered into the growing stillness, "There, there, my poor troubled soul."

A week later, a man named Conrad Jones called and introduced himself as the Sanders family's attorney. He wanted to meet to discuss the trust that was being set up. Documents needed to be signed. He sounded impatient.

The night before their lunch, she stayed up reading *Peter Pan*. She finished it that morning on a spread-out towel on the fire escape, her fingers sooty, marking pages. By the time she jumped in the shower to get ready, she didn't know who she felt more sorry for: Peter, when he realized Wendy was an old woman, or Wendy as an adult, realizing that her daughter would replace her. Was a heavier heart always a more loving heart?

She met Mr. Jones at a downtown restaurant. He set an ominous black briefcase on the table and began taking out papers as soon as they placed their orders. He had dark eyebrows and a neatly trimmed gray mustache. He took a pair of reading glasses from his jacket and shuffled some pages. He arranged his water glass and silverware so that there was room in front of him.

"Robert speaks very highly of you," she said.

"Miss Reilly, you should take these home to read."

He didn't look at her. Lunch had been his idea, but he seemed bothered by the distraction of it, the waiter pouring water, the salads arriving. One of the pages was out of order, and he fixed it with perfunct coolness.

"I'm sure it's fine," she said.

He pushed the papers across the table and double-clicked a pen and held it out. He was staring at a group of Japanese businessmen who were toasting one another, their heads slightly bowed.

She took out her own pen and left him with his arm extended. She could understand his not wanting to make small talk. Surely he had more serious business to attend to than this. But she wanted acknowledgment, at least politeness.

"Mr. Jones, you haven't touched your salad."

He pocketed his pen and picked up his silverware and started to eat.

"Aren't the walnuts a nice touch?" she said.

No response. She took another approach. "I understand you have two children. Do you get to spend much time with them?"

She could hear him chewing.

"You missed one," he muttered, pointing with his fork to a line on the page.

She stared at him in disbelief. His mustache twitched as his jaw moved. A phone was ringing. She finished the last signature and stood up.

"I expect copies of these," she said.

She took her purse and turned before he could speak. She brushed past the waiter, who was just bringing the entrées. The maître d' looked up from his desk.

She walked the entire way home, consoling herself: It's not me that he hates. It was just business.

She'd worn a new pair of shoes, and now the left one was causing a blister. With each step it dug into her heel, but she didn't stop. She passed the courthouse. She wandered through Chinatown, crates of packed ice crammed full of slippery silver fish, ducks hanging like wind chimes. She blocked out the briny smells and the chatter. A man bumped her. She was past him before he could apologize.

Mr. Jones had suggested she take the documents home. That was thoughtful, wasn't it? She'd only wanted to save him work, not drag it out. But she'd come off like a gold digger, eager for the jackpot. Maybe he'd fought with his wife or children that morning, or had an awful meeting, or a deal had fallen through. Suddenly it struck her as odd—Robert's absence from the lunch—strange and unfair. Stranger still that it hadn't bothered her until now. How differently Mr. Jones would have treated her. Perhaps he'd recommended that Robert not be present, that experience had proved . . . had there been others? Had she seemed like all the rest? She'd wanted to plead, But this was all Robert's idea. I've worked my whole life. Mr. Jones would have been even more revolted.

Once she'd begun to sign her name, there was nothing dignified
she could have said, and she didn't know which hurt more, enduring
his disgust or that she'd been so foolish as to desire his respect in the
first place.

And so it goes on, she thought as she walked, her heel stinging,
remembering the last line she'd read that morning on the fire escape.
Children could indeed be innocent and heartless. She might have
quoted Barrie. Would Mr. Jones have understood or even cared?
Perspective always came too late. She should be thankful. She
should be happy.

—

After she left her job with the airline, it became easier to accept
money she had not earned.

The days were wide open, vacationlike weeks, sleeping in, afternoons at the movies. No one telling her what to do. No more carrying trays and cleaning up wrappers. No putting up with rudeness.
No headaches from the air pressure, or chronic colds, surrounded by
sneezing and runny noses. She could stay up the entire night reading, knowing she wouldn't pay the following day. She could always
catch up; time was her friend.

One afternoon, she walked to the park at Sutton Place to watch
the sailboats coast down the East River. Children scampered about
with balls, pulled wagons, climbed on the statuary until their nan-
nies summoned them. With wide, helpless eyes, waking babies
wailed, searching for their mothers, seeing only the colored faces
that occupied their days.

She liked it here. She could sit on the park bench and read, work
her way through the accumulating stacks of books in her apartment.
She had been reading about knights, men who possessed titles like
the Good or the Lionhearted. There was one who ran away into the
forest and emerged stronger than before, one who risked his life to
rescue a maiden from a tower, and one who was pure, who deprived
himself and in the end discovered what all the others sought but
could not find. Hadn't they all been spurred by the strength of love?

She thought of her father in the war, living by instinct, a code of survival. He had fought that many might live. Her mother had had the Catholic Church, with its dictum of ideals. They both had their quests. They'd both made great sacrifices.

Kim closed her book. A barge floated past, low in the water from the weight of its load. Where was it heading? Somewhere.

Kim wondered: What had she ever truly sacrificed? She didn't believe in anything. Still, she had come this far. Had she ever relied on anyone? These men, their gifts—she had not asked for them. But she had accepted them. Wasn't it an accomplishment that she had just managed to survive? Robert would say yes, but what would her father say? She drifted like the leaves in the current below her. What did Robert see in her?

In the last light of the sun, couples stopped for a view of Roosevelt Island and a fast embrace. A woman she'd seen once with one man, she saw again with another, flipping her hair and staring longingly the same way. Ants swarmed a melting Popsicle, filing in a line to and from a sandy hole between the cobblestones. The sun receded and she walked home.

The next morning she stopped at the bank. As usual, her balance had increased.

The trust yielded sixty thousand dollars a year. Robert figured it was about what she had made at the airline. He laughed when he learned it was much more. The irony was that Robert still paid for her shopping, their weekend trips, dinners. . . .

"If you pay for everything," she said, "what's the point of the trust?"

He laughed again.

"To watch it grow."

She bought a green damask sofa with alternating stripes of holly and ivy leaves stitched so finely that they weren't noticeable unless she put her nose right up to the fabric. It took up an entire wall. She bought a divan for sheer decadence. It was designed not for sitting or even lying, really, but posing.

It's "Come in" furniture, she told Robert: the type of piece one ran to when the doorbell rang and then, after arranging oneself, called, "Come in."

Garbo, Dietrich—they'd all been photographed on divans. Now she had one. The dark mahogany frame bowed up to a spillover of carved flower petals. A million gold studs pinned the olive cushion at the edges.

"My Olympia," Robert said, the first time he saw her in it. "You know, the painting."

"I look like a painting?"

"A masterpiece," he said.

She bought four-foot-tall iron candlesticks and placed them at the ends of the divan, as though it were a great velvet tabernacle. The candle by the window burned down faster, wax rising off the side of its stem like a fin.

She forced herself to go through the *Times* every morning. She read about the death of Wallis Simpson, the Duchess of Windsor, and how in love she and the Duke had been, how he used to wait patiently at the foot of the stairs while she dressed for dinner, so that he would be there when she descended. What a noble gesture, she thought, and pictured him reading a book in the waning half-light of a hall, turning an ear every so often to listen for his wife's footsteps. Her jewels would be coming up at auction, and there was wild speculation about their worth.

—

If she wanted to, Kim could kill half a day at the salon. She'd even bought her own set of tools, stored neatly in a black lizard case.

She tucked the case under her arm like a pocketbook and slipped on a pair of open-toe sandals. Off to Bergdorf's. She liked to think of the 58th Street side entrance as her secret, even if it wasn't. Robert had shown it to her. It was more glamorous than the front entrance. There were never crowds, the out-of-town shoppers milling in from the avenue. It led through the Chanel boutique, and the salespeople recognized her. They'd call out, "Hello, Miss Reilly," or "I put aside something I thought you'd like. Stop back on your way out." On the elevator she thought how they didn't have to do that; it wasn't about selling, or status, but sharing. Yes, she could afford certain items now, but the currency exchanged was taste, not money. They were trying to help.

The salon was on the seventh floor along with home furnishings. She walked past Chinese lacquered tables, two standing mounted elephant tusks that arched over a zebra-skinned love seat, the same spot that only weeks ago her green damask sofa had occupied. She pushed open the large glass door at the end of the hall. The black leather banquettes were crowded with waiting women. They peered at her over their magazines. Kim didn't have to check in. Her account would be automatically charged. She walked past the doughnut-shaped reception desk, past Frederic's, the salon owner's, station. He was in mid-cut, standing directly behind a sitting woman with his hands flattened to either side of her face like blinders. "Do you see it?" he was saying. "Do you see it?" The woman had tiny bits of shiny foil twisted into her hair. He saw Kim in the mirror and waved with a comb.

An assistant whisked her off to a private room. A mini-tub of warm sudsy water waited. Kim rolled her tights up one turn and slipped off her sandals. She dipped her feet in slowly and eased back in a chair. Nadia rushed in. She was Romanian, with night-black hair and smooth, creamy skin. Her fingers were long and muscular from years of massaging feet and calves.

"Did they call?" she said, the words rolling off her tongue. "I could have taken you at nine."

"It's okay."

"Are you sure? Ach! Now I make you late. I could have taken you."

"Late for what? This is perfect. Don't worry."

An assistant came into the room with an espresso on a saucer and a small cup of steamed milk. She set it on the table next to Kim and left. There was a magazine rack and a telephone, a folded copy of the *Post*.

Nadia knelt and lifted one of Kim's feet from the tub. She gripped Kim's calf and kneaded the muscle for a second and ran her fingers down to the ankle.

"A moment longer," she said, rising. "I don't even say hello, darling!" She wrapped her arms around Kim and kissed her on both cheeks. "All morning like this—rush, rush. My head is crazy. Don't let your espresso get cold."

She ran out of the room. When she came back she sat facing Kim. She took one of Kim's feet from the water and placed it in her lap and began dabbing at the nails with a swab, removing the existing polish with a mild acid. When she finished, an assistant took away the tub. Nadia opened Kim's lizard case and took out a gold shark-nosed scissor and snipped at the dead skin on Kim's heel. She scraped the calluses with a razor-sharp knife and gouged at the corners of the nails with a trowel-tipped pick.

"Did you read about the Duchess?" Kim said, trying not to wince.

"Yes," said Nadia, stroking Kim's foot. "Oh, those jewels." Her eyes widened as if she were looking at them in a case. "I can't wait to see the catalog."

"I think Robert met them once."

Nadia wrinkled her nose. "I hear she was very boring."

"I'll have to ask him," said Kim.

"Are we waxing today?"

"Do you have time?"

"I never have time. That is silly question, but you, I do anything for, anything. You remember that. Other foot. We do the hands after, or you want them now?"

"After."

Nadia finished the toes: two coats of red. Kim always skipped the base and top coat. They took too long to dry. She spread her toes and Nadia carefully slipped on the sandals.

"Now up."

Nadia pulled on a roll of white paper, stretching the long sheet across a black padded table by the window and tearing off the excess. Kim lifted her arms. Nadia tugged at the elastic waistband of her tights. She pulled them down to Kim's ankles and Kim shimmied onto the table, careful not to smudge her toes.

"I'm always afraid they can see me," Kim said.

"Who?"

Kim pointed out the window to the building across 57th Street.

"The people over there."

"Where?"

"In the Crown Building."

They both peered out the window. Kim had her knees apart and her feet splayed, her pelvis tucked so that Nadia would have a better angle. They looked at each other and laughed.

"The windows are tinted," said Nadia.

"Really?"

Nadia shrugged and they laughed again.

"We put on a good show, eh?"

She began to smear hot wax between Kim's legs with a wooden spatula. Nadia liked to talk as she applied the gauze strips. Her purring voice was a welcome distraction.

"Meryl Streep was here yesterday. She's shooting a new movie. I did her eyebrows. They had to be like so." She cupped a hand like a crescent moon. "I think she is fabulous, no?"

Kim caught Nadia peeking out the window.

"I promise nobody is looking," Nadia said, her eyes dark and shimmering like her hair. She smiled.

That moment just before the rip of the first strip, nothing ever seemed funny.

"Nadia, a little lower." Kim drew a line with her finger. "He likes less," she said.

"We give him what he likes. . . . As long as we are getting what *we* like."

———

On her way out she stopped back at the Chanel boutique. Tim, the clerk, was busy with a customer, but he excused himself to come over.

"I have a jacket for you in the back," he said. "It's *that* gorgeous." He nodded in the direction of the other woman he was helping. "This may be a while, though."

"You don't have to show me," she said. "I trust you. I'm on my way home now. Just send it over."

"Timothy." The other woman was calling.

Kim thanked him. "I don't know how you do it," she said. "You have the patience of a saint." Her fingers were fanned so that the nails wouldn't touch. "Hey, do I look like a scarecrow?"

Tim laughed.

"I feel like one," she said.

On the way home, she stopped at a liquor store and sent her father a case of his favorite scotch. After every airline incident now he would call, forcing her to lie.

One time a 727 skidded off the runway at Kennedy. "How could you not have heard?" he would say. "I was afraid you were on that flight." He was relieved to hear her voice. Then he started in with the questions, expecting her to know information that hadn't yet been made public, details she couldn't fabricate. He'd hang up and then call later to apologize.

If she told him how she really passed the days, would he be proud?

That same year Averell Harriman died, survived by his wife Pamela.

"*La grande horizontale,*" said Robert, on the telephone.

"What?"

"Darling, we should take French lessons together. Mine is so rusty."

"There's going to be a new museum in Paris," she said. "I just read about it: the Musée d'Orsay. It's in an old train station. Listen, let me find the article."

She flipped pages and sipped her coffee, cradling the phone against her shoulder.

"Enough news. I want to see you."

"So come over."

"I have a better idea. How quickly can you be ready?"

"For what? I'm not even dressed."

"Lunch."

"What kind?"

"Formal."

"I need time, say two hours."

"One."

"An hour and a half."

"Okay. There's more, though. I have to give you instructions."

"A lunch with instructions?"

"Those are the best kind, darling."

"Where are you right now?"

"I'm not in the city. I'm in Banksville."

"Banksville? What are you doing there?"

"You'll see."

—

There seemed to be no end to the wealth of surprises, the stolen moments.

She had to call the Banksville Police Department.

"You're what?" said the chief of police. He put her on hold. He came back on with a chuckle. "Well, if it's okay with the restaurant, I don't see why not."

She wore a simple black dress with gold earrings. Joseph met her downstairs and dropped her at 60th Street and the river. There was a tiny fenced-in tarmac with a square cinder-block office. The pilot was waiting, a short man dressed in khaki with wraparound sunglasses. He waved when he saw the car and climbed into the helicopter and started the engine. *Wup-wup-wup:* The blades turned, their long sweeping shadows growing faint as they sped faster and faster, then disappearing altogether. The tall grass at the edge of the tarmac flattened, and bits of garbage, a paper cup and the page of a newspaper, swirled and blew against the fence and stuck there.

"I've never done this," she called to Joseph, ducking and clutching the hem of her dress to keep it from blowing up.

"Don't be scared," he shouted.

"Of flying? You should know better."

He waved and his lips moved, but she couldn't hear him.

A tall man in overalls held the helicopter door open and helped her in and latched it shut. There was a seat beside her and two behind. The front windshield was curved like the side of a goldfish bowl. The man in the overalls slapped the glass and gave the pilot a thumbs-up.

"Welcome aboard," said the pilot, looking back over his shoulder. "My name's Mitch."

He was strapping on a heavy pair of headphones.

"I have a basic idea where we're headed, but you're gonna have to steer me."

"Banksville?" she said. "It's right on the border of Greenwich."

"The city I can find. It's the restaurant I'm worried about. I have to say this is a first for me. Are you buckled in?"

"Roger," she said.

The helicopter lifted and she clutched the armrests. She expected the movement to be jerky, but it was smooth, as if riding in an elevator. They rose, and the tarmac shrank beneath them.

"I've got no coordinates," he said, "so we're gonna wing it. I figured we'd head up the Merritt Parkway."

"Just like we're driving."

"Yeah, but there's no traffic, and I gotta be honest with you, the view's a hell of a lot prettier."

She opened her purse and took out a pad on which she'd written the directions.

"Okay," she said. "Hold on. Take the Merritt to North Street."

"Gotcha."

"Go north a couple of miles. The restaurant's right on North Street. We should be able to recognize it."

"Sounds like a good plan."

They were heading up the East River, the FDR speeding beneath them and, ahead, the Triborough Bridge. The side windows were like a car's, so she pressed her face to the glass and gazed down at the water, at boats that seemed so close she could touch them, and at the whites of the choppy waves. They were flying so low—"Low as a crow," Mitch said—so they wouldn't get lost.

They headed toward Connecticut and eventually picked up the Merritt. The nose of the helicopter pitched forward slightly and they accelerated. The force pressed her back into the seat.

"Can you see the exit signs?" she said.

"Crystal clear."

Trees spread beneath them like bushes, the parkway like a stream. The sky was a clear and steady backdrop to the undulating flash of foliage; this whooshing, roaring roller coaster of a ride. It was preposterous: wonderful and preposterous. The restaurant, La Folie, was every bit as good as, if not better than, the finest restaurants in the city. "An experience," Robert had said on the phone. What he was doing in Banksville, she didn't ask. To her these impromptu meetings were part of a grand design, his plan of showing her a life that few could see but he was privileged to offer, and which she would never question.

They banked at the North Street exit and followed the break in the trees, the shadow of the helicopter shooting up the sides of houses, leaping across rooftops. They flew another two miles and then slowed, creeping through the air, hovering over any building that resembled a restaurant.

"He said we'd have no problem spotting it," she said.

"Things look different from up here."

"It's in a big colonial house."

"What's that?"

Mitch spun the helicopter and tipped sideways. Below, in what appeared to be a backyard, a man dressed in all black was waving a napkin.

"Bingo. Let's take it down."

"Can we fit?" she said.

"We'll make it."

He leveled out and began the descent as gradually and steadily as they'd taken off. The tips of pine trees rose to meet them and slipped upward past the window as though they were growing before Kim's eyes, getting higher as the helicopter sank toward the ground. The man in black had cleared out of the way and was standing at the foot of a short flight of porch steps. Waiters and busboys were crowding the porch now, leaning over the rail to see. They applauded as the helicopter touched down and Mitch cut the engine. He jumped out and came around for her door.

"Here we are, ma'am."

The man who had signaled them was corralling the others with sweeps of his arms.

"Back inside," he was saying, as they turned and piled through a screen door. "Excitement's over. Back to work. Miss Reilly," he called. Now he was coming toward her. "You made it. A pleasure."

She nodded to Mitch, and he took off his glasses and smiled.

"I'll be waiting," he said.

"This is an extraordinary pleasure," said the man. "Let me escort you around to the front. I am Charles, the maître d'. Everything is ready for you. Did you have a pleasant flight?"

"Very smooth."

The restaurant was an old brick house that had been converted, with ivy growing up the side and red rosebushes clinging to a white painted lattice, the last blooms of summer beginning to unclose.

"I am afraid our secret is out," he said.

"Secret?"

"The noise. I am afraid the other guests are aware of the mode of your arrival. There is much excitement—talk, talk."

"Oh," she said.

"It is an honor."

He held the front door open and nodded for her to enter. She stepped into a long blue-carpeted hall.

"This way," he said, taking the lead.

They passed through what had once been the living room. A fire was burning in a large marble fireplace. Everyone was smiling at her.

"Bravo," said a woman. The man she was sitting with was Senator Gary Hart. Kim recognized him from the papers, which were already proclaiming him a Democratic hopeful.

"Enjoy your lunch," he said.

She followed Charles through what had been the original dining room of the house into a library with floor-to-ceiling book-lined walls. There were only two tables. Robert was standing at one of them.

"We are here," said Charles.

Robert touched Kim's arm just above the elbow. His lips grazed her cheek. He said nothing and smiled, and she thought how dashing he was. He looked the same as the day they'd met, and if there were more lines around his eyes—he complained that there were—they only added to the sincerity of his expression. His eyes never broke from hers as they sat. Charles welcomed them yet again and signaled to the headwaiter, who was standing at attention.

The food could have been awful and it wouldn't have mattered. Nothing could undo the thrill, because in a way, the moment was already in the past and she could see herself looking back on the lunch as magical.

"Did you see who was in the other room?" she said. "He's even more handsome in person."

"You mean the senator?" He shrugged.

"You're more handsome, though," she said, extending her hand to touch his.

The soup was vichyssoise. They shared a T-bone steak and a bottle of red wine.

—

When she told the whole story to her manicurist, Nadia, she described the food as magnificent, but honestly she could not remember a single taste. She could not describe the decor or the presentation. The only details she remembered after sitting down to lunch were Robert's satisfied smile and the moment they were finishing espressos when the maître d' returned to the table and announced, "Mr. Sanders, Miss Reilly, the pilot would like to know, should he start the engine?"

Each fall, the tree in front of Kim's building flashed a gorgeous yellow before fading. The sidewalk became slippery with its leaves. Every morning the doorman from the neighboring building hosed them into the gutter, and every afternoon there'd be more. They'd catch in the hood of Kim's coat or stick to her shoes and she'd find them in the apartment hall.

The grocery stores stocked up on turkeys. Soon it would be Thanksgiving, then Christmas. She was always alone on holidays. Robert had to be with his family.

"We'll celebrate the day after," he would say. Sometimes she would wait a week or two. Browning Christmas trees would lie out by the curb with the garbage bags and slush.

"You do understand?" he would say tenderly, as though prepared to explain why he had to preserve the facade of his marriage. It was something he had built and was a part of, which she could benefit from indirectly but could not share. She could appreciate when his children made him happy, the compliments from Christine's schoolteachers, the tales Davis would tell about sneaking girls into the dorm and almost getting caught. Their problems drew out a paternal side of Robert, which made Kim feel involved, even if only as an onlooker. And certainly that had its advantages as well. Perhaps she would never meet his children in person, but she knew them through stories, which was to say she knew them through the extent of Robert's affection.

Robert's clothes took up a section of her closet. His toothbrush stood in a cup in the bathroom. If she wanted to, she could go to the medicine cabinet and smell his cologne. His belongings reminded her that she was not alone. There were others who were less fortunate, who had no one to think about but themselves.

She tried to remember the first Christmas after they were together—what she had done to pass the days waiting for Robert to return so they could celebrate. She tried to remember holidays before Robert, when she was truly alone.

She saved all her shopping for Christmas Eve now. It gave her something to do. In the morning, she went to the corner and picked out a tree. A young man took it up by the trunk and heaved it over his back and carried it to her apartment. He even put it in the stand for her. She gave him twenty dollars, and he took off his ski hat and thanked her.

"Merry Christmas," he said.

There was a bookstore she liked on Madison Avenue. An antique wooden mannequin decorated the window. It was always posed differently. There was also a small mouse, standing on its hind legs, waving a paw. In some of the displays the mouse was not easy to find, and she would stop to look for it, amused by the game. One time it wasn't there and she had to ask a clerk. He went to the window and found it for her. She laughed and clasped her mouth, embarrassed.

"I thought it was gone," she said.

"It's there."

She picked out books for Robert and cheated, choosing one for herself as well. She had it wrapped with the others. All the books would be staying at her apartment anyway.

She went to a store on 55th Street and Park and bought Robert several ties and a pair of chamois dress gloves. Then she picked out shirts to go with the ties.

"Can you carry all that?" the clerk said. She could barely fit through the door.

"Maybe you could help me get a taxi."

It took him five minutes, and he didn't have a coat. He was shivering but still managed a smile.

When she arrived back at the apartment, the doorman from next door waved and told her to wait. He was always helpful and accepted deliveries for her. He appeared with a gigantic package under his arm.

"It came today," he said. He helped carry her bags up to the apartment. She had an envelope for him.

"Merry Christmas."

There were plenty of things to do: presents to wrap, the tree to decorate. She took her time. She ordered in Chinese food and turned on the television and opened a bottle of red wine and sat on the floor. She watched a movie, sorting boxes of decorations during the commercials. Most of the ornaments she had found at street sales in Chelsea, put out because they were old and damaged in some way. There was a copper wire angel she loved, blowing on a bent trumpet, and a round Santa with a cotton beard and one eyebrow missing. She imagined the stories behind them. She would never dream of putting new ornaments on a tree.

When she was done, she plugged in the Christmas lights and turned off the overhead and lay on the couch. She fell asleep with the television on, staring at the tree, the red, yellow, and blue reflection in the ceiling and the shadow of the star.

—

In the morning she plugged in the coffeemaker. She put in a fresh filter and spooned in grinds, spilling some. She wiped the counter with a sponge and tossed it in the sink and went back to the living room. She puffed up the sofa cushions, straightening them, and opened the blinds and looked out over the fire escape at the building beyond the courtyard. The windows across from hers were dark. It was still early. There was a small round barbecue she'd bought and never used. It sat next to a frozen bag of charcoal, dark like the rusty iron rail. By the time she poured her coffee and returned to standing before the window, lights were coming on.

She decided to open her package. She got the bow off and the lid open and peeled back layers of tissue. She sat for a moment clasping her chest. Then she unfolded the coat and jumped up and ran to the mirror. She slipped it on and pressed the brown fur to her cheek and shut her eyes and felt the weight of the coat on her shoulders. She twisted her hair up and stood on tiptoe and turned sideways, looking at herself. She went to her bed and spread the coat out and lay down on it, squirming to feel the fur against her flesh; then she opened the blinds and rolled onto her stomach, supporting herself with her elbows, and watched the apartment windows across the courtyard—the shadows of people moving about.

The phone rang. She knew it would be her father, because he always called. He was living in a small town outside of San Francisco, close to the base where he'd been stationed years ago. He liked it there.

"Never wanted to leave the first time," he told her. "Did you get the present I sent?"

"It's under the tree. I'll open it now."

She set down the phone to unwrap the package—a sky-blue cashmere sweater.

"It's beautiful, Dad."

"How's work?"

She folded the sweater back into the box. He would ask about benefits, insurance, whether the recent strike had affected her. She had answers for every question. She would reply quickly, without hesitation. What she said didn't matter as much as the way she said it. He cared, but he didn't. He listened only for the things he wanted to hear—that she was secure, moving up in the world, and her colleagues looked up to her.

"Are you still with what's-his-name?"

"Robert, Dad. That's why I'm not there with you, remember?"

"What does he do again?"

"I've told you."

"He's a trader, right?"

"Yes." It was easier not to explain.

"When am I going to meet him?"

"You'll come to New York sometime."

"Is he there now? Put him on."

"Dad, he can't come to the phone."

"I want to talk to the man."

"He's busy."

"Ask him to come to the phone."

"I won't do that."

"Ask him."

"Dad, I'm going now."

He went quiet.

"I have to go now, okay, Dad?"

"Did I tell you I can see the Golden Gate from my kitchen window?"

"Dad, Merry Christmas."

"I love you," he said. "You never come see me."

"I love you too."

—

She shut her eyes and listened to the engine sounds of traffic coming from the bridge nearby, motorists on their way to visit family.

Profound loneliness—people confused it with self-pity. But loneliness could be beautiful. There was an illustrated Bible that she used to look at as a child. Her mother would be in the kitchen, making dinner, and she'd lie on the floor, looking at the pictures, tracing them with her finger so as to remember them. There was one of Jesus on the cross, mourning women at his feet with their arms thrown up. When Jesus died, did Mary cry for her loss or for the suffering her son had endured? For the loneliness of the world? Was she ever as breathtaking as at that moment? The loneliness was pure grace. The slightest drop of self-pity would have defiled it.

There was one Christmas when she was young. The tree had seemed especially large that year, thick, reaching to the ceiling.

"It's too big," her mother had said.

Her father surrounded it with packages. In slippers and a robe, he sat next to her on the floor. She remembered the hardness of his knee as she leaned against him, turning to his glowing smile as he marveled at each present she opened. She received everything she'd asked for.

"Santa knows," he kept saying.

That Christmas was her ideal. Her mother had puttered around the room in her robe, collecting bits of wrapping paper and folding them, smoothing them.

"What are you doing that for?" her father had said.

"It's perfectly good paper. It can be used again."

"Are you kidding me?"

She could see her father's eyes rolling conspiratorially. She had been so happy, so pleased by the attention, the approval. Santa knew.

Years later, from the hospital bed, her mother had confided that that Christmas had been the hardest. "The Christmas of the sure thing," she called it. Her father had lost his year's savings at the track. All the presents had been bought with borrowed money.

Even the finest memories were fragile. Why, after so long, had her mother decided to tell her? Before, her mother had been at the periphery of the memory. Afterward, she was the highlight. Instead of the tree and the presents, the expressions of her father's love, she now saw only her mother, sulking, silent, presentless, picking up the used wrapping paper in an effort to save it, and her father having the audacity to call her mother cheap.

—

Afternoon turned to evening. She was well into a second bottle of wine. There was nothing on television worth watching, but she kept switching channels. She started to think about the fur coat. Why hadn't Robert called? The card that accompanied the gift wasn't even in his handwriting. *Until we are together,* it read. She took it into the living room and looked at it again in the silvery light from the window and then tore it to pieces.

Robert could tell her how good she was, but he could never say that she was better than Nicole, even if he wanted to believe it. He always returned to his wife. He could take off his wedding band, but the mark on his finger would be there. He could rub it, but it wouldn't go away.

She scooped up the coat, bundled it into a trash bag, and knotted the opening. She dragged the bag downstairs and out the door, stuffed it into a trash can, and slammed the lid on it. A gust of wind blew a shower of icy droplets down from the waving tree branches. Then the tree became still. The sky was the color of the street. She stood there until she realized how cold she was.

The next morning her head hurt. She lay in bed with the lights off and her eyes closed, waiting for the throbbing to subside. Robert called. He was free for a few hours and wanted to come over. She stumbled out of bed. The bathroom tiles were freezing. She stood on a towel as she rinsed out her dry mouth and examined her eyes. She sifted through the medicine cabinet for something to take and filled her cupped hands with water and splashed her face and looked at herself. Then she clutched the edge of the sink. She hurried to the living room and saw the empty coat box and went to the bedroom and spun around and bit her lip and tried to think.

She threw on a robe and rushed down to the street. The garbage cans were filled beyond capacity and she staggered back a step, pressing her lips to the back of her fist. She dug through trash, bits of potato, and bones, cold against her knuckles. "Thank you, God," she stammered, finally finding the knot of her bag. She pulled on it and the whole can fell over. Somebody yelled. "*You* keep it down!" Kim shouted back. A window banged shut. She dragged the stinking bag up to her apartment, dumped it in the bathtub, and washed herself off. Then she ripped into the bag. The coat smelled a little, and she sprayed it with perfume. She hung it to air out and washed her hands again, leaning against the sink. She lowered herself to the floor and sat with her back to the wall. The sash to her robe had come undone and snaked across the tile.

"What's wrong?" Robert said when he arrived. Specks of mascara dotted her cheek. She shook her head against his shoulder.

"I'm so glad you're here," she said.

"Did you open your present?"

"I had to," she said. "It was too tempting."

"Well?"

"It's beautiful."

"It's sable. Let me see. Mmmm, like a princess."

"Open yours now."

He put his hands on her cheeks. "Can't they wait?"

Kim began receiving messages on her answering machine from people she'd never met, offering unneeded services. "Robert Sanders recommended me."

That's how she met Michael.

"He's a decorator," Robert said. "I told him you were redoing your apartment."

The man called and they met for lunch. He strolled up to the table in white linen pants and a blazer with a patch over the breast.

"This?" he said, looking at the patch. "My high school emblem." He shrugged. "I was feeling old. Voilà, young again."

He took a cigarette from a case and offered her one. They talked briefly about a house he was working on in Southampton. There was a man he recognized at the other end of the restaurant.

"Quite the naughty one," he sang under his breath. "Hearts will be broken."

He leaned across the table.

"I know the man he's with. He has the most horrible taste in shoes. You can't see from where you're sitting, but if you get up, take a peek. They're exceptionally hideous."

"Do I really want to?"

"Oh, you must. It's like my patch here. Those shoes will make you feel better about yourself."

He sat very straight with his shoulders back, as if he were regarding himself in a mirror. He looked her age. His short brown hair was parted on one side, perfectly combed. His smile was thin. His lips could almost disappear. He gazed at her with sweet brown eyes. It was the rest of the world he scorned, and he seemed so pleased when she got up to look at the man's shoes.

"Aren't they glorious?" he said when she returned, rolling his eyes from one corner of a whitening smile to the other. "They belong in a medicine cabinet."

He amused her with stories and didn't bring up her apartment until they were finished eating.

"So you're not redecorating?"

She began to apologize, but he stopped her. His eyes were still bright.

"You're lucky you're such a sweetheart," he said.

A week later, he invited her to dinner.

—

He took her to lunches, introduced her to women clients. He drove her up to Tuxedo Park to show her one project. The foundation of the house hadn't even been poured yet, but he walked her around, describing the insides of the rooms as he envisioned them. Bits of orange tape fluttered from the ends of stakes. Pine needles blanketed the ground. He told her to imagine herself sitting just so before a window facing a gap in the pines. The lake glittered below. They dined that evening with the couple that was building the house, newlyweds. For both, it was their second marriage, their second home, and the woman kept raving, "Isn't Michael the best?"

After dinner, Michael drove Kim back up to the lake. They parked and walked along a road by the water and stopped and sat on a stone wall. The moon was almost full and starting to sink. It lit the edges of clouds. He told her that both his parents had died in a fire.

He was twenty-two when it happened, just out of college. His parents owned a beach house in Nantucket, the number written with whale's ivory on the door. He was visiting for the summer. His room was on the third floor. He'd been out drinking with friends. The doors were locked when he got home, and he'd forgotten his key, so he climbed in through a living room window. He remembered looking up the stairs and thinking he'd never make it, then stumbling back to the living room and collapsing on the couch.

The fire started upstairs. Both his parents smoked and liked to drink. Perhaps they'd passed out. One could imagine the fluttering curtains, curious, stretching to the nightstand to see what was smoldering in the ashtray. If Michael had made it up to his room that night, he surely would have died. It was the ceiling crashing down that stirred him, his parents' bedroom collapsing into the study and part of the living room. He only just managed to escape through the same wide-open window by which he'd entered.

"I owe my life to gin," he said. "And people say it makes you mean."

He'd returned to New York to his job as though nothing had happened. When asked about his vacation, he told people it was uneventful. How were his parents? "We're finally getting along," he'd told them.

Knowing the extent of Michael's suffering made his affection for Kim seem even more flattering.

They watched the moon sink, its light skipping down the hill from treetop to treetop to the lake, where it scattered like bits of broken porcelain.

"Some people die without ever knowing tragedy," he said. "Others pass their lives in catastrophe's shadows. Yet we live in the same world."

He held out his hand.

"You and I," he said, "we live in the shadows."

She would recommend Michael to anyone who needed a decorator. In return, he would send her bouquets, bracelets, and earrings with notes saying he'd gotten a job thanks to her.

She began to meet his friends, a circle of men, many of whom he'd known from the Rhode Island School of Design. They would start the evenings out as a group. Knees and shoulders touched as they packed around tables that by the end of dinner looked like ransacked villages. An ever-changing collage of appetizers passed from place to place in the spirit of sharing and tasting. Kim would go to the powder room, come back, and find herself sitting on the opposite side of the table. Couples changed. They would play at seeing who could wear their napkin more creatively, tying them into ties or tucking them into shirtsleeves, ruffled about their wrists like lace.

"A six," they would vote.

"No, a five and a half."

"As usual, Bertrand doesn't want to play."

Bertrand, a sixty-four-year-old ad executive, stood up as though insulted, revealing a huge bulge in his pants.

"I guess I won't be needing this," he said, reaching into his trousers and pulling out a wadded napkin. The laughter was comforting and infectious.

"I was watching him this time, too," said a man.

"Bertrand, you dirty old sneak."

The joking would give way to gossip as the group thinned, stories brought out like expensive liquor at the end of a party, after most of the guests had gone. They were the merry-go-round spottings, the who-had-seen-who-with-whom rumors that everyone ached to tell and give life to.

Michael and Kim would wind up alone in dim downtown after-hour clubs and bars, lining up martini glasses, dueling with plastic olive swords. Michael loved to dance, "to lose himself in a crowd," he claimed, so long as Kim was watching. It was an endearing contradiction. Either he was performing for her, or her presence really was liberating.

There was a new disco he was keen on trying. Robert had already tried to go with Kim. It had taken Joseph thirty minutes just to find the place. It looked like a deserted factory, except that the sidewalk was mobbed, crowded around double metal doors and a man standing on a box. She'd watched Robert confidently push his way through the crowd and saw the bouncer's eyes look straight past him. Robert returned to the limo. "Maybe next time." She heard later that someone had died trying to get in, just like in the old 54. The police found a man's body stuck in a ventilator shaft. He was dressed like a woman.

When Kim went with Michael, they had no problem. Michael knew the owner's brother. She couldn't wait to tell Robert. Or maybe she wouldn't.

Inside, mirrors resembled icicles. Bodies were frozen behind back-lit plastic walls, shadows poised to groove to the steady bass and sax, the boyish voice of Evelyn "Champagne" King pleading through stacked black box speakers, "Momma just don't understand, oh, how I love my man." It was disco night. A bouncer led them over crowded platforms and across the dance floor to a mirrored wall. He rapped the glass twice with his knuckle. A panel opened. A woman greeted them with drinks and pulled them in, shutting the door behind. The door was a window to laser light and strobe-flash chaos. People shook and squirmed, writhing to a dampened thud, a vibration in the dark shag-carpeted walls.

Kim recognized some of Michael's friends and stepped aside, squeezing past the kissing and hip bumping to an open spot on a banquette. She sat next to a man dressed all in white. He was bent over a table with a woman asleep on his shoulder. Kim set her drink down. Encased in the glass tabletop were lines of white powder.

"How clever," she said.

The man didn't answer.

"Do you think—?"

She was talking to a statue. White hands clutched a straw. Tiny gold pin lights flashed in rapid succession up the straw to its nose.

The dozing woman stirred and stroked the statue's thigh.

"My white knight," she cooed, and slumped back.

"There you are," said Michael, leaning over Kim. He stared down at her, wrinkling his nose. "That dress—"

"Yes?"

"It's hideous."

"You know just what to say to a girl. Besides, you're one to talk."

He had on a zebra-skin jacket that matched the fabric of the banquette cushion. It was no coincidence. He owned many costumes and loved to dress up. He would put on a sari to go out for Indian, a kimono for Chinese.

"You'd probably wear a kilt to McDonald's," she said.

"You should see my tartan. Move over."

He sat, elbowing her teasingly, waving to someone.

"Did you read about the Great Wall in space today?" he said. "I know you like that sort of thing. How could you miss it? Right on the front page." He flipped his cigarette case open and snatched out a cigarette and offered one. "They've detected a narrow 'sheet'— yes, that was the word—of connected galaxies frolicking through space. Imagine, a giant sheet in space and, on either side, inexplicable emptiness. The astronomers are perplexed. They can't figure out the gravitational attraction. So." He lit his cigarette. "How long has it been?"

"What?"

"Robert—the two of you."

"You shit. Are you high?"

"Please."

"I've told you everything."

"What's it like being with a married man? Answer the question, Miss Reilly."

"You're awful."

"Curious."

"Have you ever been with a married man?" she said.

"Of course."

"And?"

"He was always looking over his shoulder."

"I'm sure."

Michael stuck out his tongue.

"He can't cheat on you," she said.

"Only with you. I know the rules of infidelity well: no thank-you notes to the apartment, no lipstick kisses after he's washed up. . . . How many years has it been?"

"I like to be alone. I have everything I need. I can do anything—"

"Not quite anything."

"I'm living a man's life, free to see anyone."

"Is there someone else?"

"I don't want anyone else. I told you, I have everything I need."

"I believe you."

"You don't."

He kissed her forehead.

"Did you make up that stuff about the wall in space?" she said.

"Of course not, darling."

—

By the end of the night, most of the room had cleared. Kim lay on the banquette with her head in Michael's lap. She formed binoculars with her hands and looked up at him.

"You're so close," she said.

He mussed her hair. She made no effort to straighten it. She folded her hands beneath her cheek and shut her eyes.

"Good night, love," she said.

"I'll wake you if something outrageous happens."

"So wonderfully outrageous."

If Joseph wasn't driving Robert or Nicole, he was available to Kim. She had the car number and called as needed. If Robert was in the car, Joseph would pass the phone back and they would talk. If Nicole was in the car, Joseph would just say, "I can't."

Joseph would lie to Nicole and say it was his wife on the phone. Later, when he'd pick up Kim, the car would smell of perfume. Even with the windows down, the lily-of-the-valley scent would linger. Sometimes it was fresh, as though Nicole had just gotten out. She might be around the corner or down the block.

"Joseph?"

He glanced over his shoulder.

"Her perfume," she said. "She's wearing a lot today."

Joseph was more relaxed when Robert wasn't in the car. Not that he wasn't professional, but Robert imposed a speak-when-spoken-to rule that Kim disregarded.

The traffic light changed and they barely moved. Then it turned red again. Kim was in no hurry. She gazed out the window at the Park Avenue drifters, residents on their way home from shopping, and the after-work herd stampeding from their midtown businesses, men with jackets slung over their shoulders, shirts wet under the arms from walking. A foreign family stood in front of Delmonico's posing for a photograph, four- and five-year-old children in topcoats. Doormen whistled for cabs, helped with bags, receded into limestone buildings.

At night, driving home, the avenue would be empty. She'd see doormen standing sentinel under the glare of awnings, light spilling across green Prussian coats with brass buttons, and she wondered about their lives. Did they wear their coats home at night, like a costume, or change into something less noticeable, something plain for the ride out to the boroughs, eyelids heavy, beer in a bag?

There was a solace she felt sometimes in the backseat of the car, the air on, a white noise that silenced the outside world, turning it into a silent picture: the flowers in the center divider streaming by, daffodils and tulips in spring, bending in unison from a voiceless wind, then straightening, blooms straining on their stems, drinking up light, shivering bushes. She'd see tipsy couples arriving home late after parties, elderly husbands and wives, shadowy clusters moving inward from the curb with the doorman assisting. It was easy to imagine the banter: the good-evenings and thank-yous; the doorman's name uttered several times as a reassurance, as if to say, We made it; conversations that ended at the elevators.

"Good night, Joseph," she would say when they arrived home, because it was comforting to add the familiar. Then sometimes she would start a conversation and they'd sit in the car in front of her building, because she wasn't ready to be alone.

—

A woman crossed in front of the car. She wore sunglasses and carried a briefcase. A blue and gold scarf draped across her shoulder. It rippled behind her as her hips swayed, floating on a sudden updraft, then settling against her back.

Kim's father had given her a silk scarf once. Her mother had argued that it was too extravagant, too grown up, and it didn't really go with any of her clothes. He thought Kim didn't like it. Two days later at dinner, he made her bring it to the table. He took it to the stove and lit it with the burner and dropped it in a pot. The stench was foul, but they finished eating. Her mom didn't say anything. It took her ten minutes to get the pot clean later.

Kim pointed to the woman.

"Joseph, do you like what she's wearing?"

He shrugged. "I don't see colors very good."

"When I was a girl, my dad gave me a scarf like that."

The light changed.

"He should have given it to my mother," she said.

Joseph eased forward, then stopped. The light changed and the car behind them honked.

"Fifth will be just as bad," he said.

"Where did Nicole lunch today?"

"She didn't."

"Shopping?"

"She had a doctor's appointment."

———

In front of six people at a dinner, Nicole had ground a lighted cigarette into the back of her hand. At the time, Robert was afraid she was nearing the edge again. So it was with a sense of urgency that Robert confided to Kim the history of Nicole's suicide attempts.

"I want you to be prepared," he'd told Kim.

"For what?"

"I guess for how I'll feel."

———

Both incidents involved pills and had occurred before Kim had come into Robert's life. Twice Nicole had locked herself in their bathroom. The paramedics who saved her the second time were the ones who'd broken down the door to rescue her the first time.

"What's the probability of that?" Robert said. "I couldn't look them in the eyes."

They found her clutching a torn note. *Without you I am nothing,* it read. Only the signature was another woman's. Robert had thrown the letter away. Nicole had dug it out of the garbage.

He described how in the days preceding he would come home and find Nicole going through his dresser drawers. He didn't have the stomach to ask what she was looking for. One night he caught her on her hands and knees, sifting through the ashes in the fireplace.

He could see the whole thing coming, like driving a car into a brick wall. He gripped an imaginary steering wheel, jerked his head forward, and flared his hands.

"You made it through the wall," Kim told him.

"The letter was careless."

"I'll never write you."

"The paramedics did such a number on the bathroom door we had to have a new frame put in. Then we couldn't match the paint. Three times and it still wasn't right. Finally we had the entire apartment repainted. It took weeks to air the place out."

"What about Christine and Davis?"

"I can't bear the smell of paint."

"Do they know?"

"Davis was away at school. Christine was with friends."

"You never told them?"

"They know."

———

Robert tried to laugh when he told Kim about Nicole's first attempt.

"You will think it's funny," he told her.

Robert knew people in the film industry. They were always telling Nicole she should act. "Most people disregard such flattery," Robert said. Nicole dwelled on it. She begged Robert to allow her to try. After some time, it began to make sense. With Davis and Christine out of the apartment, she needed a constructive distraction. Her therapist even agreed it was a sound idea.

"Of course as soon as I gave my consent, she dropped the notion. Like anything she sets her mind to, once she has my support, there's no romance in it."

He continued to encourage her, though. At last she allowed him to hire a coach to come to the apartment.

"She would never admit that she was enjoying herself," he said.

Things went smoothly. Then Robert arranged a test for a small part in a film. Nicole didn't get the part. That ended the acting.

She began telling everyone how Robert had forced her to take lessons to humiliate her. "Citizen Sanders," she was calling him. She wouldn't forgive him for the embarrassment she had suffered. Then, when the film opened, she dragged Robert to the screening.

She insisted he take her so she could watch the actress play the part she'd failed to get.

"After we got home, she locked herself in the bathroom," he said. "Pills don't leave scars."

—

Kim leaned her head close to the window. There was little breeze. Noise flooded the cab.

"Is she sick?" Kim said.

Joseph shook his head. He was straining to see a light.

"I probably shouldn't ask," she said.

He shrugged.

"She has many friends, doesn't she?"

"She knows lots of people," he said.

Kim took out a compact and looked at herself. Joseph had seen Robert's lovers come and go. She snapped the compact shut and slipped it back into its felt case. She wondered if he bragged, if he was proud of the secrets he knew. He didn't seem the type. He was more concerned with his daughters' education. One of them liked to write. She was going to be a famous journalist someday. The other loved animals and wanted to be a vet.

"I think she should be a surgeon," Joseph said. "She's got steady hands." He jiggled the wheel and grinned. "They don't come from me."

His toothy smile filled the mirror.

The only time she could recall Joseph showing regard for Robert's affairs was the previous summer, when Davis, Robert's son, lost an internship at a New York law firm. There were rumors of drug use. That fall, he would have been a junior at Brown, but he didn't go. He took time off. Robert sent him abroad to stay with relatives. The following summer, Robert called in favors and found Davis another internship at a more prestigious law firm. He returned to Brown a full class behind. She remembered Joseph saying that the boy had no will, and she could see that he cared. He said nothing outwardly critical of Robert. His sympathy was his judgment.

—

"Robert's last girlfriend—" She paused.

Joseph looked over his shoulder to change lanes.

"Monica Hartley—did you really have to drag her from the car once? Is Robert making that up?"

Joseph looked over his shoulder again.

"She wasn't very nice," he said.

There was a line outside the theater. Joseph pulled up to the curb.

"It gets out in two hours," she said, checking her watch, pausing. "Does she ever call?" Then, before he could answer: "Joseph, I don't want to know."

She opened the door and got out. He rolled the passenger window down and leaned across the seat.

"I'll be circling," he said.

—

Robert had found ways for Kim to attend events. He gave money in her name to charities and introduced her to committee members so she would be involved. The first time Kim saw Nicole in the flesh was at a benefit at the Museum of Natural History.

She met Michael at his apartment beforehand for cocktails, a small gathering of friends. He was anxious to introduce her to someone.

"Be nice," he warned. "I really think I've fallen."

He kissed her at the door.

"Now quick," she said, "which one is he?"

"Guess. No, don't. I might be devastated. There, in the corner."

The man was olive-skin tan, dark at the chin and above the lips, and shadowed around the eyes as though he'd slept little. He was leaning against the wall, his jacket pulled back off one hip, a hand dangling, hook-thumbed from a gold-plate belt buckle.

"Oscar—my black-haired Swede. What do you think?"

"I think you're very handsome," she said.

Michael pulled his money clip from his pocket and licked his thumb.

"Now a little louder, so people can—"

She pinched his arm.

"You!" she said.

"Think of me as a squirrel. Your kind words are like nuts stored away for my winter years. Some gargle, sweets?"

Michael plucked a glass off a waiter's passing tray. Music started. Kim had to lean close for Michael to hear.

"This is hardly a small gathering," she said.

"Here." He served her caviar. "I made it myself."

A woman grabbed him by the arm and introduced herself. She had on a blue and green hat with a long trailing peacock feather. Every time she nodded, the feather would graze the head of the man behind her. At first the man reached back casually, as though brushing at a mild itch. Then he began to swipe the air with his palm. People were laughing. Michael liberated himself and returned to Kim.

"A rule of thumb," he said. "If it comes from a walking bird's ass, don't put it on your head. Shall we meet Oscar?"

He took her by the hand and led her.

When they left the apartment, they took caviar with them. They squeezed into the back of the sedan with the tin and a small spoon. Kim was trying not to spill her drink.

"So decadent," she said, as Michael fed her.

"It's fairy food, darling."

"First time in a car."

"Now we're in the club," said Oscar.

Michael dipped his pinky into the dish. "Sometimes I eat it in the backs of taxis when I'm blue," he said, smacking his lips.

—

The dinner itself was held in the cavernous marine-life room of the museum, beneath a life-sized model of a blue whale. The replica dangled from the ceiling like an immense chandelier, back arched, its tail fanned wide, chin ridged and flecked white. Kim stood by the rail of the mezzanine, watching couples file through the roped opening past photographers. The same faces appeared in print week after week. So many smiles, cut and tossed to the floor.

Nicole arrived without Robert, swathed in a chartreuse velvet wrap. She greeted some photographers by name. Friends pushed toward her, a swell of faces and fleeting introductions, flashes flickering. She hesitated a moment at the head of the stairs, easing the wrap back off her bare shoulders. Then she descended, one hand tickling the broad silver rail, the length of her left leg exposed as she stepped and the dress slit parted. She was terribly thin, beautifully thin.

Below Kim, a kaleidoscopic image of tables waited undisturbed, its settings and assorted wineglasses shimmering beneath the bulk of the whale. The band played "Take Five"—drummer and sax trading improvisations. People packed the bar. Curaçao margaritas were the specialty of the night. Guests held them up to the light.

Glass cases lined the perimeter of the floor. They showed an evolution of marine life. A model white shark loomed above Michael and Oscar, its mouth a wide dagger-toothed leer. Michael bared his own teeth and snapped at Oscar's extended finger.

"You two seem to be enjoying yourselves," she said.

"He's hungry," said Oscar.

Michael pressed his lips to her ear. "Did I tell you how beautiful you look tonight? I could almost kiss you."

"Tease."

She pushed him away, and he nodded in Oscar's direction.

"I'm putty," he said. "See you at the table."

His hand brushed Oscar's hip as they moved away.

The displays on the floor below showed marine life in its natural habitat: a killer whale bursting through a sheath of ice, the murky form of a sperm whale, a giant squid locked in its jaw.

"The bottom dwellers," said a man, leaning over the rail.

He caught Kim staring and smiled.

"You weren't supposed to hear that," he said.

"Right. We're above it all."

He moved closer. "And you are?"

She looked away. People were sitting. The photographers had dispersed. Roving flashes lit crescents of arm-locked guests.

"Are you here alone?" the man said.

Kim spotted Nicole. She was following her champagne glass to the bar, trailing the luminous wrap behind her like a train. People cleared to avoid stepping on it, leaving her a wide space that moved wherever she did like a personal stage. Heads turned in her wake, ears bent to mouths.

"I'm with someone," she said.

She descended the stairs and headed for the bar. She ordered a margarita and edged around for a clear view of Nicole. A waiter passed with a tray of salmon squares. He offered the platter to Nicole and her friends. They each tried one, except for Nicole, who declined with a demure smile. Instead, she set her drink on the bar and took a silver cigarette case from her evening bag. The bartender had a lighter out before the cigarette touched her lips. She shielded her hair from her face and leaned into the flame. A strand of almond-cut diamonds lifted from her pale chest, dangling yellow white, sparkling. She drew smoke and exhaled it toward the ceiling and thanked him. Her friend was telling a story. Nicole set the cigarette in an ashtray and, not taking her eyes from the friend, scooped up the velvet wrap, pulling it around her shoulders, adjusting it so that the ends hung evenly. She retrieved the cigarette and champagne and laughed when the others laughed. She held her glass delicately. The others seemed to squash theirs with chubby fists.

Kim finished her drink and moved closer. She had to hear Nicole speak.

"Darlings," she was saying, her voice smooth and accentless, "you know I love her to pieces, but half of Fifth Avenue's worked on that face."

"Including the husband."

"So they say."

Instead of reaching the cigarette to her lips, Nicole turned to her hand and leaned gently, wrist bent, fingers straight. Her wrap didn't shift.

Kim left the bar and hunted for her table. Michael and Oscar were seated. Appetizers were served.

"Spying, are we?" said Michael, helping with her chair.

"How's the food?" she said.

"Downhill, I'm afraid."

Robert didn't arrive until the end of the main course. Kim saw him on the stairs. He hesitated to survey the floor, and she stood. He started in her direction at first, but he wasn't looking at her. Then she saw Nicole. Robert was straightening his tie as he approached, palms out in greeting as the guests at his table noticed him coming, some rising. He put his hand on Nicole's shoulder, and she ripped her arm away.

"Everything okay?" Michael said, handing Kim her napkin, which had slipped to the floor.

A finger grazed her shoulder. She cringed. The finger belonged to the man from before. He kept walking, calling back, "I'm still trying to figure out who you're with."

She settled into her chair and gazed up at the whale, silent and serene. It seemed even larger from below. What if it were not hollow? She imagined its gaping ribs and fatty flesh, its great gentle heart beating above so much frivolity: so many beautifully dressed couples, their hearts full of desire, expectation, hate, love. . . . How many of them, even the worst, still longed for that unspoken tenuous sentiment, fragile beneath fabricated layers of skin, surrounded by so much glass, so many animals, and all the while above, this unassuming creature staring down with lovely eyes. In a single breath it could exhale more love than a hundred men, and to them it was an ornament.

———

"I'm helpless when she's like that," Robert said later. "She kept asking if you were there."

"She knows?" said Kim.

He shook his head. "Suspects. She's always suspecting. She doesn't know specifically."

Kim described watching Nicole. "I felt horribly for you," she said.

Robert took a photograph from her dresser top and wiped a smudge from the silver frame with his sleeve.

"Sometimes I don't recognize her," he said. He ran a hand across his face. "It's not even the drink anymore, it's the excess of that cover-up she uses."

"Come," Kim said, patting the bed and sliding over.

He set the picture down. "If you'd seen her when we married, the difference . . ."

"I used to wonder—"

"When she was a little girl, her father would sneak her drinks at Christmas parties. What does he think now when he sees her?"

"She's probably his little girl still."

He shook his head. "In the beginning, I saw my future, right? I guess I still see my future when I look at her."

"You used to hold back telling me things."

"Am I disloyal because I want you?" He sat on the edge of the bed. "Are we ever more alive than when we're fucking?"

"You need a drink," she said, half rising.

He stilled her. "That didn't come out right. I mean—"

"You're loyal, Robert. There are things I wanted to know that I don't need to know anymore."

"Because you don't care?"

"We're past them."

"You can't care. Just as there are things I want to tell you but can't."

"There's nothing you can't tell me, darling."

"There are more wicked transgressions than infidelity."

"Yes, there are."

"Still, no matter how good or caring, or what one accomplishes over the years, all that is snuffed when—"

He rubbed his temples with his thumb and middle finger.

"Everything I say makes me sound like an ass."

"You don't have to say anything."

"I'm a bad person," he said. "I know it. You know it. There's no way I can prove otherwise. Imagine what it's like to sit down at a bar and have people get up and leave, because they know, because they're her friends . . . people you've never met, who hate you. Joseph Kennedy said, 'It's not who you are, it's who people think you are.' They're right to hate me."

"Stop feeling sorry for yourself."

"Kim, I'm still with her. The only way I can redeem myself is to deny my own desires. I don't want that. You deserve more. You deserve everything. I want to prove to you that I'm good."

"You never have to. Actions don't always mean what they're supposed to. I believe in intentions. I know you're good. I know you want me to be happy. Cheer up."

She could see he didn't believe her. He kissed her forehead and lay back. They listened to footsteps from the apartment above.

"Do you wish it were different?" he said. "Do you ever think about having children?"

She stroked his arm and pressed her cheek to his chest. She listened to his breathing, the rustling of his shirt. She listened for his heartbeat.

"I never want children," she said.

For Robert's fiftieth birthday, she bought him a new town car. It cost more than she had to spend, so she sold a painting that Robert had advised her to buy the previous year. The car was black with black leather seats and a silver Tiffany frame to mount the license plate. She had their initials engraved on the underside of the frame like a smitten teenager and didn't tell him. It would be her secret, just as the origin of the car would be a secret from Nicole. Robert would say he'd bought it for himself. It thrilled Kim to think Nicole would be riding in it. Her perfume might get into the seats, but they would be Kim's seats and that made the difference.

She did not expect to see Robert on his birthday. Nicole had planned a dinner. The day before was hers, though. He'd promised to be free. He had a cocktail party to go to early, but after that Nicole was attending a dinner he had long ago declined.

"Come here before drinks," she said.

"That doesn't make sense."

"It will. Don't ask questions."

At five-thirty he arrived. He was breathing heavily from the walk up.

"Those stairs are killing me."

"You said you needed more exercise."

"I was delusional."

She'd given Joseph a ticket stub to the garage around the corner so he could exchange the old car for the new. She'd left a huge red bow in the trunk for him to stick on the roof. He was to wait downstairs.

"I'm going to be late now," said Robert. "What's the surprise? Aren't we meeting in two hours?"

"You're right. I don't want you to be late. Come on, I'll walk you down."

They opened the door of the building and stepped out onto the sidewalk. Joseph had parked the car in front. The bow was two feet tall. Long curling ends dangled down over the windows, reaching nearly to the curb.

"Happy fiftieth," she said.

"Oh, darling!"

He walked a circle around it, running a finger along the silver trim.

"How did you know?" he said. "I was going to get a new one."

"Don't be late."

"It's marvelous, just marvelous."

"Joseph, you better get that bow off so you can get going."

Robert came over and put his hand on her cheek.

"I don't want to leave now," he said.

"Don't."

He kissed her.

"I've made reservations for dinner," she said.

"I'll cut out as soon as I can."

He looked at the car, smiling, and then back at her.

"I can't wait to kiss you in it."

"I have to start getting ready."

"I never would have guessed. How did—"

"I sold a painting."

"Not the—"

"Yes."

He shook his head. "Do you know what that would have been worth in fifteen years?"

"This is now."

"*Ma petite folle.* It's perfect."

"Pick me up when you can."

"Where are we going?"

"You'll see."

———

Joseph called before she even made it to the shower.

"It was a surprise party," he said.

"What do you mean?"

"She's here. He can't leave now."

"Sure he can."

"He didn't know."

"Put him on."

"He got the message out to me."

"Joseph, where are you?"

"I don't think—"

She insisted. "He owes me, Joseph."

"Miss Reilly—"

"He owes me."

He was parked around the corner from the Sherry on 59th Street. She threw on sneakers and a coat.

The liar, she thought. That fucking liar.

She cursed as she walked, willing herself to action, to do something he would regret, anything instead of nothing—the usual gift of her inaction, which he took for granted or which he relied on. Not this time, she thought. She would go into the club and disrupt the party. She would confront Nicole finally. She would demand— what, her fair share? Was that what she was asking for?

She walked straight across town and reached the car. Joseph came toward her, patting the air with his hands.

"Don't go in," he was saying.

"I'm not. Give me the keys."

He halted and she put out her hand.

"It's my car, Joseph."

He reached into his coat and took them out. She snatched them.

"He deserves this," she said.

Joseph backed away, turning his head as though afraid to watch. A man passed. He didn't stop. Kim stood over the hood of the car with the key wedged between her fingers.

"It's a beautiful car, Miss Reilly."

She looked at Joseph and then back at the car, the gleaming black reflecting light from the building across the street. She knew what to write. He did deserve this, something to make him regret. Still, she stood poised with the key. She had every right, didn't she? She had every right to humiliate him. . . .

Joseph came closer. She dropped the keys and covered her ears, as though the car horns were suddenly unbearable, taxis and limousines fighting to make the turn.

Joseph stooped to retrieve the keys. She couldn't stand to see the relief in his face and turned and walked. He followed to the corner to see if she would go into the building after all, but she didn't stop. She walked past the revolving door, the men in their green coats and the clock on its post like a captured moon, lighting the curb. She walked to Michael's building and went into the lobby.

"He's out at the moment," said the doorman.

"Can I wait?"

He shrugged.

She sat in a leather chair and folded her hands. The doorman checked on her periodically and, when his shift ended, asked if she wanted coffee.

"I'll bring it back," he said.

"No, thanks."

She counted the seconds and gradually found her head nodding, her eyelids wanting to close. Michael startled her, putting a hand on her knee.

"What's wrong?"

She looked at him and didn't say anything.

"Do you need a good cry?"

"No," she said.

"I gather it didn't go well."

"Do I look bad?"

"Of course not."

"I need a drink."

"Darling, I'm afraid I have company."

"Oh."

She looked over his shoulder. The lobby was empty.

"He's upstairs already."

"Oscar?"

He didn't answer. She looked at her hands. The knuckles were chapped and she rubbed them and let them fall again to her lap.

"I'm sorry," she said. "I'll go. This can wait."

"Are you sure? I can ask him to leave."

She shook her head.

"Darling," he said, taking hold of her arm.

"Michael, am I that awful? What did I do?"

"Don't think like that."

"At the charity where I help—they look at me sometimes. . . . He says it's him. It's me they hate, and they don't even know me. Everyone hates me."

"That's not—"

"They don't even hate me for the right reasons."

"Come now, you're talking crazy."

"I just wish it could be different," she said.

"That's not what you usually say."

"Tonight, I felt so . . . seeing you, I'm better."

"If I say something, promise not to be mad?"

"Yes."

"You made the decision to leave your job. Perhaps you shouldn't have."

She looked down.

"But then I wouldn't have met you," she said.

The envelope contained another envelope: an old yellowing letter from her father, addressed to her mother care of Kim's grandparents. There was no accompanying note saying where he'd found it or what it was. The postmark was smeared. The edge had been cut carefully with an opener. She slipped it out and unfolded it and read:

Tommy Gillespie lost his arm yesterday. Before the medics got him on a stretcher, his flailing had carved out a section of the grass like some kind of deformed angel. We raked the ground a bit, thinking we might turn up something. The arm was just plain gone. He was a quarterback at Michigan before the draft. Now he's heading back there. A month before a letter had arrived from his fiancée saying she'd left him. "I don't know which I miss more," he said, when I went to see him off. Wanted to know if he should get word to her. About the arm, he meant. If you tell her, I said, and she comes back to you, it's on account of the arm. You want that hanging over you the rest of your life? You may have lost a part of you, but you're still a marine. That seemed to buck him up.

Why am I telling you this? I'm wondering myself. Couple days ago Sam Tucho got his Dear John. Billy Dilesio's gal quit writing back. Twenty-six men died yesterday. I knew twenty-four of them. There's sand in my eye that feels like it won't ever come out. I know I'm asking a lot. I just gotta know somehow. Is there any way I can beg you to stick by me that won't sound like old Tommy with his arm? Say you won't leave me, that you'll wait, and by God's grace I'll make it back.

She tried to imagine what it must have felt like, thousands of miles away, fighting, not knowing if your love back home still cared, finding out that she didn't. To be in the middle of a war, she thought, and find oneself completely alone, and then continue to fight. All those brave hearts. But then on the home front, wasn't that too a battle? She wondered whether Robert considered his marriage a home front or war. Was Kim the front line? Had she ever not been a part of some conflict? Could love exist without war? Perhaps her father was not trying to confess anything but, rather, warn her?

She called him, and the first thing she asked was where he'd found the letter.

"How's the weather there, cold?" he said.

"You just thought to send it?"

"Warm here, but then you wouldn't know."

"It's raining here."

"Rained this morning, but now it's sunny."

"Don't go out without sunblock," she said.

"Suddenly you're concerned?"

"The letter, Dad—it didn't sound like you."

"How am I supposed to sound?"

"I could imagine you writing it."

"She'd want you to see."

"It was beautiful."

"Seeing my boys die was not beautiful."

"Is Tommy still alive? Did you stay in touch?"

"He got shot holding up a liquor store."

"I'm glad you sent it, Dad. Thank you. And hey, you got your wish, didn't you? Mom stuck by you."

"And never let me forget it," he said.

———

She counted the years since she'd last seen him: twenty, more than half her lifetime, old enough to go to war but not old enough to drink. And so she told him finally that she'd left her job.

She had imagined the moment many times, playing out the dialogue, the reaction she'd been avoiding for so long. In part, she told him because she thought he'd caught on, that his seeming apathy was a concession to accept her lies.

"So you're finally getting married?" he replied.

"Robert doesn't believe in marriage."

She tried to explain. So much time had passed since she'd actually left her job. She couldn't remember the rationalizations. She could hear herself rambling about commitment and promises. Her father said nothing.

"Honestly, Dad, I'm not afraid. I know I've made the right decision."

On the table by the phone were framed photographs, crystal column candlesticks with silver Corinthian caps, a bronze figurine of a ballerina that she used as a jewelry stand, necklaces draped over its shoulders, bracelets around the feet. The towers of books virtually covered the walls now. Posters had long ago been replaced with artwork: a blue and pink pastel of Fred Astaire dancing with his shadow, a life-sized charcoal of a woman, her head reared back in ecstasy, hair, thick like an Egyptian headdress, sweeping her shoulders. She could not justify over the phone what a hidden life had proven over time.

Having told him, she volunteered to fly to San Francisco. He insisted on coming to New York. He wanted to meet Robert, to see what she'd forfeited her life for.

—

"He knows no other way," Robert said.

She refused to believe he was defending her father. Her past was so alien to him, like a play unfolding. He was attracted to the drama.

"You were never in the war," she said.

"I didn't have to be."

"How can you say he's the way he is because he fought? How do you know he wasn't a bastard to begin with and would have been no matter what?"

"I know that fighting makes men hurt inside."

"Then you're okay with this?" she said.

Robert agreed, almost too willingly. "Just tell me what to do."

He listened in as she made reservations.

"You put him where?" he said.

"Then what about—"

"Too grand."

"I want grand."

"He wouldn't like it. Have him stay with you."

"Are you crazy? That's my—no, that's . . . he's not going to even see my apartment."

She suggested three other hotels, all of which Robert rejected. Either the rooms were poorly furnished or the service was inadequate or the location was inconvenient.

"Inconvenient to what?" she said.

"I'm excited to finally meet the man. I want it to be right."

—

As the day grew closer, her father began to call with regularity. He asked the same questions again and again, checking the flight numbers and times, rechecking where they were to meet.

"Dad, you have the tickets. All that information is on the tickets."

"Not where we're meeting."

He had always prided himself in his ability to commit such details to memory—an entire week's schedule in his head. "Never write anything down," he'd tell her. It was just one of many military precautions that spilled over into life and had lost its usefulness; like pinpointing a position on a map.

"The gate," she said. "I'll be at the gate."

—

Kim arrived at Kennedy early. Three flight attendants glided past in navy suits, chatting happily and wheeling their overnight bags behind them. They moved at a fast clip and disappeared into the shifting crowd. Kim flattened her hand over a jeweled strawberry brooch that was pinned to her lapel. Ruby flakes prickled her palm reassuringly. She leaned against the window, looking out over the tarmac and the retractable tunnel that would connect to the plane.

—

Once when her father was due back from a trip, Kim's mother insisted that she sit on the front steps of the house to greet him.

"He'll be here any minute," her mother said. "It will mean so much."

The minutes piled up and Kim remained sitting like a prop in the twilight, a welcome-home mat. When he finally arrived, he jumped out of the car with the engine running and bolted up to the step.

"This makes it worthwhile," he said, scooping her up and holding her above his head. Her mother was watching from the doorway, like a director standing in the wings.

Once after a big fight, when he was leaving, she was forced to put on an even greater production. First she had to stand in the kitchen door, waving as he idled the car. Then, as he backed out, she had to run through the house to the living room window and wave again. He waited at the foot of the drive until he saw her.

"He won't leave unless you're there," her mother said, holding the curtains to one side, beckoning. "You're making him late."

She jumped up and waved, broad sweeps of the hand as though she were cleaning the window.

"Fine," her mother said. "Now frown all you want to."

———

The plane nosed right up to the window, the deafening accordion blast of its engines screeching through the glass, sustained for a beat, then cut off. The sudden silence was immediately filled with the faraway roar of a plane taking off, the familiar rush and ripping of air. She watched the tunnel navigate its way to the hatch, hydraulics pumping it higher as it adjusted to the opening.

An attendant wedged the gate doors open, and the first passengers appeared. She wished her father would hurry. Then she saw him, caught in the shuffle, narrow eyes locked ahead as if he knew where he was going. She called, and he didn't hear at first. He stopped. She waved and he saw her.

He cut back against the flow, blocking people. His face and scalp were red from the sun, the skin on his neck even darker, thick as animal hide. What hair remained was razor-cut—stubble salted around the ears. He stopped in front of her. The shoulder pad of his jacket had caught under the strap of his bag. She reached out to fix it and he clenched the strap.

"Is that your only bag?" she said.

He stared her up and down.

"You look thinner," he said.

"Since when?"

"Since a photograph you sent."

"The strap's caught." She gestured with her chin.

He stepped forward, his frame in no way slighter than she remembered; invisible strength that seemed to dictate the space around her. She remained still for his kiss, licked lips closing on her cheek, the sandpaper chafe of his chin. His hands locked on her hips, firm, familiar, fingertips pinching as though he might try to lift her.

"Still doing push-ups every morning," he said, stepping back.

"I have a car outside. Can I carry your bag?"

"No."

She hesitated a moment and then realized he was waiting for her. She only remembered seeing his profile slightly ahead, never behind, his hand reaching back to draw her along. He fell in beside her, fumbling with the strap of his shoulder bag, glancing at Kim to see if she was looking.

Joseph saw them and popped the trunk. He was taller than her father. She introduced them and her father put out a hand. She noticed the firmness of the shake, the assessing stare. It was a ritual he claimed was unintentional.

—

An hour later, they arrived at the hotel. Her father refused to give up his bag to the porter, who simply shrugged and held the door.

"It's his job," she whispered, as they ascended a short flight of stairs to a wide marble landing. Spiky palms bowed toward them from both sides. Limestone columns rose five stories to a translucent marble ceiling.

"They could've landed the plane right here," her father said.

More steps led up to the lounge and tearoom respectively, filled with people, their lips moving in conversations made silent by the dimensions of the lobby. Floor-to-ceiling framed mirrors reflected the vast spaces between.

Kim lifted the bag from her father's shoulder and handed it to the porter. Her father did not argue. At the front desk, she did the talking. Her father waited until they were in the elevator to speak.

"Who's paying for this?" he said.

"I am, Dad."

The room was one of four corner suites on the fiftieth floor. The walls were paneled, upholstered in cream-striped silk. A fax machine sat on a wheeled end table. She followed her father to the bedroom. The window overlooked Central Park. A cloud drifted by. He took in the view with his hands in his pockets.

There was a brown spot on the side of his forehead, a vein that bulged, spiraling like a heating coil. She had never noticed it before.

She pointed out the roller rink and the zoo.

"You can see the Met," she said.

"Do I have time for a nap?"

She left him and went to the bar and asked for a martini. A mirror reflected the tables of businessmen, flattened them out like a picture. Cigar smoke and laughter clung to the curtains, the rolls of material gathered into tight bundles. A woman next to Kim asked for a light. Her accent was thick, Spanish, or perhaps Portuguese. She was trying to figure the tip. She asked a man what to leave. "All day my husband is in meetings," she said. "I find things to do."

———

Kim's father was dressed and sitting when she returned, drumming the arms of his chair with his fingers. The windows had darkened. The city fell away behind him.

"The bed's too soft," he said.

She set her evening bag down, went to the phone, and dialed the desk and asked if there was a way of making the bed harder.

When she turned, her father was holding her evening bag in both hands.

"It's so small," he mumbled. "What can you fit in here?"

"Lipstick. Here."

She took the bag from him and he followed her to the door.

Robert had chosen the restaurant. The maître d' was at the door when they arrived.

"Miss Reilly, always a pleasure."

"Good evening, Bruno."

"This must be your father. An honor," he said, clicking his heels. Her father did not appreciate the act.

Bruno ushered them to their table, sidestepping to let a waiter pass. Unsure of where to stand, her father backed up. A seated couple's hands shot out to protect their drinks. The woman shifted the bracelets on her wrist and whispered into the man's ear as he stared at her father's spit-shined patent-leather shoes.

Robert rose to kiss Kim. He winked and looked past her.

"Mr. Reilly," he said, putting out his hand. His smile was wide, too generous for a first meeting, she thought. "Wonderful to finally meet you."

She looked away and took her seat.

After they settled, the captain brought the wine list.

"Is that what we're drinking?" her father said.

"Would you prefer a cocktail?"

"Doesn't matter."

Robert thought for a moment, then ordered. Her father asked for the wine list. He was curious about the prices, Kim was sure.

"A white Burgundy to start," Robert said. "After that, a fine second-growth Bordeaux."

He described the Bordeaux, pinching his thumb and forefinger for emphasis, tapping the air.

"It's often compared to Palmer." His hand was still bobbing. "Unfairly, I think, for it's superior. Some would disagree."

He tugged his shirt cuffs and rested his hand on the table. His nails were perfectly manicured, and he'd removed his wedding band.

"It gained its reputation during the reign of Louis Fifteenth," he said. "Or was it Sixteenth? There's a delightful story about the Marquis de Rauzan, who owned the estate at that time."

His hand was active again, palm up, as though feeling the weight of some invisible object. She'd never seen him gesture so much.

"Have I told you this?" he said.

She shook her head.

"Supposedly," he went on, turning back to her father, "the marquis sailed to England once with hopes of obtaining better prices. Right there in the harbor, from his ship, he held an auction. At first nobody was interested. The prices were outrageous. Rauzan was infuriated and threatened to pour every last barrel into the Thames. In fact, he started to. Picture it: one, then another, and another; wine dribbling down the hull of the ship. The horror. The Brits became so nettled, mortified, to see good vintage wine going to waste, that they caved in and paid the asking price."

He laughed and looked at Kim.

"Of course, Château Margaux is my favorite. It's the parent of this wine. The vines were originally cut from that estate. That's what I mean when I say second growth."

"Mr. Sanders," said Kim's father, "you know a lot about wine."

"Call me Robert, please."

"After the war, I spent some time in France. A buddy of mine was interested in starting a vineyard. He had money, but he didn't want just any old vines. So we traveled, tasting more wines than I can recall the names of. One morning, I remember waking up in a barn with hay up my nose and a mule staring at me. That one wasn't good, I think. But we finally found one we liked and my friend made an offer."

Her father held his glass to the light. He wiped the rim with his napkin and set it down.

"I forget the Frenchman's name," he said. "Stubborn old bastard. I can see him smoking a pipe. He was the caretaker. Every day for a week we went to that man, begging, raising our bid each time. He'd open a bottle and sit us down and ask us to tell stories about the war.

His English wasn't so good, but he could understand enough. You know, he gave us the vines for free. Turned out not to be a question of money. He'd lost two sons in the fighting. It was his way of thanking us. We smuggled the vines back to the States, and my friend took them out west and planted them."

"Dad, I never heard that story before."

"That's how I know what a second growth is."

"You should have stopped me," said Robert.

"I did."

Robert laughed. The sommelier was opening the wine.

"Did you keep in touch with your friend?" Kim asked.

"Jim Burr."

"I'd remember that name," she said.

The sommelier presented the cork and poured Robert a sip.

"Stayed on as a reserve."

"What about the vineyard?" Kim said.

"One foot in, one out."

Robert nodded for the glasses to be filled.

"His helicopter veered unexpectedly and smacked into a tree."

Her father clapped his palms. The sommelier jumped, spilling wine on the table.

"I'm so sorry," he said. Her father said nothing as the man folded a napkin over the wet spot and finished pouring.

"At least that's what I heard," her father said finally. "Korea hadn't started yet."

Robert thanked the sommelier, paused, and lifted his glass.

"Semper Fi," he said.

Kim's hand trembled as she clutched her glass. She wanted Robert to smile somehow or nudge her under the table; some discreet sign to show he wasn't so painfully serious. No matter how insulting, it would have been a relief. But he kept his drink aloft and held her father's stone-jawed stare.

"To Jim Burr," she said, hastily drinking.

Her father still hadn't moved. Then, slowly, he took up his glass. He held it rigidly before him, eyes locked on Robert's, lips moving slightly as though in silent grace, then jerked the wine to his mouth, snapped it back, and drained it. He brought the glass down hard, rattling the silverware, and wiped his lips with his napkin.

"It's very good," Robert said.

"Look," said Kim, "there's George Davis. Doesn't he own a bison ranch near Denver somewhere?"

"He says bison's the meat of the future. Cheaper and healthier than beef. I still haven't tried it."

The headwaiter appeared with the menus, and she opened hers quickly. They were written in French. She sipped her wine and started through the appetizers: crab cakes with mustard sauce on a bed of sweet-pea greens, tuna tartar, white asparagus tips with truffles. She didn't look up until she'd finished reading all the entrées.

"Do you have any questions?" she said, glancing at her father.

"I don't."

"You should try this," she said, leaning over and pointing.

He glared, but when the waiter returned, that's what he ordered, holding out his menu and pointing just the same.

"It's very good," said the waiter.

Robert handed his menu to the waiter. "So, Charlie—may I call you Charlie? Your daughter has told me some harrowing stories. Do you miss it?"

"Miss what?"

"I mean the edge. Life after war must pale."

"I miss having a gun pointed at me."

"I don't mean that, obviously. I know people who have had your sort of experience, and the period after—"

"You know someone who fought in Korea?"

"I mean from the accounts I've read, articles—"

"I haven't read many articles."

"You didn't fight in Vietnam, I understand."

"I was too old."

"You almost sound disappointed."

"I'm not."

"Would you have wanted to if you could?"

"Would you?"

"Well, I don't think so."

"I didn't want to."

"You didn't believe in it?"

"Of course I believe in war. I fought in two of them."

"Can we talk about something else?" said Kim.

Her father put his hand on her arm.

"No, sir," her father said. "Don't mistake me. I would have fought if they'd asked me. I trained soldiers to go there."

"Was it the politics of the war?"

"Sure it was politics."

"I mean, when you say you didn't want to go."

"No."

"It wasn't?"

"What are you aiming at, Mr. Sanders?"

"Most people I've talked to share your sentiment. They were ambivalent."

"I don't follow."

"That's why it was so horrific."

"No worse."

"It tore our country apart," Robert said. "I'd say that's pretty horrific."

"Horse shit."

"Yes, but—"

"You can point to specific fights and details, and I'm here to tell you, there's no difference between any of them."

"That wasn't—"

"Whether it's Bunker Hill and you're staring down two hundred and you've got just the stones at your feet, or you're lying face first in mud, trying to pick a sniper out of a tree and you've pissed your pants you've been still for so long."

"Dad." Kim turned away.

"War is war, six of one and half a dozen of the other—all red in the end. I trained marines to be men."

"Yes, and then they didn't receive any support from back home."

"A marine doesn't need support."

"You didn't feel sorry for them? If they didn't believe—"

"Mr. Sanders, do you pity me?"

"Of course not."

"All those so-called whining veterans—they're just a bunch of candy-assed momma's boys who thought they deserved a pat on the back because they had to shoot people and then found out their long-haired friends back home didn't respect them for it. All they did was insult my memory. If Patton had been alive, he would have slapped each and every goddamn one of them."

"Certainly you respected—"

"For that matter, if he'd been alive, we would have won that damn war."

"You respected the men you trained, though, didn't you?"

"That's the difference. People only care about themselves now."

Kim stood abruptly. She excused herself and went to the powder room. She shut herself in and sat down, clutching the folds of her dress in her lap, gathering them to her chest and face.

To see her father side by side with Robert—to observe Robert's finery, the sharp points of his perfectly folded handkerchief, gold conch-shell cuff links, stiff starched collar, and Windsor knotted tie—then to see her father, his brown puckering suit, matted shoulder pads sitting off his shoulders, that took nothing from his piercing expression, was to acknowledge that his dignity came from somewhere else, a place she hated to respect but trusted, where limbless men lay propped against trees, faceless, tags on chains torn from their necks. Robert could be stripped of his dignity. Her father could stand naked, hobbled and slouched, eyes glazed and full of drink, and nobody—nothing—could deprive him of his. There was no denying it. It came from the inside, from lasting memory. Her father's stern gaze, the lines in his face—cut deep like driftwood, split by the ocean, dried by salt and sun, and washed ashore—and his inability to discuss the trivial set him apart from Robert's eagerness, his fluff.

She pulled up her stockings and straightened her dress and wondered if a little of the light her father cast on Robert didn't fall on her as well. She checked her hair.

When she returned, they were talking easily. The subject had changed to Robert's investments. There was a play he was considering backing. Her father was grinning.

"You'd think I'd have learned my lesson," Robert said, rising and helping Kim with her chair. "My first brush with theater production was a disaster. Darling, I was just telling your father about my past foolishness, that gangster musical I thought would be a smash."

He turned back to her father.

"There are much wiser uses for a million dollars."

"A million?"

Robert sipped his wine. The dinner came.

"So what's this play about?" said her father, taking up his knife and fork.

"Charlie, it's far too embarrassing."

"Tell me."

"You'll say, 'Robert, why not just give the money to me?' "

"Should we order another bottle?" Kim said, finishing her glass.

"We did, love, remember?"

"Give me a clue," said her father. "Who's the star?"

"No one."

"No one?"

"No one you would know. I'm afraid it's all about cars. The actors play cars and wear roller skates like that play a few years ago, and skate on ramps. They sing about being cars, what it feels like to sit in heavy traffic or get rear-ended."

Her father's mouth hung open.

"There you have it."

"You're right," her father said. "You should just give me the money."

"I can't even say I had a boyhood fascination with cars. I know it sounds preposterous, but you have to admit, if you had the opportunity to invest in something so positively absurd . . . a grown man on roller skates singing about getting his oil changed. . . . As a conversation piece alone, the investment's worth it, don't you agree?"

Her father nodded.

Kim stared at him. His nose had reddened. His lips were pale. The second bottle of wine had been decanted. The waiter brought new glasses. Her father watched expectantly as the wine was poured, tapping the rim of his glass for more. The waiter continued to pour, filling the glass uncomfortably full. Robert beamed. Usually such a stickler about etiquette, he seemed not to care.

He talked about other investments, brushing off losses as mere amusement and savoring the successes. There was so much her father seemed willing to overlook. Was it the gambler's thrill? Horse races or paintings—was there any difference? Only with Robert there was no losing all his money because there was too much. It was there in the end, handed down like a blessing. To see her father's wide-eyed gaze undid all she had credited him with. She thought about the nights he stayed out, with her mother alone in the kitchen, watching the clock, taking his plate from the table and wrapping it in foil and going back to the chair and waiting.

When the check arrived, her father took out his wallet. But Robert had given his credit card before dinner. The slip was already prepared.

"You will treat when we visit you," Robert said, and this satisfied her father.

They stood up. Bruno was at the table to help.

"You will come back again," he said to her father, smiling. He escorted them to the door and shook Robert's hand.

"Now, where's Joseph?" Robert said, looking up and down the street.

"Did you like dinner?" said Kim.

"You have to tell me what I ate," said her father.

Robert was smiling. "Goose liver."

"Goose?"

"That's right."

Her father nodded. "It was good."

Kim looked away.

—

At the hotel, Robert waited in the car. She rode the elevator up with her father and saw him to his room. He stood in the doorway, swaying from side to side, his face flushed from the wine. She stepped forward to kiss him and he put his arm out.

"Robert—" He raised a finger. "There's a lot he can give you."

She bowed her head and was silent.

"Don't go screwing it up, now."

She leaned over quickly to kiss him, and again he put his hand on her shoulder to stop her and stared at her and made her look straight at him.

"Before you were born, even, I did things," he said. "Anything to make the world a better place."

He clutched her in a tight embrace, bumping her as he tried to steady himself.

"You're a big girl now," he said.

He turned and leaned against the door frame with his back to her.

"Dad?"

He seemed to be nodding.

"'Bye," she said.

He closed the door behind him.

—

Her heels echoed in the lobby and scraped against the sidewalk outside. She got in the car and Joseph eased out into traffic.

"You made it," said Robert, putting his hand on her thigh.

"How dare you bring up the subject of money with my father?"

"Pardon me?"

"What were you thinking?" she said, her voice rising.

"I don't appreciate your tone. There's no reason—"

"Fuck my tone. You had no right."

Joseph watched in the mirror. A taxi careened past them and shot through a yellow light. Joseph stopped short. Garbage bags lined the street, piled high before dark store windows and pulled-down gates.

"This dinner was for you," Robert mumbled. "It was your idea."

He was quiet the rest of the drive. Only as they pulled up to her apartment did he turn to her.

"Would you like me to come up?"

He touched her leg again. When she didn't respond, he nodded to Joseph, who got out and opened the door.

"Good night, Joseph," she said.

She started to climb out. Robert grabbed her wrist.

"What?" she said. She stared at him. "What?"

He didn't move.

"All that you know, and you still said those things. Now let go!"

She threw his hand away. It lay dead on the seat. Joseph nodded to her and shut the door. She stood on the steps, watching, as he climbed back into the car and pulled away, the back of Robert's head in the rear window.

She opened her evening bag for her keys and found an envelope. It hadn't been there before. She turned it over and peeled back the flap. There was a check. A note slipped out and fluttered to the sidewalk. She stooped to retrieve it and held it up to the lamplight.

I know it's not much, it said in her father's hand, *but—some walking-around money.*

The check was for two thousand dollars.

PART III

RESIGNATION

As time went on, Kim heard more about Nicole's severe episodes. Like the time she broke fifty thousand dollars' worth of Ming porcelain, or when she doused Robert's favorite saddle with lighter fluid, nearly setting fire to their barn.

Robert would call in the night and come over after Nicole had taken a Valium. Sometimes he showed up without notice. Once she woke to find his lips against her forehead. Gasping, she swatted him away, and he had to grab her flailing wrists to calm her.

"It's me. It's only me," he said. After that, he made a point of always ringing the buzzer so as not to alarm her. It would sound like a gunshot, startling her awake. She would have seconds to ready herself as he climbed the stairs.

He would omit the precipitating details of the evening and start mid-story, pacing at the foot of the bed as she shielded her eyes from the light.

—

"What am I supposed to do?" he said. "Today she spent a hundred and fifty thousand dollars on a sports car."

"I must look terrible. I hate it when you don't call."

"You know her license was revoked four years ago? Well, today she drove the floor model out of the dealership and was stopped for speeding."

Kim laughed.

"It's not funny," he said.

"I know."

She took a clip that she kept by the bed and gripped it in her mouth as she gathered her hair and pulled it back and fixed it in a choppy ponytail.

"The car was impounded. I had to get her out of jail." He sighed.

"Should I make coffee?" she said, flattening the covers next to her, smoothing out the wrinkles. She slid over to give him room.

"Did I tell you Davis quit his job?" he said, staring at the space she'd created on the bed. "He told us at dinner. I thought Nicole was going to stab him with a fork."

"I'll fix us drinks."

She climbed naked out of bed. He seemed not to notice. She wrapped herself in a silk robe and went to the side bar by the dresser. She poured a finger of scotch from a square crystal decanter and tipped the glass back, palming the heavy carved cap as the tingle spread through her body and rushed warm to her head.

"He does these things to spite her," he said.

She refilled her glass. The bedsprings squeaked. He was lying on his back, staring through framed fingers at some imaginary scene on the wall. Kim crawled onto the bed and sat cross-legged, sipping as she waited for him to continue.

"You can't blame him," she said.

"For what? For pouring gas on a fire?"

"For crying out, I mean."

"He knows I'll get him another job."

"Don't."

"I have to."

"Silly."

"No, I have to. I know he's crying out. Of course I know. I'm not the one holding back here, and I'm not about to start."

"Well, he's rebelling against you too."

"I can see I've caught you in one of your moods."

"Robert, it's two in the morning."

"Nicole's always commenting on how Christine's perfect."

"Fine."

"And all I can think about, all I can hear, are these endless tapes in my mind, these incessant conversations we had about just this sort of thing: before Davis was born, and then when Christine came along. Wasted breath. She thinks she's being constructive with her praise—healthy sibling competition. She's punishing him. I can't stop her. The least I can do is stick up for him."

"The ways we ask for love," Kim said.

His cheeks creased and his mouth bent as though he'd tasted something bitter. "Are you listening to me?"

"It's not spite."

"Christine's about to graduate summa cum laude. She's a shoe-in for the law school, I'm told. You know how many Harvard undergrads are accepted into the law school? Do you know how hard she works? Ten times harder than Davis ever did. You'd think it would be the other way around."

"You're judging him, too."

"Imagine a mother who's barely articulate half the time telling him he's a miserable failure. Why would he want to spite me?"

"I didn't say that."

"Sure you did."

"Darling, you don't have to yell."

"Tell me."

"You're right. You're right. I was wrong."

"Go on, tell me."

"I said I was wrong."

He lurched from the bed and went to the window and pulled up the blinds. She went to the bathroom, shut the door quietly behind her, and leaned against the sink. He was angry because she had intruded. But he had led her there. She knew one thing: Knowing and doing were completely different. Michael was right. She had to make herself useful. She'd cheated herself out of something long before she'd left her job. Perhaps she could go back to school. Was that too drastic? She might take a class just to try it, sit in on a summer course. Slowly, she began to outline her lips with a pencil. She thought back to her last years of schooling, the anxiety, the derision. Would it be different now? Would she feel stupid? She filled in with lipstick and kissed a Kleenex, then looked at herself more. She plucked an errant lash, turned side to side, then dabbed her neck with perfume.

When she returned, Robert was pouring another drink.

"I'm sorry," she said, going to his side.

"I didn't come here to be rebuked."

She pressed against the length of his body.

"Would you like another drink?" he said. He began to loosen his tie.

They made love urgently that night. She took his penis in her fingers, coaxing him until his hips worked alone and he thrust into her hand, casting off the weight he carried to the bed. That wasn't enough. He wanted to hear her cries.

At such times he would put his finger inside her and feel his way and study her. Her spasms made him forget, soothed, touched him someplace else. All this she saw in his face, a specific and definite hope. She would concentrate every muscle. She would focus on his finger and shut out the world and pray that she could. As his arm tired and lost rhythm he would brace it against her thigh. He would switch hands and begin again with renewed vigor, and she would encourage him, pleading for patience, telling herself as his hand fluttered that he had chosen her over others and what that signified. Fear made it difficult. Fear made it possible. Her body would fill and shudder, and she would cry sometimes with relief. She would look up and Robert's face would seem small, as though she were seeing it from far off, the sweaty satisfaction.

They lay separately afterward. She imagined what it was like being married, sharing a bed night after night without escape. She listened to Robert's breathing as he drifted off to sleep.

—

He woke a few hours later, fully exhilarated. He was brimming with news, as though he'd just returned from a long workday or trip. "You know that painting I bid on?" he said. "I got it for a hundred thousand under the asking price."

He sauntered into the bathroom, whistling a Vivaldi concerto. She knew it was Vivaldi and not Bach because he'd made her listen to the difference many times. "It's more languid," he'd say. "Not as mechanical." Maybe it was Bach. It sounded familiar, and then it didn't.

She got up and went to the closet and began to dig through clothes that she'd bundled on the floor, piles that she was too lazy to take to the cleaner. She pulled out single shoes that had become detached from their mates and tossed them aside. She sifted through folded-up overnight bags and more clothes until she finally found the shoe box she'd been looking for, which contained all her notes. She opened it nervously. It had been so long since she'd read any of her own writing. The bits of paper had yellowed and curled. Robert came out of the bathroom, still whistling.

"Sorry about earlier," he said. "How do you put up with me?"

He bent over her and pecked her cheek and noticed the box in her lap.

"What are you doing?" he said.

She read one of the slips to herself:

A shell full of water can hold the sky.

"What are those?" he said.

"Writing."

"Whose? Yours? Let me see."

She shook her head.

"Imagine," he said. "A little trove. What is it, sort of an old journal? You don't want me to see? How long have you been keeping a journal?"

She sat on the floor and he kept asking questions, as though finding and opening the old box had opened some door in his mind, some dark room that began to fill with pits and torture devices.

"My little secret one." He laughed. "My little brilliant one, writing away."

He wondered what she'd written and he encouraged her now to expound on matters of her childhood as a means of guessing at the box's contents. Of course he wanted to know if she'd written about him. Did her writing contain information that didn't belong on record? He kept smiling, but she could see that he was worried, that knowing about these scraps, just knowing they existed, even locked away, conjured up feelings he hated to admit. The scraps were shameful, sometimes beautiful, maybe shameful because they were beautiful. They felt like lies. She couldn't take a course, she realized.

"What if I told you you're not in them at all?" she said.

His smile was full of confidence. "Of course I'm in them," he said, beaming like a child. "If your father's in there, then I am."

"Why's that?"

He shrugged as though the whole thing were of no matter, as though he'd been teasing her. She wondered whether he knew why he was right.

"Now, now," he said. "Don't look so cross. I didn't mean to hurt your feelings. It's only right that I should be curious. You've been holding out on me. What do you say we make a deal? I promise not to bring up reading your little private bits so long as from time to time you read me a few little parts that you feel comfortable sharing. How's that?"

She took a slip of paper from the top of the pile, unfolded it, and stared.

"He wishes he could turn back the clock. He wishes for even a small surprise."

She looked up at him. There was an odd mix of hurt and pleasure in those blue, blue eyes. He smoothed his drying hair back.

"You wrote that?" he said. "I'm not sure whether I should be flattered or ashamed."

She held the piece of paper up and turned it over to reveal that it was blank. He nodded slowly.

"I'm ashamed," he said.

She put the lid back on the box and stood and set the box on the nightstand. "No, you're not."

"I deserve to be."

He reached out and touched her mouth and tried to draw a smile.

"How do you put up with me?" he said.

———

After he left, she took off her makeup and moisturized her face.

Back in the bedroom the comforter was half on the floor. She straightened it and climbed under the sheets with the television on and the lights out. The sheets smelled faintly of sex. She hugged the pillows and kept to her side of the mattress. The relief that came at Robert's departure always faded.

On the rare occasion that Michael wasn't invited to an important party, she couldn't resist teasing him. The public library was having a Black and Gold ball in the courtyard in Bryant Park. She called him a week before.

"I'm sure your invitation got lost in the mail," she said. "It's okay. I put your name down as my guest."

Then she had to beg him to join her.

—

They had set up tents in case of rain, but the sky was clear. Gold spotlights nestled among the roots of trees, shining up the trunks and on the lowest limbs. The foliage above the illuminated canopy was dark, like a charcoal cloud hovering at the feet of the imposing chalk-lit skyscrapers that surrounded the park. Women in assorted gold gowns stepped delicately, slowly, careful not to catch a heel in the mossy cracks between stone slabs.

Two giant draped boxes stood behind a carpeted platform atop which a man in a gold bow tie with wispy gray hair was delivering a speech. As he finished, he turned to one of the two boxes and threw up his arms. The covering dropped away to reveal a cage and two pacing lions. After the applause died, he extended his thanks to Ringling Brothers for loaning the animals. The circus was at Madison Square Garden that week. The second draped box sprang open, releasing hundreds of doves. For a moment the birds flew together, a swooping cloud of white beating wings above the guests. Then they dispersed and there were only pigeons left. The man climbed down from the platform to another round of applause, and a band began to play.

"Can we leave now?" said Michael. "We're going to be late for Bertrand's party."

Kim was watching Robert and Nicole from a distance. If he were to glance over, she wanted him to see her laughing.

"Is he looking?" she said.

"Yes," said Michael, and she emptied her glass and tossed back her head.

When she glanced over, Nicole was pointing a gold silk-gloved finger at a dove that had settled on a park bench. Robert and the other guests were admiring the bird.

"He's not looking," Kim said.

"He was. Come, darling, let's go." He put out his hand.

"Wait!"

She brushed past him and started toward Robert's group. The first few steps were cautious as she crept from shadow into the glare of a spotlight. She wanted to see if Robert would notice her, but he didn't. She found her pace quickening until she was close, then beside them, reachable, an arm's length away. She stretched out a hand to touch Nicole's shoulder. Robert turned and almost dropped his glass. His eyes flared, strained for a beat in their sockets as though struggling to escape the body that had cemented very suddenly around them. As the leaves of a plant set too close to an intense heat, Kim's fingers seemed to curl and wilt.

Nicole whipped around.

"Your dress is beautiful," Kim said.

Nicole nodded, a twitch of a thank-you. Anxiously she spun back to the conversation she'd left. "That's not what he said. That's not what he said at all."

She was wagging a gloved hand.

Kim walked away. She could feel Robert's stricken gaze following her.

Michael had his arms crossed like a scolding nanny.

"Pleased?" he said.

She looked back to see Robert, his eyes now darting from her to Nicole.

"I doubt she could pick me out of a lineup," Kim said. "Anyway, she looks terrible."

"Only to you."

"Those gloves are over the top."

"They're fun. Can we please go? I'm afraid one of those birds is going to shit on me."

"Now I'll have to see their photos and hear the comments."

"What comments?"

"In the magazines, from people."

"You don't have to look at those photos, and you don't have to stand here watching. We could be downtown at Diva now, getting drunk with Bertrand. I think he turned a hundred and fifty today. You're being hard on yourself. On second thought, I take it back. It's me you're being hard on, keeping me here."

"You don't get it."

"Of course I do. That should be you over there by his side."

"No."

"And in the magazines."

"No."

He checked his watch. "You *are* torturing yourself, though."

"Okay, we'll go."

They steered clear of Robert. He had his arm hooked around Nicole's waist, an ear cocked to a man who was speaking. One laugh set off a series. They were all laughing, Nicole clutching her stomach, then dabbing a tissue to her tearing eyes.

Michael tugged Kim's arm.

"No dillydallying."

She hesitated a moment longer—enough to see Robert lift his head and peer in the direction of where she and Michael had stood before. That was the image she clung to as they left.

Michael couldn't understand. It was not jealousy she felt, seeing Robert with Nicole, but fatigue. Jealousy was too black-and-white. For Robert to come to her in the night, complaining of the same wounds week after week, craving salve; to tell him simply to leave Nicole, or to even think that was a viable solution—that would have been jealousy. She never suggested that he desert her. Rather, she dug deep. She found examples in their relationship of his generosity, the ways he took care of her, and used these to contradict Nicole's portrayal of him, to reassure him. She reminded herself that it was love that kept him at Nicole's side, and love that brought him to her door, and that love, unlike jealousy, was an endless combination of true and false, a sweet painful Godlike gray. She had to find new ways to offer the same encouragements, to overcome the dim knowledge that she rarely saw Robert at his best, but always in some troubled state. All this she could bear. She certainly did not wish to be in Nicole's shoes, but there was no way of proving that to Michael.

—

Robert called that morning at four-thirty, whispering, begging her not to be so daring.

On Fridays in the summer she would ride out to the Hamptons. Sometimes Michael would drive her. Other times she took an upscale shuttle bus called the Jitney. They offered sealed cups of water and juice and small bags of pretzels and handed out magazines containing photographs of celebrities and wealthy residents seen the previous weekend. It was cold on the bus, and she would wrap a sweater around her neck and shut her eyes and listen to the crackle of pretzel bags tearing open, the anxious chatter that usually only lasted the first third of the trip, until they hit heavy traffic and people began to doze.

Michael would be waiting at the stop in Bridgehampton with his car running. He'd roll down the window and cry out loudly so that everyone would stare, "Hey, you on the shitney!"

The trunk would pop and she'd load her bag and creep around to get in. He'd be laughing.

"I don't know how you take that thing," he said. "They treat you like steerage. Look at you, you're shivering."

"Glad to see you, too."

"You know, if you stay on, the next stop's the meat factory. You're lucky I pick you up here."

———

She lunched with Michael and groups of women, clients of his who were mostly married and in their late thirties. The husbands were off playing golf or at home on conference calls with an office overseas.

Conversations gravitated toward money: donations of note, the cost of incompetent help, recent acquisitions and how much was saved, when really it was the amount spent that counted. In sandals and frog-eyed sunglasses, clingy silk beach dresses and wide-brimmed hats, they sipped Chardonnay and nibbled at cucumber sandwiches and tuna fish on Ritz crackers, growing more gregarious as the lunch drifted by. They marveled about increased land values, tiny houses that were selling for well above their worth, and the enormous tasteless houses that were going up, Napoleonic statements of wealth, until by the end of the meal they were anything but discreet and spoke openly about spending as though it were the weather, as if what they revealed were no more significant or personal than the rolling clouds or the possibility of rain. By the time they broke from the table they were stumbling. They hugged and kissed and weaved back to their cars, off to collect the kids and the nanny from the beach or home to change for afternoon cocktails, all the while tossing back invitations for future weekends, offers to stay at their houses that by dinner were forgotten.

Kim surveyed the different shades of lipstick marks on the glasses. Stacks of dishes filled the sink. Some plates sat on the counter with food that had hardly been touched: a sandwich with just the corner bitten off, one lying open-faced with some of the insides picked out. One woman had left a pile of neatly peeled-off bread crusts. Another had eaten only the *cornichons* from atop her salad.

"You should hear the things they tell me in private," said Michael.

"Like?"

"How Daphne's husband is like this." He stuck out his pinky. "That's why they own a twenty-million-dollar house with thirty bedrooms. Or how Wendy's husband likes to videotape her with Asian prostitutes."

"Get out!"

"I choose their drapes so they tell me these things."

"I think they're in love with you."

"Judith Haines, whom you just met—the one in the white skirt that looked like a dust ruffle—a month ago she gave birth to her third child. Today, she'd just come from giving her personal trainer a blow job. Supposedly, her husband's sleeping with Daphne in one of those thirty bedrooms. That's unconfirmed."

"They're all crazy."

"No, they're normal. You're crazy. Everyone cheats but you. We're all a pack of horny baboons."

"I'm hardly moral."

"Nonsense, you're the most moral person I know. It's almost boring. You should have heard Oscar the other night talking about you and Robert. He called it true love. It nearly brought up my stuffed quail from dinner."

"Is love so distasteful to you? You liked Robert once."

"Oh, look, a piping plover." He pointed. "That bird there."

"You know everything."

"I do, don't I."

Poolside afternoons: Michael reclined in a chaise longue, sipping daiquiris from foot-tall glasses. He'd started a collection of tiny paper umbrellas and stuck them between his toes. "To keep them cool," he said. She did the same.

" 'Love looks not with the eyes, but with the mind,' " he said. "Shakespeare."

"I thought love was blind."

" 'The course of true love never did run smooth.' "

"So they say."

"Shakespeare again."

"Enough already with Shakespeare."

"I forget who it was who said, 'When you look at love it disappears.' "

"Is this your idea of a lecture?"

" 'If in your fear you would seek only love's peace and love's pleasure—' "

"Am I afraid?"

" 'Then it is better for you—' "

"You've been busy."

"You're making me forget. Something about nakedness; nakedness, I always get hung up on that word, wait. . . ."

"Then it is better for me—"

" 'To pass out of love's threshing-floor into the seasonless world where you shall laugh, but not all of your laughter, and weep, but not all of your tears.' "

"Impressive. You've memorized a lot."

"I've collected a few ditties. Daiquiri musings, I'm calling them, for your edification."

Michael's friend Oscar was playing tennis with three other men. The court lay at the far end of the lawn. From where they sat, they couldn't see much, but they could hear laughter, the pop of shots, and the racing footsteps.

Michael brought up the end of the century. He was planning his eve.

"You already know where you want to be?" Kim said.

"No, but I know how I'd like to be."

He ran off a list of cities.

Machu Picchu: "There's magic there."

Madrid: "They give a very good party."

Venice: "Everyone in masks on boats. I have a cape I've been saving."

"Why not be sailing?"

"I want to be someplace specific."

"Under the stars."

"A palazzo on the Grand Canal. I know someone. I should call him tomorrow."

"It's seven years away."

"Darling, have you tried calling some of the restaurants? They're filling up. Maybe I should stay home that night and just take a bath. That's where I shall be, in my tub. I'll call the maid in and have her take a picture. Where will you be, love?"

"Maybe I'll take a bath too."

"Excellent choice. All the world will be bleary-eyed and sweaty, and we'll just be rising from our warm soak, smelling clean, ready for the new millennium. I'm going to call all my friends and tell them. They'll be jealous."

Oscar had peeled off his shirt and shoes and was sprinting barefoot across the lawn to the pool. He launched into a high arching dive, feet perfectly pointed. There was hardly a splash. Bubbles marked where he'd entered the water.

"Very dramatic," said Michael when Oscar surfaced. "Now let's try to keep some of the water in the pool, shall we?"

Oscar gave him the middle finger.

"Look at him," said Michael. "Like a little boy." He called out, "How about a cannonball now?"

Oscar began swimming laps. A swell of water preceded his gliding body and slapped the end of the pool as he flipped and pushed off and surfaced, coming back the other way. Kim sipped her drink and watched his hands, the steady reaching, the rhythmic slicing of the clear surface. The years had been like this.

Her thoughts returned to the millennium, to people's place in time. Her father had been to war. Even Robert had his place: the son of a son, an heir in a line of heirs dating back to the 1300s, Northern Scotland, and the Conquests. He could recite his lineage, the deeds of his forefathers. Kim had no lineage or defining experience. Two generations back, a boat ride erased the past. What had she contributed to history? Time was running out on the most obvious of possible legacies. Soon she'd be able to say that her womb really was a spare part. There was no point trying to attach more significance to one year than another. The millennium would be the same.

Oscar burst from the pool, dripping. He shook himself vigorously and wrung water from his hair with both hands and grinned.

"My black Lab," said Michael.

—

The following week Oscar met her at the bus stop in one of Michael's cars. He had the top down. He jumped out and helped with her bag.

"Michael had to meet a client in Montauk," he said. "He'll be back for dinner."

"He's probably at the beach."

"I do all the cooking anyway."

"Nice sunglasses."

"Thanks, they're his. I stole them."

When they got back to the house, Oscar had a bottle of white wine open. He plunked an ice cube in his glass.

"Want one?"

"It's already too cold," she said. "Leave the bottle out for a bit."

He shrugged.

She sat at the kitchen island and watched him go through the refrigerator, laying out salad items. Three steaks were already marinating in a large glass dish.

"Would you like to shell the walnuts?" he said. "For the salad."

"I'm not very good."

"I'm sure you're better than his majesty."

He took a nutcracker from a drawer and brought her an extra bowl for the shells. Then he set to slicing vegetables.

He asked about Robert, but she was tired and didn't feel like a drawn-out conversation.

"Tell me something about Michael, then. A deep dark secret."

"Like what?" she said.

"Like what does he say about me?"

"How wonderful and gorgeous you are."

He threw the vegetables in a frying pan and fiddled with the burner, bending to see the flame. He spilled a little wine and laughed, dropped a rag on the floor, and pushed it around with his foot.

"Tell *me* a secret," she said.

"About Michael?"

"Something about you."

"Like what?"

"Anything. Tell me about your parents."

"They don't talk to me."

"What do you mean?"

"I don't exist anymore."

She wanted to say she was sorry, but thought it would sound in poor taste. Still, she said it because she couldn't think of anything else.

"What about Michael's parents?" he asked. "Does he talk to you about them?"

"How do you mean?"

"What they're like—he won't say."

"Have you discussed that with him?"

"Have you met them? C'mon. It's okay to tell me."

"If Michael doesn't want to talk about it, you should respect that."

A car sounded in the drive, saving her. Oscar checked the vegetables. Michael breezed into the kitchen, tossing his keys into a basket.

"So much money out there, so little taste," he said.

He pecked Kim on the cheek.

"Oscar pick you up okay? He wasn't late, was he?"

"Right on time."

"Want some wine?" said Oscar.

"Is there any of that iced tea left? I'm going to jump in the shower."

He headed upstairs.

"I'll get it," she said to Oscar. "Keep an eye on the vegetables."

She filled a glass with ice from the dispenser in the door of the fridge and took out the pitcher of tea.

"Too much ice," said Oscar. He came over and removed two cubes, tossing them in the sink. "He likes four. Hey, don't look at me."

"Better start those steaks."

———

After dinner, Michael took a large bottle of vodka from the freezer. "Now, a game of pretend."

"This should be good."

Michael paused. "Okay, everything you say has to be a lie. Understand?" He set three glasses on the counter. "If by accident you actually tell the truth and someone challenges you, you take a shot. If no one challenges you, of course, you're fine. You've passed the truth off as a lie. That may be the funnest part."

"What if someone challenges and they're wrong?" said Oscar.

"Then *they* have to do a shot. Anyone can challenge."

Oscar was already sitting on the counter. He put his feet up. Michael nodded for him to put them down.

"How long does the game go on?" said Oscar.

"I don't want to play," said Kim.

"Do you mean that, or have you started playing?" said Michael.

Oscar poured a shot and downed it.

"I'll go first," he said.

"It doesn't work that way. There are no turns. It's everything you say from the moment we start."

"Who wins?"

"Nobody," said Kim. "You two play without me."

"You have to play," said Michael. "Darling, don't quit us. We're so used to lies. Won't it be nice to spot the truth for a change?"

"So everything has to be a statement?"

"No, just every statement has to be a lie."

"Sounds boring," said Oscar. "There should be a way to win."

"It sounds boring to you," said Michael, "because you don't like to think."

"I think anything that requires one to think is boring," said Kim.

"Ah, she's entered the fray with flying colors."

Michael smiled. She didn't say anything.

They went back and forth. Mostly Oscar got stuck doing shots. It became difficult to tell if he was really trying or just playing to get drunk. Michael would say, "I think designers these days aren't using enough rayon." Then Oscar would pipe in, "I love rayon," and Michael would challenge. Oscar would giggle and down his shot and Michael would roll his eyes.

"The things we're learning," he said.

"I've got one," said Oscar.

"One what?"

Oscar refilled his glass, then glanced at Kim. "He likes to look at pictures of naked women."

"Only one woman," said Michael. "There's only one woman for me, Oscar. Didn't you know that? Ever since we met. It's you, Kim. I'm madly, deeply, head-over-heels in love with you."

A smile played on his lips.

"Well?" He stared at Kim. "Aren't you going to challenge?"

Kim stood and turned. "I knew this game was dangerous."

"You're not going to challenge?"

"I'm going to bed."

"But—"

Oscar shushed him. "Sometimes you're cruel for the sake of it."

"Now that I'm going to challenge."

"Asshole."

"Double challenge."

She heard them laughing as she walked up the stairs. Then she heard footsteps.

Michael stood in the center of the foyer looking up at her. His shirt was partially unbuttoned.

"You should have challenged," he said.

Oscar was calling him.

"Go play," she said.

"French toast in the morning?"

She nodded.

"In bed?"

"I'm not playing anymore."

"Sweet dreams," he said, turning.

"Michael?"

He stopped and looked back.

"Have you never told Oscar about your parents?" she said.

"That would have been a good question for before."

"Have you?"

"Let's not talk about it. Sleep tight, darling."

———

Kim learned to play bridge, took tennis lessons from a sandy-haired Australian at the Meadow Club, and drank Southsides made with real crushed mint. She stood at the outskirts of brick patios during endless cocktail hours, gazing out over barberry hedgerows and Scotch broom as the sun kissed the sea. Sometimes she would bump into Robert. He never seemed surprised.

"Who are you with?" he would ask.

"Michael."

Ends of summer felt like endings.

She cut her hair short, after a style she'd seen. At Michael's urging, she let it go dark, and it was odd at first, the reflection she saw, like an awkward memory. Robert refrained from commenting. She could tell he hated it. When she discovered gray hairs, she dyed it blond again. She started going to the gym.

The hours, the days could seem so full. But there was rarely any spillover of activity from one day to the next. Sometimes she liked that feeling, the freshness of the morning and what lay ahead. Certain things were the same, though: the afternoon light creeping across her living room floor, the blinds clicking from a draft, the brick and cement apartment buildings buried beneath decades of soot, dull chunks of sky outlined by a thousand jagged rooftops.

Wind gathered, stirring the courtyard trees, shaking the window in its frame. Her tea grew cold, the mint smell strong, enveloping, then unnoticeable.

Michael had called that morning to cancel lunch. He had sounded distressed on the phone, but then he usually sounded cross in the mornings. She had trained herself not to take his moods personally. She spent the afternoon running errands, then returned home to get ready in case Robert was free for dinner.

—

Michael phoned again that evening.

"I'm waiting for Robert to call," she said.

"Don't want to go tying up the line for the old *all's clear,*" he said. "Don't want to impose myself, botch the romantic fun, third wheel, and all that fiddledeedee."

"Have you been drinking?"

"Why, do I sound like I've been drinking?"

"A little."

"I've been a little drinking."

She asked if there was something the matter; then, after a long silence, "Michael, dear, are you there?"

"I need to get out."

"Shall we meet somewhere?"

"I don't want to go out."

"You're not making sense. Do you want to come here? I'll tell Robert I'm busy."

When Robert called, she canceled. He seemed more amused than concerned when she told him why.

"Another hangnail?" he said.

"That's not funny. You know if you didn't trust Michael, you'd be more respectful of him."

After that he became serious and promised to check up.

An hour later she buzzed Michael into the building. She left the door unlocked and went to the bathroom to brush her teeth. She dried her hands and checked her makeup. Still he hadn't knocked. She cracked the door and discovered him sitting on her umbrella stand.

"It was open," she said. "What are you doing out here?"

His hair was matted on one side, short spikes curling up with no part. He stared at her a long moment, then seemed to remember himself and produced a bottle of champagne from under each arm. "Dinner!"

She held the door wide as he shuffled through.

"I thought we might go out," she said.

Her jacket was hanging from the doorknob.

"Not a good idea." He waggled a finger and headed for the kitchen. "Tonight, I am not meant to be seen . . . no, you're . . . you shouldn't be seen with me. And I can see I've ruined your plans."

"Nonsense."

"You're lying. Good. Let me crack these. Stay out there. Go. I'll be damned if he gets them."

She stood in the hall, debating whether to put on her jacket. There was a loud pop and splatter, a curse. She peered around the corner. He was on the floor with a sponge.

"Here," she said.

She pulled the sponge from his hand and squeezed it out in the sink. She added soap and ran fresh water into it and got on her knees. Champagne had dripped down the side of the cupboard, collecting at the base—a small puddle of popped bubbles like the shell of an abandoned honeycomb.

"Has anyone told you how lovely you look this evening?" he said, hoisting himself up by the refrigerator handle.

"Dear, go lie on the sofa."

"Does Robert forget to tell you how nice you—look at you there: the very picture of scrubbing. What brand is that sponge? I want to buy it. All right, all right, I've got the bottle."

He put a hand out to steady himself and veered around the corner as though the floor had tipped. The doorjamb was shiny where he'd touched it and she wiped it, then wiped the refrigerator handle and tossed the sponge in the sink. She dried her hands on a rag and took down two glasses.

"Oh, dear," she heard him say, and then a volley of thuds like trampling hooves. He'd knocked over a tower of books and lay sprawled on the pile, the bottle of champagne in one hand, an open book in the other as though he were reading. He looked up innocently and took a swig from the bottle.

"*Tender Is the Night,*" he said. "Loved it." He tossed it aside and picked up another. "*The End of the Affair?* I always like to poke about, see what you're reading."

"Robert gave those to me."

"How very maudlin."

"I won't read them. They're not . . . he keeps giving them to me and I feel guilty. I just add them to that stack."

"A stack of self-pity."

"Well, now you're covered in it. Are you going to stay on the floor all night?"

He raised himself and came over to the sofa and collapsed.

"I've got it," she said, peeling his fingers from the bottle and filling his glass.

His tie knot was twisted up under his shirt collar as though someone had yanked it like a leash. His eyelids were swollen and red. She
gathered his feet, propped them on a crushed velvet pouf, and pulled
off his shoes.

"I'm impossible," he said. "Hopeless and impossible. I keep telling
people. I warn them. They don't believe me. They insist on getting
close. They can't resist my charm. . . . Oscar's leaving me."

He pulled a throw pillow to his stomach and stroked the gold
braided fringe.

"I like this pillow."

He touched the tassel to his nose.

"They always leave," he said.

She sat on the pouf and cradled his feet to her side so that they
wouldn't slip. His knees were wet from the floor.

"There was one a few years back," he said. "We saw a bald man
at a restaurant, and I told him I'd never fucked a bald man and
thought it might be exciting. You know what the fool did? The next
night when I came home, he'd shaved all his hair off—all his beautiful black hair—and I laughed. I can still see him in the foyer, grinning like a seal, the light glaring off his head." He rubbed his eyes.
"Poor fool."

"Did you say something to make Oscar leave?"

"He insists it isn't me. I don't believe him. I just can't let well
enough alone. He wears the most appalling clothes. I feel an obliga-
tion to convert his tastes. You spilled on your tie, I say, and brush at it,
then act surprised that it's only the pattern, and he always believes me
at first. He slaps my hand away. He was always slapping my hand."

"You tease me about my taste."

"Are you leaving me too?"

"I know you don't mean half the things you say."

"Half? That's better than I thought."

He pressed his glass to his forehead, eyes tightly shut. Condensation ran down his nose, and he opened his eyes and wiped his face
on his sleeve.

"I must want him to leave. Otherwise he wouldn't be packing."

"What's that supposed to mean?"

He shrugged.

"Michael, do you love Oscar?"

"Do you love Robert?"

She stared at him. "We're talking about you."

"Let's talk about you for once. Let's talk about anything, anything at all, but not about me, me, me."

His toe touched her side.

"I don't know if I love Oscar," he said. "How upset do I seem?"

"Very."

"Then I guess I do love him. The first time I saw Oscar was at a party at my apartment."

"And where was I?"

She pinched his toe.

"Probably at some fancier party that I wasn't invited to."

"You said you met him through a friend."

"In a manner of speaking."

"Go on. Tell me."

"I've told you this before. He kept staring all night. We never so much as exchanged a word. Later, I went to fetch someone's coat. He was waiting in the bedroom. He pushed the door shut and we just looked at each other. I had my back to the door and he put his arms out to either side of my head, pinning me. I thought he was going to hit me. I don't know why. It was the look in his eyes. Like I'd betrayed him somehow. Then he kissed my forehead."

She poured more champagne and got up and sat next to him on the sofa. He held the glass to his eye, staring sideways at her through the gold liquid.

"Maybe I'm saving Oscar from myself," he said. "I couldn't watch him pack anymore. He triple-folds his shirts."

"Poor sweetie. How horrible."

"Someone said to me once, Do you love me for being me, or because I remind you of you? Truthfully, he wasn't anything like me at all. It's always the ones that leave that I care about the most. The ones that stay, I can't forgive."

He covered his face with the pillow, the tassel clenched in his hand. She thought he was crying, but when he took the pillow away, his eyes were dry. He spit lint from his mouth, let his empty glass slip to the sofa cushion, and rubbed at his eyes again.

"Stop." She caught his hand. "They're red enough already."

She clutched tighter when he tried to pull away. His arm tensed; then his whole body seemed to sigh. She pressed her mouth to his ear and whispered, "Stop hating yourself."

"I hate myself."

"I won't let you."

"Don't let me."

He started to shake. She held his heavy head to her lips, the comfort of silent words. She covered the side of his head with kisses and turned him to her and touched the smooth skin of his forehead, wet to her cheeks and chin and hand. He kissed her hand, pressed it to his cheek, and then kissed it again, nuzzled his head against her arm, turned his lips to hers.

"Michael—"

His mouth grazed her neck. His eyes were closed.

"Don't let me," he whispered.

He kissed her breast through the sweater.

"I won't," she said.

She took his head in her arms and imagined him with his lover, curled, cradled—they were her arms.

"I won't let you," she said. He started to undo his pants, and she let her legs swing over, straddling his lap. She felt him struggling with the belt and clasp, the zipper, his fingers, knuckles pressing.

"I want you," he said.

She wanted desperately to lessen his pain. She lifted herself on her knees so he could kick his pants down and tug at his underwear and unbutton her pants. He raced to put himself inside her, sharp fleeting resistance.

"Okay," she said, curling over him, breathing into the hollow of his mouth. She ground her hips faster, fighting an already slow softening that she could feel, and then he was out of her.

"I want to make you happy," she said.

He put his finger to her lips. She clung to him, his chin digging into her shoulder. Then she rolled off. His penis rested against the base of his stomach, foreign and unexplainable, white under the ceiling light. His breathing slowed. The air in the room was warm, soured by their champagne breath. She could hear a truck in the distance coming over the bridge; its engine a *whoosh* growing louder like a downdraft of wind, that first curtain of rain, countless droplets forming one steady voice. The city's cries at night were the same, constant if one listened.

"Well, that's that," she said, snatching the fringed pillow. "It was time we got that out of our systems."

She flung the pillow across the room, tassels whipping. It rattled a picture, knocking it aslant, and landed on the pile of books. Michael labored to stand. He steadied himself against the sofa arm and rubbed his eyes. His pants were tangled about his ankles, black socks, pale calves. He pulled his pants up slowly, tucking in the tails of his shirt. He tried to smile.

She started. "Did it suddenly occur to you that I—"

"Darling, you're very beautiful."

"You should go," she said.

"Always beautiful."

He slid his belt through the buckle and centered it to his fly. He stood before her, then stooped, and she turned her cheek to his lips.

"Maybe Oscar will still be there," she said. "Make up. Finish what you started here."

"Forgive me," he said. "It's not you. I'll call."

He stopped at the door to rest, bracing himself for the flights down. He was too drunk. He was going to smash his arm or his leg, wake up in Emergency, a fitting end to the evening. Even if he did make it down to the street, where was he going to go? She imagined him curled up on a grate, shivering the night away. She should ask him to stay, she thought.

"Michael, did you come here tonight to make love to me?"

The door clicked shut behind him as he left.

After a while, she got up and bolted the door. She stacked the fallen books and straightened the picture on the wall. She picked up the pillow and her pants and tossed them on the sofa, went to the kitchen for the second bottle of champagne, and took it into the bedroom. Robert never called.

She wanted to stay mad at Michael, but she couldn't. She saw him two nights later. He said everything was fine, and she wanted to believe him. Then he said it again, and the repetition suggested he'd already determined otherwise. She was too tired to talk, and he was talking to avoid the silences. He had left her already, as had all the other men she'd ever given herself to. All but one.

"You seem upset," said Robert that night. "You're hiding something."

Were her eyes different, she wondered, windows that Robert could see through? She met his gaze unflinchingly.

"I'm tired."

"You look tired."

She tried not to blink. Her emotions were a dark tangled ball wound up in her gaze for all to see. Could she turn her eyes into walls?

"Tired, but beautiful," Robert said, and she leaned over to kiss him.

—

A week later, she saw Michael again.

"Oscar left a pair of silk pajamas behind. You don't suppose it's his way of getting me to call?"

She imagined Michael's apartment, the long hall to the bedroom with its many hidden closets and cabinets, the pristine living room, always ready for entertaining—all unchanged by Oscar's absence.

The next weekend she went to the Hamptons alone. She shopped for dinner and spent the evening cooking. She opened a bottle of wine and sat on the porch counting fireflies. She felt she owed someone an apology. She didn't know for what.

She called Michael on Monday and they met for lunch.

"There's Edie," he said, glancing over Kim's shoulder. "What is she doing with that necklace?"

Michael waved. Show us, he mouthed. The woman pretended not to see. He waved again. She nodded to the man in sunglasses who was with her. He closed the case, tucked it under an arm, and left the restaurant.

"Did you see the size of those diamonds?" said Michael.

After lunch, Edie came over.

"You miser," said Michael.

"Darling, I couldn't show you. I'm selling it for a client."

"Who?"

"I can't say."

"Let me pinch that naughty tush. Do you know Kim Reilly?"

"We've met."

"Who was the thug?"

"The driver. I said I couldn't meet today. She asked where I was dining and sent him over. The audacity. He was supposed to be here an hour ago."

"The lot of the first wife," said Michael.

"No clues." Edie kissed him on the cheek. "But only in New York, right? I'm late." She headed for the door.

"Next time share the goods," he called after her.

"I'm late too," said Kim.

"Where are you off to?"

She didn't answer.

"You didn't want to see the necklace?"

She reached for her pocketbook and stood.

"You're still angry."

"I'm going."

"Who's stopping you?"

To see his almost smile, as though there was something left to say, reminded her that there was only the same thing to say, a false assurance that somehow couldn't express the sticky, saplike feeling of what had passed.

"Forget about it," she said, half to herself.

He had vanity to retreat behind. She had Robert.

—

In the weeks following she avoided parties Michael might attend. She steered clear of Fifth Avenue near his apartment and the street where he worked. New York was such a small city. That she managed not to see him for so long surprised her. She stopped worrying. Certainly he was avoiding her too. There were other people she knew to fill tables with. Finally, one night at a dinner, someone mentioned seeing Michael arrive.

"By the bar."

They pointed.

"Upstairs."

She looked.

"By the coat check," said another.

She couldn't find him. Why was she looking? She never mentioned to Robert that they weren't speaking, and it never occurred to him that Michael was missing from her life, because in his mind nothing was ever missing from her life.

Purple Noon was playing at the Paris. She had a popcorn lunch in the back row and didn't get up to leave until well after the credits had rolled and the house lights had come up. Outside in the shade under the marquee, she took her sweater off and draped it over her shoulders. A woman in a wide-brimmed straw hat drawled on to another woman about a bulletin she'd seen at her church on finding "giftedness." The other asked what that meant. They began to discuss volunteer work.

"I knew I just had to hold those little HIV babies," said the woman with the hat.

She made them sound like some kind of candy, or an animal she'd seen in a pet-shop window.

Kim thought of her mother. After deciding not to go back to school, Kim had wondered about working with the elderly, perhaps cancer patients, or whether that would dredge up too many painful images. HIV babies were different, she thought.

The woman with the hat told the other to call up volunteer services at Saint Vincent's Hospital, and that afternoon when Kim got home, that's exactly what she did. She asked the person in charge how she could get involved.

"I want to work with children," she said.

"That doesn't narrow things much."

"A friend told me that you have a program."

"What's your friend's name, honey? We've got lots of programs."

"I want to hold babies," said Kim.

"Have you worked with infants before?"

"No."

Kim could hear papers shuffling.

"I could schedule you for orientation this Thursday, eleven o'clock."

"That's fine. Do I need to bring anything?"

"Just yourself."

Kim gave her name and number and felt a surge of relief.

Kim could feel Robert's energy rise when he described the car he'd bought for Davis, the vacation he'd planned for Christine. She deserved it; she'd made law review her first year.

"And she's seeing someone," said Robert. "We finally met. Nice young man from Virginia. He's also a law student. Imagine that—two lawyers in the family."

In contrast, Davis had changed jobs for the third time.

"We had a long talk," Robert said. "It was good."

"Darling, I knew if you just sat down with him . . ."

"You were right."

"He needed that."

"Wait till he sees the car."

"He needs you. When you reach out like that, it's just . . . he wants it so badly and he doesn't know how to ask."

"Sometimes it's difficult."

"They're going to love their gifts."

"I guess." Robert stood at the window with his back to her.

"A moment ago you sounded sure," she said.

"I've spoiled him. It doesn't matter what I give him anymore. A car—he'll ask if I'm paying for the insurance as well."

"Robert, please."

He shrugged. "What do I know?"

"What if you give him the car and take it on a trip together? Do something with it. Make him drive you somewhere: up to Saratoga for the weekend or anywhere, so it's not just about the car. Let it be an excuse to spend time together."

"It always comes back to that."

"It's what matters."

"What if he doesn't like the idea? What if he doesn't want to spend time together?"

"Robert, he's going to love the car."

"No."

"He will."

Robert faced her, startled by the urgency of her tone. "Are you okay?" he said.

"Yes."

He stared at her. "You're always telling me to spend time with Davis."

"I know."

"It's important to you."

"He loves you."

Robert nodded and looked back out the window. The lights in an apartment across the courtyard were on and the curtains were open. A man was washing dishes.

"I remember when my father would take Mom and me on picnics," Kim said. "He'd pack the basket himself with sandwiches and iced tea and cherries and plums. I'd watch him spit the cherry seeds into his fist and he'd show me how to hold my hand to do it. He was so handsome. He'd pick dandelions and flick them at me and I'd try to run away, with Mother laughing. He caught me and tickled me and rubbed buttercups under my chin. Then he'd stick his chin out and let me do it to him, and ask if it was all yellow. 'Now let's get Mom,' he said. He would tuck me in at night and rub my back and sing me to sleep. He had the most beautiful voice. Sometimes we'd sing together. I used to know so many songs."

Kim went to the window and stood next to Robert, watching the man across the way.

"For some reason I'm remembering more and more good things about him. The presents—Dad would give me the best birthdays. I'd wake up and find gifts laid about the foot of my bed: fancy bows and brushes, white gloves for church, a music box once, and a stuffed bear we called Patton. One morning he brought me orange juice in bed, and ice cream—'Don't tell,' he said—and a little honey jar for Patton. Then he read to me about Winnie the Pooh and Piglet, all before Mother was even awake. I was his precious one those mornings. That was written on the cake every year. I should never have doubted. I guess I knew he loved me."

"I love Davis," Robert said.

"He's going to love the car."

They watched the man across the way dry his hands on a rag and go to the refrigerator. He took out a can and popped the lid and reached for a light switch. The window went dark.

"All those apartments," Robert said, "and I've never once seen anything exciting; not even a man and woman so much as kissing. Have you?"

"Maybe if you were here more. . . ."

He smiled.

"So tell me about Christine," Kim said. "What's this guy like?"

"He thinks Christine works too hard."

"Good, he's old-fashioned."

"He was genuinely concerned. I said, 'Son, she's always been that way. If you figure out how to slow my baby down you have my blessing.' "

He took out his wallet and flipped it open. There was a small photo of Christine jumping a horse in riding pants and a velvet coat, the horse's mane blowing against her concentrated face and arched hands.

"She was eleven then," Robert said.

He'd shown Kim the photo before.

There was another tiny black-and-white from the night of Christine's debut. She was standing between her mother and brother with a smile that made up for theirs.

"Isn't she beautiful?" he said.

Thursday morning arrived. At ten after eleven Kim crept into the volunteer office at Saint Vincent's. She waited in a plastic chair and filled out a form. When she'd finished, a nurse introduced her to the director. Hetty, the woman she'd spoken with on the phone, weighed two hundred pounds and looked like she could lift a bus to save someone.

"You're late," Hetty said, scanning Kim's information sheet. "Have a seat."

Kim sank into a tattered sofa and crossed her legs, watching nervously as the woman read.

"New York Hospital's much closer to you," Hetty said.

Kim said nothing.

"You want to hold babies," she said.

"Yes."

"What does that mean?"

"Well." Kim swallowed. "I heard about your program."

"Okay, let me tell *you* what it means. You decided on an age group: toddlers. You will be assigned to a pod, a floor, looking after a constantly changing number of children with a variety of problems, soup to nuts, mostly respiratory and gastrointestinal. Responsibility is based on a baby's need. That could involve holding, changing, or just sitting. We ask for a commitment of time, a minimum of about four hours a week. You pick a day. Now, I see you don't work and that you're not married."

Kim nodded.

"You think you could honor this kind of commitment?"

"Yes, ma'am."

"Parents—living, deceased?"

"My father's alive."

"Mother?"

"Died of cancer."

Hetty scribbled something on Kim's sheet.

"Any history of mental illness?" she asked.

Kim shook her head.

"Other illness? Are you on any medications?"

"No."

"I have to ask these questions."

"I understand."

"Why children?"

"They have their lives ahead of them."

Hetty's brow dropped like a beam.

"A lot of these infants will require primary care for the rest of their lives. Some of them will die." She took a sheet of paper from her desk and handed it to Kim. "That's a list of the tests you have to take," she said.

The list was long.

"If the results are clear, you come back and we'll get you started."

"That's it?" said Kim.

Hetty stared at Kim's Chanel jacket.

"For now."

———

Kim left the hospital holding the sheet and was still clutching it when she got back to her apartment. She stuck it on the refrigerator with a magnet and tried not to look at it. It bothered her to know it was even there, but she couldn't throw it out. She needed it to aggravate her.

For Robert, words were never enough. Kim had accumulated presents from weekend trips, holidays, and the anniversary of their meeting, which he never forgot. There were artifacts from his travels: blue and pink Roman perfume bottles from the first century B.C., icons from Jerusalem, flat slit-eyed saints and supplicants, palms up with gold-leafed halos, ruby-star skies. He would surprise her with tickets to a show, or a messenger would drop off a book, another tragic romance that she'd put away. *Everyone was talking about this at lunch,* the note would read.

He would ask her later what she thought. "You can always exchange it."

No matter how small the gifts, they had meaning for Kim. She never considered returning anything, and she told him so. This contradicted with the nature of his upbringing—the rite of his privilege. No gift was too special that it couldn't be improved upon. Why settle for anything unwanted? But if the gift became irrelevant, the original thought did too. She tried to show him that.

For her fortieth birthday, they flew up to Martha's Vineyard and stayed at the house of a friend. They walked on the beach and watched the sun go down. A kite was climbing steps of red cloud and then diving, climbing again and diving. A woman's voice carried on the breeze, calling her son in for dinner, away from the blackening sea. They went in themselves and popped a bottle of champagne and scrambled to the bedroom, their laughter echoing in the big empty house.

"Sing to me," said Robert.

She tossed her T-shirt to the floor and began to hum.

"Do you know this?" she said.

Robert shook his head and grinned. She undid the button on her shorts. Her voice was soft.

"Please darling don't ask me to marry you yet . . ."

The shorts dropped around her ankles and she stepped out of them, hiking her underwear up over her hips. She climbed onto the bed. Robert laughed.

She sang teasingly as she crawled catlike toward him, kneading the covers with arched fingers. She dipped her head so that her hair brushed his chest—a tickling touch for each pillow-talk promise, anticipating the risqué discovery of the song's last line:

"I'll get up and get dressed and go home."

She licked his stomach and reared back, smiling sideways at him with a final flourish.

"Bravo." He clapped.

He pulled her to him and hugged her and rolled her over, the sheets twisting around their feet.

"This is for you," he said, reaching under the pillow.

He produced a necklace: strands of diamonds woven to form intricate interlocking spiderwebs. She covered his face with kisses and jumped from the bed and ran to the bathroom.

"Wait," he said.

She closed the door behind her and rushed to the tub and turned on the water.

"What are you doing?" he called. "The champagne's getting warm."

She filled the tub with suds and put on the necklace and eased into the water and called to him. The door slid open, and he stood with his shoulder against the jamb looking down at her.

"You're beautiful," he said.

She splashed him, and he came over and knelt beside the tub and kissed her.

"Sing some more," he said.

His lips traced her neck. She closed her eyes.

> "The minstrel boy to the war is gone,
> In the ranks of death you'll find him.
> His father's sword he has girded on
> And his wild harp slung behind him."

"It sounds Irish."

"My father taught it to me."

"Don't stop."

He kissed her shoulder.

> " 'Land of song,' said the warrior bard,
> 'Tho' all the world betrays thee,
> One sword at least thy rights shall guard,
> One faithful harp shall praise thee.' "

"So beautiful."

"There's more."

"Sad."

> "The minstrel fell, but the foeman's chain
> Could not bring that proud soul under;
> The harp he loved ne'er spoke again
> For he tore its chords asunder."

"I love you," said Robert.

She kept singing:

> "Said, 'No chains shall sully thee,
> Thou soul of love and bravery.
> Thy songs were made for the pure and free,
> One faithful harp shall praise thee.' "

He kissed her soapy breasts and took the necklace between his teeth like a horse's bit and brought it to her lips. It was tasteless and cool. He continued to kiss her as he swung his legs up over the edge of the tub and in, water slapping the sides and splashing onto the tiled floor, soaking the bath mat.

———

For her forty-first birthday, they were to fly to London. Somehow he'd forgotten a dinner Nicole had planned for the Swiss ambassador and some recent winner of the Pulitzer Prize. He couldn't back out. He gave Kim an emerald parure worth twice the necklace from the year before. It was a less significant birthday, but he didn't think in those terms. Gifts dictated future gifts. He had to outdo himself. The extravagance should have lessened the sting of her age. Perhaps in London it might have. She wore the necklace and earrings while she unpacked, dumping the neatly folded contents of her suitcases onto the bed.

———

She turned forty-two and forty-three.

One Sunday afternoon, Robert was to join her at the movies. She bought tickets and waited outside. Finally, she went in and sat in the back row. Halfway through the picture she got up and left.

When the doorman from the building next door saw her, he called out.

"I've got something for you."

She waited on the step as he ducked into his lobby and came out holding an envelope.

"How was the movie?" he said, handing it to her.

"Bad."

She opened the envelope on her way up the stairs. There were two tickets to the opera and a note: *Sorry—8 P.M. tomorrow.*

———

The following week they arranged to meet in the park. She bought a basket and some cheese and packed a bottle of wine and two glasses.

She waited for him on a bench near the boathouse and watched couples line up to row out on the lake. After thirty minutes she unwrapped the cheese and cut herself a slice. A jazz band began to play and a crowd gathered. She could no longer see the players. During one loud crescendo, the trombonist's slide jutted above the dense wall of onlookers, the curved brass tip white in the light from between the trees. The slide poked at a low-hanging branch, disappeared, and then shot up again as though something were caught there and needed to be knocked free. She left the basket on the bench and walked away.

"Miss," someone called.

She didn't turn back.

There was a message on the machine at home apologizing.

"Be home between three and four," it said.

At three-thirty a messenger arrived with a gown and an invitation to a party the following night.

To see you in it, the card read.

She went to the party the following night but didn't wear the gown.

"It made my arms look funny," she told him.

"Your arms? Never."

———

She left a message with his secretary.

"Odd," he said.

"You didn't get it?"

She left several messages with his secretary.

She could not say if there were more canceled plans that year than before, but there were more gifts. Instead of Robert, a book. Instead of Robert, a ruby pin. The buzzer would ring, and it would be Joseph with a bouquet of roses. Robert was with Nicole.

———

"Lunch tomorrow won't work," said Robert, as he kissed her good night.

"Now you tell me?"

"The wine auction's tomorrow. Perhaps I can send you a case."

"It's only lunch."

"I've pored through the catalog. There are some amazing years."

———

The following afternoon, a case of Burgundy arrived.

"From a Mr. Sanders."

The deliveryman set the crate on the floor and handed her a form on a clipboard to sign. She stared at the blank line and tapped the pen.

"I don't want it," she said.

"Lady, I just carried it up four flights of stairs."

"You can have it."

"Are you trying to get me in trouble?"

She signed the form and held out the clipboard.

"There, now you can have it."

"You're setting me up."

"Now if you excuse me."

She shut the door. He whistled. Through the peephole she could see him heft the crate back up over his shoulder. He looked at the door a second, whistled again, and started down the stairs.

The next day Robert sent peonies. Two nights later, after a missed dinner, he sent a beaded bracelet from Africa.

———

"What about yesterday?" she asked.

His eyebrows shot up. "Did we have plans?"

"No, I just wondered what you did. Were you free?"

"I was so busy."

"With Nicole?"

He slipped off his shoes and put his feet up.

"Among other things." He sighed.

"Why don't you make us drinks."

He went to the side bar. "I wish I could have seen you," he said.

He came back to the bed and held out her drink.

"New glasses?" he said, loosening his tie. She rolled onto her side, her back to him.

"Did you hear the Dewesons were rejected from the board?" he said.

"Do I know the Dewesons?"

"Jane and Frank."

"Of course—a pity."

—

When he left, she listened to his footsteps on the stairs, then quiet, only the patter of rain against the window's thin glass. Could rain be patient? she wondered. The wind was always callous the way it blew hard-edged down First Avenue, like bracken whipping at the skin as one ran through woods, too intent to ward off scratches that would appear later, red-lined skin raised: that delayed sting like a vodka burn, that muscle-tensing convulsion of the throat as it was poisoned and subdued in one gulp.

In the living room, she stared at the poster of Garbo. It was the one poster she'd saved amid all the artwork. She remembered framing it years ago, those big watery eyes filled with despair. I'm not a recluse, she thought. She put on shoes and dragged the picture from the wall, flung open the front door, and left the poster in the hall to take down the next day. She poured herself another drink and got the vacuum from the closet and started to clean the apartment. The man from downstairs banged on his ceiling. She didn't care what time it was.

For her forty-fourth birthday Robert planned a dinner.

"Where's Robert?" she said to Joseph, when he picked her up.

"He's going to be late."

"I don't believe it."

She sank back into the seat, then bolted upright.

"Stop the car."

He pulled over.

She threw open the door, telling him to pop the trunk. It was empty.

"I was afraid there might be something for me," she said when he came up beside her. "We'll go somewhere first."

"I'm to take you straight away. It's a surprise."

"A surprise? What is it?"

"He doesn't tell me that."

"Then it's his problem. We're stopping off first."

Six blocks later, she pointed to a bar with a fake stone front and a blacked-out window.

"Don't be on his side," she said. "Wait here."

Joseph parked. "Not long."

The bar was dark with a stained-glass light above the register and a jar crammed with tips. A man offered his bar stool.

"Can I buy you something?" he said. He wore a baseball jersey half buttoned.

She squeezed into the space he'd cleared.

"Three double vodka-on-the-rocks," she said.

The bartender slung a rag over his shoulder and put his hands on the bar as though he were about to lecture her. She held out a hundred-dollar bill, creased it, and laid it in front of him. He put it in his pocket, not the jar.

"Rough day?" said the man in the jersey.

"You can have your seat back in a second."

The bartender's lips moved as he counted out shots.

She snatched up the first glass, swirled it a little, and gulped it.

"Where you gotta be in such a hurry?" said the man.

"I'm late for my birthday."

"You don't wanna miss that."

She drained the second drink.

"So you're on your way to a party?" he said. "You're sure dressed real nice."

He signaled the bartender.

"What she's drinking," he said.

He cracked his knuckles and tried to slip off a wedding band without her seeing. She tipped her glass back and let the third double vodka run slowly down her throat.

"Gettin' older's no fun," he said. "You sure don't look—"

"What's your name?"

"Ralph."

"You've got someone who cares about you, Ralph?"

"I—"

"But suppose you didn't. Let's pretend you only think you do. Deep down you know you don't."

"Maybe you better lay off the booze, lady."

"Ralph, imagine nothing you do matters. Nobody needs you. Nobody wants you. You're a worthless piece of garbage. But—"

She opened her purse, peeled two hundred-dollar bills from her clip, and crumpled them into a ball. She grabbed the man's hand and slapped the wad of money into his palm, closed his fingers around it, and gave the fist a pat.

"Now you know how I feel."

She slid from the stool and the floor seemed to rise up to meet her. She steadied herself against the bar and saw Joseph at the door, watching. Ralph started to unball the money.

"I can't—" he was saying.

She headed toward Joseph, who held the door. She wanted to scream.

"So what's the surprise?" she said.

—

The maître d' met her with outstretched arms.

"I am older and you—you are younger and younger. It is unfair."

He led her to a round table in the center of the room. "Happy birthday!" came the chorus. Then she saw Michael.

"Birthday girl!" He slipped a hand under his jacket lapel and held it there as though feeling for his heart. "You look like you've seen a ghost."

She leapt forward and wrapped her arms about him and squeezed.

"Have you been drinking already? You sneak. Say hello to the others," he whispered. "They're waiting."

She circled the table, shaking hands with the Stevensons and Johnsons.

"Robert's running a little late," she said. "Any minute now."

She sat opposite the empty chair reserved for Robert. The waiters brought pink champagne and a smattering of *amuse-gueules.*

She hung on Michael's shoulder. "I don't know if he's even coming."

"Shh," he whispered. "Don't worry. Focus on the positive."

She gulped champagne.

"That we're here together," he said, "like old times. It's been too long."

"Who are these people?"

She knew who they were, though. John and Ellen Stevenson were just back from a tour of California; Robert, fishing for an invitation to Ascot, was having them up to Westchester for the weekend to play golf before they headed back to London. George and Elaine Johnson lived in Palm Beach year round, less than a block from Robert's house there. They'd flown up to visit their son and see a few shows. They were sponsoring Robert at a country club.

"Strangers," she said.

"What about me?" said Michael.

Kim leaned on his shoulder again. "Robert doesn't know we're not speaking."

"Were we not speaking? I thought you were just so fabulously busy."

"He's not here, but you are. You're my gift. I looked for you in the trunk earlier."

"You *have* been drinking. Pity. I've got catching up to do."

"Hurry, hurry."

"Kim," said George, sitting to her right, "Robert's sung your praises for a longer than long time."

"And here we all are," said Kim.

Elaine, who sat to Michael's left, clutched a sun-blotched hand to her freckled chest. Bangles tinkled down her wrist. Her face was like a porcelain mask.

"To meeting on this happy occasion," said George, raising his glass. "And to the Stevensons for surviving the West Coast."

The Stevensons sipped their drinks in unison like a pair of synchronized swimmers, trying to ignore the empty seat between them. It was like a charity dinner, Kim thought. She should have turned Joseph around from the get-go.

George's voice boomed in her ear. "You know what Frank Lloyd Wright said? The country slopes down toward California, and eventually everything loose winds up there."

Kim felt as though the table were tipping. Robert needed her to be stronger than his wife. What if she couldn't be?

"Michael," she whispered, "he's not coming. Tell me what to do. What would Nicole do?"

"Nicole?"

"I don't know anything anymore. You—can you—?"

"Why don't we go ahead with the appetizers," he said, signaling the captain. "We'll wait until Mr. Sanders is here for the entrées."

"Tell him two magnums of Pétrus," Kim said.

Michael turned. "Now I can't hear you."

"What's with the whispering?" said Elaine, pushing the bangles up her arm.

"Kim's plotting our inebriation."

"That needs plotting?"

"Tell 'im, sister," said George. "Let's get that sommelier off his can."

"Michael normally abhors extravagance," Kim mustered. "He's quite the Buddhist."

"You're not really a Buddhist, are you?" said Ellen, eyeing his black velvet jacket.

"After dinner, we get to rub his tummy," said Kim. "I'm first because it's my birthday."

"Speaking of bellies," said George, holding his own.

The sommelier brought the magnums already decanted. He poured and Michael tasted. Kim decided to go ahead with ordering the entrées. The appetizers arrived. For what seemed like hours, George droned on about golf. Periodically, he would mold his hands into a grip, waggling his wrists. The Stevensons listened, their faces disappearing behind the rims of their Bordeaux glasses. George named the eighteen toughest holes in the country and how a group of pros had jetted from one to the other over the span of a week. Then he described the different architects: Tillinghast, Ross. . . .

A dab of butter had stained Ellen's sleeve.

Kim willed Robert to walk in. She dared him. She would humiliate him in front of everyone. She thought of the time she'd intended to scratch the hood of his car. How many times had Nicole thrown a drink in his face?

Six waiters appeared at the table. Glasses were shifted, plates rearranged. The waiters plucked the covers from the plates.

Kim asked the captain to remove Robert's setting. They took away the chair and cleared the space, but the Stevensons made no attempt to shore up the gap between them.

George demonstrated a chipping technique.

"Just stroke it," he said.

Elaine burst into laughter, covering her flushed cheeks.

Kim waved at the decanters. "Two more."

"Eat," said Michael.

"I am."

"Are you okay?"

"Splendid. Splendorous."

"Darling—"

"I didn't tell Robert about us."

"Of course."

"If I had, you probably wouldn't be here."

"That's true."

"You hate him, don't you? That's okay. I'm supposed to be satisfied with our little party here, my prize, my bone."

"Easy, now."

"I can't forgive him." She turned to George and laid a hand over his arm. "I want you to swear: No more golf talk. I forbid it."

"When we were in Los Angeles," said John, "we visited the new Getty Museum. There was a most shocking painting of a—"

"Penis," Ellen blurted.

"We were the only ones in the room actually looking at it. The room was crowded, but no one looked. Everyone seemed more concerned with whether they were being *seen* looking."

"Get that chap more wine," said George.

"It's like what you said before about the slope," said John.

George stared blankly. "The slope?"

A waiter passed, and Kim reached for his arm. "More wine, please," she said.

"We've ordered it already," said Michael. "Remember?" He nodded to the waiter.

"There's the sommelier. I—"

"It's coming," said Michael. "Trust me."

He took her hand and held it. Ellen stared. Kim looked away. She imagined Robert's apology like a hastily written note, dangling carrot promises of future evenings that would undoubtedly fail. She imagined him with Nicole, checking his watch. "Who do you have to call?" she'd say. "No one. No one, darling." Kim could hear him clearly in her mind.

Everything—the wine, the dinner, the endless parade of art, tickets, coats, dresses, pins, bracelets, earrings, and necklaces, even poor Michael, for he, too, was something to occupy her—were all reminders of Robert's absence. She wanted to clear the table with one swipe of her arm. She wanted Robert to see the evening he'd planned destroyed, see the pain he was conveniently never present for.

"When you're fucking," Michael was saying, "*any* view's a good view. Even a bare lightbulb hanging from the ceiling looks great."

She'd heard Michael disarm acquaintances with the same jokes a thousand times. Elaine's laughter validated something stale. She wanted to tell Michael to change, to shake him and beg him to say something original. He was her surprise. He was her only friend.

"I'm not wearing underwear," Elaine whispered.

George was describing a golf course in Monterey.

"You're handsome," Elaine whispered to Michael.

"Louder, please, so everyone can hear."

A glass dropped at a far table. Waiters scattered in all directions like crows at a gunshot. Somewhere a light flickered.

"I keep a set of clubs in each of our houses," George said.

"Michael, make it stop," said Kim.

The room was blinding.

"Michael—"

Startled, she drew back from a cake. The neighboring tables joined in song: more strangers. She remembered the officers' voices at her mother's funeral grinding out hymns to a body in a box. She thought of her father crying.

There were hundreds of candles. She couldn't see her name.

"Wish for something good."

"A slice of wicked dreams," said Michael.

Kim blew, driving the flames, diving, shivering, beaten. Laughter—more applause. Smoke streaked to the ceiling. She watched as though she herself were floating away.

"Michael, I need to lie down."

"A little longer," he said. "You have presents."

He had to help with the bows. She opened his first—a costume bracelet: gold shells embedded in plastic.

"For when you come to the beach," he said.

She received a silver frame from Tiffany's and shell-shaped bath soaps, a picture book full of society photographs, and a silver-sequined eyeglass case.

"I have to wear reading glasses now," said Ellen, "and I just fell in love with it."

"I don't wear glasses," said Kim.

Michael gathered the gifts. Half a magnum of wine remained.

"Aren't you even a little embarrassed?" Kim said to the table.

"Those soaps were expensive," said Elaine.

"What if something's happened to Robert?" said Kim.

"You want us to call?"

"I just wanted to see him for my birthday."

She got her purse open and pushed back her chair. She stood and almost fell. She tried to press a credit card into Michael's hand.

"Darling, I'll take care of everything."

The captain was at her side.

"Here," she said, giving him her card. "Don't let him pay."

"I'll call you," said Michael.

She stumbled over the bag of gifts as she left the hushed room.

Joseph was waiting by the curb. He froze.

"Get me out of here," she sobbed.

She collapsed in the back of the car and buried her face in her hands.

"He's with her, isn't he? Isn't he, Joseph? Fuck him. Fuck him!"

She lay on the seat with her legs tucked and her dress twisted. Shadows danced inside the car. Streetlights whited out the rear window.

—

When they reached the apartment, Kim was half asleep. She propped herself on one elbow and rubbed her eyes.

"Home," said Joseph, opening her door.

"My head's swimming. Let me sit a little."

Joseph watched her eyelids sag.

"I need to rest," she said.

Joseph shut her door and stood on the curb. It was cold. He blew into his hands and lit a cigarette, and the smoke and his breath were the same. A couple passed, their coats snug to their chins. Laughter skipped up the block. Joseph stared at Kim through the window, his forehead knotted with concern. After a while, he climbed back into the car and waited some more.

"My father always gave me the best birthdays." Kim sat on her hands. "He did lots of nice things," she said.

She touched the fogged window, drew a cake, then smeared it.

"You're shivering," she said.

He shook his head.

"I'm so sleepy."

"It's almost two," Joseph said.

"I can sleep right here."

"C'mon, I'll help you upstairs," he said, before she had a chance to lie down again.

He lifted her and got the door closed with his foot.

"The keys are somewhere," she mumbled, dangling her open purse. Her eyes were half shut.

She leaned against him as he studied the door. The keys looked tiny in his large hands. He tried two.

"The pointy one," she said.

He supported her up the flights of stairs, an arm cradling her. He unlocked her apartment door and dropped the keys in her purse. She stood in the doorway. He gazed at her. For a moment he looked as though he were about to turn. She touched his shoulder. He didn't move.

"You smell nice," she said. "Did Robert give you that cologne?"

She could feel his arm twitch. Her mind reeled.

"Joseph—"

His mouth opened.

"Kiss me," she said.

His eyes widened.

"Do it," she said.

She had liked his hand on her back—stronger than Robert's.

"I said kiss me."

Slowly he bent forward, his face intensifying as it neared hers, as though he were leaning into the spinning blades of a fan. Was he thinking of his wife? Was he thinking of his daughters? Their lips met. His body was rigid.

"Stop!" she said.

He fell back.

"What are you doing?"

He shook his head.

"What do you think you're doing?" she said.

"I—"

He turned and ran down the stairs, echoes of echoes. The building door slammed.

She went to the phone and dialed Robert. Her head was whirling.

"Is he there?" she said, recognizing the maid.

"Who?"

"Is he there? Please, it's urgent. Please."

"Hello." He came on. "Who is this?"

"Robert," she said, "you have to—"

"Wait." He covered the receiver. There was muffled talk, then his voice became clear. "I'm so sorry, darling. I'm so, so sorry."

"You have to come over. Joseph just tried to kiss me."

She was crying. She could hear Robert's breathing. She could tell he was stunned. She had hurt him.

"He kissed me, Robert. He drove me home and tried to kiss me."

———

Kim stared at the clock and guessed how long Robert would take. Time moved quickly, then the moment passed. After that, the waiting was harder.

There had to be a lie, a lie to undo this terrible lie. He was trying to comfort me, she could say. He was wishing me happy birthday. She dug her nails into her thighs, bile rising in her throat.

When the door bolt turned, she ran to Robert's open arms. Her hands raked his back as he fumbled to pocket the key.

"It's okay," he said. "I'm here now. It's okay."

"Robert, I just feel—"

"Don't worry."

"What are you going to do?" she said.

"He's gone."

She didn't look up.

"I fired him," he said.

He shut the door. She hugged him tightly and tried to breathe, to still the pounding in her chest. She pushed past him to the bathroom.

"Kim?"

She dropped to the tiles and braced herself against the toilet seat and retched. Finally the vomit came, bloodlike, wine gushing from her throat and nose. Robert reached over her shoulder to flush. He pulled the hair from her gaping mouth. So many times she'd stood behind her father's hunched body at the sink or the side of the drive as he shamed himself—the curses and pleas. Robert mopped her chin. Her face fell heavily against her forearm and she stared at the vile bits of food under the rim that the flushing couldn't wash away.

When she finally could stand, Robert put his hands on her hips to steady her. She jerked back and punched his shoulder.

"Where were you?" she said.

She leaned close again, pounding his chest softly with her fists. She grabbed his coat sleeve and twisted and tugged and balled it. Then she smoothed it out.

"Nicole broke her arm," he said. "I spent the night at the emergency room. By the time the doctor saw her, she was vomiting everywhere. I promise you, no one is more sorry than I."

"I didn't—"

"I'm heartbroken I couldn't be there. The whole thing's a complete shambles. I wanted it to be special."

He stroked her forehead and spoke softly.

"Happy Birthday, my love."

A fter breakfast they showered and dressed. They went down to the street and signaled a taxi. Robert mumbled an address that she couldn't hear, and she hung on his arm, begging him to tell.

The taxi turned up Park Avenue and pulled over to the curb at 59th Street. She followed Robert into a building, and they rode the elevator up and stepped out into a private foyer that led to a single apartment.

He dangled a key and dropped it into her outstretched hand.

The door swung quietly on well-oiled hinges to reveal an enormous gallery with antique boiserie panels. The living room was twice the size of her entire apartment. She clasped her hands and turned to Robert, who was leaning against the door frame.

"You!" she said.

He came toward her. She kissed his hands and tossed them away like confetti and ran through the other rooms. Robert followed slowly, calling when he couldn't hear her footsteps anymore. He found her in the bedroom, arms spread, her whole body pressed tightly to the window, dark against the glare. He came up behind her.

"You deserve this," he said.

He nuzzled her hair. Cars streamed noiselessly up and down Park Avenue, specks of light, glinting in the morning sun. She could see the horizon unobstructed. Buildings that at street level possessed no luster flourished at this height. How like flowers they were, plain stems rising up and up with the inexplicable promise of something greater. Above ten stories the city was all bloom: patios and penthouse gardens, carved stone animals and small bits of copper and tile-arched roofs, gargoyles lurking above windows, converted top-floor pools and sky, building tops falling away like rolling terrain. A whole countryside perched above the fray—above the alleyways and streets, the sidewalks and the labyrinth of steel-girdered subway tunnels—a gentle high-up suburb. She could see Queens, the factories and bridges, planes taking off and landing. At this height the days would be longer. After the streets were cast in shadow the sun would still show itself. It would pause those few extra minutes, for her, as if to bid her good night in private.

"Darling, who does this sort of thing? Who but you?" she said.

"You're crying."

"I'm happy."

"What's wrong?"

She shook her head and turned around to him, folding his arms about her like a net. The sun beat against her face—red through her closed eyelids.

He touched her cheek.

"It's cold from the window," he said.

They stood awhile.

"We've been together a long time," he said. "Wonderful years."

They stared out the window some more, before they locked the apartment door and rode the elevator down. The doorman hailed a cab.

"Welcome to the building, Miss Reilly," he said.

Two weeks later, Kim marched into Saint Vincent's Hospital. When she reached the office of volunteer services, she handed a brown envelope to the nurse at the desk.

"My test results," she said.

"Do you have an appointment?"

"Hetty told me to come back when I finished them."

The woman took the envelope and disappeared. Hetty emerged from her office, rocking side to side as she walked, the nurse following.

"I'm in a meeting."

"I came back," said Kim, pointing to the brown envelope. "The results."

"Took you—what, four years? There weren't that many tests, sister." She nodded to the nurse. "This is Lila. She can get you signed up."

Hetty turned and lumbered off. Lila opened the envelope and checked the results to make sure they were in order. She handed Kim a clipboard and asked her to fill out an information sheet.

"But I did this already."

Lila rolled her eyes.

Kim filled out the form again and Lila looked it over. She handed Kim a stapled pamphlet of rules and guidelines. "Any questions?" she said.

Kim shook her head.

"When are you available?" said Lila.

"Nights!" Hetty barked, coming back into the room.

"Okay," said Kim.

"Fridays are tough for us," said Hetty. "People like to go out, leave town. How about Friday nights from seven to eleven?"

Robert usually spent Friday nights with Nicole.

"That's fine," said Kim.

Lila wrote on the sheet. Hetty left.

"See you Friday," said Lila. "Hetty'll show you the ropes. She'll trail you the first night."

Kim turned to leave.

"Oh," said Lila. "Bring a picture with you for your ID."

Kim decided that Robert needed Michael more than she did, needed her to have the diversion, to shoulder the burden of her feelings. He had returned Michael to her under the very pretext that had brought them together in the first place. She wondered if Michael knew about the apartment before her birthday, if that had prompted him to accept the invitation. In the end, did it matter?

They talked every day about design, met regularly to go over fabrics or look at photographs, catalogs of furniture coming up at auction. Silk damasks, taffetas, and failles all began to look alike.

She asked him if he was seeing anyone.

"No one in particular."

She'd never known him not to be in a relationship.

"You don't want to tell me?" she said.

He held a swatch of fabric to his face like a veil.

"What do you think of this?" he said.

There were so many fabrics.

—

Friday at six-thirty she arrived at Saint Vincent's. She sat on her hands and waited. Hetty crossed the hall and noticed her. She nodded but didn't stop. At seven, Hetty reemerged.

"Let's go, let's go," she said, barking like a drill sergeant. "You got your picture?"

Kim handed her an envelope. She gave the envelope to a nurse.

"Follow me," she said.

She took her into a back room. There were lockers. Each locker had a padlock and key.

"You put your stuff away; then you get washed."

She pointed to a sink. There was a pump dispenser filled with antiseptic soap. Kim put her purse in a locker and pocketed the key. Hetty watched her wash her hands.

"All the way up the arms—good. Now your apron."

She showed Kim where the aprons were stored.

"Wash first, then put the apron on. You forget, and it could cost a life. . . . You listening?"

Kim tied on the pink-striped apron and nodded. She followed Hetty from the locker room down a long hall to an elevator.

"You will always come to my office first. Ninety percent of the time you will be working the same pod, but that can change, and you need to check in and make sure."

The elevator door opened and they stepped in.

"You're gonna find a sink in every room," said Hetty. "By every sink you'll find gloves and masks, if you need one. You must wear gloves at all times. Got it? Every time you enter a room, you wash your hands, you put on fresh gloves. You finish with a baby, throw out the gloves, wash your hands, and put on a new pair. Don't ever touch a baby with gloves you've used to handle another baby. No germs, understand?"

The elevator door opened to the sound of babies crying. They stepped out into a brightly lit ward. The walls were decorated with murals of flowers and fish and animals. Hetty led Kim to the nurses' station. A gray-haired woman with thick glasses looked up from a row of monitors.

"Denise," said Hetty, "this is Kim Reilly. She's our new Friday night."

Another nurse appeared, carrying a tray of IV packs. Hetty introduced her. Hetty explained how Denise was the head nurse on duty this time, but that would change from week to week. "Find out who's the acting head nurse and report to him or her," she said. "You listen to them. They're gonna tell you where you're needed. Most of the time, you won't be the only volunteer on duty. Volunteers are dressed like you. Nurses are in white. You got a question, ask a nurse, not another volunteer. That's for your own good. Let's get started. We're late."

Hetty turned to Denise.

"Denise, tell me where to go."

"Room Four, Bed Two. Cynthia."

"Is there anything I need to know about this child?"

"Upper respiratory. Wear a mask."

Hetty nodded for Kim to follow. They passed an open door. Kim saw a woman in a pink-striped apron sitting in a rocking chair, a bundled-up baby pressed to her chest. The soft glow of a television lit the room.

Hetty lowered her voice. "You always ask if there's anything you need to know about the child, anything unusual, any background. There are two beds to every room. You will find the medical records at the foot of each bed. Check the name to make sure it's the right one."

They entered Room Four. There was a sink in the corner. They scrubbed their hands and arms and put on hospital gloves and masks and went to the bed. Hetty showed Kim where it said CYNTHIA on the chart. There was a rocking chair in the corner. A television hung from the ceiling.

Cynthia was crying. Her legs were kicking under the covers; her tiny hands were patting the air. One of her arms was bandaged to a splint, which secured an IV line.

"Pick her up," Hetty whispered.

"How?"

Hetty looked at her. Kim's face was perspiring under the mask.

Hetty scooped up the baby, keeping the blanket wrapped about her. She showed Kim how to cradle the head, how to keep her upright, and how to keep the IV line from catching and tangling.

Cynthia coughed.

"That's okay," said Hetty, showing Kim a box of tissues. "She's gonna keep coughing. That's why she's here."

She wiped Cynthia's chin. Cynthia continued to cry.

"Sometimes you rock a little," said Hetty. "It's soothing. That's right. You're getting it."

Cynthia's head felt too heavy in her hand. Her face was red, her chin raw from drool.

Hetty studied Kim. "You've never held a baby before?" she said.

Kim shook her head. She was afraid to talk with the baby in her arms.

"So you've never changed a baby before? I better show you. Watch the IV."

The medicine bag hung from a tall pole on wheels. "Never move the baby without keeping a hand on that," said Hetty.

Everything Kim needed was in a cabinet by the sink. They used special diapers that were sanitized.

"Normally, you'd use powder," Hetty said. "With respiratory, you can't. It'd get in their lungs."

There was a special lotion, and she showed Kim how to wipe the child and fasten the diaper.

"Don't be afraid to have a nurse watch the first few times," she said. "Don't be afraid to ring for any reason. *Any* reason, mind you. There's a buzzer on each bed."

She stayed a few minutes, then told Kim she had to leave for a bit.

"If she falls asleep, check with Denise and she'll assign you a new one. I'll be back."

Kim stood by the bed, not wanting to move. Cynthia was still whimpering. "Shh," Kim said softly, then again later, "Shh." She moved her thumb gently against the side of Cynthia's head, caressing it over and over. She had no idea how much time went by. She sensed the shadows of passing nurses. Her neck stiffened. She didn't turn. How long did it take her to realize that Cynthia had stopped making noise? She gazed down in astonishment. Her lips were no longer moving. Was she breathing? She didn't seem to be breathing. Kim reached for the buzzer to signal the nurse. She could not feel her arm. In seconds, Denise appeared, Hetty right behind her.

"She's not breathing," said Kim.

Denise rushed to the sink and scrubbed her hands. She snapped on gloves and covered her face with a mask and rushed to Kim.

"Set her down," she said. "Move."

She leaned over the child and put her ear to Cynthia's mouth. She straightened and turned and motioned Kim and Hetty from the room. In the hall, she pulled down her mask to reveal a broad smile.

"Sister," she said, "she's just sleeping."

Another nurse hurried up. "Denise, Room One."

They took off together.

Hetty looked at Kim. "Don't feel stupid. Remember, don't ever be afraid to ring that buzzer. Because the one time you don't—"

She turned and started down the hall.

"Well?" said Kim. "What do I do now?"

"It's eleven-thirty. Go home. See you next Friday."

———

It was well after midnight by the time she reached her apartment. She was exhausted, but she couldn't sleep. She lay in bed for what seemed like hours. Finally, she got up and went to the kitchen. She took a pen and a pad of paper from a drawer. She wrote the date, and then beside it she wrote *Cynthia*. This would be her list.

After that, she could sleep.

The months blurred. She read books on French furniture, studied pictures of the undersides of chairs, the nails and joints and studs, what to look for to tell if a piece was authentic or fake. She'd never had a dining room before. Now she owned a table with leaves that could make it longer.

"You can have dinners for eight, even twelve," said Michael, collecting his books and his briefcase.

Robert nodded. "That's right. You'll finally be able to entertain."

As though she'd been embarrassed to show people her old apartment? What made him think she would want to entertain?

As soon as Michael left, Robert pulled a drop cloth from a bergère and slumped in the seat with a tumbler of scotch.

"Why can't it be comfortable?"

"You said Louis Sixteenth."

She told herself that his impatience was with the process and scope of the job, the endless deliberations and consultations.

—

She was still sleeping in her old apartment, even though the bedroom of the new one was finished. There was the painting and the smell, which Robert loathed. She'd put most of her things in storage. There were boxes in the living room.

"I've lived here forever," she told Michael. "I never thought I'd be in one place so long."

She stared at the bare walls.

"It doesn't feel like home anymore," she said. "It's as though it knows I'm leaving."

"Think about the fabulous new home you're going to have. You've traded up." He checked his watch.

"I don't know."

"Are you saying you're not happy with what we're doing?"

The sharpness of his tone surprised her.

"I just want Robert to be happy."

"He doesn't like it?"

"Can I confess something?"

His lips shut so tightly they seemed to disappear.

"It's not about the apartment," she said.

"I'm already late."

"Remember on my birthday, I—"

"Darling, we're so close to being finished. You know that, right? Everyone I've ever worked with gets the jitters near the end. It's hard. I understand."

"Robert's driver, Joseph. He was fired."

Michael inched toward the door.

"No more second thoughts," he said. "It's going to be perfect."

He undid the latch.

"I called Robert that night and told him Joseph tried to kiss me."

Michael stopped. His eyes filled with derision. "What are you telling me?"

His hand was on the doorknob.

"I had to tell someone."

"You're under a great deal of stress. Stop worrying."

His voice was icy. He stepped out into the hall and she held the door open behind him.

"When the apartment's finished," he said, "you're going to move in and I promise it will feel like home, like you've never lived anywhere else."

He started down the stairs, his shoes clicking on the steps.

"And darling," he called, "don't forget to get over to see those curtains. They're perfect for the library."

The building door opened and slammed. She went to the living room and sat on a box. She shouldn't blame him for being disgusted.

She didn't want a library.

She arrived early for her shift at the hospital. Two volunteers had just finished. They were laughing about a movie they'd both seen.

A nurse passed. "Hi, Ruth. Hi, Gail," she called. "Good work."

They waved. They were more assertive, Kim thought. All the other volunteers were. That's why they were recognized. Only a few nurses knew Kim. Sometimes she liked the fact that she was relatively unknown. No interferences. No distractions. She'd show up and do her job. She washed her hands and put on her apron. She washed her photo ID card and clipped it to her breast pocket. Anyone who didn't know her could read her name off the card.

Kim rode the elevator up alone. Some nights were calm. Others were more stressful. On a bad night, the door would slide open to a cacophony of cries, and she'd know it was going to be a long one.

She'd been so naive those first few times. She'd thought most of the babies were orphans, abandoned by drug addicts, prostitutes, AIDS victims. Not so. She'd come to meet many of the parents. She'd been afraid at first.

"They're going to hate me," she'd said to Hetty. "It's like I'm taking their child from them."

"You're crazy, sister. They've been sitting with that child all day. They're exhausted. Sometimes they're too scared to leave. But then you show up. They see you and they're grateful. You're like a little bit of sunshine."

She was right that they were grateful. They'd thank her and offer to bring things.

The elevator door opened. The sound was deafening. There were more nurses than usual. There'd been two emergencies.

"Who's the head nurse on duty?" Kim said.

"That's me," said a man, hustling up to the station with a chart.

"I'm Kim Reilly," she said, "the Friday night."

He showed the chart to a woman behind the counter.

"Call Dr. Jacobs," he said. Then he turned to Kim. "How 'bout Room Five, Bed One. Her name's Angela."

"I know Angela."

"Okay, Kim. Thanks."

She headed down the hall and into Room Five, closing the door gently behind her. The baby in Bed Two was asleep. Kim washed her hands and put on gloves. She pulled a chair up to the side of Angela's bed. She checked her IV bag. It was nearly full. The other baby's IV bag was almost full as well. She'd keep an eye on both and let the nurses know when they needed to be replaced. On busy nights, these simple things might make the nurses' lives easier.

She settled into the chair beside Angela and reached out and touched her tiny hand.

Angela was a drown victim. Kim didn't know how it had happened. She didn't want to know. Some time ago, she'd stopped asking a lot about the children. The stories were too painful, and if there was anything she really needed to know, the nurses would tell her. In Angela's case, she'd been under water long enough to cut off the oxygen supply to the brain. As a result, she'd become deformed. She was a year and a half old. Her arms were crooked and her legs were bent. Tiny pillows kept her propped so as not to put pressure on her joints. She could not be picked up. Kim could only touch her. If she cried, Kim would stroke the back of her hand.

She stayed an extra hour past her shift. When she couldn't keep her eyes open anymore, she whispered, "Good night." Before leaving, she checked on the baby in Bed Two and read his name off the chart.

The halls were so bright compared to the rooms. The head nurse on duty had changed. Denise was working. Kim asked about the new baby in Bed Two.

"Where's Derald?" she said.

"He didn't make it," said Denise.

When Kim got home, she took out her note pad. She wrote *Angela* next to the date. There were scores of names. She'd filled five pages. She scanned back a few weeks and found Derald. She drew a little cross by his name, because that's what she did when a baby she'd held died.

She spent four days with Robert in the Cayman Islands. She tried to water-ski. Seven attempts and she still hadn't stood up. She preferred sitting in the boat with the driver drinking Sea Breezes. The hair on his arms was bleached from the sun.

—

There were other trips: days on a two-hundred-foot yacht, drifting through the Bahamas, nights in Lyford Cay, drinking frozen daiquiris from coconuts, eating vodka-soaked watermelon. She wore a silk scarf and dark wraparound sunglasses to the beach. She could see Robert eyeing the young girls in their thongs.

He seemed to spend more time at the mirror, tying and retying his tie, fussing over the points of his pocket handkerchief, chasing his reflection until pleased. One night, halfway out the door, he noticed a wrinkle in the back of his shirt collar. He stood close to the mirror and then got his reading glasses from the nightstand and inspected himself in the mirror again. Off came everything. He started over. To sit through the process nightly, seeing the excessive, almost effeminate care he took, and then watch him in the presence of a young woman, someone he might never exchange a word with, sit up straighter, become conscious of his hands, hold a door, make eye contact . . .

The night they left port, they opened a rare bottle of wine and left it on the deck table to breathe. Kim sprawled on long blue terry cushions, watching the radar gun at the top of the boat turn in slow, steady revolutions that defied the wind. An anvil of clouds was rising in the east, flattening, and the boat began to slide on the growing swells. She took a pill for her stomach. Robert slid the glass door open.

"The captain says you better come in," he said.

"What about the wine? My stomach's turning."

"Don't drink, then."

"It's such a waste."

"There will always be more. Leave it."

She followed him into the cabin and stayed sitting half the night to keep her head from spinning. She thought about the wine they weren't going to drink, how few bottles of that vintage still existed: the vineyard they came from, gentle faraway hills, dusty wheel-tracked roads slipping between rows of gnarled vines. She pictured herself wandering a musty cellar, dark wood barrels lined up like eggs, comforting cold wet pockets of air. The boat's rocking wrenched at her insides.

In the morning, the sky had cleared. Louanne, the mistress of the boat, was already hard at work. The white fiberglass table had been scrubbed down and showed the sun and the pure blue sky like a still-water reflection. She came out onto the deck with a vase of cut flowers and a basket of silverware and napkins and place mats. She had blond boyish hair and wide dimpled cheeks and smiled and said hello. Her white shorts were pleated and heavily starched, cinched with a white canvas belt. Her legs were darkly tanned all the way down to her bare toes. Kim stared at the woman's sturdy calf muscles as they tensed, countering the slow shifting of the deck so naturally. To look at the woman's face, she could see no change, no adjusting, only an unwavering young smile.

Robert stood behind the glass sliding door, his hair unmussed, safe from the blowing wind. He was also staring at Louanne. He held a half-smoked cigarette and watched until the table was set. Then he tightened his robe and came out onto the deck. He flicked the cigarette over the side of the boat.

"I left some shirts on the bed to be ironed," he said.

"I'll see to it," said the mistress. "How do you feel this morning?"

"Better."

He took a seat at the table, straightening his knife and fork.

"Louanne," he added, "be careful with the cuffs and collar. There were wrinkles before."

"I'll be extra careful, sir."

"Well starched."

"The way you did them last time was fine," said Kim. "He's cranky because he's famished."

The mistress took a breakfast menu and a list of the boat's wine stock from her basket and held them out to Kim.

—

Too many nights on a boat.

On the flight home, a stewardess recognized Kim. The woman's lashes were heavy with mascara. The skin around her lips was soft and powdered. Her hair was piled into a graying bun.

"Kim Reilly, is that you?"

Kim stared blankly.

"Jennifer," the woman said. "Remember?"

She was pushing a drinks cart, holding in her hand a pair of silver tongs for the ice.

"Can I get some coffee?" said a man on the opposite side of the aisle.

She turned her back to the man and bent over Kim, hands between her knees. "I don't believe it. You look fantastic."

She stared Kim up and down, taking in the shoes, peach satin pumps with creamy unscuffed soles. "Wow, are you still in New York?"

Kim nodded.

"I moved back to South Carolina. I just . . . look at you. Can you believe it? I always wondered about you."

Robert was reading. Kim tapped his arm. He lowered a pair of glasses on his nose and shook Jennifer's hand. It was as he readjusted his glasses and turned back to his book that Jennifer must have made the connection.

"*The* Robert? Did you . . ." Then quickly: "We've come a long way." She was smiling still. "I'm divorced now, but I have the most beautiful seven-year-old boy. He's so smart. He wants to be a pilot when he grows up. I gave him one of those flight simulators for the computer. I can't do the thing, but you should see him. Like he was born with a flight stick in his hand."

Jennifer sneaked a sideways glance at Robert.

"Seven. What grade does that put him in?" said Kim.

"First. He leaves me crayon drawings for when I get home," Jennifer said. "And no matter where I am, we talk on the phone at least once every day."

"Does he look like you?"

"My coffee?" said the man across the aisle.

"Coming." Jennifer whispered, "I only wish I didn't have to spend so much time away."

She took a cup and poured coffee and handed it to the man.

"With milk, please."

"Oh, yes, of course."

She opened a drawer and took out a carton of milk and set to opening the spout.

"They get old so quickly," she said to Kim.

Robert grunted and shifted toward the window.

Kim lowered her voice. "Jennifer, is there any other champagne on board?"

"Just what you're drinking."

"Sometimes there's an extra bottle stashed away, something better, for certain passengers."

Jennifer looked confused. "I don't think so," she said. "At least not on this flight."

When they landed in New York, Kim gave Jennifer her card.

"I haven't seen her in years," she told Robert.

"She could use a face lift," he said.

———

Kim went to her apartment. Robert went to Nicole. In two days he called Kim from Palm Springs. She got on a plane.

That evening, she sat on the patio with a towel wrapped about her. A grassy slope ran down to a peanut-shaped pool, deck chairs, and tables, shadowy forms like animals come to drink. Sprinklers gurgled, choked, and spluttered on. The fine spray of soft hissing water was the only sound.

She went inside to the study door and listened. She could hear Robert's muffled voice. She turned the knob and peered in. Robert held up a finger without looking. She went back to the patio and watched the moon rise from behind the dark ridge of mountains. Light spilled over the jagged rim of rock, running softly down its face—a new shade of blue. The moon broke free and continued its ascent.

"You're still not dressed?" Robert said. He stood in the door.

"I'm watching the moon."

"Hurry up. I have good news."

"Well?"

"Christine's engaged."

"To that boy?"

"David Winthrop."

"You approve, don't you?"

"I do."

"You seem calm."

"Let's celebrate."

She tightened the towel about her and reknotted it.

"One more call," he said, turning.

"I thought you were ready to go."

"Go get dressed. I'll be out here on the cell."

"Who do you have to call?"

"I don't ask about your Friday nights."

She didn't say anything.

—

Where once there had been sandy fields of smoke trees and spiny ocotillo, now there were rows of car dealerships with glaring spotlights and swarms of bugs, big as locusts. Half-vacant stucco minimalls required parking lots that stretched back from the highway to the foot of the mountains. At last they reached the restaurant. Gold pin lights spiraled up the trunks of the palm trees that lined the curved drive.

Robert ordered margaritas. The glasses came trough-sized and rimmed with salt. A mariachi band crooned "Malagueña." A young clean-shaven man stood at the edge of a fountain strumming a ukulele, his falsetto floating up to the bamboo ceiling. Aged brick and wrought-iron balconies decorated the inside to look like an outdoor courtyard. Kim cradled her drink with both hands.

"You don't seem happy," she said.

"Of course I am."

"You haven't said whether you like my dress."

A waitress took their orders, a light-skinned Mexican with a single long braid bisecting her back.

Robert asked about the shrimp fajitas.

"I thought you were having chicken?" said Kim.

"The chicken is very good," said the waitress. "The shrimp are my favorite. I can bring you some of both—"

"Bring him the shrimp," Kim said. "Apparently he wants the shrimp."

"And for you?"

"Ah, now it's my turn."

The ruffled collar of the woman's dress hung loosely at her chest, the gentle rise of her breasts, more almond skin.

Kim drank without talking. Old plates hung from the wall alongside a photograph of a bullfight, the matador leaning into the bull's driving shoulder, horns jerking back in an attempt to snag the streaking cape.

Kim went to the rest room. When she returned, the waitress was at their table, Robert smiling wider than he had in years.

It was a relief to be back at the hospital. She put away her handbag and washed up and put on an apron. Hetty met her coming down the hall.

"I have a huge favor to ask you," Hetty said. "One of my volunteers had an emergency and couldn't make it. I need someone to work the cancer ward. Is that a problem for you?"

Kim shook her head.

"It's an older age group."

"That's okay."

"Think now, honey. You can say no."

"It's fine."

"You're a doll."

Hetty chugged back to her office and returned carrying a folder. She was breathing heavily. She briefed Kim in the elevator on the way up. This would be no different from what she'd been doing.

"There's no moving around, though," said Hetty. "You'll be sitting with the same girl the whole shift. Her name is Brittany. She's seven. You wash up. You wear gloves like normal. Her immune system's shot, so the slightest exposure to germs—"

Kim nodded.

"She'll probably sleep the whole time, she's on so much medication. If she wakes up, she may get sick. Don't panic, just ring for the nurse. She may ask you to read to her. That's okay. Try to keep her from talking too much. She gets excited, and that's a strain."

The elevator door opened. The halls were painted a light green, but there were no murals and no sounds of crying. Hetty took her to the nurses' station. The nurse led her to Brittany's room.

"She's sleeping now," said the woman. "Just make yourself comfortable."

The room was filled with colorful balloons and pots of fake flowers, plastic daisies and tulips. Kim scrubbed her hands and arms and slipped on the gloves that had come to feel like a second skin. She looked about the room. There were get-well cards and a poster of a water-soaked kitten. A small painted dresser stood against the wall opposite the bed.

"Mommy puts my clothes in there."

Brittany had raised herself and was looking at Kim. She had no hair. Her scalp was smooth and white with a large brown spot over her left ear. She had no eyebrows. Her eyes were wide.

"She bought me a new dress today. It has a frog on it. The doctors say I can only wear these."

She tugged the sleeve of her gown.

"Mommy doesn't listen. She keeps giving me new clothes. Do you want to see?"

Kim nodded. Brittany pointed for Kim to open the top drawer. Kim found the frog dress neatly folded.

"Can I see?" said Brittany.

Kim held it up, then folded it carefully and put it back. She went to the sink and took off her gloves and rescrubbed her hands. She put on fresh gloves.

"You didn't have to do that," said Brittany.

Her head was resting on the pillow again.

"You're new," she said.

"I'm usually on the floor right below this one."

"Where's Lucy?"

"Is Lucy usually here Friday nights? She couldn't make it tonight, so I'm here."

"That's okay."

Brittany closed her eyes.

"Would you like me to read to you?"

No answer. She'd fallen asleep. Kim sat down in the chair by the bed. There was a little round table covered with books and scattered papers that had been drawn on and covered with scribblings. A pack of crayons lay open.

Kim picked up a book and began to read.

When Brittany woke again, she was sick to her stomach. Kim rang for the nurse, who wheeled in a new bed. Together, they helped get her face cleaned and changed her into a fresh gown. They lifted her into the new bed. She was light as a bird. Instead of changing the linens in front of Brittany, the nurse removed the soiled bed.

"It's nicer that way," the nurse said.

When she'd gone, Kim sat back down.

"Sorry," said Brittany.

"It's okay, darling."

Kim opened the book she'd been reading to her saved place.

"Would you like me to read to you?" she said.

"Which book is that?"

Kim showed her the cover.

"The Wind in the Willows," Brittany said.

"I bet you're a really good reader."

"My daddy says I read on a fourteenth-grade level. Read me the part about the baby otter."

"Which chapter's that?"

"Where Ratty and Mole look for the little missing otter."

Kim found the chapter and began to read. From time to time she'd look up to see if Brittany had fallen asleep. Her eyes were open, staring at the ceiling. The brown spot on the side of her head was shaped like a rain cloud.

When Mole and Ratty finally found the baby otter, he was nestled in the rushes. Pan had shown them the way, and after, he made them forget that they had seen him.

"Who's Pan?" said Brittany.

"He's like God."

"Why does he make them forget?"

"Because he's too beautiful," said Kim.

"So?"

"They might miss him too much."

Brittany's eyelids began to sag. Kim checked her IV bag. It did not need to be refilled yet. She didn't wake up again. Kim read a little more, then put the book down and rubbed her eyes. She looked at some of Brittany's drawings. There was a poem written in wobbly purple block letters:

> The sun rises the sun goes
> The moon high the grass below
> So deep down in my heart I feel your soul in me
> And when I feel your soul I think of others. Amen.

In the bottom right corner of the page, an adult, probably Brittany's mother or father, had written *Brittany, Fall,* and then the year.

It was two in the morning. Kim touched Brittany's forehead. She touched the brown spot on the side of her head, and her shoulder. Then she left.

She added Brittany's name to her list that night and stayed up to watch the sunrise.

———

Three days later, she got a call from Hetty. She asked if Kim could attend a staff meeting the nurses were having that afternoon. "Sometimes we invite volunteers," she said. "Their input's important."

Kim agreed to be there. Hetty gave her directions to the nurses' lounge and told her not to be late.

Kim arrived on time, but the meeting was already under way. The room was crowded with nurses, many she'd never seen before. A couple of the women she recognized as volunteers. Ruth was sipping coffee from a Styrofoam cup. Hetty was speaking at the far end of the lounge. She saw Kim and nodded. Kim tried to melt into the corner.

"For our last item of business," said Hetty.

Kim wondered if she'd mistaken the time. She'd clearly heard 3 P.M.

"As you all know," Hetty continued, "we have many volunteers on our staff. These people give up their time so that our hospital is a little brighter, a little nicer, so that children and adults get the kind of attention they need, that doctors and nurses can't always give. Every year, we at Saint Vincent's like to recognize the work of one volunteer. This isn't an easy job. It's hard to single out just one person. But this year wasn't so hard. This year's special person is someone I have to admit I had my doubts about. I get a lot of bleeding hearts who come and see me about work, but not all hearts bleed."

"Amen, sister," someone shouted.

"You all know her by her work. She doesn't say much—just helps. She gives more than her time, and that's what we're all here for. This year's award goes to Kim Reilly."

Everyone turned, strange smiling eyes, happy teeth, and clapping hands, a wave of sound that made Kim feel faint. Hetty was calling to her, waving for her to come and accept the award. Everyone reached out to touch her as she passed, patting her shoulders and squeezing her hands. Hetty handed over the plaque with a smile. Kim started to speak. "Shut up," said Hetty. "Don't make me cry." She kissed Kim on the cheek. The plaque read KIM REILLY—VOLUNTEER OF THE YEAR, with the hospital insignia and the date.

The throng parted to reveal a large rectangular cake.

—

For half an hour, people kept congratulating her. She didn't know what to say. She smiled so much her face hurt. When it was all over, Hetty gave her a hug.

"Do you have someone special to celebrate with?" she said.

"Yes."

Kim had never told her anything about her private life. It seemed strange not to have said something.

"First I want to go upstairs and see that girl from the other night," she said. "She was asleep and I didn't get a chance to say good-bye."

"You mean Brittany?" said Hetty, her smile vanishing. "Child, she didn't make it."

When Kim got home, she went to the end of her list. She'd written two hundred names. Brittany's was the last. She drew in a cross.

PART IV

PARIS

The apartment had taken a year. Halfway through the installation, Robert admitted to not liking the color scheme. They had to start over.

"It's not as if we're not paying for it," she said to Michael.

When the apartment was complete, Michael wouldn't return her calls. Change, she thought. She needed to get away.

—

Nicole left for Hawaii. Robert and Kim had planned a few days in Paris. It was late May. The trees would be blooming, the weather starting to thaw. They would stay at the Ritz as they had in the past. But this time it would not just be for a weekend. This time she wanted to see the city, see the moon from Sacré-Coeur, wet her feet in the fountains at the Louvre, and walk barefoot under the stars. She wanted Paris beyond the landmarks she knew, the scattered restaurants they always went to, the fashion houses and the four corners of a bed.

The night before the flight, she took out her suitcases. She laid trousers across the bed, many with the price tags attached, still unworn. If she liked a style, she usually bought two, sometimes three. She pulled down shirts and piled them one atop the other over the pants. She poured herself a vodka from a crystal carafe that sat on a gold-leafed side bar. She shook the ice in the glass and went to the closet to survey the racks of suits. The hangers were evenly spaced. No two suits touched and the sleeves fell freely, pearl and gold and jade buttons all in a row. Her father would approve.

She wouldn't have answered the phone, except that she was expecting Robert for dinner. She thought he was calling from his cell phone.

"Hello?"

There was no reply.

"Hello?" she said, louder, thinking Robert would come on momentarily.

"Miss Reilly?" said a strange voice.

"Who's calling, please?"

"Joseph."

He sounded official, as though he were waiting downstairs with the car, as though no time had elapsed since his firing.

"What do you want?" she said.

She pictured him in traffic on the 59th Street bridge, girders like prison bars creeping by, a steel-covered street with no view of the night sky, only flashing glimpses of the city left behind. And what ahead? Cramped car-lined streets, sooty brick duplexes with aluminum strip overhangs above the front steps—the back roads to the airport, Joseph's home. How many times had he stayed up all night driving her to parties, then returned to a sleeping wife and children, foil-wrapped cold dinners? She could still see his eyes that last night when they kissed, the shock, the helplessness as she robbed him of his dignity, abandoning her own. Did he need money?

"I'm calling," he said, "because I thought you should know you're not the only one. I thought you should know."

She hung up and stared at the dress she was holding, black with Robert's imperative slit up the side. She spun around and whipped it away, the hanger shooting loose, tomahawking across the room, nicking the cream wall, a wisp of plaster dust. The dress dropped like a weight, a hole in the carpet. The phone rang. It stopped and then started again. She rubbed her temples and looked about the room at the sweeping yellow curtains and the armoire with the retractable shelf and the television half pulled out, open drawers, stockings still in their packaging, and mounds of folded cashmere sweaters, a stray highball she'd poured earlier that evening and forgotten. She rushed to answer the phone.

"You're lying!" she shouted.

"Who's this?"

Kim sat on the edge of the bed. She began to untangle the cord.

"Yes?" she said.

"Kim?"

"Yes?" she said louder.

"This is Rose, your grandmother."

The voice bore no resemblance to the voice she'd heard on the phone years ago. It was weak.

"I was expecting someone else," said Kim.

"It hasn't been easy tracking you down."

There was a long pause.

"Your father is sick. A neighbor found him in time. They say it was a mild heart attack. He's back home but scheduled for surgery in two days. I just wanted to let you know. I have the number of a priest who—"

"For what?"

"Well—" She paused. "I thought you'd—in case—"

"There's no *in case.* What do the doctors say?"

"They say he'll be okay."

"Why are you calling then? Why isn't he calling?"

"I thought you would want to know."

"Did he ask you to call me?"

"No." Her voice trembled.

"Because he will be okay. He knows."

"But—"

"You don't understand. Nothing can kill him. He'll outlive you and me, everybody. He'll be fine. He'll fight and win this time and he'll fight it and beat it the next time and the next. You have no business calling here. If he needed me, he'd call himself. If he wanted me to come, he'd call. He's conscious, right?"

"Yes."

"And he didn't say he wanted me to come?"

"Your mother didn't want us to come either."

"I don't care."

"She told us not to."

"I don't believe you. I was there. I was by her side. I know why you didn't come. Don't presume to know what she really wanted or what my father needs. And don't you dare think you know what I should do. You don't know my father or me or anything. Don't ever call here again. Do you understand?"

"I'm sorry," she said. "He's been very kind these past years. There was nobody else. He loves you very much."

Kim hung up and reached for the glass on the nightstand and shook the ice loose. She circled the room, staring at the phone as though it might ring at any moment. She refilled her drink and went around the room again, rubbing her forehead with her free hand. The television was loud. Finally she returned to the phone, picked up the receiver, and dialed.

"Hello?" came the voice. Did he sound out of breath?

"Daddy—"

"What's wrong?"

"Nothing. Grandma Rose called."

"What did she want?"

"You've been taking care of her?"

"I haven't been taking care of anyone."

"She seemed grateful."

On television, a weatherman pointed to a map of the states. There were patches of rain and wavy lines, fronts with arrows showing direction and movement. City temperatures began to flash: Los Angeles, San Francisco, Seattle. . . .

"Is it really eighty degrees in San Francisco?" she said.

"Huh?"

"Dad, I want to come."

"What?"

"To be there."

"What did that woman tell you?"

"I can be on a plane tomorrow."

"Don't go doing that."

"It's serious, Dad."

"Goddammit. In, out—that's what the doctor said."

The weather report ended and cut to a commercial. The television seemed to grow even louder.

"So what are you doing?" he said. "Everything fine?"

"I'm supposed to fly to Paris," she said.

"That's perfect. That's grand. You do that."

"Tell me to come, Daddy."

"I never got to take your mother. That fellow going with you? What's his name, Bob? I have to have a talk with that boy."

"I don't want to go now."

"Damn it. Don't start worrying about something that ain't worth—" He took a deep breath. "Look at what you're doing. I told you—"

"I want to be there."

"No! I don't want you here. If you show up, I swear . . . don't."

"What hospital? At least tell me the hospital. Please. Don't make me call Rose back."

"You promise to get on that plane to Paris?"

"I promise."

"Cross your heart."

"Yes, Daddy."

He would be fine. She would know when the time came, she told herself. And it was true; nothing could kill her father: bullets, hate, disease, love, not even prayer.

—

Robert was late picking her up. His new driver, Angell, sat in the front seat, beating a rhythm against the wheel with flat palms. She could hear the radio through the windows. He looked slowly in her direction, then looked away as though he hadn't seen her, hands smacking the wheel, head bobbing, sideburns below his ears. She waited for him to get out of the car and open her door. He whistled through his teeth as he swung his legs out and moved slowly. His hand lingered over the door handle as though daring her to say something. Robert had his head turned. There was a lot he was willing to overlook to be able to say he had a driver named Angell, a former state trooper. He would boast of Angell's tattoos over cocktails. "He shot a man. I don't know if that's what got him removed from the force." Then, fueled by the shock such statements would elicit:

"He carries a Beretta." He'd pat his calf. "Right here." He seemed proud, almost, as if he were living dangerously, performing an act of courage in hiring such a man.

"You're late."

She turned her cheek to his brisk kiss.

"Can you turn the music down?"

The car smelled of lemon rinds, not Nicole's lilac standby. She lowered the window and tried to forget Joseph's call. Soon her own perfume would seep into the leather, leaving its mark.

"Do you have to go so fast?" she said to Angell. Then, a moment later: "Why are you cutting across here? There's always traffic on this street. Robert, say something."

"You sound like Nicole."

She saw Angell's face in the mirror, the splinter of a smile.

———

She drank vodka martinis during dinner. They numbed her throat and warmed her hands. Robert never lifted his eyes from his food. He chewed mechanically and redistributed portions of meat and vegetable about his plate, avoiding her gaze.

"My father's having surgery," she said.

For a second, the muscles in his forehead relaxed. Then his brow leveled and he set down his silverware.

"Is it serious?"

"He doesn't think so."

"What happened?"

"Mild heart attack."

"That is serious."

"In, out, the doctor said."

"A heart attack is serious."

"My grandmother called."

Robert stared blankly.

"I shouldn't worry," she said.

He nodded slowly, but she could see that he disagreed.

"We'll have to postpone Paris," he said firmly.

"Why?"

"Why? You should be with your father."

She shook her head.

"You don't want to be there for the surgery?"

"He doesn't need me."

"Are you sure you've thought this through?"

"Of course."

He sipped from his glass.

"He said I should go to Paris," she said. "And I want to more than before."

His eyes dipped from hers.

"Nicole's back," he said, after a long silence.

He stopped a waiter and ordered another drink.

"She's not feeling well," he said. "She wanted to be near her New York doctors."

He stared gloomily into his glass and finished the remains and looked about impatiently for the waiter.

"Where has he gotten to?" he said.

"So that's why you don't want to go."

"This should blow over in a couple of weeks."

She set her fork and knife down.

"I know. I'm sick about the whole thing," he said.

"If I had flown to San Francisco to see my father, you wouldn't have told me."

"We'll still go. I promise."

She reached for her drink, and her jacket cuff touched her dish. Robert dipped his napkin into his water and offered it.

"What?" she said.

He shrugged. A busboy brought a fresh napkin and replaced his water. Kim saw the stain on her jacket and rested her arm in her lap so Robert wouldn't look at it.

The table next to them emptied. The maître d' watched as the busboy cleared saucers and cups and smoothed out fresh linen.

Just then, Angell walked in with the sleeves of his suit pulled up to his elbows. He pointed at Robert and started in their direction. The maître d' cut him off.

"Your convict wants you," she said.

Robert wiped his lips.

"What now?"

He threw his napkin down and got up. The maître d' stepped aside as Robert approached. People were looking. Angell was not smiling his usual proud, crooked grin as he cupped his mouth to Robert's ear. Robert didn't seem as concerned.

"What was that about?" she said, when he returned to the table.

"Nothing."

"He barged in here to tell you nothing?"

"Darling, I'm sorry about your father, really. And I'm just sick about the trip. I know it will work out. Please forgive me. I know how upset you are. You should go to see your father."

He straightened his napkin in his lap and tugged his shirt cuffs until they were satisfactorily revealed and looked up.

"You're firing daggers at me," he said.

"I'm going."

He paused and she repeated herself, sounding more sure.

"Good," he said. "It's the right thing to do."

"Like you know right from wrong."

He shrugged. "I know about this."

"You think I mean San Francisco."

"Go tonight. I'll have Angell take you," he said.

"Robert, I mean Paris."

A waiter approached the table.

"Is everything all right?" he said.

"Yes," Robert said. "You're going without me?"

"Yes."

She ordered dessert and coffee. The busboy cleared the glasses. Robert pursed his lips against his closed hand. He stared a long time at the check before signing it.

The busboy grinned at her as she went to stand. She'd forgotten about the stain on her jacket and she quickly covered it with her hand.

The maître d' hurried to assist with her chair.

"So sorry, Madame," he said, glaring at the busboy.

Then back to Kim: "You must forgive him. Today he is a father."

The busboy beamed.

———

Robert insisted on dropping her off.

"I wish you wouldn't go," he said. "Aren't you being a little cruel?"

She lowered the window. She was sweating, and the air chilled her forehead.

"Darling, did I say something? Just tell me. I'm sorry about the trip. I would have told you about Nicole."

He stared at her.

"It's getting cold. Why don't you—"

She pressed the button to raise the window.

"Tell me," he said. "What can I do? Say something."

She shook her head. "I don't know what to say."

———

The bedroom was a wreck, clothes strewn about, her closet wide open, every light glaring. She collapsed on the mound of clothes on the bed and waited for the phone to ring, for the continuation of Robert's pleading. She stayed up all night thinking, staring at the art on her walls, botanical prints that Michael had chosen because she'd instructed him to, because she'd liked the idea at the time. "No, for the bedroom," she'd said, as though they were relevant to her past and she needed them close for comfort. Pretend hand-me-downs. Souvenirs of a stranger's life, a false travel log of memories, connecting her to random places—nowhere, nothing, no one. She opened a drawer and took out the plaque she'd received from the hospital. She went to the wall and took down one of the prints and hung the plaque in its place. She stood back and gazed at it, stuck between two Redoutés. Volunteer of the year. So many names. So many crosses. It occurred to her to pray and forgive, to ask for the strength to bless her father's soul for any pain he might endure.

She finished packing before Robert finally called.

"I'm still going," she said. "You can call me at the Ritz."

"I wish you wouldn't. Your father—"

"Don't you dare pretend to be concerned."

In his voice she heard exhaustion. It was not in him to put up a fight.

"Perhaps I can join you. I'll have Angell take you to the airport," he said.

"Don't bother."

She phoned Saint Vincent's. Hetty was not in. Kim left a message explaining that she wouldn't be able to make the following two Friday nights. . . . Maybe three. She was leaving the country. Not to worry, she'd be all right. She would make up the days as soon as she got back.

She called for a service to meet her and take her to Kennedy. Within a few hours, she was on a plane. She woke as they were landing. It was early morning in Paris. It was the day of her father's surgery.

At the Ritz, a broad-shouldered valet carried her bags from the taxi. Another held an umbrella. People huddled under the overhang of the hotel entrance, waiting as porters in long raincoats ventured across the cobbled Place Vendôme, whistling for taxis and waving their arms in the rain. A wet foot-marked red carpet led to the revolving door. She was too tired to attempt French. She gave her name at the reception desk and the man responded in English. He welcomed her and asked about the flight. A room was ready, a beautiful one overlooking the inner courtyard.

"I know you specifically requested one in front," he said, but explained that for early check-in there were no front rooms available. If she preferred, she could take the room that was ready and they would move her that afternoon.

She could think only of lying down, of shutting the door to her room and being alone.

"You've had a long flight," the man said. "You will feel better after a bath and some breakfast."

A porter led her to her room and pushed open the door. Light from the hall fell on hundreds of white roses, bunches upon bunches in porcelain vases on the night tables, on the dresser and vanity, and a gilded writing desk. He went to the window and opened the curtains. Blooms the size of grapefruits perfumed the long room and sitting area. The walls were upholstered with silk, the color of the clouded sky. She called down for a bottle of champagne and searched for a card, stretching the phone cord across the room as she went from bouquet to bouquet. The porter set her bags in the closet. By the time she got off the phone, he had gone.

She found the card at last: a small envelope and a typewritten note. *I miss you already. Robert.*

She closed the curtains and slipped off her shoes. She turned on the television, calculating the time in the States: 3:20 A.M. in New

York, 12:20 A.M. in San Francisco, almost eight hours to her father's prep. She sat at the edge of the bed, her hands crossed in her lap as she waited.

A man arrived with the champagne.

"You are alone?" he said, looking around.

He popped the cork and filled one of the two flutes, tucking the other under an arm. He put the bottle in a silver bucket of ice, rolled a napkin and draped it across the rim of the bucket.

"It is early for you, *non*?"

"Do I sign?"

"Compliments of the house," he said. "For a little confusion."

She gave him several francs and he left. She drank to the lilting sound of the television, words strung together seemlessly. Occasionally she'd catch a word. In the beat it took her to interpret, so many more had flown by. She drank quickly and ordered another bottle before she'd finished the first. It was a different man this time, older, with a thin mustache.

She checked her watch again and reset it. She dragged a suitcase from the closet to the middle of the room and sat on the floor, sifting through it, pulling out pieces of tissue paper that she'd packed between layers of clothes to keep them from wrinkling, folding them for reuse. Robert had taught her the trick. Kim leaned against the foot of the bed and sipped her champagne. Piles of clothes were scattered now about the floor.

———

The phone woke her. It was the concierge calling to say that her other room was ready. He'd rung earlier but she hadn't answered. She couldn't think of moving now. She remembered how much she had wanted to bathe. Somehow she'd forgotten. She wanted only to rest her head, to clear her mind. The champagne glass lay on its side.

She looked at her watch and picked up the phone again. She asked the hotel operator to dial the number of the hospital in San Francisco and waited to be connected to patient information.

"Reilly. Charles Reilly," she said. "He's just had surgery. I'm his daughter."

"One moment."

There was a long pause.

"He's in recovery."

"Is he conscious?"

"Let me connect you to someone there."

The line went silent. It hummed and clicked. Kim had spent so much of her life on the telephone, it seemed. She stared at the glass on the floor, so fragile, waiting to be stepped on, tripped over, shattered.

The operator put her through to a nurse. They paged the doctor who had performed the surgery, and she continued to hold.

"Mrs. Reilly? I'm Dr. Sturgess. You should know that the operation went smoothly."

"He's okay?"

"We're optimistic."

"What does that mean?"

"We expect no surprises. Medication should take care of the rest. It's just a question of monitoring him."

"So he's going to be fine?"

"Stronger than before, I think."

"Can he talk?"

"He's still heavily sedated. Say hello, but then let him rest. Do you have my number?"

She copied it down on a piece of hotel stationery.

"Thank you, Doctor."

There was another silence, then a muffled grunt.

"Daddy?"

"Is that my girl?"

He sounded drunk.

"The doctor says you did great, Dad. I knew you would. I'm in Paris."

"That's my princess. You're a good girl."

"You need to rest, Dad."

"What do you think I'm doing?"

"Okay. You get better now."

"Already am."

She set the receiver down on its base, went around the room turning off all the lights, and climbed onto the bed.

She draped an arm over her eyes and fell asleep thinking of the candles she'd lit as a girl, the dancing lights and smell of wax and incense, her mother's voice in prayer, and childhood wishes.

She woke to the smell of roses. Her clothes were wet with sweat. She rubbed her eyes and sat up. It was nine in the morning.

She called for coffee, shed her clothes, and started a bath. She was getting out when room service arrived. She slipped into a white hotel robe that hung from the door.

A short gray-haired woman brought coffee on a tray.

"On the bed is fine," Kim said.

The woman went to the window.

"Oh, *non*," said Kim.

The woman opened the curtains anyway. Light flooded the room.

"Ahhh," said the woman, smiling. *"Il fait beau."*

She unhooked the latch and swung the window open. She stood on tiptoe and leaned out and waved to someone. She turned and smiled, nodding to the window.

"It is nice. *Écoutez*—the birds. They are pretty. Perhaps you leave the window open."

She collected the champagne bottles and the glass. Kim wandered over to the window and rested her arms on the sill. Sunlight filtered through a yellow awning. A breeze blew cool against her still-wet ears. Tiled ivy-covered walls and columns enclosed the busy courtyard. A fountain gurgled. Geraniums and roses spilled from giant urns. White marble statues, their smiles unchanging and silent, gazed demurely at the white set tables and white iron chairs and the bustling waiters in tails.

"It will be like this all morning," said the woman. "Later, it rains."

"Yes, *oui*," said Kim. "I plan to be out."

The woman nodded to the side of the bed Kim hadn't slept on, still undisturbed. She held up the single champagne glass.

"Paris will be your lover," she said, and left.

—

Kim finished her coffee. It grew thicker as she neared the bottom of the cup, a pattern of grounds clinging like tea leaves for a fortune-teller to divine. She checked herself in the mirror and switched earrings, then sorted through hatboxes, switched earrings again, and listened to the birds. She was overdressed, but there was always the possibility of running into someone from New York. Finally she went down to the lobby and stopped at the desk to say she was happy with the room.

"*Attendez,*" the man said. "There is a message."

He searched. A man in a white coat was on his knees polishing a brass floor grate. Even in the dim light the fixtures shined. A series of vitrines lined the lobby, containing necklaces and bracelets from select jewelers. On previous visits she and Robert had always stayed at the Ritz. They would browse these vitrines after dinner, and she would point out what she liked.

"There are better," Robert would say, as though she were worth more.

"Ah, *oui,*" said the man, having located the note. "I thought not to disturb," he said, passing it across the desk.

M. Sanders, it read, and the time.

She folded the note and dropped it in an ashtray on her way out the door.

———

The day had started out fine, as the maid said it would, but already clouds were gathering. The breeze picked up. Kim stood at a corner of the Place de la Concorde, dizzied by the swirl of traffic. Fountains spilled in the wind, dousing the cobblestones. She had an umbrella but left it down, turning her face to the wet wind, the first raindrops pricking her cheeks, the gray obelisk in the center of the square and the tip of the Eiffel Tower rising like twin spires above the city line.

It began to drizzle. She wandered east under the protection of an endless arcade. The street was sad, dark, and full of hurried people, tourist shops, and metal carts and freezers full of long dry sandwiches. T-shirts with emblazoned red, white, and blue fleurs-de-lis screened windows like curtains. Rows of shiny Eiffel Towers of assorted sizes were stacked as many as shelves would fit. Kim watched a family choose the biggest one. The store woman didn't go to the shelf. She produced a shrink-wrapped tower from behind the counter.

Kim veered off the main street. The rain fell harder. Cracked terra-cotta pots sat in a blue rusted-metal window box, flowerless, clumps of oozing mud piling on the sidewalk beneath like sand castle beginnings. The outside tables of a café were deserted. Plastic ashtrays flooded. The windows reflected the street except where a man sat just inside, his long burning cigarette hanging from his lips, ash ready to fall. A hand supported his tired head, pushing a tweed cap off center. A car rattled by and the man sat back, his figure shrouded by the stormy reflection.

Up ahead another woman walked at the same pace as Kim. Together they left the avenue's sighs behind but grew no closer to each other. Two smoking men in overalls leaned against a miniature green garbage truck. Their heads followed the other woman, then swung back. They jeered at Kim: "A passing cloud." One man blew a kiss. She walked faster.

A sharp gust of wind bucked a red store awning. It swelled and strained against weary metal arms. A loud crack drew a clerk out into the rain, cursing. He hurried to crank the awning shut with an old dark lever. The side flaps snapped wildly like a loose sail.

By chance she found herself on the rue Saint-Honoré and set out for the couture houses she knew. She was relieved to strip off her wet coat and sip espresso as young women modeled gowns and suits for her. She bought freely and had everything delivered, but what used to be the thrill of returning home in the afternoon, to find garment bags spread out like gifts, now only emphasized the fact that they were *not* gifts. They were things she could purchase just as easily in New York. She blamed herself at dinner for not being courageous, for not venturing out into quarters she'd never seen before.

The following morning, she ate in the spa by the pool. Bathers plodded down the marble steps in white terry robes and slippers—celebrities she recognized from television, Americans from the flight she'd come over on, skin glistening, all smelling of chlorine. A man with a long sloping nose stopped to talk. His eyebrows were thick and tangled, and he had a copy of the *Herald Tribune* rolled under his arm.

"You are staying at the hotel?" he said, surveying the pool. He turned back. "Not everyone is."

She asked if he knew any restaurants she should try, and he suggested they meet for drinks that evening.

"What is your room number? I'll ring you."

"I can't this evening," she said.

He gave her his business card and she thanked him and tucked the card under her breakfast plate.

The man at the table next to her had small round spectacles that made his eyes appear soft. A stack of newspapers lay at his feet. She asked if he knew a good café she might try.

"I don't want to feel like I'm on holiday," she said.

"But you are, *non*?"

"Oui."

He seemed happy to share a part of his city, perhaps a personal, secret part.

"You are American?" he said. "You will like this place."

"Why?"

He wrote the address on a napkin and handed it to her.

"Many beautiful people go there," he said.

"So?"

The man laughed. He asked if she was free for dinner and frowned when she declined.

"You are here long?" he said.

"Only a day."

"Well," he said, gathering his papers, "I hope your stay has been nice," and he got up and left. She realized he was referring to the length of her visit. She hoped she wouldn't see him again.

—

The driver didn't need her napkin with the address. He was eating lunch as he steered, a brown bag flattened in his lap. Something on the floor stirred and she saw two large brown eyes looking up at her.

"Say *bonjour,* Titi," the man said. The dog put its face on the seat and sniffed the air and then stared at the man's hamburger.

"He is quiet today," said the man. "Usually he is not this way. He is not so good. Are you, Titi?"

Two gold statues of warriors on horseback ushered them across a bridge. The man turned down a tree-lined boulevard. Branches arched across its width, joining and twining to form a continuous shimmering canopy that stretched for blocks. It was like looking through a garden hose, the green translucence and circle of light ahead where the boulevard intersected a square. One summer, her mother had planted petunias by the stoop of their house. Every day Kim watered the cluster of flowers. She'd put her thumb over the nozzle and mist the water until she could see a rainbow; she remembered thinking how the colors were always there, all around her, even though she couldn't see them all the time. She had only to mist the water to prove it—even when they moved and there were no longer flowers by the stoop.

The driver parked and motioned to a green-and-gold-trimmed awning.

"*C'est là,*" he said. Then suddenly, "*Merde.*" A bit of hamburger had tumbled into his lap. "*Merde.*"

He needed her napkin after all.

On the other side of the square was a church, its bells ringing the end of mass. Worshipers filed out, joining the roaming hoards. Roads converged from several angles. Scattered stoplights held cars in check as they funneled into the chaotic intersection, making sur-

prisingly little noise; or, if there was much, Kim didn't notice, because the engines idled at a different pitch from those in the States,
a distant siren sounding silky as a mother's hushed lullaby. There
was a softness to the city's hum, the street chatter and clatter of silverware and tables being served—notes of a chord.

She liked that the sidewalks were wide and one could sit outside
without being in the street. There were no free tables that she could
see, and she went to the entrance and asked a waiter. He swept his
arm impatiently, a silver chain looped from his vest to his belt jangling as he gestured to the whole of the café. A woman in a sooty
bowed hat got up, clucking to a dog on a leash to follow. Kim started
for the table but was cut off by a man, who gave her a tight-lipped
smile and sat.

Nearby, another man leaned against a thin tree trunk. He read
from a folded copy of *Le Figaro,* looking up from time to time to
scan the tables and re-adjusting a brown linen coat draped over his
shoulder. Two women stood in casual, almost surprised conversation, as though they'd just bumped into each other. One held a plastic bottle of drinking water between pointed fingers like a cigarette.
The other had short raspberry-colored hair and a black lace choker
about her neck. They too were waiting to sit, keeping tabs on new
arrivals, nodding politely to imply an order.

At last Kim squeezed toward a table without competition and collapsed into the chair. It was ten degrees cooler under the shade of the
awning. She took a handkerchief from her purse and dabbed at her
forehead and neck.

Her waiter was the same one she'd approached before. He
seemed not to recognize her. She asked for white wine: *"Peut-être
un Montrachet—"*

"There is nothing like this," he said.

"Un Corton?"

He shook his head. "Shall I choose?"

A tall, lanky young man sat at the table next to her with an open
book, one eyebrow cocked like a crow's wing as he read. His hair was
still wet, drying in long black streaks that threatened to fall in his face.

Sloppy, she thought, but caught herself. Maybe he just wasn't trying to impress anyone. He had a scar running from his left eye to the side-burn, like a wrinkle from squinting or Egyptian makeup, paler than his already pale skin. He was clean-shaven, almost too pretty except for the scar, which made him look older than he probably was.

The waiter brought her glass on a round silver tray. He slipped the receipt under the corner of her ashtray and stood waiting for her to sample his selection. It was fruity like an after-dinner wine. She thanked him.

Condensation beaded on the side of the glass.

The book the young man was reading had a long French title with a peacock on the cover, its fanned tail feathers superimposed over the outline of a woman's legs. Kim sipped her wine and wondered what kind of a story would have such a jacket. What would a man be reading on a weekday morning at a café in Paris? His cheek was laid across the knuckles of a supporting fist, his expression shifting from troubled to serene: a ripple of concern in tired dark eyes, then still-water smooth. What was he thinking?

He glanced up, saw her staring, and looked away, then looked back, this time at her hand—her emerald ring, she realized. But he didn't say anything. He dove back into his book.

Kim adjusted her hat.

There was a girl at the street corner with bony knees, dressed in a sheer flowery dress. A sweater so small that it couldn't possibly fit was tied about her waist. She flirted with a boy in leather biker pants. His hand caressed the seat of a sleek crimson motorcycle. Every few seconds he wiped it as though dust had collected.

A Chinese gentleman with a white silk ascot and cream linen jacket sat with his dog. He threaded the leg of his chair through the handle of his leash and took out a pipe. A Gypsy boy crept up to him. There was a girl not far behind. They peddled carnations. The boy's tray was full, stems held in a frame of wet cardboard. The girl had sold all of hers but one, and the Chinese man was her final taker. He clipped the stem near the bud and stuck the flower in the lapel of his jacket.

The girl curtsied and skipped away in pink plastic shoes.

The boy pressed on, calling out, tugging at people's legs.

Across the street above a pharmacy, a large billboard promoted a film. It showed a woman with stricken eyes and a bleached white face, her front teeth pinching a fleshy lower lip.

"Excuse me," she said, touching the young man's table as if it were his shoulder. "Do you know who that actress is?"

She pointed to the billboard.

He looked at it a moment. "Camille Claudel?"

Kim shook her head. "Who is she?"

"I'm sorry. Camille Claudel is not the actress."

"Oh."

"She was Rodin's lover."

"The sculptor?"

"She was an artist too."

"You are an artist?"

"I mean like Rodin. Some of her finest work he took credit for. She broke free finally."

"She left him?"

"It was always *his* greatness, being his lover and all. No one could judge her on her own."

"And who's the actress?"

He paused and smiled. "I forget now."

"You're American?" Kim said.

"From Los Angeles."

"My father lives in San Francisco. Have you been here long?"

"A bit."

"May I ask what you do?"

He shrugged. There was a notebook on the table in front of him.

"Are you a writer?"

He looked down. "This?" he said. "No, this is just . . . there's a lot of garbage in here." He patted the notebook.

"Are you on vacation?"

"I'm trying to be a painter."

"So you are a painter. I'm always jealous of anyone who can draw. I should think you either are one or you aren't, though. A painter, I mean. Why *trying*?"

His coffee arrived and he glanced at the bill and reached into his pocket for some coins. He picked up his book and began to read again. How rude, she thought, to start a conversation and stop like that. She ordered a second glass of wine. It tasted more mellow, like a pear without the skin.

The young man finished his coffee.

"Can I buy you another?" she said.

"No, thanks."

He stuck his book in his jacket pocket and began to collect his things. He pointed to her umbrella. "I see you're staying at the Ritz." He stood and stretched his long arms, gazing up at the sky.

"I keep getting caught in the rain," she said.

He peered up the boulevard, turned as though he were about to walk away, and paused.

"You look lost," she said.

"There's a story about Einstein. He's walking across campus and stops a student. 'What direction am I heading?' 'Why, Mr. Einstein,' the kid says, 'I believe you're heading north.' 'Good,' he says. 'Then I've had lunch.'"

She hadn't expected to laugh and the young man seemed relieved that she had. His eyes didn't run from hers.

"Did he really say that?" she said.

He shrugged. "At least it's how I feel today," he said. "By the way, that is a beautiful ring. Is it an emerald?"

"Yes."

"Enjoy your wine," he said.

She watched him go, his jacket slanting across the backs of his thighs. A bit of the lining had come unstitched in one of the tails and showed, a lick of silk smiling at her. At the corner, he stopped the small Gypsy boy and bought a carnation. The young man walked on with his hands at his sides, his pocketed book swinging, bumping his thigh until he took it out and tucked it under his arm with the flower.

Kim paid for the wine and thanked the waiter.

"It was good?" said the man.

"Oui, oui."

He stared at her.

"Very," she said, more seriously.

She wandered along the boulevard, pausing in front of a movie theater to inspect the posters. There were those same stricken eyes again staring back at her, the pouting red lips. They were everywhere. She considered going in, losing herself in the dark, but pressed on. She turned up a hilly street lined with galleries and rare bookshops. A wooden half-open book dangled on chains from a copper arm above a door. In the window were rows of stern red leather volumes. One was two feet tall with latticed gilt running up the spine and no title. Browning paperbacks lay about it like fallen leaves, nothing but text on their jackets.

She came to another busy avenue. There were more bookstores with shady outdoor tables and hundreds of art books and whirlybird maple seeds raining down on the stands and sticking in her hair. Signs with arrows pointed to a garden across the street. Two grim-faced gendarmes stood to the side of an iron gate.

Who had the young man at the café bought the flower for? she wondered. Maybe just to buy it from the boy.

In the center of a sprawling sandy square was a boat pond and fountain. Flower beds wrapped the perimeter: swaths of red and pink zinnias and snapdragons against a green backdrop, a sharp rise of grass that led to the surrounding tier of park, potted palms and allées of chestnut trees. Boys and girls huddled at the pond's edge with sticks, leaning against the molded rim, stretching, beckoning to several miniature sailboats that dotted the pond. Wind pushed the boats to the edge, toward the anxious sticks, then shifted mischievously, turning the boats on themselves, sails dipping into the water, then springing up, filling, turning. It was a race to see whose boat would reach the edge first. When one did, it would be poked out with a stick after a mere moment's glee. Then a wild dash to the other side of the pond, pebbles kicking up as the children ran.

There was a girl with crooked bangs and a black cotton sweater with lace at the neck. Her cheeks were pale and she stared but not at anything in particular, her little stick at her side. Kim smiled but the girl did not smile back, and then Kim realized she was blind. The stick was not for the boats. Her mother guided her to the pond, a hand, inches from her shoulder, ready in case she should stray. She reached down into the water and spritzed the daughter's face, swept the panorama of the park with her arm, drawing it in the air with gestures that her daughter could not see.

"She is very beautiful," said Kim, moving closer.

The woman stooped to button the girl's sweater. A large moth hole near the neck showed her undershirt beneath. The lace collar had browned and was stitched sloppily in a spot where it had frayed.

"Qu'est-ce qu'elle a dit?" said the girl.

"Tu es très mignon," said the woman. "You are nice," she said to Kim, finishing the last button and running her hand across the girl's cheek. There was a scar on the back of the woman's hand, pink and round, the size of a dime. They started to go.

Kim opened her purse and took the first few bills she could find and held them out to the woman.

"Please," she said.

The woman hugged her daughter to her leg. The girl stumbled, then caught her balance and held on to her mother. *"Maman?"* she said, and the mother shushed her.

"I want you to have it," said Kim, holding the money out, taking a step toward her.

The woman rattled off a string of sentences, snatched the money, and threw it down, bills scattering in the breeze. She took her daughter by the shoulders and steered her.

"Maman!" the girl cried, reaching out with her stick, money fluttering about her feet. A bill blew against her leg and stuck for a second, then fell away.

"Wait," said Kim.

They hurried off, leaving Kim frozen with her hand outstretched like an unsuccessful pickpocket. The woman's voice had drawn attention. People stared, their faces full of alarm. Kim abandoned the swirling bills, marched straight to a park bench, and sat, cradling her purse in her lap, looking ahead.

"Madame," said a man. He handed Kim a fifty-franc note and walked away.

Kim woke before the sun, dressed, and went down to the lobby. Robert was calling at ridiculous hours, leaving messages with numbers she didn't recognize.

"Madame does not wish to be bothered?" said the man at the desk. "You will let me hold your calls?"

The sun had not climbed above the buildings yet, and the street lay in shadow. Taxis lined up, their headlights still glowing. The bakery at the corner was crowded with people. Armloads of fresh baguettes were heaped into baskets, emptied and refilled, selling faster than they could be baked. The smell of oven-hot dough wafted out whenever the door opened, the rich warm scent lingering.

Up ahead an iron sailing ship swung from a door sign. She reached the store and pressed herself to the darkened window, cupping her hands at either side of her head like elephant ears, peering in. There were rolled-up maps bundled into barrels and small wooden models of ships, tiny squares of sail like tissues and thread for rope. Her breath fogged the glass. Her hands left prints; she stared at the smudges. A gust of wind rattled the sign above her, which settled into a slow, rocking rasp.

She passed brass doorknobs the size of pineapples, and two wooden knobs carved like sunflowers. She walked by a store window full of umbrellas: cat-faced carved handles and duck bills, a crystal ball gripped in silver talons, and an intricately engraved sword handle. She was so engrossed that she nearly tripped over a woman sprawled on a piece of cardboard, gnawing on a hunk of bread. She stuck out a swathed hand and grumbled. Her eyes were black-rimmed and hollowed and her four front teeth were missing. Crumbs had collected in the layers of cloth bunched between her knees. When Kim looked back, the woman was tossing the crumbs to pigeons, cooing to them like pets. The gloomy birds waddled toward the bits of bread but left them, and the woman cursed, her shrill words lost in a burst of ungracious beating wings.

Kim wandered aimlessly, beginning to trust that around each corner lay a secret waiting patiently to be revealed. Bit by bit the sun lit one side of the street, etching the jagged shadows of garrets, gutters and pipes, ducts, and slanting roofs on the listing walls of opposing buildings. New sights, new details: the carved stone around a doorway, grapevines clinging to an arborlike crossbeam, a building's perfect facade, cream-walled with black shutters and iron rails—but through the windows, clouds, sky, and the steel frame of a ten-story crane, rising out of the center of the gutted building like a ravenous dinosaur attacking the city, the exterior walls preserved like a movie set, a shell of the past. Everything competed for her attention. She quickly forgot the signs she read, remembering only that she'd wanted to remember them. But all interesting things were replaced by an endless supply of new interesting things, the remembrance of remembrance and a longing to hold on to experiences.

She tried to go on. In Paris the roads angled so that one could never see far ahead. Now the bakery windows were emptied. Baskets that at dawn had contained scores of baguettes now held only a few. One had to rise early.

—

Clouds streaked the sky. The sun disappeared. She came to a park. She could hear cries, see small colored forms scrambling between tree trunks. A boy with a book bag charged with his head down, clumsily, as though this were a rare opportunity.

"Arrête," a woman called, and he stopped. His eyes were still wide, chasing after the pigeon or the leaf or whatever it was that his heart had attached to momentarily.

A raindrop hit Kim's hand. A group of waiters stood outside a bistro at the corner, shoulder to shoulder just under the edge of an overhang, smoking. They gazed up at the churning sky, the park lanterns swinging from their curly posts, cigarettes glowing in turns.

Behind them, a man in white trousers waved to get their attention. "Excuse me," he was saying. They smoked on, talking quietly without emotion. Finally, one flicked his butt away. It arched through the air, trailing smoke like a launched firework. She imagined shimmering colors, a thunderous boom. It landed without a sound. The waiters still looked up, as if there were something there, something promising in the colorless wash.

Kim walked under her umbrella. She stopped to admire an octagonal crocodile handbag. It had a keyhole latch and a tiny key on a chain that hung from a gold-scaled handle. The store was a puzzle. There were other old handbags, a white fitted short-sleeve top and knee-length black skirt, yards of puddling material, green satin and silk, Schiaparelli pink, and scarves the color of blood-soaked tourniquets draped across the back of the window display. Kim entered to find a maze of racks on wheels and more racks hanging from the ceiling.

A man in a turquoise angora cardigan with no shirt underneath was talking on the phone. He looked up at the sound of the door and then went back to picking lint from his sweater. His fingers were covered with silver serpent rings and a horned skull that clicked against the glass countertop.

She found an eighteenth-century gown that smelled of mothballs and smoke. Its hooped skirt was turned up on end and mashed, looking as if it wanted to explode. A white-powdered Madame Pompadour wig sat atop a plaster bust, rows of tight curls pyramiding toward a butler's coat that hung above. The Comédie Française, she knew, was nearby. Many of the outfits were probably discarded costumes from past productions.

She pointed to a pair of patent-leather military boots beneath a row of clothes.

"Are these from a performance?" she asked.

"Un moment," he said into the phone. *"Quoi?"* he said to her, his voice deep. *"Ah, oui. D'accord.* Those are real," he said, putting down the phone. "There is a uniform that goes with this."

He pushed a rack aside to reveal a panel where all the ropes from the ceiling racks converged. He rubbed his hands on his hips and stared at the ceiling.

"*Oui,*" he said, and untangled a knot like a clenched fist. The veins on his neck rose as he let the rope out slowly, the pulley squawking.

Once he'd lowered the rack and secured it, he wedged both hands between the hangers to get at the jacket. He laid it across the rack and beat dust from the deep navy shoulders with the flat of his hand. It was single-breasted with a belt at the waist and a high collar that hooked. She slipped her fingers under a button and pulled it taut, staring at dulled gold that was like a coin that had sat at the bottom of the sea for many years.

He lifted a flap of the jacket. There were trousers, too, with red piping along the seams.

"A man's name on the label," he said. "*Tiens.*"

He unhooked the collar and folded the lapel back. In faded black ink it read ROTH.

"It is an officer's," he said.

She would never forget the image of her father in his formal uniform on Sundays. Even after retirement he still wore it, he told her. Possibly he went to it out of habit. There were the annual parades, the march down Main Street with kids waving flags. Did he have his name inscribed in his as well? She squirmed at the thought of his uniform ending up in a boutique, strangers fondling it, buying it for parties, wondering if it was worth the price. She remembered the day a stranger came to dinner. He'd known her father from years back and was passing through. "Is your father home?" he'd said, clutching a baseball cap in both hands, turning it. She remembered the sweat stain in the brim, the salt line at the edge of the wet. He was bigger than her dad and ducked to get through the front door. He took up most of the sofa when he sat, springs jostling as he sank in, popping when he struggled to stand to salute her father. After dinner the two of them rehashed the years, the deaths, the devastated lives. They were still in the kitchen when it was time for bed. She went to kiss her father good night. The visitor was crying—three hundred pounds shaking in a tiny metal chair. She remembered great swatches of raw tear-soaked cheek and the adoration in his eyes to be in her father's presence, hearing his assurances: "There's nothing you could do, Lou."

There were people out there who loved her dad.

"You like?" said the salesman. "It is real."

People respected her father for reasons she would never know, for deeds he kept secret. They loved him. The stories he told were for her imagining: the seeds of reasons to love. Distance made them grow. Twice he'd returned to her mother. Dedication, loyalty—they counted for something. Her mother had stuck by his side. Out of love? Had her mother ever said to him, I love you? All the time, she was sure.

"Maybe I hold it?" said the man. "You come back?"

Kim hesitated.

"You don't think it is so fantastic?"

"Okay," she heard herself say.

"Oui?"

"I'll take it. For Roth."

"Roth? *Ah, oui,* Roth."

"But I need it delivered."

He pursed his lips.

"I'll pay whatever it costs, of course."

"To where?"

"The Ritz."

"Of course."

"Today?"

"When I close."

He held the jacket up, admiring it.

"Fabuleux, non?"

She took a taxi to the café opposite the church. Even in the rain there were people waiting, clusters of umbrellas touching and bumping. The awning was rolled out all the way for cover. She spotted the young artist, alone at a table in the corner. He sat as she'd first seen him, in the same blazer, with wet hair, face tipped across a fist, book in the other hand, as if he'd never left. There was something sad in his sameness, his stillness.

She remembered he'd been rude. Perhaps his time at the café was a routine, and perhaps she had interrupted that routine. She didn't care. She'd do it again. She squeezed through to his table and hovered. He looked up, then straightened, his cheek mottled with marks from his supporting knuckles.

"Mind if I join you?" she said.

He looked at the open chair next to him, then stood. He cleared his notebook and book to one side of the table and pulled the chair out for her.

"If you're in the middle of something . . . ?"

He signaled for a waiter. She could see he'd already finished his coffee. She ordered wine and offered him a glass, but he declined.

"I'm Kim Reilly."

"Evelyn," he said. "Call me Scott, my middle name."

"No surname?"

"McKay."

"Is that Irish?"

"Scottish."

"Isn't Evelyn a girl's name?"

"If you're a girl."

The waiter brought her glass. Scott reached for his book.

"I'm right at the end of a chapter."

She sipped and watched him read. Sometimes his lips moved. He looked up at one point and stared at her face, not directly so much as pondering, perhaps matching an image to the page, savoring it, and then continuing. When he finished, he opened his notebook and wrote something. He checked his watch.

"So you came here to be a painter," she said.

He nodded. "They let me into the Louvre. I've been copying some things there."

"Yesterday I bought macaroons at Ladurée. I was wicked. Today I'm paying."

"Are you here with friends?" He looked at his watch again.

"Yes," she said. "Am I keeping you?"

"The rain's let up."

"Share a glass of wine with me."

He buttoned his coat and reached under the table, pulling out a wooden box. He touched her shoulder as he stood.

"I have to be disciplined," he said. "Have another for me."

She didn't think she had said anything wrong, nor did he seem angry. She waited a moment, then stood. She left money under a glass so it wouldn't blow.

He was already at the other side of the square. There was a saw musician: a woman on a bench with the tool wedged between her legs, bending the end and stroking the back of the blade with a violin bow. Scott had stopped and was listening, but before the light changed he was off and Kim still had to wait. There were no cars, but a gendarme was nearby and the DO NOT WALK sign was lit: the little red silhouette of a scolding man that amused her, as though he were wagging a finger. Now it wasn't amusing. She wanted to see the little green man, the cheery figure putting one foot happily in front of the other. She strained to see over people's heads and hurried across the street as soon as the light switched, past the woman with the groaning saw and down the side street after him.

She thought they were heading toward the Seine, but then she wasn't sure. She couldn't see the tip of the Eiffel Tower to orient herself. Her footsteps echoed, so she took off her shoes. The cobblestones were slick and cold. She didn't care. Once, Scott stopped to look over his shoulder. She ducked under an arch and covered her mouth. She was laughing into her hand with her eyes pressed shut. If Robert could only see her now. What was she doing? Why was she following this young man? She'd never chased after anyone, she thought. She found herself staring at a set of blue initials someone had spray-painted on the limestone wall. She stepped into the street. Scott was gone.

She rushed around the corner and discovered the Seine: a flood of space, the exhilarating roar of motorists, and a host of budding trees. She was just in time to see Scott's head disappearing down a flight of stone stairs. She ran partway into the street. A car honked and swerved. Another refused to stop. She froze and it careened by, the driver's face twisted and scornful. No one would let her go. She was stuck between lanes, traffic flashing past on either side. Finally, an opening; she dashed for the curb, pressed herself to the thick wall, gasping, and leaned over to see if she'd lost him.

He stood at the edge of the quai like a man looking out to sea. He set his box down, paced off several steps to his left, and stopped and looked across the water again. Then he came back for the box and paced off the same number of steps and settled. He took off his jacket and folded it into a crumpled square and laid it beside the box. He swung his legs over the edge and sat motionless. She wanted him to point, to indicate what held his attention. A large green and blue boat approached. Passengers waved. Scott's head didn't move. She thought he might be asleep, but then his hand crept out for the box. He took it by the handle and set it on his lap, each movement unrushed. He cupped his hands to his mouth, breathed out, and rubbed them; then he unfastened the latch. He gripped the box lid delicately at the corners with his thumbs and lifted.

Scott's head was in the way so she could only see the edges of his canvas. Parts were still white. He propped it against the lid and removed a piece of cellophane from a small square palette. It fluttered and stuck to itself and he peeled it apart, folded it exactly, and tucked it under the corner of his coat. He blew into his hands again and unbuttoned his shirt cuffs and rolled them back. Then he produced a rag and a brush and hunched, hugging the box close, shielding the canvas from the world.

He stayed like that, his body compressed. Only his right elbow moved. He set his brush down and took out a thinner one, so small she couldn't see the bristle, just his fingers caressing it, coaxing it as though drawing a thread through a needle, molding the shape to his liking. The wind gathered, and he put a hand on the canvas to steady it. The brush he'd set down rolled up against his leg, dabbing paint. Again he hunched over his work, curling into a tight ball, a single spot on the desolate quai. Beyond him to the left, the Louvre stretched endlessly.

On the opposite bank, there was so much for Scott to paint: black-shuttered buildings blue without the sun, peeking above the green, windows between the trees, the tops of cars slipping from trunk to trunk through this quiet landscape. Perhaps he was painting it all, or perhaps he was focused on a single image, a single stone or floating branch or bit of foam. Or what if he were not painting the panorama before him but rather some image he carried in his mind, and he'd settled here not for the view but for a feeling, for the solace, to find himself away from people but in the middle of things, alone but not so alone that he wasn't still immersed in this precious world? In that setting, finding peace, he could truly turn into himself, fold into a more private untapped place that he was careful to shelter, closing his body around the canvas, protecting it from all intrusion, focusing, focusing like the heart of a flower clothed in petals.

Suddenly he stretched. His spine straightened and he seemed to grow, holding his arms out like wings, rising, standing—taller than she'd remembered, imposing himself into the overall picture. He touched the sky and stooped to his toes and rolled his head like a runner loosening up for a race. Then he sat again, head bent, shoulders slack, receding once more into himself until there was no evidence of any disturbance, no clear sign of passion. It was contained so eloquently in stillness, in the surroundings he seemed again to be absent from.

Kim climbed onto the stone ledge and crossed her legs. She watched him as if in a dream, car engines doppling behind her. She didn't mind that her pants were wet from sitting. It felt good to rest. Minutes drifted by. She thought of the uniform she'd bought. She pictured her father in it, walking these same quais after the war. He too had sought peace here in Paris, reconciliation with a changed world. Whatever he'd found, whatever bit of truth he'd salvaged on these aged stones, though, surely he'd lost again in the fighting that so soon followed. But at that time he could not have known what lay ahead, what wars were left to be waged, and possibly there had been hope. And this boy, Scott: were his battles behind him? Was it hope he saw there on the far bank, in the trembling reflections of the trees, the windows of dry between the rains guiding his hand? It was there. She could feel it too. She wondered if the uniform she'd bought would fit Scott and how he'd look wearing it; if he stood straight and kept his shoulders back. She imagined him with short hair, but she liked his long hair, how it fell freely.

———

She watched him put the cellophane back over the palette and wipe the brushes with the rag and close them inside the box without its even occurring to her that he was finished, that he was leaving. And then it struck her. He had his jacket on and was walking. She snapped to attention.

She slipped on her shoes and hastened to the stairs. The steps were worn smooth and she trailed a hand along the wall to keep from slipping, fighting the urge to leap the steps two–three at a time. She hit the bottom and tried to run. Her shoes clattered against the uneven stones. Just before she reached him, he turned.

"You walk too quickly," she said, putting her hand to her chest. "I'm not here with friends. I lied. I'm alone. Do you think I'm crazy?"

He stared at her. "Because you're alone or because you followed me?"

He smiled wider than when he'd left her at the café, and not to himself. He touched his cheek, smearing paint.

"Join me for dinner," she said.

"I can't."

"Perhaps tomorrow?"

He shifted his box from one hand to the other.

"Do you go to that café every day?" she said.

"I only go for coffee."

"I'll see you there," she said.

He looked away and then back, smiling. "You really followed me?"

"Until tomorrow, then," she said.

She put out a hand and he stared at his own. He wiped his palm on his pant leg and they shook. He turned after he'd gone several steps.

"It's just that I'm busy," he said.

She waved, then savored the blue-green smudge on her hand.

The next morning, she woke early to the squeaky wheel of a maid's cart in the hall. Undefined shadows crowded the room. Not the slightest light showed at the edges of the curtains. The flowers seemed remarkably still, as though in anticipation of a sudden happening, a change perhaps, for she felt close to something new, as though she were traveling toward a strange, formerly distant place only now within reach.

She dressed hastily and descended to the lobby.

"You look much rested," said the man at the desk. There were messages from Robert. She stuffed them in her coat pocket and dashed out into the damp cold.

She bought a warm baguette from the patisserie at the corner to take away the chill. The woman at the register greeted her with a singsong *"Bonjour,"* two happy notes, a tune Kim carried with her as she left. She stuck the baguette under her arm with her umbrella and broke off pieces, scooping out the hot insides, savoring the bites on her tongue and tossing away the crust.

"Bonjour," Kim sang. *"Bonjour!"* She hopped over a thin stream of water that hugged the curb.

At a café outside the Louvre she took a seat on a wooden banquette. She cradled a cup of coffee and then warmed her ears with her hands and looked out over the drenched stones of the square. She'd seen the pyramid in pictures but never in person, not even from a car in passing. She remembered Robert was asked once at a party whether he approved of its construction, and he answered that it was too modern and demeaned the history of the setting. Later he confided that he'd only said that to avoid a fight with the woman. Robert loved art, but he abhorred museums.

The pyramid rose up from the center, interlocking triangular windows, and she tried to picture what it must look like on a sunny day:

blinding light beaming off a thousand facets, shining on the carved exterior of the museum. Without light, it was like the thousands of standing puddles, all mirroring nothing except the smoky gray sky that was itself like glass.

Then a bus let out and there were people piling toward the pyramid. A line formed, extending past the velvet ropes away from the entrance, yellow slickers and olive flannel, tweed hats, shiny dashes of red and blue windbreakers like the scales of a great snake, slithering from the curb, bending in an arc. Colors bled into the flat stone. Puddles lapped at the browns and blacks of shoes. The sky seemed not as empty somehow, as though it were absorbing and reflecting the palette of these welcome tourists. However improbable, she would swear it was true; she imagined tiny brush strokes, color so subtle that it could only be felt, caressed into the heavens by passionate hands and a desire to see. She paid her check and headed for the line.

—

She wandered halls the size of ballrooms. She sat on a green velvet bench and stared at a ten-foot-tall painting of Christ on the cross. His ribs seemed about to burst, as though there were no muscle in the chest to brace them, only a veil of pasty flesh. In the same way, the stomach seemed an afterthought, too thin to contain organs, a lacerated strip from which the jutting hipbones hung. A group of tourists passed, blocking her view. Smiles, muffled conversations on the verge of becoming loud, backpacks and swinging cameras, and half-folded maps streamed past her bench on both sides, following a tiny red pennant on a stick.

She looked at the crucifix again but it seemed different: as though an intimacy had been lost, and whatever it had been on the verge of showing before the interruption, suddenly now was withheld. The eyes gazed upward through a tangle of thorns, avoiding her stare. But wasn't that the point? Frozen there, the face contorted in agony and turned with such extreme longing, oceans of empathy painted into the eyes to the extent that it hurt to look at because they were fixed and could not meet her own, could not recognize the sadness that filled her eyes at seeing his torment.

—

The Mona Lisa was marked on the guide, but she didn't want to consult a map. She asked people and they pointed down an endless telescoping hall.

"I just came from there," she said.

"The crowd, the crowd."

She turned into a side chamber and stood listening to the sounds of the main hall behind her: floorboards cracking like sticks on a forest floor, the whir of air through a metal grate. At the far end of the room a man was painting. From a distance he seemed small, tucked away in the corner with his easel. There were more pictures of Christ; scenes from his life hung one above the other as on some vast rectory wall. There was a John the Baptist waist deep in water, muscles like red rock, straining to raise a dripping Jesus. Throngs of people stood watching from the sandy bank, one man's forehead notched with disbelief, his mouth round and wide, a dark hole the color of the river. Kim began to cross the room. She wanted to approach quietly, but each step sounded her presence. She stopped a short distance behind the man.

He was sweating in brown corduroy, a spare brush clenched between his teeth. He was copying a Madonna and Child, leaning a hand against a thin wooden stick that he propped against the canvas.

She looked long at the original, the whiteness of Mary's skin and the blue of her robes like snow at midnight, shadows of bowing drifts humbled beneath stars. How could one paint grace? she wondered. And yet, each soft fold of the robe, the hands cradling the child, the extreme and gentle calm, somehow seemed right. She thought of her own mother's eyes, the masquerade of emotions contained in them, permanently shrouded by her death. The Christ child had dimpled knees and bulging sides, cheeks like melons, and eyes that probed as though aware of the trials ahead. They seemed less cool than the mother's, more reciprocating. Mary's eyes could not be disturbed from their peace.

The man squeezed paint from a tube, smeared it on his palette, and mixed it with a knife. She imagined Scott's hands performing the same tasks, the details hidden from her by his back that afternoon on the quai. The man dabbed his brush into a small tin and mixed the paint more, then lifted it to the painting and took one last look at his subject, hand poised. Kim breathed in the overripe smell of the oils. The man's brush touched the canvas, then pulled away. He seemed satisfied not to have drawn a line or changed a shape, but simply to have added red to the red of Mary's veil. She thought she did see a glimmer of knowing in the baby's eyes.

"Do you speak English?" she said.

The man nodded.

"Do you know Scott McKay?"

He took the brush from his mouth. "Scott?" His accent was Irish. "Not here this morning."

"I'm seeing him later," she said.

"Are ya now?"

He wiped his brush and touched it to a caterpillar gob of blue on the palette. It was darker than the blue of Mary's robe.

"Why this painting?" she said.

"Raphael?"

When he raised his brush, he touched it to the red part of the veil, then took it away. Did the veil look any different?

"You've really got his eyes down," she said. "Do you try to make it exact?"

She looked at the original again and then at the man's copy. Something about Mary's eyes was off. The aloofness was missing. She didn't want to offend him.

"Her eyes seem happy," she said.

"Aye."

Kim looked at the original again. No, he'd missed it.

"Her mouth is hard," he said. "I still don't have it."

"It's almost flat."

"How did he do it? It's a lying smile."

"You think she was pretending to be happy?"

"It's about Raphael, not her."

"Did he have a sad life?"

He tapped Mary's mouth with the handle of his brush.

"When I have this," he said, "the eyes will be right."

"I saw a friend of yours at the Louvre today," said Kim. "It was my first time inside. Isn't that absurd?"

"Who'd you see?" said Scott.

"I didn't ask. You must think I'm crazy. I was going to ask him to say hello, but then I was afraid you'd think I was stalking you again. We talked about his painting."

He motioned for a waiter.

"What did he say?"

"He was copying a Raphael."

"Ian. He's been working on it for three weeks."

"I didn't tell him, but I thought he'd gotten Mary's eyes wrong. Then out of the blue he said it was the mouth, not the eyes. Have you seen the painting?"

"It's good."

"He insisted he could change the eyes by redoing the lips. I was so focused on the one thing, you know, it never occurred to me to look that way. And then why stop with the lips? What about the fingers? They would have an effect, too. Suddenly I was searching the painting for anything that might make the eyes more sad. Is life that way? Do you change by looking in the less obvious places?"

"You wanted the eyes to be sad?"

"Like a mother's. Like the original. So there I am hanging on poor Ian's shoulder while he's trying to work. . . . I'm rambling."

"He probably enjoyed the attention. Do you want wine?"

A waiter stood over the table.

"*Deux*," said Scott.

The man turned without nodding. Kim gazed after him.

"Sometimes this waiter gives me a free coffee."

"He has a nice mustache," Kim said. "Tell me about your painting."

Scott shrugged. It had begun to sprinkle.

"We can talk about something else."

"Tell me why you've come to Paris alone."

The waiter brought the wine.

"I'm not alone now," she said, picking up her glass and sipping. "Mmmm."

"It's steady," he said.

"Steady?"

"My own term. So why Paris?"

"My father came here after the war."

Scott sipped without looking into his drink.

"I thought everything would be wonderful," she said. "Look, you can see the church steeple in the carafe."

He leaned over to see, and she pulled the feathered collar of her coat snug around her neck, shivering.

"It's cold," he said.

"Would you like to walk a bit? You're not dressed warmly either."

He regarded her shoes: black satin heels. The soles were lipstick red.

"We'll stop if they hurt," she said.

She opened her purse, but he made her close it. His pocket was filled with coins and he counted out the amount and a little bit more.

They walked past the doors of the church and he asked if she'd ever gone in. She thought he might suggest a look, but he continued to walk, folding the lapels of his jacket up to shield his neck from the wind.

"This way," he said, pointing down a narrow street. It opened onto a shady square. The surrounding buildings had settled inward, their facades slanting deferentially toward the trees that grew in the center. There was a wooden bench and a tall iron lamppost.

"The middle used to be grass," he said, "but the homeowners got tired of all the artists and musicians. So they put in cement, and the artists stopped coming. It's still a beautiful square."

They walked in silence until they reached the Seine. Scott wanted to browse the bookstalls. Most of them were shut because of the weather. A couple were open. Plastic drop cloths kept the books dry.

A man sat in a chair with a green poncho covering his head and his hands folded over the handle of a cane.

Scott held up a brown leather book. The binding was crusted, the cover dried and crumbling at the edges.

"A Bible," he said, putting it back. "These stands are a graveyard for Bibles. I find them all the time, sometimes in Latin. Guess they belonged to dead people."

He returned it and thumbed through a stack of vintage photos. He showed her one of a bony-kneed boy in shorts, staggering under the weight of a magnum of wine.

She struggled to think of the photographer's name. So well known; it was on the tip of her tongue.

"The kid's very strong," said Scott. "This one's a keeper."

He gazed lovingly at the postcard. The boy's toothless grin was genuine and full of pride, spreading across his face like a banner.

He paid the man, and they walked back to the café. He put her in a cab, and she rolled down the window, and he leaned on the door.

"See you around," he said.

"See you around," she said.

He patted the roof of the car and waved. The taxi began to move. She felt sure she would see him again. And she wanted to.

The wipers squeaked. The driver had his side window cracked to prevent the windshield from fogging. Droplets of rain splattered off her armrest. She asked him to close it and he tried to explain that he couldn't. He rubbed the window emphatically with his shirtsleeve and took his hands off the wheel to shrug with both shoulders.

"*Arrêtez,*" she said.

"*Ici?*"

He stopped at the curb and she jumped out. He started to shout, but she quickly climbed into the front seat. There were papers and she shoved them to the middle.

"*Qu'est-ce que vous faisez?*" he said.

She had her handkerchief out and leaned over as far as she could and wiped the front window until it was clear.

"There," she said.

The man looked at her and laughed. *"Vraiment?"*

"Allons-y," she said, and he pulled into traffic. Every few minutes she would reach across to blot away the fog. Droplets of rain beaded on the windshield. Tiny round shadows dotted the man's smiling face.

———

The bedcovers in her room were turned down, folded at the same angle each night. She took off her coat and ran her hand a last time across the feathered collar and let it fall to the floor, not caring if it wrinkled. She kicked off her shoes and wandered dreamily to the bathroom, undoing the buttons of her blouse. "This one's a keeper," she murmured, as she knelt beside the tub. The porcelain was icy, and she tried to reach the faucets without its touching her bare stomach. A quick nip and she let out a shriek. But then it was pleasant, cool against the skin, and she pressed against the side. The faucets chirped and gave and the water exploded into the tub. She chose a vial of bath salts from a tray, blue crystals that turned the water turquoise. She added soap and watched as the bubbles mounted and spread and the pitch of the gurgling seemed to climb.

She was eager suddenly to throw off her shirt, so she yanked her arms free and cast it rippling toward the bidet. It settled around the base like cotton snow under a Christmas tree. She dropped her pants to the floor and kicked them into a heap and lifted her bra above her head without unfastening it and shot it into the sink like a rubber band. She stretched her hands toward the ceiling light and breathed the steam, feeling the heat deep in her throat. The mirror was fogging. She thought of the taxi driver and laughed.

She shut off the water and went naked back into the room for a magazine. The phone began to ring. She stared at it, waiting for it to stop, but it kept on. At last she plucked the receiver from its hook.

"Hello?" she said.

"Madame Reilly, there is a Monsieur Sanders on the line from New York."

"Please tell him I am in the bath."

"He is calling several times and says it is an emergency."

She took a deep breath.

"Madame Reilly?"

"Put him through."

There was a click, then the line seemed clear, empty.

"Kim?"

"I got your messages," she said.

"I thought you would never answer."

"It's just that I've lost count of the days. I don't even know how long it's been. I'm walking everywhere. You don't realize how huge the city is until you walk it. I spent hours in the Louvre today. You would have died. I'm doing all the things you hate to do."

"Wait."

Someone else was talking on Robert's end.

"It was like going to church," she said. "So many religious paintings. I'm learning about art—"

"Kim, she's tried to kill herself."

Again Robert's voice broke off.

That explained Nicole's skipping her trip to be near her doctors, Kim thought. Like a hammer descending on a glass bowl, the break was inevitable. She had seen it happen again and again in her mind, had imagined Nicole's suicide with each desperate warning, each paranoid threat and changed plan. Expectation lessened the shock, the shattering jolt and crash. The fragments were there, nonetheless. She was rooting for her, of course.

"I'm losing my mind," Robert said, returning.

"Are you at home?"

"I'm at the hospital."

"Which hospital, Robert?"

"Mass General."

"Where?" she said disbelievingly, with a touch of sarcasm that she couldn't help, because it seemed ridiculous and typical that there would be some bizarre circumstance to the tragedy. Boston?

And then it caught her like a current. Clarity and calm vanished as the event transformed and she tried to backpedal. With less than a year of law school left, she thought.

"He broke off the engagement. That bastard Winthrop called off the wedding, and she slashed her wrists with a broken bottle. She's in intensive care. I'm going to lose my baby."

"Robert—"

"I don't know what to do. I need you here."

"She'll pull through."

"What do I do? It's all my fault, Kim."

"No."

"It is. I feel so guilty."

"Darling, you didn't do this."

"Then why does it feel as if I did? What am I supposed to feel?"

"I'm so sorry, Robert."

"I don't know what to feel."

He seemed willing to accept her emotions in place of his own.

"Is Nicole with you?"

"She's down the hall. She got here on an earlier flight. Just think if I hadn't arrived in time."

"Don't think that way."

"I got on the first flight I could."

"You made it, Robert. That's what matters."

"But if I didn't get here in time? If Christine had died with only Nicole at her side? Imagine how it would be. She'd never let me forget that."

"Robert, just worry about Christine."

"Please fly back," he said.

"I can't."

"Damn it, I need you. I'm falling apart."

"But there's nothing—"

"Kim!"

"If Nicole's there—"

"I need *you,* Kim, *you.*"

"Okay."

"Christ, I—do you hear me?"

"Yes, yes, okay."

"You're coming?"

"I'm coming."

She promised to be on the next flight. She promised anything, listening to the sounds of her own voice churning out assurances, the assuaging effect of her words as she took down the hospital number and information.

She hung up the phone with every intention of calling the airline.

She thought of pictures Robert had shown her, of Christine with her horse, with her mother and brother. She stared at the note pad and realized that along with the number, she'd written the date and Christine's name.

Her foot snagged the crumpled pants she'd left, dragging them a step, and she realized she was back in the bathroom. She could not remember having moved. Time elapsed in bursts. She stared at the tub and shivered, thinning suds popping like bubbles of saliva: a gaping, rabid mouth waiting to consume her. She sank in, water sloshing over the side, and lay back, staring at the ceiling. Her ears filled and echoed the prayers her lips formed. "Please let her live," she pleaded. But Kim knew whether Christine lived or died, she, the mistress, was irrevocably a part of her sorrow, and to ask God for some reprieve . . . no, she would not mock him with a conscience.

—

Her fingertips were crinkled and numb when she climbed from the tub. She allowed the bath to drain and wrapped herself in towels. She went to the closet and took out a pair of tapered tuxedo pants and a black knee-length jacket with thirty tiny pearl buttons up the front. She laid them on the bed. Then she returned to the bathroom. She combed her hair out over the toilet and flushed down the loose strands. She blow-dried bending at the waist so that her hair touched the tiles. It was straight when she finished, and she patted it away from her eyes and sprayed it to stay. She chose black heels, thin as nails, dressed, and left for dinner as planned. She had to be out. Everything would be fine. Stay in motion, she told herself.

Tour d'Argent was one of Robert's favorite restaurants, one of the handful of pit stops from their few previous weekends that suggested no city between. The head chef had left to open his own restaurant. Earlier that day she'd called and used Robert's name.

The chef made a point of coming to the table. He was disappointed not to see Robert.

"He could not make the trip," she said.

"We will take special care of you. You are more beautiful than in my memory. If you please, I will prepare for you the duck. It would be a pleasure if you would allow me to cook it at the table."

"Thank you."

"Would you care for wine? *D'accord,* allow me then. I will offer something to start and the wine will accompany. We are going to make Monsieur Sanders a jealous man tonight. *Oui?* That will be our prize."

The walls of the restaurant were stone, as thick and impregnable as a fortress. The building had been a medieval convent. There were two stained-glass windows, alternating gold and red diamonds with a king's crest in the center, and heavy velvet curtains that matched, red facing in, gold out, the last of the evening light slanting across the rippled folds. There were four other tables in the room. All were filled. Hers was adjacent to a portable stove. It was covered in white linen. The chef stepped behind it and began to inspect an ornate silver and gold press, spinning the gleaming propeller-like handle to the top of its screw, lifting the lid, and peering in. He smiled a wide bullish smile. His chin was shadowed, even though he was clean-shaven. His white jacket was spotless.

"Monsieur Sanders works too hard," he said.

The sommelier introduced himself. His face was as thin as the chef's was broad. He started to describe two Burgundies, a red and a white.

"You will like both," he said.

The chef was at her side again, holding out the duck on a large dish. The skin had been removed and the meat was the color of a fading bruise. The wings hugged the sides. The neck was tied off. She nodded her assent and the chef swept over to the stove.

The chairs were high-backed and she stayed very straight and stared only at the chef, focusing on each step.

Now the pan was on the burner. Blue flames licked bronze. The sommelier was pouring the Burgundy: swirling green-yellow-gold, the hazelnut aroma at her nose, a tinge of truffles. "Hazelnuts— *Corylus avellana,*" she could hear Robert saying. Thin tendrils of wine slid down the glass side like the oil in the chef's pan as he tilted it right, then left, to coat it. The sommelier's smile. A plate before her: fish finely chopped with tomato, herb like green mist, cupped in endive with wine and a touch of vinegar. She raised her glass to the chef, and he smiled, not taking his eyes from his work. He slit the bird down the center of its breast. The two sides sprang apart, and she thought of the Roman, moved to drive a spear through Christ's side, that crescendo of guilt.

The chef carved slivers that he laid across a plate. He cut off more pieces, which he placed in the press. Each twist of the handle thickened the trickle of blood, which flowed from a gold duck-bill spigot and collected in a cup. The waiter brought another plate: firm white *asperge,* a single line of dressing banding the stems like a silk thread. The red Burgundy was breathing now in a crystal silver-rimmed decanter. She could no longer hear voices, only the sizzle of the blood simmering, the crackle as the chef added wine and tipped the pan to even it. He repeated these steps, putting more meat in the press, drawing more blood, exorcising the last drops of life from each remaining piece until there was only the carcass, the choice slices saved, and the hissing blood dark as an unlit window. The ritual took an hour and a half; the actual cooking time, only a few minutes. Two of the tables had emptied. He served the plate himself and bowed his head, and the husband and wife next to her and four businessmen applauded. The front of his white jacket was sprinkled with blood like a thousand tiny pinpricks.

A waiter served the businessmen coffee. A man with dark side-burns stubbed his cigarette in a small silver ashtray and picked up the check. They all rose to leave. Minutes later the husband and wife were finished. The waiters were helping with the chairs.

"Was it worth the wait?" the man said to Kim, stepping aside so that his wife could pass before him. A gold leopard brooch with ruby and sapphire spots was pinned to her lapel.

She nodded.

"Enjoy," the man said.

Kim ate in silence. The waiters watched. She ordered dessert and coffee. A busboy went from table to table, snuffing out the candles. She paid and stood to leave. A waiter ducked into the kitchen and reappeared with the chef. The chef, the sommelier, and the maître d' all saw her to the door.

"*Merci, merci,*" she said. "*Merci mille fois.*"

"It was to your liking?"

"You are truly an artist."

Outside on the step she gulped air. For the first time it seemed the night sky was visible, cleaving through cloud like a deep blue blade. She swallowed, forcing cool air to her lungs, her stomach so burdened it hurt to move. She forced herself—one block to the Seine, two more to the nearest bridge. She leaned against the stone rail staring down at the black water beneath. Wasn't it here at Île de la Cité that Marie Antoinette was held prisoner? She remembered reading so long ago at her mother's bedside. There'd been a drawing of a woman sitting on a crate with other women kneeling at her feet.

Kim stumbled across the bridge and turned to walk along the Seine, passing from darkness to light to darkness again, ovals of lamplight and the gaps between where the cobbles were black and grabbed at her heels. Small parked trucks jutted into the street. There were voices, two teenagers coming the other way with a bottle in a paper bag, singing "*Cluck, cluck, cluck*"—animal noises. Their laughter momentarily drowned out the staccato of her footsteps. She rounded the corner.

Notre-Dame loomed at the far end of the vast square like a crouched animal ready to spring, a sphinx with its head to the ground, towers rearing into the night like hunched shoulders, fearsome and hulking. Taller and taller it grew as she neared until she was standing at the guarded entrance. She gripped the rough iron bars and shook the gate on its hinges. The eyes of saints looked back at her, unblinking, one holding its severed head in its hand, embedded in the cold, dark facade.

She backed away looking up, gazing at what was surely the altarpiece of the city. Stones upon stones, a structure born from many deaths, many accidents that did not matter because they were in the name of faith. She turned. A man and woman approached, walking arm in arm. Like her, they stopped before the gate, two silhouettes in the faint moon shadow joined in a kiss, worshiping unwittingly with their love.

—

It was past midnight when Kim staggered into her room. She went to the phone and dialed the hospital in Boston. After several connections and transfers, she reached a nurse.

"I'm calling from overseas," Kim said. "I'm trying to find out the status of a patient."

"What name, ma'am?"

"Sanders, Christine Sanders. She was brought in yesterday."

"Yesterday? I'm not showing—"

"Today, I'm sorry. The time change."

"What is your relation to Ms. Sanders?"

"A friend. Is she all right? It's very important."

"Sorry, but I can't give out that kind of information."

"I'm calling from France. I need to know if I should fly back."

"I understand, ma'am, but if you're not family . . . look, Mrs. Sanders is here. Let me see if she's available to come to the phone."

"Can't you just tell me if she's stable?"

"Mrs. Sanders is right here. If you hold on a minute—"

"You can't just tell me? Tell me if she's okay? That's all I need to know."

"I told you—"

"How about Mr. Sanders, is he there?"

"I don't think so. Listen, do you want to speak to Mrs. Sanders or not?"

Kim put back the receiver. She forced herself to be logical. Nicole was there alone. Robert wouldn't leave Nicole alone unless there was some reassurance from the doctors.

Slowly Kim slipped the top button of her jacket from its eyelet. Her fingers found the next pearl down as though they were linked by a thread. She didn't have to look. With each button, the note of her prayers changed. They were no longer needy or wanting; they were illuminating. She could not fly back to Robert. He wanted her to hold his hand, but any support would be a distraction. What he needed was her absence, regardless of his desire. She would not contribute further to Christine's unhappiness. The damage was now irrelevant. What mattered only was that she take responsibility for her own anguish and return Robert to his family. By not flying back, she was helping.

She continued to unbutton her jacket, fingers tracing the buttons in succession, repeating silent thanks, and grieving, not for what was lost but for seeing so late.

"I've been involved with a married man," she said.

Clouds had crept back that afternoon. The streets were shadowless, and she could not see the rain, but she could hear its patter like impatient fingers. Scott held her umbrella between them as they walked. He pointed to a dip in the sidewalk.

"His daughter attempted suicide," she said. "I found out yesterday. The mother—she's tried before, and if it had been her, I wouldn't have cared. . . . That's the despicable part, that I can rationalize her suffering. Now this girl's one step closer to becoming like her mom. I'm ashamed."

Kim sidestepped a long puddle.

"At what point did my life become part of theirs? I wasn't even supposed to exist. But I did. I need his daughter to be okay."

A car pulled onto the curb, its whole frame rocking as the wheels bumped and the chassis went aslant. The headlights showed the rain for a second, then were shut off. The door opened and a woman emerged, dark and featureless, shopping bags in both hands, balancing on one foot to kick the door shut.

Kim and Scott walked on. She tried to read his silence. He maintained the umbrella a safe distance above her head, eyes locked on the pavement before them, watching so they wouldn't trip. She thought of him painting, the stillness she'd observed. Now, even in motion, there was a stillness about him—a surface concentration that left his senses free.

The road led to the Seine. They crossed a bridge and descended a flight of worn marble steps. The quai was deserted; they stopped at a bench. Scott wiped the wet surface with his sleeve and they sat.

"Your arm's soaked," she said.

On the opposite bank, the streetlamps had begun to glow. The rain fell harder, drops visible as they slanted across the scattered islands of yellow light. Rain hit Scott's shoulder.

"When I first came to Paris," he said, "I had these fantasies, romantic ideas of things to do to make the thrill of my time here permanent in some way. I wanted to drink wine with someone on the Pont des Arts and throw the glasses into the Seine—the nicer the glasses, the better—or even to pour some of the wine into the water; I felt that would connect me to the city somehow. It's because I was alone. Sometimes when you're alone, you fool yourself into thinking a city can share your sadness. You believe it's giving back, but you're only taking from it."

Scott's shoulder was a deeper shade of blue now, the wetness spreading like an epaulet.

"Have you left him?" he asked.

"It doesn't end like that. There isn't really an end."

She moved his hand so that the umbrella covered him more.

"Did you come here to get away?" he said.

"It will always appear so."

A *bateau-mouche* was approaching, a tour guide's nasal voice droning above the chugging engine. "On the left, zie Hôtel de Ville. *À gauche, L'Hôtel de Ville*—" Glaring green and white lights bulldozed the darkness. They covered their eyes until it passed and the banks were again dark. Black waves slapped stone. She kept her eyes shut, feigning blindness.

"Les yeux, les yeux," she said, rubbing them.

Scott laughed.

The choppy water settled, fragmented slivers of reflected lamplight becoming whole again, gold shafts reaching toward them. She hunched and shivered.

"There was a blind girl in the park the other day," she said. "I tried to give her mother money." She dropped her hands in her lap. "Why do people refuse things? I never have. Did I ever think about love?"

"This man—"

"Robert."

"You didn't want him to leave his wife?"

"I don't know. I never thought I wanted to get married. My father used to hit my mother."

"Did he hit you?"

"It doesn't matter now."

Another boat approached and they turned their heads. She could see their shadows cast on the ivy wall behind them side by side. An empty wine bottle lay in the dirt.

"She would intercede," said Kim, "absorbing blows until she caught his wrists. Even the simplest memories change. The years make you see differently. One time, Father was furious. I think over clothes, how I'd hung them in my closet. Of course Mom was there in a flash. I still hear her clearly: 'Charlie, what did she do?' She'd calm him that way. 'What did she do?' "

"She was your savior."

"She always wanted me to forgive him, but I did already. I can say this now: I never doubted his love. He never apologized for being the way he was. He knew he was a monster. He never admitted it, but he knew. That was the difference. She felt so sorry for herself. I never asked for protection. Something made me think she was blaming me. I couldn't understand. She died when I was seventeen."

"To have to watch someone you care about—"

"An excuse. I felt like an excuse."

Scott was silent.

"After she died," said Kim, "I moved out. I got as far away from my father as I could. That was running. I'm not running from Robert. Now it's different. I can feel it's different. But I'm not going back to him."

Scott shut his eyes. He put a finger to his lips, then reached out and gently cupped a hand over her mouth.

"Have you ever heard rain before?" he said. "Have you ever really heard it?"

There was rain in his hair, his lashes, dripping from his ear, coursing down his neck. Her chin was wet now from his palm. His eyelids shivered. Was he fighting to keep them closed? she wondered. She could not close her eyes. The sight of him transfixed her, his face like a diver's surfacing, and the touch of rainwater from his absolving hand. His eyes opened and he saw that she was staring.

He lifted his hand away and slowly leaned his face toward hers. Their foreheads almost touched.

"Sorry," he said, and he shifted the umbrella so that it was covering her more.

Perhaps he didn't wish to kiss her at all, and this was only what someone looked like who cared. She had said things that she felt she'd said before but knew she hadn't, or at least not as clearly, and she tried to remember the past, how she had expressed confessions and how men had reacted. She thought back to Robert the first time she'd shown him her photo album and how after he'd left she didn't even pick it up off the floor. She thought of Sam in the back of a rented limo, taking the cigar from his mouth to say "Don't cry," after she'd talked to her father: damp tobacco kisses that were supposed to cheer her. Then the nameless ones who came before, faces she recalled vaguely, a beard, groping fingers, the chill of a watchband against her breast.

Scott had only to lean over to kiss her, to break the precious distance that had already been disturbed by her want. Would his kiss be grand? Or would she find what she had countless times? She felt close to an explanation. Yes, the gap, the narrow space between them that was itself a form of skin, a membrane that they shared.

"I want to see you tomorrow," she said.

"Then you will."

"You're not busy?"

"I can make myself free."

"Join me for dinner. But we'll still meet in the afternoon."

They climbed the steps to the street and walked to the nearest taxi stop.

"Here," he said, handing her the umbrella. His one whole side was soaked. He turned his face to the cloud-covered night, his cheeks covered with droplets, tiny gold dabs of reflected lamplight, like stars, like Paris.

"Do you know your way from here?" he said.

"I'm learning."

In the morning she sipped coffee with the curtains pulled back, sunlight warming the tops of her feet. The glare was so bright she stood to the side of the window, watching as the waiters prepared the courtyard tables below, setting them for the first time since the day after she'd arrived: billowing white linens, glinting silver.

She unlatched the window and stuck out her hand. The dampness was gone. The air was still cool, but with the promise of warmth. Her hand was pale.

She refilled her cup from a silver pot and stood before her closet, curling her toes and stretching. Blue capri pants and a blue cashmere sweater, a blue and cream hat with a wide sloping brim that could turn up in front, and no handbag—sandals; Scott had never seen her dressed casually. She would surprise him with this side of her. There would be other sides.

Paris could seem like two cities. In the rain, everyone was anxious to get somewhere. In the sun, there were no destinations, no deadlines, and people scattered along the banks of the Seine like shells. Love was no longer a private matter that could be detained.

She walked along the quai past a woman with a pink parasol and a tattooed man whittling soap, shavings about his bare feet and poking from his shoes, which he'd set to the side. A boy with orange hair slept with his head propped on a green canvas knapsack. A man had a young woman in his lap. Her skirt was hiked up and her thighs were white. Black spaghetti straps left her shoulders exposed. She was holding seed out to a bird. *"Voilà!"* she exclaimed, when the bird landed and snatched the seed. The man gazed up at a straggling cloud, then kissed her shoulder blade. No rain could touch him.

Scott was sitting on the edge of the quai, leaning back on straight arms. His pants were rolled to the knees and his shoes were off. His jacket was folded beside him. He hadn't seen her, and she stood for a moment watching. She thought of sneaking up behind him, perhaps throwing a pebble or a twig to get his attention. Instead she walked quickly to the edge of the quai and sat down beside him. He didn't say anything at first. He just nodded and smiled. His cheeks were red as though he'd been sitting in the sun all morning. He lifted his legs and pointed his toes, and she did the same. He crossed his legs and uncrossed them and she copied him. The trees on the opposite bank swayed in the breeze.

He reached into his jacket.

"I brought you this," he said.

It was a rolled piece of paper tied with a shoelace.

"Should I?"

"Sure."

She undid the bow and regarded him and looked down. It was a sketch of a young boy and girl on a bench. The boy held an umbrella. He stared at the girl. Her gaze was down, her head tipped toward his chin, yet pulling away as though tickled—two simple lines for lips. Her hands were folded, her socks uneven. The light shined from below, casting their shadows on the ivied wall behind, inflating their dark silhouettes, joined to envelop them in their own night.

"I'm going to cry," she said.

"The eyes aren't sad."

"No, they're not."

He'd made the umbrella big enough to cover both of them evenly. The boy didn't have pupils. There was only the faintest dark, not enough to take away the softness of his stare, which was also in the angle of his face, as though he was deferring to her. What, though?

She rerolled the drawing carefully, tying it with the shoelace and clutching it to her chest.

"No one has ever given me anything like this."

"It's a reminder."

He ducked under the brim of her hat, close so that his hair fell against her ear. His lips touched her cheek—the sound of drawing air as they withdrew.

She put the drawing to her eye and looked at him through it.

"What do you see?" he said.

"I see a person who's about to go shopping with me."

"Oh, no."

"You promised me the day."

"A different kind of day."

"You said you would let me take you to dinner, and that means I get to choose the restaurant."

"But—"

"It's very formal."

She looked at him through the rolled drawing again.

"Is that a smile?" she said. "It's a little blurry, but . . . come on, how often does a woman offer to buy you a suit?"

"It's our first dinner and you want to dress me?"

"I don't. I swear. Think of it as going to a costume ball. We're going to put on masks and pretend we're very serious. But inside, we'll know that we're really sitting here bare-shinned, licking ice cream from our fingers."

"That sounds more fun. Why can't we do that?"

"Because Berthillon doesn't have a 1982 Margaux on their wine list. We can do both. I'll race you!"

She jumped up and tried to run as fast as her sandals would allow. Scott was scrambling to get his shoes on. His coat was gripped in his pumping fist, and she could hear his pounding footsteps closing. Then he was past her. She stopped and dropped her hands to her knees and panted, and he slowed when he saw that she'd given up. He walked back to her, grinning.

"If I were wearing sneakers," she said.

"I've never had Margaux."

"I've never had Berthillon ice cream."

"What time is the ball?"

"There's plenty of time. Can you carry this to keep it safe?"

He shook out his jacket and slid his arms through the sleeves and tucked the drawing into the inside pocket. Then he rolled down his pants.

"First things first," he said.

—

They bought two cones, three scoops each, and traded as they walked so that Kim could taste all six flavors.

"*Framboise,*" she said.

"Raspberry. That's on mine."

"What's strawberry?"

He passed her his cone. "*Fraise.*"

"*Frais fraise.*"

"How about *ananas*? Rhymes with bananas."

"I like the coffee."

"The *framboise* is the best."

"It almost sounds more like a raspberry than raspberry."

They had to walk underground to get to the other side of the busy Quai de l'Hôtel de Ville. The ramp was long and their footsteps echoed. When they rounded the corner, half the tunnel was flooded.

"Here," she said, gripping her hat and balancing her cone. She jumped to a small island of dry cement and began searching for the next one.

"What now?" he said.

"Follow me."

"You're going to have to move off that spot."

"Join me."

Three women had entered the tunnel from the other side. They surveyed the flood, shook their heads, and retreated.

There was another dry patch near the edge of the wall, and Kim braced herself and jumped and leaned against the cool cement side. When she looked back, Scott had taken off his shoes. He was rolling his pants up again.

"That's not fair."

He dangled his shoes in one hand and held his cone in the other and marched very matter-of-factly, spraying water right and then left with each long, intentional sliding step. She hugged the wall to avoid the splashes, shielding her face with her cone and squealing, the sloshing and her laughter reverberating like the pool noise of children playing.

"I'm waiting," he called.

He was standing at the end of the tunnel. He dropped his shoes and kicked drops from his feet and rolled his pants back down with one hand.

"You're right, the coffee's good," he said, licking his cone, slipping into his shoes and fixing the heels. "There's going to be none left."

She undid her sandals and threw them, sending him ducking. She ran through the water, clutching her hat, kicking showers up before her, drenching her thighs. Scott had retrieved her sandals.

"Mademoiselle."

"*Merci.*"

"Your coffee ice cream." He extended the cone and bowed his head slightly.

"*Merci.*"

Her sweater stuck to her skin and she flicked water from her fingers and laughed. Scott offered an arm and they turned the corner and headed up the ramp. There was a gendarme at the exit of the tunnel. He looked them up and down as they walked past, and they tried to maintain a straight face. Then they dashed across the fountained square for a taxi, tossing their finished cones in a green trash can. Even Kim's hair was wet. The driver complained and they tried to appear grave and apologetic.

They drove to the rue Saint-Honoré and got out and she led him eagerly, as if she were taking him to a special unknown place. He stumbled behind her, dragging, then relenting. They stopped first at the Valentino Boutique, still wet, Scott's pants soaked up to the knees. A salesman glared at them, the corner of his mouth twitching.

"But it is nice out, *non?*" he said.

Kim stepped forward. "We need dry clothes."

The man glanced at her ring. "May I ask what sort of dry you are considering?"

"Very dry. Evening dry."

—

She sat in a leather chair outside the fitting room, Scott's folded jacket in her lap. A short woman in a black linen dress with a starched white collar brought her mineral water with a slice of lemon. Kim leafed through fashion magazines, looking up whenever Scott appeared, the man standing just behind, watching for her approval.

"You like the three buttons?" she said.

"It's sort of twentiesish, or is it fortiesish? I don't know."

"My friend Michael says, 'If it's ish, don't buy it.' "

"Everything can be ish."

"Classicish?"

"A two-button, then?" said the man. "With the same pinstripes?"

"Do you like the pinstripes?" said Scott.

"They're beautiful, and the fit is perfect."

Scott turned sideways to a mirror. He unbuttoned the jacket and the man lifted it from his shoulders. They disappeared back into the fitting room.

In her magazine there was a photo shoot of actor George Clooney's apartment. She thought of her apartment and how impersonal it felt: bits of chopped-up scattered collections, like wilted garnish, that reflected neither Michael's taste nor her own in the end—nor Robert's, for that matter. She would call Michael, try again to apologize. Perhaps he would take her call. Perhaps he would even come to visit.

Then she thought of Joseph, his phone call the night of her departure. Had he really intended to hurt her? What if the call was a warning, because he cared? Because he felt all along that she deserved better, that she could *be* better? Could he ever begin to forgive her? She would call him too. Perhaps he would even allow her to hire him. Maybe not. Hopefully he'd gone on to a better job. And his daughters, were they following their dreams? Two people who had been nothing but nice to her. Why, she hadn't a clue. She had known only hurt and how to hurt. She would call them. She could change. She was learning.

Scott emerged in a two-button charcoal suit, the pinstripes thin with the faintest texture.

"That looks exactly right," she said.

The man crossed his arms. He brushed a thread from Scott's shoulder.

"Are you comfortable?" she said. "I want you to be comfortable with this."

"It feels great. I mean, I feel a little like a schoolboy."

Kim looked at the man. "Can you excuse us for a moment? We will need a shirt as well, and a tie. Oh, and shoes."

"I will pick out a few things and return."

Scott leaned over her, bracing himself against the armrests of the chair.

"I don't need anything," he said.

"Anything?"

He lowered himself over her so that his face was inches from hers. "I saw the price tag."

"But this is my drawing for you," she said.

He nodded, almost imperceptibly.

"You're not a schoolboy. I want you to feel deserving."

"That's not what you want."

"I want you to be happy."

"I am."

"Then I am too."

The man reappeared with three shirts and three ties. He stood at a distance, waiting for Kim to signal him over. Scott stared at her.

"You look great," she said.

He stood straight.

"This is an expensive dinner," he said.

"I promise you, it's not."

———

Scott picked a blue shirt and a dark navy tie with silver stitching that formed squares, and a silver dot in the center of each square.

"That's the combination I would have chosen," she said. "They need to hem the pants. Don't forget shoes."

"This is for tonight?" said the salesman. He crouched behind Scott, tucking the excess of pant leg up and under, working the fold to the right length, checking the mirror. "Like so? Then, if you please, step into the other room. The tailor will attend to you." He turned to Kim. "Say, two hours?"

She looked at Scott.

"Do you mind if I leave you here? I have to get ready."

"No problem."

"You'll be okay? When they finish, come to the hotel. Just ring me from the desk and I'll meet you."

"I'll see you in a bit, then."

"Before you know it. I don't want to go."

She reached into his jacket and took out the drawing and waved it.

"I'm taking this with me."

"Wait."

He came over to where she was standing. The space between them vanished. The union of their lips lasted no longer than the time it took Kim to close and open her eyes: but in that electrical flash of not seeing but tasting, and then his eyes staring back, still close, green, vibrant, she felt as though he'd filled her lungs with the warm whispered innocence of kept promises.

"Hurry," he said, and went back to the fitting room.

The salesman took an imprint of her credit card and she signed the slip.

"We will take very good care of him," he said. "*Bonne soirée.* Enjoy your dinner."

—

Not enough time, she thought, as she raced back to the hotel. The valets stared at her as she dashed up the carpeted steps and through the revolving door.

She surged into her room, Frisbeeing her hat onto the bed.

She unrolled Scott's drawing and laid it flat on the vanity, weighting it at either end with a compact to keep it flat.

He'd said, "Hurry." He was right. She couldn't break the tempo of the day, this effortless rush. If lost, how would she find it again?

She had already set two jackets aside. One was green satin, cut like an overcoat, an upside-down V that buttoned once just below the bust. It showed her stomach. She looked in the mirror and rejected it. The other was black. She wanted color.

She rifled through hangers, wood and metal clattering, velvet and silk brushing her knuckles. She stopped at a silverish thigh-length jacket. It shimmered like the inside of a shell. The buttons were abalone. She held it to her chest and swayed side to side. Yes. She stood before the mirror on tiptoes, imagining the jacket with tapered black pants, or perhaps none at all—black stockings, stilettos. Then she hung it on the door and dashed to the bath.

She showered with the detachable gold nozzle, the massaging spray beating against her closed eyelids, soap running down her neck and chest. She wrapped herself in towels and wiped steam from the mirror. Her nails would need touching up. She sat on the closed toilet seat with the door open so the bathroom could air, the warm terry towel bunched between her legs, another capturing her hair like a turban. Carefully she dabbed on polish, holding her fingers straight to the light, blowing on them gently. She willed them to dry. She started to perspire.

She unwound the towel from her head and brushed her hair straight. Then the phone rang.

"There is a Monsieur McKay to see you."

"Tell him I'll be right down," she said.

The hair dryer roared like a jet turbine. She tried the jacket without pants. Her thighs were white. No, only after she'd tanned. She reached for a black lace camisole and a pair of black cigarette tuxedo pants. She buttoned her jacket and sat at the vanity to do her lips, steadying her hand to paint the outline. She looked down at Scott's drawing.

"Slow," she said, looking at herself in the round mirror.

She lifted the lipstick to her lips and filled in carefully, blotting them on a tissue. She turned her head right, then left. She dabbed on perfume, touching the glass top to the base of her neck and wrists. She would wear no jewelry, only a watch—a diamond bracelet band with a mother-of-pearl face. She checked her black satin evening bag for lipstick and a compact and snapped it shut and went to the door. She looked once about the room.

—

The elevator opened onto the landing. The concierge nodded down the short flight of steps to Scott, who was sitting very straight, a garment bag slung over his shoulder, dangling from a hooked finger. He saw her and stood. His hair was combed back, his suit buttoned. He moved to the foot of the steps.

"What's that?" she said.

"My clothes."

She skipped down a step and took the bag from him and carried it to the desk.

"They'll keep it for us," she said, coming back. She stood at the top of the steps and stared at Scott a moment before descending.

"Where were we?" she said.

He reached out a hand and she stretched toward it. Their fingers met and he guided her down to him, as though they were dancing, as though he were about to turn her, a gentle spin.

"It's not fair," she said. "The suit, it was supposed to be for you, but it's for me again. You look so beautiful."

"Shhhhh." He put a finger to his mouth. "You're too generous. If you knew how I've been thinking about you."

"You have?"

"Today on the quai, then when I was waiting for the suit . . ."

"What were you thinking?"

"The day you followed me—I knew you were there. I felt you watching me."

"You sneak."

"I was afraid."

"Why?"

"I couldn't believe you'd be interested in me."

"That's silly."

He lifted both hands to her face and drew her forehead to his lips. She looked up at him.

He offered his arm and they walked past the vitrines, past gilded statues and floor-to-ceiling curtains. The maître d' led them through enormous doors onto the courtyard. Two waiters held their chairs.

"My room is right up there." She pointed.

Scott was staring at her.

"What?" she said.

"You are so beautiful."

—

They drank an '82 Margaux. The sommelier approved.

"C'est très fort," he said, pumping his fists for emphasis.

"It's beyond what I imagined," said Scott.

"It's like sitting in front of a fire," she said. "You taste the wood, the smoke, the tickle of wool from an old hand-woven blanket."

Her napkin slipped from her lap. Before she could pick it up, a waiter was at her side. He removed the napkin and stuffed it under a cart. Using a spoon and fork like tongs, he placed a fresh folded napkin onto a silver tray and carried the tray to her table. He used the utensils again to set the napkin neatly before her. His hands never touched it.

At the next table, a family was celebrating. The father was in black tie. The mother wore a sparkling silver evening gown and smoked a cigarette through a long filter. Their two daughters were dressed alike with pink skirts and blue sweaters, pink taffeta bows in their hair. They each held a large present. The father nodded for them to open the gifts: identical dolls. They jumped from their seats and rushed to him, kissing his cheek, one and then the other, and then they went to the mother, who blew smoke and smiled, and leaned down to Eskimo-kiss their tiny noses. The father was signaling for the check.

Scott watched.

"This is the first night it hasn't rained," she said.

—

They ate and talked about Los Angeles, what it was like growing up near the ocean.

"I used to know a surfer," she said.

"Have you ever tried?"

"I wanted to."

"I couldn't stand up. It's all timing."

"You did other things."

"I did other things."

His father was an architect. He would take Scott to construction sites as a child, hoist him onto his shoulders, and walk through wood-framed skeletons of houses, pointing out hints of structure, describing things to come.

"There would be a slab of poured concrete and a chalk-marked outline of a fireplace. My dad would describe the fireplace in such detail that I could swear I was looking at it. One minute, nothing; the next, sun-reddened rocks rising like a massive potbellied stove to a forty-foot-high ceiling. I got good at seeing things that weren't there. It was different for him. He knew the plans."

"Is that where you get your creative genes?"

He laughed. "I suppose."

"He doesn't approve of your painting?"

"He tries."

"At least he tries."

"He doesn't see it turning into anything." He set his silverware down.

"You must come up for champagne after," she said.

He looked at her and wiped his mouth on his napkin. "I want to."

She ordered a bottle to be sent up to the room. Then the captain came with the dessert tray: assorted cakes and tarts on gold-rimmed plates. She ordered crêpes suzette and a half bottle of Sauternes. A busboy wheeled a cart up to the table. There was a burner and a pan. The captain lit the burner and set to cracking eggs.

—

They spilled into the room and she felt for the light switch. The draft from the door caused the nearest vase of roses to stir, petals trembling as they sweetened the air. Kim plucked a rose and clipped it with her nail. She tucked the short stem through the buttonhole in Scott's lapel.

He smoothed her jacket.

"It's almost too perfect to touch."

She unbuttoned the jacket and dropped it to the floor, never taking her eyes from his.

"I don't like it, then," she said.

She turned to switch off the overhead, the only light now coming from the window and the lanterns in the courtyard below. Scott explored the room, trailing a hand along the carved edge of the armoire, up the side of a vase, and over the round cluster of blooms. He saw his drawing and looked back at her. She sat on the edge of the bed, arms out. He crossed to her, touching her bare shoulder, then running a finger from the strap of her camisole to her hand, closed his hand around hers, and with the other grabbed the cold bottle.

He didn't move. Their fingers remained interlocked.

"You have to let go," she said softly.

"You first."

Their hands came apart slowly, the hair tickle of separating fingertips.

He peeled off the foil seal and unwound the wire in steady turns. She stood and held out flutes. The cork shot across the room and he quickly tipped the bottle to her glass, a wave of foam rushing up the neck over the rim. She caught his cheek in her hand, felt the day's stubble of his chin, touched the scar by his eye.

"How did you get this?" she said.

He finished his champagne in one long gulp and turned to set down bottle and glass.

"On one of my dad's construction sites," he said.

She kissed the scar and he closed his eyes.

"Edge of a crossbeam," he said. "I was running—didn't see it coming."

She kissed the corner of his mouth, licked her fingers, then the moist blush of his cheek, tasting champagne.

"Whether tonight, tomorrow, or a week from now," she said, "this is going to happen."

"I know."

She ran a hand up through his hair, pointing her fingers until they emerged like the tips of a crown. She pulled on the knot of his tie, ran a hand under his jacket, feeling his chest. He kissed her neck.

"Tonight," he said.

Her mouth opened to the ceiling, drinking the silence, the rustling of his kisses like wind through a sleeping house, swirling in the corners, whispering through keyholes. She felt her flute tip, heard the splatter, the fizz. She let go. The glass dropped. She was falling back over his arm as he kissed her breast, floating in fields of moonlit grass, silver bobbing dandelions; peacocks preened, gathering the stars in the net of their feathers; clouds like snow castles stretched to heaven.

Suddenly they were on the bed, racing, peeling off clothes, a tangle of arms and bumping elbows, cycling feet, kicking off shoes, laughter like champagne bubbles popping off the ceiling, sprinkling down cool on their naked skin.

He reached for the instep of her foot, ran his hand up her calf and thigh and between her legs, beneath her, turning his palm to support her back, inching farther, farther, until his hand was between her shoulder blades, the bend in his arm braced between her legs, lifting her as though she were weightless toward the pillows.

Then he was on top. She felt the flex and tension in his arms as he planted them and ran her hands down his sides, feeling the press of his pelvis and the bowled hollows of his moving hips. He lifted to allow her to reach underneath, to take hold of him. He swallowed air. He gasped and looked into her eyes with what she thought was love, because there was humility there, and shame, and desperation, a smoldering need for affirmation, as though he had yielded too much too soon.

Her hands were caught in front of her, folded between them. She freed them and reached around and hugged him, holding tightly as though she were falling, as though they were both tumbling, rolling down a hill in quickening, dizzying turns.

"What should I do?" he said.

"Lie with me."

She stroked his back and listened to his breathing, watched his eyelids fall, then flutter open. Soon she was able to slip him inside. They made love slowly, without nervousness. She reached to the headboard, brushed at its edge in languid swimming strokes, gliding to his rhythm—a wake, slapping the banks of the Seine, clapping in the middle. She imagined Scott's face through closed eyelids. Opened her eyes to remind herself, quick flashes. She saw him on the quai, painting, rising up from his sitting position, stretching to the sky, splintering into a thousand shimmering pieces of light. Then he was above her, his face like the moon, blue, blue hair falling in waves over her cheeks, blue lips lapping at her ears, bathing her in night. There was no final dying thrust. It was a drawn-out sigh from somewhere deep, that came separate from their movements, from the contractions, like a traveling sound that lingers in the ear long after its passing.

She could hear it still, far off, winging out over the rooftops, echoing in the drainpipes, drifting wayward as she curled into his arms and slept, the effortless sleep of a child.

When she woke, he was standing by the window in his underwear, his head tipped somberly to the glass. The outline of his face and hair glowed in the dawn light—a sliver of sun emerging from behind the moon.

She sat up, pulling the sheets around her.

"Did I wake you?" he said. He stared at her a moment, then looked again out the window.

"Come here," she said, patting the bed.

The glow of the sun left his skin as he turned and faced the shadowed room, the half-light that absorbed all color and sound, as though stillness were itself a color, cool as the dawn gray, a slow breathing shade tone away from a whisper. Outside, she imagined words strung together in full tones, the full-color chaos of rising, flowers cupping open, insects flitting between blooms, shops opening, sunlight hitting glass, infinite motion blinding white—the color bleaching the senses.

Scott lay down beside her and rested his head on her shoulder.

"You're my beautiful painter," she said, kissing the top of his head. "I'm going to frame your picture. When I look at it, I'll always see last night."

He squeezed her leg.

"It's so good," she said, "being good at something. You . . . I wish . . . I'm making no sense at all."

She kissed him again, stroked his hair, and thought for a while.

"So you're studying now?" she said.

He nodded.

"Is it a special program they offer?"

"Who?"

"The Louvre."

"No, they let me bring my paints and easel."

"You're not going to school?"

He shook his head.

"But you said you were."

"No, Kim. I should be going now."

"I don't want you to leave. Do you have to?"

"I don't want to, if that's what you mean."

"Can I see you later?"

She clutched his arm. He kissed her hand and climbed from the bed. He went to the closet and came out holding an open garment bag.

"These aren't my clothes," he said.

She laughed. "That's mine. Take it out."

He slipped the uniform from the garment bag and held it up.

"It's real," she said. "I found it in a vintage store. Try it on."

He looked at his watch.

"For me," she said. "Let me see what it looks like."

He removed the pants from the hanger and shook them and slipped a leg through and then the other and buttoned the waist. They hung low on his hips.

"Too big," he said.

"Now the jacket."

The sleeves reached to his knuckles. He fastened the buttons up the front and buckled the belt, then started to roll up the sleeves.

"No, leave them," she said. She jumped from the bed and guided him to the window. She turned him so that the morning sun lit the buttons. The lapels puckered. The pants dragged.

"I don't like it," he said.

"Just a little second."

She felt his shoulder and imagined a military tailor circling him with a tape measure. Scott's neck was white. The collar was loose.

"This doesn't feel right," he said.

She dropped to the floor and hugged his knees, pressed her cheek to the hard sinew of his thigh, and looked up at him. She reached up his chest, under the jacket, feeling his ribs. The jacket fell open and she kissed his stomach and unbuttoned his pants.

"I have to go," he said.

"Someone wants to stay."

"I—" He leaned down and kissed her forehead, twisting away from her groping hands. "I have to."

He went to the closet and came out with the right garment bag, quickly stripped off the uniform, and started to dress in his old clothes. She stood at the window and watched.

"We can meet later," he said. "At the café, say around four-thirty."

"Four-thirty it is, then."

He took his jacket from the hanger and swung it over his shoulder. She could see that he'd fixed the lining with a safety pin.

"I can have the hotel press your suit," she said.

"Great."

"Should I bring it?"

"Keep it here." He came over to the window. "Four-thirty," he said.

She touched his cheek.

—

She should have felt hung over, but she was too excited. The ice in the bucket had melted, but the bottle was still cold. She filled her glass and drank and stooped to retrieve Scott's rumpled suit jacket. The rosebud fell from the lapel, a soundless scattering of petals. She called down for the suit to be picked up and ordered breakfast: bacon and eggs, and orange juice for mimosas. She put the uniform in the closet and went to the bathroom to shower. She couldn't shake the feeling that Scott was still in the room, that he'd left a piece of himself behind for safekeeping; as if it would be four-thirty for the rest of the day.

She spent the morning going through her address book, searching for the business card of a friend of Michael's, Stefan, who owned a gallery in Soho. She called and left a message on an answering machine. At three-thirty she still hadn't heard anything. At four, he called.

"It *has* been a long time," she said. "You know Michael did my apartment. When I get back I'll have you over."

Then she told him about Scott. "Of course he shows at a gallery here," she lied. "I don't remember the name. It's French. I own one

of his drawings. Yes. . . . I'm sure he can send you something. . . .
Slides? I'm sure he does. . . . Yes, he's amazing. He's young. You'd
be doing me a favor."

"How young?" he said.

"Young enough to make me feel young."

"You naughty girl."

—

She felt flushed from her news, her secret surprise like a bubble in
her stomach wanting to pop. She hurried down to the lobby and sent
the porter dashing out across the square for a cab. She didn't once
doubt whether Scott would be at the café. She didn't question the
night or the morning; she didn't wonder if it had all been merely a
glimpse of a faraway fantasy, a new language that she'd fooled herself into thinking she could speak. The day had been real, as true as
water spray between her toes, as her hands circling Scott's head in
the dark like a halo, or the drawing on her vanity back at the room,
living proof of a beautiful sleepless dream. He was at the café at the
time promised, so still, so engaged in his book, yet not so removed
that he didn't look up at the exact moment she was stepping from
the cab and see her. He set down his book and stood.

"My beautiful painter," she said, kissing him on the lips.

"Aspiring painter."

He held her chair and signaled a waiter.

"We have to get champagne," she said. "I have a surprise."

"Uh-oh."

"Trust me. It's great news."

The waiter came to the table and Scott ordered.

"Do you sell your work?" she said.

He didn't answer.

"Scott?"

"No."

"But you're so good."

"Not yet. Soon, I hope."

"I would buy your work."

"Well, we've made love."

"Seriously."

"Let's talk about something else, Kim, something fun."

"This is fun. That's why I'm bringing it up."

"I need to create work before I can sell it."

"You must have lots by now. Do you have slides? Listen, I talked to a friend before I came here, and—are you ready?—he wants to see slides of your work to consider putting you in his gallery in New York. Can you believe it? I'm so excited for you."

Scott looked away.

"If you don't have slides, we can make them. That's no problem. Scott, he's going to use you for a show."

"What are you doing?" he said.

"I'm helping."

"No, you're not."

"C'mon, be practical."

"My life is not about practical."

"But the drawing—you're gifted. This is a way—"

"To ruin everything."

"There's something wrong with my wanting to help?"

"Help what? With what?"

"Sell your work. How can you pass up—"

"I want to paint," he said. "It's all I'm ready for now, that and being in Paris . . . with you. Don't you see, I could do that drawing for you because of the choices I've made?"

"Well, I could take you to dinner because of the choices *I've* made. What's wrong with being practical? You're acting like a boy."

He put his book on top of his notebook.

"Scott—"

"No."

"Scott, I'm sorry."

He shook his head.

"Don't go," she said.

"Who followed who?"

"What?"

"You followed me."

"When you run out of money, what then?"

He smoothed the sleeves of his blazer and patted his pocket for his wallet.

"This is why I don't discuss art," he said.

"This is a chance to show your work. You want to pass that up? What's wrong?"

"Thank you for dinner last night," he said, standing.

What could she say to make him stay? She couldn't understand why he'd suddenly turned hostile.

"Please sit," she said.

He didn't move.

"You play the pauper," she said, "while drinking five-dollar coffees, pretending you don't like gifts. I don't understand."

"You don't."

Hadn't she seen his eyes light up at the store yesterday?

"At first you turned up your nose at the clothes," she said.

"Keep the suit. I don't want it."

"Admit that you liked getting that suit. You admired it because you are an artist. It's your nature to appreciate it. Who's being foolish? I understand more than you think."

His cheeks reddened. She knew she hadn't been the only one wrapped up in the previous day.

"You must let my friend see your work," she said.

She wished he would not be so rash. She was pointing the way. His eyes were like stones.

"When you get to be my age—"

He snatched his notebook and book so suddenly she flinched. Her hand shot to the side of her face.

"Scott, don't go. I'm sorry." But he was too far off to hear.

The waiter appeared with the bottle of champagne and the bucket of ice. He watched Scott go, then looked at her. She nodded for him to uncork the bottle.

She would not chase after him. He would come back.

The next day, she went for an early manicure. She got her hair trimmed and combed into a flip and returned to her room to change. She took extra care dressing, choosing a forest-green wool jacket with a sheen that shifted color depending on the light. Sometimes it appeared black, sometimes more yellow. She thought Scott would appreciate the aesthetic, the color, the texture. She slipped on the emerald ring she'd worn the day they met, the ring he'd noticed.

She went to the café at the usual time and drank wine. She waited for Scott. He never came.

All evening she waited. The phone never rang. Around midnight, she took out a pad of hotel stationery and began to write. She crumpled the first two attempts, then began again. No lies, she thought.

Dear Scott,

How do things become other things? I wanted only to give you the most wonderful dinner, and then it turned into something else. Did I do that? How many gifts have I transformed, I wonder? You see me as owning a great deal. Can you believe me when I say that nothing I own is what it seems, or that whatever meaning these things once held has recently changed? I came to Paris empty-handed, knowing that everything I possessed amounted to nothing. I knew this in some way before I came, but I am even more sure now. You bought a postcard of a boy the other day. I was so afraid you were going to ask who the photographer was, that you knew and wanted to test me. I was scared because I couldn't remember his name, and I wanted desperately to impress you. But you didn't seem to care. I know now that it wouldn't have mattered, because all that counted was the picture, the boy, his strength, his courage. That's what you were telling me—not to change it into something else. You asked me to listen to the rain. I wanted to know what you heard, because I wanted to hear the same way. But that wasn't the point either. Whether you knew or not, you were informing me. Did you know how badly I needed to see? I can't thank you enough. Then I went and destroyed everything. I was afraid again. I fell back on what I knew, and look at the mess. You gave me so much, and I wanted to give back. I only knew one way and that turned out all wrong. Please forgive me. I'm so naive. All my life I've blamed myself. I want to stop this. Scott, we hardly know each other, so I can't presume to understand, but trust my intention when I say that I didn't want to turn you into something you're not, or make you into something I'm more used to. And if it seemed like I did, I was deceiving myself. The things I have that lack meaning can only have value if they bring someone like you happiness. I want to offer myself because it is the only thing I can give that won't turn into something else. Give me the chance to prove to you that I mean something. Promise me you won't feel pity if I say that I love you. I want you always to remember that, because I'm going home.

When she woke, she didn't shower. She put on black leggings, a long black jacket that flared at the knees, and a thin leopard Alice band to hide her messy bangs. She took out earrings, setting them on the vanity, but then didn't bother to put them on. She took a taxi to the café and sat and waited, wiping sleep from her eyes.

"You are meeting someone, yes?" the waiter said. It was the man with the mustache.

She was afraid to answer.

"Maybe he will come today?" he said.

She sipped coffee and waited.

She watched the early morning crowd leave and the lunch crowd gather. She ordered more coffee and a salad.

The people next to her finished and left. The man getting up had brown hair. The man sitting down had black hair. No further details mattered. People came and went. They fit into one another's absences, adopting the same anonymous form as the one before, smiles, mere facial contortions, void of possibility. She observed this familiar, faceless crowd as an outsider: the motorists and the tourists with their shorts and white sneakers; the musician with his bony cat and dog, who lay at his feet, preying on the hearts of the churchgoers who passed.

There was an old woman with thick-soled shoes, carrying a gray plastic bag, shuffling along the sidewalk. An expensively dressed woman breezed past her, coming the other way with plans, Kim imagined, more plans than she had time for, probably. They appeared and disappeared. They inhabited the same cobbled square, day after day until death, scattered, busy as swarming ants, leaving scarcely a mark. History changed. Impressions changed, and the square remained, through generations of rain and cold, exposed and unpossessable, for new eyes, younger eyes to love and lose.

Scott would not come, she realized.

The waiter watched her pay, stroking his mustache. He stopped her at the curb, then hesitated to speak.

"Can you give him this?" she said, handing him the letter she'd written.

He tucked it in his pocket. "I will tell him you waited," he said.

—

Her hotel room was filled with roses when she returned, vases on the commode and vanity and nightstands, a single rose across her pillow with a note from Robert. Hatboxes wrapped in blue bows were stacked on the bed. She started to undress. The phone rang.

"Madame, there is a Monsieur Sanders on the line. Shall I say you are out?"

"I'm here," she said.

"Hello, Kim?" His voice bubbled with excitement.

"I just walked in."

"I know. I had the concierge ring me."

She said nothing.

"She made it, Kim. Christine pulled through! We can breathe."

"We can, yes. God's will."

"What the last two days have been like—I needed you here."

She said nothing.

"It's okay, Kim. I understand. It would have been inappropriate. I wasn't thinking. I was—listen, I'm coming to Paris."

"Don't."

"I promise, Kim. I'm not angry. Do you love the flowers? Have you looked at the hats yet? I bet they're all over the room now. I wish I could have seen you opening them."

"Robert—"

"You don't sound pleased."

"I'm relieved about Christine."

"Davis is here. He came when we told him and wouldn't leave her side. I think his face was the first thing she saw when she opened her eyes."

"But you were there, too."

"I was."

"She'll remember that. You'll see. What about the fiancé?"

"He's here. We telephoned his parents. He flew up immediately. They're talking. He's had a rough go too. I think the wedding is back on. He's a fine man."

He took a deep breath.

"You're right, Kim. I can be better. Say it. Tell me I can. I need to hear it from your lips."

She was silent.

"Come back to me," he said. "Or I'll come to Paris. I have a whole week that—"

"Don't come."

"We need—"

"No more, Robert. I—I'm going now."

She waited, hoping he would cut off.

"You can't stop my coming," he said. "You know that. If I want to see you—"

"I don't want to see *you*."

"That's not acceptable. You owe me—"

"What do I owe you, Robert?"

"For starters—"

"What is it you deserve?"

"Now that's a different term."

"Why did you ever give me anything?"

"Why? Darling, I loved you."

"Say it again."

"I love you."

"Again."

"Kim—"

"Like you mean it."

"I—"

"Daddy used to say that. *Like you mean it!* he'd bark. Say it like you mean it. After a lot of repeating, you don't think about the meaning anymore." She listened to his breathing. "I'm not blaming you."

"What are you doing?"

"I can't see you anymore," she said. "Not anymore."

"I don't—Kim, we—"

"We can be better."

"What are you trying to say?"

"It's hope—hope, Robert."

She set down the phone. Her hand brushed one of the earrings she'd left on the vanity earlier, knocking it to the floor. She stepped back and something crunched. She stooped to pick up the pieces. The setting had fractured. The stone had come out, and she got on her knees to look for it. She imagined the sight of herself and started to laugh. If anyone asked her, she'd say she spent the week searching for a diamond on the floor of the Ritz. That's what she did in Paris. She found the stone and laughed. She stood up and set the earring on the vanity and looked at the picture Scott had drawn of the girl and the boy with the umbrella, and she remembered Bobby Streeber, whom she hadn't thought about in years.

"You can catch wind in a jar. . . ."

She rushed to the window, unfastened the latch, and flung it open. She cried for Robert's daughter, a second chance at life, and the pain she would face. She cried because of that pain she herself had always fled, the things she'd missed along the way and the things she did not yet know; for Scott's struggles and pride, and for those who were no longer part of her life. She cried to be free, not knowing how truly free she was, for she was unaware that two days before, eight thousand miles away, her father had died. The initial surgery had been successful. Complications followed, and another more serious failure. He died in the early morning, the sun just rising over the cliffs, a team of doctors crowding his open chest, ribs fractured and split apart with a sparkling clamp, sterile air touching organs that were not meant to see light, all the while his fighting—his fervent, unconscious clinging to the dawn. None of this she knew. Even still, she mourned him, because his life had been at the heart of the missing. It always had been, since she knew enough to know missing; and the missing that lay ahead that death could not alter— that was a part of rebirth.

She dropped her head back, and even her crying couldn't block out the song of the birds.

About the Author

CAMERON DOUGAN grew up in Ho-Ho-Kus, New Jersey. He attended Davidson College and New York University, and earned his M.A. in creative writing at New York University. He is assistant manager at the Madison Avenue Bookshop in New York City. This is his first novel.

AtRandom.com books are original publications that make their first public appearance in the world as e-books, followed by a trade paperback edition. AtRandom.com books are timely and topical. They exploit new technologies, such as hyperlinks, multimedia enhancements, and sophisticated search functions. Most of all, they are consumer-powered, providing readers with choices about their reading experience.

AtRandom.com books are aimed at highly defined communities of motivated readers who want immediate access to substantive and artful writing on the various subjects that fascinate them.

Our list features literary journalism; fiction; investigative reporting; cultural criticism; short biographies of entertainers, athletes, moguls, and thinkers; examinations of technology and society; and practical advice. Whether written in a spirit of play or rigorous critique, these books possess a vitality and daring that new ways of publishing can aptly serve.

For information about AtRandom.com Books and to sign up for our e-newsletters, visit www.atrandom.com.